A DANGER TO GOD HIMSELF

A NOVEL

JOHN DRAPER

A Danger to God Himself

© 2015 John Draper

www.johndraperauthor.com

Cover Design: Zoe Shtorm

www.zoeshtorm.com

ISBN: 978-1518881091

ISBN: 978-1-5188-8109-1

❀ Created with Vellum

For Monique, Dr. Minefield, and Nick. ("The jewel will cut the rope!")

CHAPTER ONE

M y name is Kenny Feller, onetime agent of the Restored Gospel on Planet Earth. All told, I've been on a mission from God once, twice, thrice, maybe four times. Depends how you count. Anyway, that's what this whole story is about: my three or four missions from God, the ones I may or may not have had. I don't know. Keep reading and see what you think. Stay open to shit. At least that's always been my policy, to the extent I've had one.

First things first. Don't worry. I'm not going to try to convert you. Those days are long gone. The way I see it, everybody's got to find their own path. If you ask me for advice, I'll give you some, sure. Maybe it will help. I *have* seen a lot. But, in the end, you choose your own path—if you're smart. That's what this whole story is about: how I came to learn that lesson, poked my head right through the diaphanous veil between this world and the next. (There. I used my new word for the day—*diaphanous*.) If this story doesn't rock your world, well, then it doesn't. No skin off my nose.

It should, though.

I feel prompted to start by telling you about the day I met Jared —a genuine holy moment if there ever was one. It was Friday,

August 17, 1979—twenty months into my two-year mission. My previous companion had been reassigned to a new senior companion, as often happens. So I had the first half of the day to myself until Mission President Dewey hand-delivered my new companion. I was home alone in my apartment in Sedro-Woolley, Washington, eating out of a jar of peanut butter with my first two fingers. I was reading a contraband issue of *Rolling Stone*, the magazine's effect, on the whole, being one of slackening my resolve. (On the plus side, I had found my new word of the day—*numinous*—as in "Supertramp's latest offering, *Breakfast in America*, is numinous.") Had it been a mere month or two earlier, you would have found me gravely digesting the Book of Mormon to no effect. Reading and learning nothing. Praying into the vacuum. Struggling mightily for the gospel without profit.

And therein lay the burr between my ass cheeks, the *vexation*, if you will.

It just hadn't worked out as advertised, the whole deal. Growing up in church, we always prayed to Heavenly Father as if He was involved in our lives—imminent, sneaking notes into the knife pocket of your corduroy pants. This was supposed to be even more the case once you were on your mission. You go on your mission, study, strive, and pray to be found worthy, and you experience the power of God in your life, in what you say and what you do. The kicker was that the whole experience was meant to launch you into Mormon Manhood, which was one miracle after another, blessing upon blessing.

So goes the Party Line.

Like I said, it just hadn't worked out as advertised, the whole mission thing. In my entire twenty months sharing the gospel, my companions and I had shepherded a total of two seekers into the waters of baptism. Two. Just one day a week, P-day, we were allowed to write home to our families. In my case, it was my stepfather, six stepbrothers, and my mother. I lied like a two-term congressman in my letters home. All sorts of miracles were happening.

By the time Jared showed up, truth be told, I was just going through the motions. I had come to the conclusion that the best I could hope for in terms of a Mormon Manhood was just being my stepfather, except for the part about being an asshole. God was real, sure, I mean in the sense that He existed. But He didn't really work in the lives of Latter-day Saints, and if not in Latter-day Saints' lives, then whose, for fuck's sake? The whole thing was a long con, a well-intended long con. The best you could hope for was just to grit your teeth and try as hard as you could to be a really good person, but don't expect a leg up from Heavenly Father—empowerment. You were fucked. All those stories you read in the Book of Mormon, they were just metaphors or poetry, object lessons we could apply to our lives as we strove to live the gospel. Or fairy tales. I don't know. At least, that was the conclusion I came to sitting on my couch reading *Rolling Stone.*

God just didn't work anymore like He did in the olden days, Book of Mormon times. If He ever did in the first place. We were fucked.

Then Jared showed up.

Anyway, that's what this whole story is about—Jared showing up and making a new man out of me. Keep reading and see what you think. Stay surprisable. At least that's always been my policy.

So, like I was saying, there I was—it was about 12:45 in the afternoon—reading the *Rolling Stone.* My companions and I lived in an apartment across a field from a loading dock of some sort. Big, banged-up trucks would pull in and pick up stuff or leave it, I assume, and then drive away, all day and into each night. They had this PA system above the loading dock and messages were always issuing from it, telling the drivers and the forklift guys what to do. Thing was, the speaker was broken or shorted out or something, and you could barely make out what they were saying. All you heard, especially at our apartment way across the field, was *Serft,*

serft, serft! Nokka-guy-rye, too-bladdum. Too-bladdum! Stuff like that.

So I'm sitting there reading and in walked Dewey, Jared in tow. I stuffed the magazine under a cushion as the door creaked open. Dewey held out his hands, palms up, and motioned toward me with a nod. His diamond chunk cufflinks glinted like the teardrops of an angel. Then he made the same gesture toward Jared. As if on cue, Jared spread out his arms and said, "Kenny Feller, as I live and breathe!"

Dewey closed his eyes and pinched the bridge of his nose. He'd clearly had his fill of the charms of Jared Baserman. "The question," he said, "is not how you came upon the knowledge of Elder Feller's Christian name. That will pass uninvestigated. Rather, let us leave such questions and pursue immediately the matter"—here he lifted his hands in front of himself delicately, like a maestro—"of proper introductions." He gestured toward Jared. "Elder Feller. This is Elder Baserman, fresh from the Missionary Training Center in Provo, and before that resident of the environs of Boise, Idaho. Famous potatoes, they say."

Then he gestured toward me. "And, Elder Baserman. This is Elder Feller, he of vast soul-winning experience and nearing the end of his mission, a fitting senior companion for someone such as yourself."

So there I was, looking for the first time upon Jared Baserman. I must say, I was stirred not in the slightest. Really, it's hard to be surprised when you first gaze upon any given Mormon missionary. You always get what you expect, thanks to the church's unflinching insistence on conformity. And Jared didn't disappoint. Everything was regulation, starting with The Suit. (I'll tell you about his hair later.) Those suits, they suck the idiosyncrasies clean out of any organism. He looked mass produced.

He looked like a dork, though it wouldn't have done you any good to point that out to him. Turns out, Jared was actually excited about the suit, seeing as how it was the first one he had ever owned.

He was like an accessory after the fact to this crime against style. He didn't care. I think It came from him being so at home in his skin. He accepted himself. Hells bells, he even liked himself.

Cap-a-dap toenum! Cap-a-dap toenum! Mala! Mala! Mala! the PA across the field announced.

I'd seen enough of Dewey's mannerisms to interpret his introduction as my prompt. So I rose and leaned across the coffee table to extend my hand to Jared. He leaned forward, keeping his feet planted on the floor, as if he was magnetized to Dewey's proximity by the mission president's personal vibrations. He shook my hand with a shy smile. I would come to see that, for all his joking and indiscretion, Jared was, at heart, a bashful guy.

"Elder Baserman," I said. "Welcome to the Sedro-Woolley mission! We're doing a marvelous work and wonder for God." That was a lie, as was Dewey's assertion that I boasted "vast soul-winning experience." Not that my previous companions and I hadn't worked hard at proselytizing. We had. It's just that, for all that work, we had a dismal baptismal record, as previously noted.

"I'm all about marvelous-ness," Jared said with the overly serious look of a county fair pie judge. "Count me in!"

The PA from across the field said, *Spig! Spig! Spig! Doe-bomb!*

Dewey stared at Jared and puckered his lips doubtfully. He appeared to think of a response before thinking better of it. "Yes, well, the fields, as the authors of scripture assert, are 'white and ready to harvest.' So, no time like the present. What say, Elder Feller, that you take Elder Baserman here and introduce him to the rewarding toil of the loyal missionary?"

Taking the hint, I tucked in my shirt, cinched up my tie, grabbed my backpack, and walked outside, motioning to Jared to follow. I squinted up at the sun.

"Nice out," I said, by way of a conversation starter.

Jared looked up appraisingly and adjusted his name badge. "Yeah. It's so nice out, I think I'll leave it out."

"What?" I said.

"Unless that offends you," he said, deadpan.

Now, looking back at that double entendre, I'm struck by how it shows just how nimble and resourceful Jared's brain was. He came up with that quip instantaneously, at the speed of thought. And, at the time, I thought it was pretty funny. In fact, myself, I've used it any number of times since. But, back then, standing there with my new junior companion—my greenie—my primary concern was to communicate something non-judgmental yet alarmed. Something that was senior companion material but also made me seem like a normal guy. I think all I marshaled was a pained, equivocal look, like my plumbing was backed up. In response, Jared was blank as a slate. The silence was his punch line. He never missed the punch line. That was one of the things about Jared.

"Okay, look, you're new on the mission," I said to Jared, trying to sound like a senior companion. "Like you were told at the MTC, when it comes to success on a mission, it's a matter of staying attuned to the promptings of the Holy Ghost. That's when God will empower you." I know that sounds really Party Line of me now, for a guy who wasn't a gung-ho Mormon at that time, or at least a guy who wasn't sure what kind of Mormon he was at the time. Realize that I could tell Jared was being coy with me—what was he really all about?—so why should I be the first to tip my hand? As far as he would be able to tell, I decided, I would be the Vanilla Missionary of Rectitude. "Everything begins and ends with prayer."

"Amen, my brother," Jared said.

"Good luck, gentlemen!" Dewey called as he stepped outside and walked to his car.

"So," I said. "Let's approach Heavenly Father in prayer."

We folded our arms, closed our eyes, and bowed our heads. After a moment's pause, I stole a glance at Jared. He was eyeing me with a friendly smile.

"Heavenly Father, we thank Thee for this opportunity to share Thy gospel," I began. "We know that Thou lovest all Thy children.

But we also know that not all of Thy children are open to Thy gospel. We ask Thee now to send us Thy guidance. Direct us toward those people whose hearts are prepared to hear about Thy Plan of Happiness. We ask Thee now to speak to our hearts and show us the way."

We stood in silence. A dog barked somewhere. I could hear a throaty car, a testosterone torpedo, no doubt, knifing through the dead air, rumbling up the street toward us. As it neared, the sound from the stereo inside grew louder. I could make out, ever clearer, the sounds of Ted Nugent, the Motor City Madman, the Ten Fingers of Doom. As he passed us, the driver yelled out of his window, "Smoke 'em if you got 'em!"

I winced and opened one eye to glance at Jared. He hadn't twitched a muscle.

"We say these things in the name of Thy son, Jesus Christ," I said as the sound of the car faded into the distance. "Amen."

"That house," Jared said, closing one eye and pointing his finger like a six-shooter toward a blue and white rambler halfway down the block.

Believe it or not, right then, standing with Jared in front of our apartment, I felt something. A stirring. My first ever. Or maybe I just thought Jared was yanking my chain and I wanted to be contrary.

"I feel impressed that we need to go in that direction," I said, pointing the way down a stately lane of hedges.

Jared squinted down the lane apprehensively. "Shouldn't we get the same answer?" he asked, scratching the back of his head. "Maybe we should try again."

The faraway dog barked again. "Yeah," I said, following Jared's gaze down the lane. "That would make sense, wouldn't it?" I adjusted my backpack and stretched my neck side to side. "Tell you what. You pray this time. I'll agree with what you pray. What do you think?"

Jared stared at me for a moment. "Sure," he said, smiling. "Let's give it a whirl." He closed his eyes, rubbed his palms together briskly in front of his face, interlaced his fingers, and cracked his knuckles. "Heavenly Father, we have this message about Jesus Christ that we want to share. You know the one. We just need someone who will listen to us. Please show us who to ask."

We stood there bowing our heads for, I don't know, ten or twenty seconds. When I looked up at last, Jared was murmuring to himself.

"What'd you get?" I asked.

"Well, what I heard was that I was wrong about going that way," he said, nodding in the direction of the blue and white rambler. Right at that moment, an older woman, bulky as a barn, came out on the front porch of the rambler and favored us with look of grim menace, squinting furiously. Then she shook her head as if in disbelief and retreated inside. "Instead, we should go to"—here, he closed his eyes—"the house next to that one." He opened his eyes and looked at me seriously. "On the money."

I pursed my lips. "Well, I didn't get anything. This time."

Jared looked at me. "This isn't working very well," he said flatly.

Indeed. There we were, two young men—kids, really—not distantly removed from our days of feckless abandon, and we were purportedly about God's solemn work: saving gentiles. I think we both realized in that instant how ridiculous the whole scene was. (It actually had occurred to me before that point.) What kind of a Master Plan was it for God to hinge the expansion of His kingdom on shoulders as sloped as ours? I think Jared and I came to an unspoken understanding right then and there that neither of us was really up to this. We were just well-meaning young men trying their best to do the right thing, to choose the right.

So there we were.

"Why don't you take the lead this time? That's what senior companions do, I guess," Jared said.

So we went about it. Here follows a distillation of the rest of that day of tracting. Interpersonally, we hit it off, as different as we were. Had I gone to high school with Jared, I probably wouldn't have pulled within a million miles of him. I had all sorts of so-called friends in high school. All sorts. And Jared would not have been one of them. As we walked from door to door, we shared our stories about growing up as Mormons. We got along famously, as my mother would say. In terms of missionary success, though— different story. Not a nibble. At most of the doors we knocked on, Jared wouldn't say a word. But he'd toss out some *riposte* after we left. (The thing about Jared: I came to learn that he wasn't always cracking jokes out of insecurity or as some sort of defense mechanism. He sincerely thought he was funny. It was only the Christian thing to do to share his gift with us, after all. "I'm the funniest man in America," was what he would tell me on his deathbed.) We'd flop at every door, and Jared would find a way to frame it in the comical. Effortless.

To wit:

Old man working in garden: We walked up slowly, and when our shadows passed over his work, he looked up and squinted. "Mormons," he said, as if we didn't know. Then he went back to his work and addressed himself to his plants. "You come out here, with nothing better to do, and pester us innocent citizens. Go get a real job!"

As we walked away, Jared said to me, "We tried, sir, but McDonalds wouldn't have us."

Young woman comes to door: "Good evening, ma'am, I'm Elder Feller and this is Elder Baserman, and we're missionaries from the Church of Jesus Christ of Latter-day Saints."

She smiled kindly. "We have our own church, boys," she said. "Thanks, anyway."

As I was taught at the MTC, I followed up immediately with, "Oh, what church do you attend, ma'am?"

"Thanks anyway, boys," she said. As she closed the door, keeping her face visible in the shrinking crack, she repeated: "We have our own church, boys. We have our own church, boys." We heard the deadbolt click home.

"She probably had to get to church," Jared said dully.

Bare-chested man scratches belly, holding side of door: When I started in, he held up his hand to stop me, as if he had something to offer. He lifted one leg and let loose with the loudest, most alarming fart I had ever heard—and I grew up with six stepbrothers. Then he nodded tersely, as if to say, "Take that!" and slammed the door. As we walked away, Jared said, "Easy for him to say!"

Older man answers doorbell: "Good evening, sir," I started. He jumped in. "So I'm supposed to take life advice from a couple of kids? I'm supposed to listen to you for the Meaning of Life? Do either of you guys even shave yet?"

"We–"

"You don't know shit," he continued. "Go live life some and then come back and we'll see if you're so cocky."

As we were walking away, Jared said, "I resent that. I've been shaving my legs for well over a month now!"

More, much more, of the same followed.

Around 6 p.m., we took thirty minutes for a dinner of sandwiches I had packed that morning and an apple a piece, sitting on a park wall and bouncing our heels against the bricks as we talked. We chatted and got to know one another some more. When it was just us, you couldn't shut him up—and he wasn't always cracking jokes. Jared told me about his family. I could tell he really missed them. His father cried when Jared left for the mission at the airport. That really impressed me, as I had never seen my stepfather cry. I mean, it's common for Mormon men to cry, often when bearing their testimony or relating some "spiritual experience." As a general rule, Mormon men have soft hearts. Not my stepfather, though. I mean, I think he think he loves the Savior. Who's to say? My stepfather had two settings on his emotional dial: Mad and Off.

"My dad," Jared said, looking up at the clouds. "He's a good guy, really good. I guess he's the kindest man I've ever met. He's really the reason I'm on a mission. I mean, I believe, but it means so much to him. I'm doing it for my family, too, my twin sister. It's really important that I return with honor. Really important."

"That's cool," I said with a nod. "My dad . . . the church is everything to him, too. But I wouldn't say he's particularly kind. In fact, I guess he's kind of a hard case. My mom, her favorite saying was: 'You just wait till your father gets home,' when she'd bust me for something. To which I'd say: 'He's not my father.' Without fail, she'd back off and later say: 'Okay, Kenny. I'm not going to tell your father about this this time.' But, I think he knew anyway. And he's not my real father. He's a piece of work, that's for sure. But anyway, I believe, too."

Then Jared told me about the "spiritual experience" he had at a family reunion, which led directly to his decision to enter the mission field. The way he described it, it was like a vision or something, just like in the Book of Mormon, and the Bible, too, I guess. I mean, in the Mormon Church, a lot of people talk about receiving "impressions" from Heavenly Father. Usually, it's related to vague matters, things not empirically verifiable or, if verifiable, of piddling significance—for example, finding one's car keys. Also, it's my experience that most people saw the hand of God in hindsight. In the middle of the miracle, they were oblivious. Heavenly Father was as subtle as moonlight. You'd look back and there would be His footprints in the damp grass. Also, coincidences—Mormons tends to see God in improbable coincidences. *That* must *have been Heavenly Father!*

"It wasn't something I was making up, you know," he said. "Like when you're at a Testimony Meeting and you say 'I know' and all that shit. I mean, this came upon me. I think it was the power of God."

"But why would Heavenly Father do that for you?" I asked. "I mean, no offense, but you don't seem like some spiritual giant, a Man of Valor. Isn't that how it's supposed to work? You know, you receive power from on high in proportion to your worthiness."

"No offense taken. And the answer to your question is I have no fucking idea why He did it. Fucking. I suppose I should say flippin' now that I'm actually on my mission."

"Hell, yeah!"

Jared laughed, which was something he didn't do much. Not that he was glum. Far from it. First off, he was funny as hell, but most of his jokes were delivered with a humorless affect. Secondly, he just didn't find other people funny—or at least as funny as he was. "I like you, Kenny Feller," he said as we sat on the brick wall. "Elder Feller, he of vast soul-winning experience."

"Yeah," I said. "That was a load."

"I had already used my spiritual powers to discern that," Jared said, placing two fingers on each temple and closing his eyes.

"Elder Baserman," I said, popping the last of my sandwich into my mouth and dusting off my hands. "You are without question the strangest companion I've ever had, and I can say that after only a half a day with you. It's only going to get weirder from here, isn't it?"

He lifted his gaze and studied the horizon. "Indubitably," he said with a smile.

A WORD, before I go any further. I want you to understand that everything you're reading, it's all provable. I say this at the outset because I'm certain that—not too far in—you'll feel compelled to dismiss it all as horseshit. Understandable. All the stuff about Jared and his visions, and the miracles, and the assorted sexual congress, the God of the universe striking people dead. But I can substantiate it all, every bit. I'm not saying that I understand everything that happened to us, Jared and me. I'm not saying that a lot of it wasn't baffling, because most of it was baffling and, by turns, titillating, aggravating and—so help me—simultaneously profane and inspirational, if such a state is even possible. What I'm saying—the point

I'm making—is that I constructed this retelling of those three turbulent months primarily from eyewitness accounts.

Not that eyewitnesses are infallible. But at least they're earnest.

That means I busted my hump to chase down all the players in this drama and gather their recollections. A number of them resided outside the greater Skagit Valley, so it took some *wayfaring* on my part to conduct my interviews. *So what did you say? Then what did he/she say to that? What were the exact words he/she used? How'd that make you feel?*

And so on.

The way I saw it, I had to reconstruct every conversation, every scene, get it perfect. After all, I was on a mission from God.

For example, I had a number of meetings with Algernon Briskey, erstwhile bishop of the Sedro-Woolley ward of the Church of Jesus Christ of Latter-day Saints—Pious Briskey, specifically. Or maybe it was Evil Briskey. There's the rub. Jerusha's the one who came up with the whole Evil Briskey/Pious Briskey thing. Just to needle me, I think. It kind of became a shorthand for Jerusha and me—a running joke. Was that Evil Briskey or was that Pious Briskey who did that? Her mind was made up: There never had been a Pious Briskey. There was only Evil Briskey, villain to the bone. I think she blamed him in large part for what ended up happening to Jared. Me, even though I used the phrases Evil Briskey and Pious Briskey, I wasn't so sure. Had there ever been an Evil Briskey?

We ended up calling it The Briskey Enigma.

After what we all went through, I've come to the conclusion that evil is tough to nail down. What is evil? I think most people who are evil—and, believe me, I think there are plenty of evil people out there—they don't necessarily see themselves as evil. That is, they have rationalized their attitudes or behaviors. It was for the Good of the Community, or something like that, perhaps Protecting the One True Church. You know. Also, I've come to believe that evil—real evil—is insidious. It comes on slowly over a person and tricks them into going down a darker path. Evil is deceptive to the evildoer. People who are in a cult don't think they're in a cult. They just think they're normal people—believers. My point is, they've been deluded by the evil itself. I think now that Joseph Smith believed some, maybe all, of his lies, in some way. Evil tries to hide, like God.

The thing about Pious Briskey—if there even is a Pious Briskey walking upright among us—the thing is you are inclined to believe him. At least I am. Reason being, he cuts down on Evil Briskey so freely. He is so upfront about how sinful he had been before his conversion to his offshoot brand of Mormonism. The way Briskey tells it, the Garden variety Mormon Briskey—Evil Briskey—was a lout. The Pentecostal Mormon Briskey—Pious Briskey—well, he isn't perfect . . . but he is aware of his failings and plainly devoted to God's glory. At least that's how he tells it. Once he was lost. Now's he's found. It makes you think, "Only an honest person would talk about themselves like that. He must be sincere." At least, that's what he makes me think. I don't know. Jerusha tells me not to be a dumbshit.

We'd always meet in the food court of the Cascade Mall.

"Tongues and visions," Pious Briskey said, putting a French fry in his mouth as the food court buzzed around us. "I remember once when I was bishop, it turned out that somehow a car in the parking lot had caught fire. Full up in flames. Well, someone in the foyer saw this going on, and ran into the chapel to tell me. When he got inside the chapel, I was in the middle of a benediction and everyone had their heads bowed. So this guy, rather than shouting out, 'There's a fire in the parking lot!' he stood in the back of the chapel and waited for me to finish. When I was done, he sneaked up to the dais and whispered in my ear. And what did I do? Instead of yelling out, 'There's a car on fire in the parking lot!' I told the guy to go get my First Counselor and have him deal with this situation. My point is, that's how stifled things were at our church. And not just ours, all Mormon churches. When I was a non-spirit-filled Mormon, I was proud of how reverent our services were, all hush-hush and sober-minded. Bah! Now I see that we were squelching the Holy Spirit. We weren't reverent. We were asleep—asleep in the light. We weren't letting the Holy Spirit move! I say Jared was a godsend. Others don't and that's their prerogative. He changed me—and I think he changed you, too. Am I right?"

"No doubt, I'm different," I said.

"He who has ears to hear . . ." Briskey said, waving grandly.

So it went.

Now, all that said, it's my own eyewitness observations from those months in Sedro-Woolley that fashion the backbone of this story. Because of the Elbow Rule—"always stay near enough to your missionary companion to hear him at a whisper while outside the apartment, and do not separate for long periods of time within the apartment"—I was present for almost all the stuff Elder Baserman, Jared, battled through.

And I'm as earnest as the day is long.

BACK TO THAT first day of tracting with Jared in Sedro-Woolley. After we finished our meal, we returned to our Holy Work. That is, until the last call of the day. It was approaching 9 p.m. Dusk was falling. As we were walking to the door of our last house of the day, Jared caught hold of me by the elbow.

"Hold on," he said. "The people in there. There have been innumerable misconstructions. Negative anagrams." He nodded toward the house. "They. They are against us. In fact, I think they followed me from Boise." At first, I thought it was one of his jokes again.

"Of course they're against us," I said. "But here we are, still knocking on their door. Welcome to the mission field. Everyone's been against us today. In fact, this was pretty typical. Get used to it because, I'm telling ya, this is what it's like. Everyone hates our guts. It's been like this for me for the past twenty months."

"No, this is different. These people have been waiting for us. They really hate us." He looked at the house nervously. "They want to hurt us, man."

"What are you talking about? Listen, it's been a rough day. Let's just make this our last call for the day. Let's just get this over with and we can go back to the apartment. You haven't even had a chance to settle in. You'll put away your stuff, get your stuff arranged. I'll make us some chili. You like chili?"

Jared stared at the house before turning his gaze to me. "The Musical Fruit," he said, with the worried look still on his face.

"So let's do it," I said with a smile. "Odds are, they aren't even going to want to hear what we have to say. Slam-bang, then we're done. Go back home. Have some chili. Plan tomorrow. Maybe get a little reading in. Slam-bang. Then lights out at 10:30, unless you're too tired, then we can sack out earlier. That's cool."

Jared pressed his lips together doubtfully.

"Come on, man," I said. "Let's do this." I motioned to the house and glared at him. He looked unconvinced.

"You do all the talking, okay?" he said.

"You want me to do all the talking? Fine. That's cool. But tomorrow, you've got to start talking to people."

Jared followed me to the door, where I rang the bell. Before the chiming had finished, the door was open, and we were looking into a woman's face. "Latter-day Saints, at our door!" she said cheerfully, speaking through the fence of a tooth-filled grin.

"Well, don't just stand there like bumps," the woman said, motioning us forward. "Come in, come in, gentlemen! My name's Lisa P. We have some refreshments waiting for you."

Jared followed me in. I looked back at him with raised eyebrows as if to say, "See? No danger here!"

"Daryl is excited to speak with you," she said over her shoulder.

She ushered us into the kitchen, and there at the table sat

Daryl, I assume, every bit as overfed as Lisa P. and polishing a handgun longingly. It was a hell of a handgun, too, a real Avenging Angel kind of thing: The Deathbringer. I looked around the room and saw guns everywhere. They were mounted on the walls like prize bass and left derelict on the counters like Pop Tart wrappers. And Bibles. Guns and Bibles. Daryl snapped his gum in his mouth.

"Sit," he said.

Lisa P. motioned for us to sit. A pitcher of water with no glasses and a plate Oreos sat on the table. "This is my husband, Daryl," she said. "Tell us all about yourselves!"

I dove into my story, putting a definite pro-church slant on matters. I knew, as all Mormons know, that we are the church's public relations agency—walking billboards, if you will. That means we had to portray the church is the kindest light possible and to present ourselves as the best, most well-scrubbed people in the land—people you'd like to be. I looked to Jared as I spoke and it was clear he didn't want to say a word. As I had been taught at the MTC, I knew my goal was to move the conversation toward spiritual matters as quickly as possible. "It sounds like you may be familiar with us," I said. "What do you know about the church?"

Daryl looked at me as if I hadn't said a word. "Now, you Latter-day Saints had some front-page news recently, didn't you? All over the news."

"Sir?"

"Well, just last year, your prophet—that's like your pope, right?"

"I really don't know about that, sir," I said. "The prophet speaks for God in this dispensation. He's a special witness for Christ."

"So, he talks to God and knows what God's thinking?"

"Well," I said, getting the uncomfortable sense I was being cornered.

"Would the prophet ever tell you—tell your Church, I mean—to do something if it wasn't, say, God's will?"

I could tell by the glee on his face that he was about to lay the whammy on me. "No, sir," I hesitated. "God would never let the prophet lead us astray."

"Well, your prophet, he had some exciting news last year's what I hear."

It was then I noticed that he kept looking at a piece of paper on the table top that looked like some kind of flyer or brochure, something like that.

"Some big news," he repeated. "He said that blacks could hold the priesthood. First time in more than 150 years."

He leaned back and snatched a glance at the flyer on the table. He spun the handgun around like a warden with his clutch of keys. "So, big news."

I could feel the sweat on my upper lip. I glanced at Jared. He looked like he had swallowed a turd.

"Finally, after 150 years, black people could have the priesthood, leastwise, black men could, right?" He nodded toward his wife. "So what does that mean now?"

I opened my mouth but he cut me off. "It means that, without the priesthood, they didn't have the power of God, didn't it? It means black folks couldn't set foot inside your temple. It meant they couldn't do your ceremonies—your ordinances—to get into heaven. Into"—here he glanced at the brochure in his hand—"into the Celestial Kingdom. No blacks in heaven. Why is it that black men couldn't hold the priesthood until 1978?" he asked, not really asking.

Finally, an opening. I recited the lines President Dewey gave us all. "No one really knows why black men couldn't hold the priesthood until 1978, but–"

"Now, that's not entirely true, is it, boy? In fact, all your prophets over the years, they've seemed to know the reason why. It says here that your prophet Brigham Young said that blacks were cursed with the curse of Cain and that they couldn't, therefore, have the priesthood. And, what's more, blacks couldn't receive the priesthood until the Second Coming. All your prophets said that was God's will, keeping the priesthood from black men. Most of them vociferously. It was God's will that blacks couldn't hold the priesthood. Period. Well, that sounded okay in the olden days, but these days it sounds downright stupid, and racist. It sounds like your Church is racist."

"Racist!" interjected Lisa P.

"So your prophet now was in a fix," Daryl continued. "He wanted to give blacks the priesthood so everyone would stop calling the church racist. But how does he do that without saying all the past prophets were wrong on this matter? Prophets can't be wrong, can they? Your whole Church is built on the prophet always telling you God's will correctly. You said it yourself: 'The prophet would never lead the Church astray.' Your prophet was in a fix. So what he decided to do was, he decided to give blacks the priesthood but not tell anyone how or why. Whenever someone says, 'What about all the other prophets who said it was God's will that blacks should not receive the priesthood until the Second Coming?' he just tries to change the subject. Did God change his mind about blacks? Were the past prophets wrong about what God thought about blacks? And if the past prophets could have been wrong, what's stopping your current prophet from being wrong about the all the other stuff he's telling you now?"

I took a deep, slow breath and considered my options.

He looked at Lisa P. and back at me. "How come your Book of Mormon says that when dark-skinned folks convert to Mormonism they will become . . . 'white and delightsome?'"

As I had been trained at the MTC, I began, "Maybe we shouldn't take up any more of your time here" and started to rise from my chair.

Daryl held up his hand to stop me. "How is it that every prophet before this prophet has said blacks were cursed with the Curse of Cain, and therefore couldn't have the priesthood? Now, suddenly, God changes His mind. Blacks can hold the priesthood."

I was frozen halfway off my seat, my hands on the chair's arms. "Sir, I–"

"Boy, here's the bottom line for Mormonism. One or more of the following people must be racist: Joseph Smith, Brigham Young, or God. Which is it?"

"Sir, the prophet Joseph Smith–"

"Joseph Smith was a lying sack of dickheads!" Lisa P. finally erupted.

"Yeah," said Daryl. "And let's talk about Joseph Smith." Here he flipped open the brochure and began reading to himself. "Here: 'Joseph Smith married more than thirty women, some of whom were as young as fourteen years of age. And he married ten women who were already married to other men.'"

"Now, that's just a lie," I began.

Here, Jared jumped to his feet, and shouted, "Joseph Smith only had one wife, Emma, and he was faithful to her to the end of his life!"

The man shot up and pointed the gun inches away from Jared's crimson face. "You little shit-eater!" he yelled. "Who are you to talk down to us?"

Jared shouted back. "I testify to you that Joseph Smith was a Prophet of God and that the Church of Jesus Christ of Latter-day Saints is the only true and living church on the face of the earth!" He bent to pick up his backpack and added, "And, in the name of the holy Melchizedek Priesthood, I call a curse against you from on high!"

"You little fucker," Daryl boomed.

Jared rose and headed for the door, leaving me frozen in my chair. Then he turned to face Daryl and Lisa P. "You have a spirit of contention!" he shouted.

"You little fucker!" the man shouted and stormed after Jared, berating him and waiving the gun. His wife followed him, leaving me alone in the kitchen. I gathered my backpack and started after them. The man shouted curses at Jared, who shouted over his shoulder, "You have a spirit of contention!" He marched ahead of them, picking up his pace, which led the man and woman to jog forward, to the extent they were able. By the time I reached the front door, they were halfway down the block, shouting at one another as they jogged. I had to sprint to catch up to Jared, and as I passed the couple, the man huffed out, "You . . . little . . . fucker!" He waved the gun weakly in my direction.

I caught up to Jared and looked over my shoulder to find that the couple had stopped, clearly out of gas.

"Come on!" I shouted to Jared, slapping him on his shoulder. We turned the corner and slowed, eventually stopping at the base of a huge tree.

"Holy shit!" I said, leaning over with my palms on my knees.

Jared gasped heavily and leaned against the tree. "They . . . they. . . had a spirit of contention," he said, dropping his backpack at his feet.

I watched Jared leaning against the tree and it hit me: He had been right. They were against us. I mean, I don't think they were from Boise. But they saw us coming up the street and they grabbed their flippin' brochure, and they put together their plan of attack. It wasn't much of a plan: just some water, some woebegone Oreos, and a brochure. And the gun. I suppose the gun was part of the plan somehow. But we walked right into it. And, somehow, Jared knew it beforehand.

"Spirit of contention," Jared said breathlessly.

And that was how I passed my first afternoon and evening in the presence of Elder Jared Baserman.

CHAPTER TWO

Anyway, let me tell you how Jared ended up on the mission field. It's a real head scratcher—enigmatic to the point of being numinous. This is where I've been able to construct my most nuanced retelling, seeing as how I had three people's perspectives to work with: Jared, his twin sister, Jerusha, and their father, Nephi.

It began as a new morning unfolded in March of 1977, outside the Regency Inn on the ragged flatland due south of Boise proper. Next to the motel, a second-hand Gremlin sputtered in a cartoonish manner. Nephi was at the wheel.

"I was praying," Nephi told me when I interviewed him years later. "I always tried to pray a blessing over the owner of the motel or hotel or apartment when we were forced to leave early. I was praying that Heavenly Father would find a way to bring the rent I owed into the owner's account. I believe God can do those things, you see. I've never really been a praying man—but I hate to leave anyone in the lurch."

Outside, seventeen-year-old Jared descended the building's exterior stairs, carrying a cardboard box full of his worldly possessions. Most of it was old magic tricks and comic books, plus his precious, precious Playboys.

"Jerusha was complaining that she couldn't find her, what is it? Her marital aid," Jared said breathlessly to his father as he climbed into the car. "Don't want to start a new life without your vibrator!" At that moment, Jerusha emerged from the corner on the second floor and headed for the stairs. She also carried a cardboard box, this one labeled My Shit. Jerusha entered the car head first and suddenly stopped.

"Oops, Dad. I left some stuff in the hidey hole. Be right back."

Nephi leaned his forehead against the steering wheel in exasperation. "Mr. Parthemer knew something was up yesterday. 'The rent's two weeks late, Baserman,'" Nephi said, mimicking the toxic drawl of the live-in landlord. "'You've got the appearance of a deadbeat about you, Baserman. You're not a deadbeat, are you, Baserman?'"

"You're not a deadbeat, Dad," Jared said, adjusting his comic books in his box. "You're an entrepreneur."

Echoes of yelling issued from the second floor of the motel. Jerusha appeared at the corner of the building, scrambling for the stairs and carrying her hidey hole box. A few seconds later, the redolent Cassius Lionel Parthemer III appeared in his bathrobe, angrily waving something in his hand—a lamp?—and shouting. Jerusha took the stairs three and four at a time. It was all Mr. Parthemer could do to carefully proceed from step to step, as if he were crossing a creek on stones.

"Baserman!" he shouted. "Give me my money, you deadbeat fuck!"

Perhaps out of alarm, Nephi gunned the car and, at that instant, it died with an ironic shudder.

"Holy Baloney," Nephi said, fumbling for the keys. Jerusha flew into the front seat of the car.

"Woo hoo!" she shouted.

By this time, Mr. Parthemer was halfway down the stairs. "I'll fuck you up, Baserman!" he shouted over the sound of Nephi frantically trying to grind the car back to life.

"Let's go, Dad," Jerusha said.

"Trying," he answered through gritted teeth.

"He's almost down the stairs, Dad!" Jared cried from the backseat.

"Baserman, you're a fuck!" Mr. Parthemer shouted from the stairs.

"Hot damn!" Jerusha hooted.

"Now would be a good time to start the car, Dad," Jared said, bouncing on his seat and watching Parthemer out the window.

Finally, when the car wouldn't turn over, Nephi, exhaled in frustration and bowed his head. "Heavenly Father, please get us out of this scrape we're in here. I'm not a bad man. In the name of Jesus Christ, amen." At this, he gave the car one more try and it kicked in.

"Praise the Lord!" Jerusha howled, stamping her feet on the dash.

As Nephi and the twins screeched out of the parking lot, Cassius Lionel Parthemer III shouted something and threw the lamp-like object in his hand. All three Basermans provided me different recollections of what they heard. Nephi recalled Mr. Parthemer shouting "Apostate!" Jerusha, she said he cried out, "Baserman, you're a fuck, you fucking fuck!" which was a joke meant to shock me, I think maybe. Shocking people was Jerusha's style. Jared, he told me Mr. Parthemer shouted, "You forgot your complimentary continental breakfast" and I definitely think that was a joke.

Nephi reached around the boxes stacked two-high between himself and Jerusha and pushed his sole 8-track tape into the player. It was *Afro-Sheen Presents the Best of Stevie Wonder*. It came with the car. Nephi had never heard of Stevie Wonder prior to buying the car. Now, he talked like the Secretary-General of the Take Stevie Wonder to the Huddled Masses Foundation.

"That Stevie Wonder, kids, he's an example of what a person can do when he, or,"—here he nodded over to Jerusha—"she attacks the obstacles life presents you with a positive attitude. Gives you the energy to battle the little hurdles that life puts in your way. If Stevie can do it, so can you. Of course, we need each other. We need to help each other. That's why we—you two and myself— that's why we have us." He tapped on the steering wheel and sang along with the music.

"This song is about God, kids." Nephi looked at Jared in the rearview mirror. "The name of the song is *Highest Ground*."

"We know, Dad," Jerusha said. "We've heard it like a million times. And it's *Higher Ground*."

"Whatever," Nephi said. "It's got a real groovy beat, doesn't it, kids? Makes me want to boogie."

"Dad," Jerusha said. "First off, no one says groovy anymore. That went out with, like, Woodstock. Number two, the term isn't boogie. What you mean to say is get down. The music makes you want to get down—as in get down and get funky."

"Dad doesn't have a funky bone in his body," Jared said. "Dad, you've got serious White Man's Disease. You're like squaresville, baby."

Nephi shrugged his shoulders and resumed his off-key version of the song.

"I think this song is about reincarnation, Dad," Jared said.

"Yeah," Jerusha added. "Mormons don't believe in reincarnation, I think."

Nephi shrugged and kept singing.

Every spare space in the car was stuffed with humans and boxes. The Basermans always stayed at hotels, motels, and furnished apartments, so they were able to gather all their possessions in the trunk and two modest bench seats of the Gremlin. This wasn't the first time they had skipped out on rent, so they had grown adept at packing. The story always scripted out the same. Nephi would struggle at selling whatever it was he was selling at that point—herbal remedies or fat blasters or kitchen knife sets. Whatever it was it was, it was always a modern miracle at the time. ("The ancient Assyrians used this to cure hyper-tension!") The unvarnished truth was that he was a terrible salesman. Nicest guy you'd ever want to meet, but a bad salesman. Eventually, when Nephi realized their funds were all but gone, they'd leave under the cover of darkness.

"I could sure use a Sugar Daddy, and a cup of coffee," Nephi said. "What about you two?"

"A Charleston Chew for me, please," said Jared.

"Coffee me, too," Jerusha said.

Nephi pulled into the first convenience store they found. The twins watched him browse the store and take his purchases to the girl at the register, who was resting her forearms on the counter and drumming her hands, perhaps in time to the store's piped-in music. As was typical with him, Nephi tried to strike up a friendly conversation with the stranger, but she was having none of it.

Back in the car, Nephi handed everyone their treats and began to take a high-minded view of recent events.

"Okay, kids," he said to the twins in the cramped car. "We're going to pay Mr. Parthemer back, you know, as soon as we can. You know that what matters is how you treat your fellow man, or,"— here he tipped his coffee cup toward Jerusha—"woman."

"Thank you," Jerusha said.

"That's what Jesus said, kids," Nephi said, holding up his coffee cup and looking from twin to twin. "He said, 'What you do to the least of these, you do unto me.' Unto me!"

"More Jesus talk?" Jerusha moaned.

"All I'm saying is that when you help someone you're really helping Jesus," he said, gesticulating with his Sugar Daddy as he made his point. "'Unto the least of these.' That's what he said."

The trio ate and drank in silence for a few minutes.

"I'll send Mr. Parthemer the money for the rent when I get it. I just can't make money appear out of thin air, can I? Money doesn't grow on trees."

"That would be sweet," Jerusha said.

"Yeah," Jared said.

"'Unto me,'" Nephi said. "That's what he said."

Nephi downed the rest of his coffee and clapped his hands. "Well," he said. "I think I'll call Jo. I'll tell the girl at the cash register I have to report a crime, a citizen's arrest kind of thing."

It was always the case that, after they had skipped out on rent, Nephi would call his older sister Jo, the only member of Nephi's expansive immediate family who would associate with him, and ask for a loan. Jo was the firstborn child of Marcus and Zena Baserman, who christened her Josephina. She owned a string of coin-operated laundries across the greater Boise area and she was wealthy as a porn star. She would invariably give in to Nephi's requests, but not until she made a point of belittling him in front of his kids.

This state of affairs, their itinerant, threadbare lifestyle, their dependency on Jo—all of it—Nephi considered recompense for the fact he wasn't raising his children "in the gospel." The twins knew he felt that way, and they tried to disabuse him of this conclusion, to no avail. There was nothing for the predicament he was in. He just didn't have it in him to follow his family's religion . . . religiously. All the rules. It just wasn't him—and he was stricken by this as an irredeemable defect, like a short leg. For their part, the twins didn't really see themselves as deprived. Life was good. Who needs religion?

The twins watched Nephi go into the store and present his bald-faced lie to the girl at the counter, who sneered and pointed over her shoulder with her thumb.

Jo was none too pleased to be awakened from a deep sleep at 6:20 on a Tuesday morning, but not surprised. She spoke in the clipped diction of someone who was constantly late for an important meeting.

"Are your kids there? Get your kids there," she chirped at

Nephi. Nephi put the phone down and stuck his head out the office door. He waved his arms at the twins in the car, but they didn't see him. He walked toward the front of the convenience store and waved his arms again.

"The police want to hear their side of the incident," he explained to the gum-snapping girl. "Jared! Jerusha!" he called to them, as if they could hear him. He waved his arms over his head until he had their attention and he beckoned them inside with a swooshing motion of his arms.

The twins walked into the store. As Jared walked past the girl, he said, "Thank you for your forbearance. We must all do what we can to stem the tide of suburban crime. My father, he's been given special dispensation to act in these types of matters. By the authorities, I mean."

"Bite me," the girl said.

"Hold the phone out so you can all hear me, Nephi," Jo groused to Nephi. Nephi did as he was told and Jo began speaking forcefully over the receiver. "I want to ask you this one question. What example are you showing to your children? Jared and Jerusha, you need to make sure you don't follow the path your father has walked down. Do you understand that?"

Jerusha grabbed her throat and pretended to be choking the life from herself, rolling her eyes and sticking out her tongue.

"We hear you, Aunt Jo," Jared shouted politely, saluting the phone. "Don't be like Dad."

"Nephi," Jo continued with a sigh, "I'll give you the money. You come to my office on Fourth at 8 a.m. and I'll give you the money. Now put the phone back to your ear." Nephi did as he was told and Jo continued. "How long are you going to keep this up, Nephi? Really. It's time to grow up. You need to go to church."

"We go to church, Jo."

"Yes, you go to church when it suits you. You go to church when you think you can find someone to scam. I swear, Nephi.

Heavenly Father would strike you down where you stand if it wouldn't mean your children would be left as orphans."

"It's a mess, no argument," Nephi responded sheepishly. "This time, though, a new start."

"How many times have I heard that?" Jo asked with a sigh. "Just be there at 8." She hung up the phone and Nephi smiled.

"Well, kids," Nephi said as he clasped his hands in front of himself. "Jo's going to help us out of this jam. Thank God for Jo. She's a blessing, no doubt. Heavenly Father has His eye on us."

"She has a bug up her butt," Jerusha said flatly.

"Jerusha, please. She is a handful, no argument from me. But she's my sister. Family is everything. I mean, look at the three of us. We're all we have, each of us. We have to stick together."

"If family's so wonderful, then why is Aunt Jo the only one of your six brothers or sisters, or your parents, that you ever see?" Jerusha asked.

"You are my family," Nephi said, looking back and forth at his two kids. His eyes teared up. "And, yes, Jo is my family too, I guess."

Jo was a frequent topic of discussion between Nephi and his kids. They really didn't know what to make of her. They all assumed she was devout, a regular attender, and a full tithe payer. However, they never heard her talk about her faith.

Jo was not the type of woman the church would put on its glossy marketing pamphlets about Happy Families. She wasn't unattractive, by any means. But clearly she wasn't someone who would turn men's heads—or cared to. She was thick-boned and large-bottomed. She had, as it turned out, the perfect body type to excel at softball and shot put, which she had done in her school days, to the consternation of her parents. She always wore her hair short and wore oval, gold-rimmed glasses, which gave her a studious look. At first, her parents were proud of the way she excelled in grade school. But when these characteristics were combined with her fierce disinterest in the domestic training her mother tried to impart to her—how to cook, how to sew, how to keep a house tidy for your priesthood holder—well, they started becoming concerned.

By adulthood, a certain gloom had started to come about her. She rarely smiled. The siblings would say to her face that she was "all business" with what was meant to be a friendly laugh. "The thing about you, Jo, is you're all business," they'd tell her. Behind her back, they'd whisper "Jo would perk up if she could get a good Mormon husband. But I don't think *that's* in the cards."

Jo was actually quite forthcoming when I interviewed her later, after everything that ended up happening to Jared. I gathered that she felt responsible for the whole mess, seeing as how she was the one who actually ended up convincing—most would say black-mailing—Jared to go on his mission. To her mind, some good came of the implosion around Jared. Since Jared's problems were suddenly fair game for family conversation, Jo felt emboldened to finally come out to her family. I think that was amazingly brave of her. No one was surprised. But neither were they warm to the idea.

"I don't think she has sex," Jared said in the Gremlin. "When the time comes, she'll just spontaneously regenerate. A mini-Jo will appear on her back like a goiter and then drop off and plop! She's a parent. No fuss, no muss. No exchange of bodily fluids."

"Yeah!" Jerusha said with a laugh.

"Please, kids," Nephi said. "She's my sister. She's really looked out for us. When she lectures us, she's just doing it for our own good."

"She doesn't lecture us, Dad," Jared cracked. "She lectures you."

"Look, you two. We have about 45 minutes to kill until we have to meet Jo. What's say we take a first look at what's out there for apartments, sort of do the first pass through?"

So the three of them spent the next thirty minutes rolling through various parts of town, looking for Rooms for Rent signs. Then they drove to the office of Sparkling Clean Inc. on Fourth.

They saw Jo standing in front of the building, her arms crossed at her chest, an envelope dangling in one hand.

"Here's the money, Nephi," she said, extending her hand with the envelope once all three of the Basermans emerged from the Gremlin. Nephi reached out to take the envelope and Jo retracted it and pushed her other hand, finger extended, into Nephi's sternum.

"I want to hear you promise," Jo said, leaning into Nephi. "Say you'll go to Priesthood Meeting on Sunday. And stay for Sunday School and Sacrament Meeting. He needs"—she pointed at Jared—"instruction in the gospel. Take the girl, too."

"Jo, you have my word," Nephi said, instinctively raising his hand in the Boy Scout salute. He placed his other hand on his heart. "Next Sunday, the whole enchilada," he said.

"They're serving enchiladas at Sacrament Meeting?" Jared asked. "I'm there. The Mormon Church goes south of the border!"

Jo eyed Jared dubiously. She pursed her lips and handed Nephi the envelope. "Make sure you're keeping track of all I owe you, Jo," Nephi said as he took the envelope.

Jo looked distastefully at the envelope in her brother's hands. "Nephi, I stopped keeping track years ago. I do this because you're family and it's my duty."

"Thanks so much, Jo," Nephi said. He held out his arms and moved in to hug his sister.

"Nephi, be serious," she said, holding up her hands toward Nephi and shooing him away. "Go find a place to live. I have work to do."

And that's what they did, roaming southern Boise, stuffed between all their belongings. They talked about their latest encounter with Aunt Jo as they drove.

"I feel sorry for Aunt Jo," Jared said. "She doesn't seem happy, even with all that money."

"Money doesn't buy happiness," Nephi said. "Look at us. We

don't have a lot of money, but that doesn't stop us from being happy, does it?"

"I think she seems angry all the time," said Jared. "Angry and sad."

"She's desolate," Nephi said.

"She's what?" Jared said.

"Desolate," Nephi said. "It means she's all alone, by herself. Lonely and sad."

"Yeah, she's that," Jared said. "Desolate."

"I think she's pissed because since she's a dyke she doesn't have a husband, and that means she can't make it into the Celestial Kingdom," Jerusha said. "Besides, I don't think dykes can get into the Celestial Kingdom, even if they are married."

"Aunt Jo's a dyke?" Jared exclaimed in mock astonishment, jerking forward and splaying his fingers in front of himself.

"We love Jo for who she is," Nephi said. "Besides, Jerusha, I think Heavenly Father would be willing to fudge to let Jo into the Celestial Kingdom."

"I agree with Dad," Jared said. "God loves everyone. I mean, I don't want to spend time and eternity with Aunt Jo, but God probably does."

"Puh!" Jerusha responded.

And so it went.

***

THE THING about the Basermans was that they could be something less than surgical when interacting with one another, blunt-edged, even. They felt free to let their true emotions show, which, if my family is any indicator, is not common in Mormon households, where unacceptable emotions and touchy issues were broomed under the rug. For example, when I was fourteen, my Sex Ed consisted of an ambiguous Sunday School talk from a member who was a doctor. The next Sunday, a Sister Teacher in Sunday School passed around an unwrapped stick of gum for everybody to hold, and then asked if anybody wanted to chew the gum that had been handled by others. Then, to drive home the point, she chewed another stick of gum and asked if anybody else wanted to chew it. The message was clear: Keep yourself pure for marriage. Whatever that meant. My mom capped it off by sliding a pamphlet under my pillow a while later.

But Nephi and his kids would discuss anything with each other. I saw it. Anything. With the Basermans, there seemed to be an unstated understanding that if a member of the family did go too far in expressing a particular uncensored emotion, forgiveness would always freely be given. You were allowed to be yourself, even surly at times. Nobody was perfect. The thing was that such emotional eruptions rarely happened among them. It's my judgment that such explosions were infrequent because they were so free to let off steam with one another. If one of them offended another family member, the offended member would quickly share the injured feelings. They'd tell each other anything. (The clear exception to this was Jared's "secrets," which came later.) As a result, there was always a good vibe around them. You could tell they sincerely enjoyed each other's company, even if they didn't always understand one another. They were all they had, each of them.

They drove around for a fair while, mostly because Nephi was picky when it came to choosing seedy rental units. They'd pull up to a location and Nephi would go inside to talk to the manager. Eventually, they'd emerge from the office and the manager would take Nephi on a tour of the facility. Jared and Jerusha would stay in the car, not because they didn't care about where they would be staying, but because they had learned that, one, they were far less discriminating than their father and, two, whatever motel he chose likely wasn't to be a long-term solution. Nephi would land different sales jobs, perform unspectacularly, and either lose interest or get sacked. Consequently, Jared and Jerusha were continually changing schools. Despite this, they were always at the top of their class. In fact, whenever they'd show up at a new school, the administrators would take one look at their transcripts and put them both in gifted classes.

Jerusha, she would always rapidly rise to the top of the gifted kids' clique. She had that something about her that seemed to say "I don't give a shit what you think." But here's what they thought. Boys, they wanted to get into her pants, but, being geeks, they didn't have the first clue about how to go about doing that. She had an animal magnetism: deep-set, intense eyes and auburn hair worn in a style that, were it a little bit longer in back, would be called a mullet today. She wasn't a tomboy but she dressed like a boy. Girls, they were cowed by her. She had a way of saying what everybody else thought. You could even call her a loudmouth, I suppose. She's what you would call Take Charge. Physically, Jerusha was smaller than average for a girl her age. However, she was always physically strong. She would always win wrestling matches with Jared. It's fair to say that she was the Alpha Twin. However, though she bossed around Jared, she was terribly fond of him.

For his part, Jared was usually on the periphery of the gifted kids' clique, to the extent he was connected to any clique at all. For her part, Jerusha would try to bring Jared into the Inner Circle of the Geek Brigade, but Jared would soon alienate kids with his strange sense of humor. Physically, Jared was less than impressive. He was sloped-backed and thin-wristed. And his hair! The best way to describe Jared's hair is to say that, when the time came to go on his mission, he didn't have to make a single change to his 'do. As far as the Mormon authorities were concerned, it was already Standard Issue. Really. Consider the guidelines for Mormon missionary hairstyling:

- Cut hair above the ears and neck. You should have a line between your hair and shirt collar.

- All missionaries must wear a part and comb their hair to the side.
- Sideburns are not allowed.

JARED'S HAIRSTYLE fit right into this scheme. The one devia-tion—the one way he flouted the rules, I guess you could say—was the way his frizzy hair would stick up in an arch from his part. It was a veritable crest. It probably would have been useful for attracting mates in the wild. If Jared had been like other wiry-haired white boys in the late '70s, he probably would have sported a full-blown afro in advance of his mission, maybe even with a cake-cutter jutting out at a smart-assed angle. But, instead, he walked around with that . . . thing . . . on the top of his head, right in front of every-body. Courageous in a way, I guess. The mission leaders no doubt thought, "Here is a young man who is bullet-proof when it comes to being snubbed by his peers. Here is a young man who seeks the Glory of God, not the Praise of Men. No friend of the world, he!"

"I discern that you're a brave lad, my son," the bishop report-edly said to Jared during Jared's pre-mission worthiness interview.

"It's not easy, sir," Jared said. "My classmates, they pick on me because I'm gifted, you know, from God. Heavenly Father. I was born with the ability to identify what member of a group has flatu-lated in a small room. It's a burden."

"Uh, well. You're a brave lad, my son," said the bishop.

"That's what they tell me," Jared said.

I don't know. I do know Jared wasn't stupid. He knew his hair-style didn't fit in with his classmates, but he liked it coiffed that way. To him, that's what mattered. Early on, I gave him grief for his hairstyle, but he didn't care. He proudly pointed out he had had the same hairdo since he was eight. Proudly. I'm sure his look didn't stick out, really, in grade school. I mean, everybody was a doofus back then. Kids would pick their nose in public and eat it. Right in class!

In junior high and high school, his hairstyle made him a target for bullies. And his hairstyle was only one of his problems during his early teen years. Jared was not athletic, and kids who weren't athletic got slapped with labels like fag and spaz in PE class. Jared told me about a time when a jock passed a basketball right into his face at full speed. It helped that Jared's family moved around a lot, so he was changing schools often. That meant he never had to bear the abuse too long at any school before he left. And every time he started a new school, he would get a couple months' grace before boys grew aware of this spaziness and started the abuse—stuffing him into lockers, pantsing him, all the usual stuff. I mean, with his hair alone, he was asking for it. And then he'd spaz out. It was *ineluctable*.

No one was more aware of Jared's dorkiness than Jerusha. But she wrapped her heart around him and stood up for him whenever she could. More than once, she laid into some troglodyte who was tormenting Jared. In fact, she broke this kid's nose once. Blood everywhere. She became a whirlwind of punching fists, kicking feet, and purple invective whenever she felt the need to defend her twin brother.

BY AND BY, the Gremlin pulled up to a two-story apartment complex. The manager, presumably, was outside watering the lawn disinterestedly, perhaps thinking about boobs he had left unfelt in his boyhood—alas—and he scowled at the Basermans as they pulled up. A teenage boy stood with his bike at the corner of the apartment dragging on a cigarette with timid derision as Nephi got out of the car and approached the manager.

"Got one left, if that's what you're looking for," the manager called out. "First and last at the start, and you don't have any pets in there, do you?"

Nephi padded his back pocket with his hand. "Do you take cash? But let's not put the cart before the horse, sir. Show me what you have and then let's talk." The manager threw down the hose, turned off the spigot and motioned Nephi to follow him. He'd get back to the boobs, undoubtedly, as his schedule allowed.

"That guy over there, he keeps staring at us," Jerusha said in the car. She pointed to the teenage boy on the bike.

"You mean he keeps staring at you," Jared responded. "He's warm for your form."

"Whatever. He looks like a schmuck."

"Schmucks need love, too."

"Puh!"

Eventually, Nephi and the manager emerged and Nephi gave the thumbs-up to the twins in the car.

"There's a tanning booth!" he called to them. "We have to drive to the back."

Nephi got in the car and drove around the building while the teenage boy followed their progress on his bike.

"You're on his radar," Jared said. Jerusha glanced over at the boy and tousled the top of her hair.

The Basermans slowly climbed out of the Gremlin and carried their possessions into their new apartment. The boy threw his cigarette into the bushes and approached them with outstretched hand.

"Welcome, new family. Glad to have you. My name's Rickey, Rickey Chalmers. My friends call me Roach, though."

"Home sick from school, Roach?" Nephi asked.

"I sell marijuana, sir. Don't go to school. But I'm not a scumbag or anything, sir."

"Well, Roach. Not too sure I like the sound of that," Nephi said, a large cardboard box in his hands.

"There's nothing to worry about, sir. Mr.–?"

"Baserman, Nephi Baserman," he said, balancing the box on his thigh and extending his hand. "These are my twins, Jared and Jerusha."

"Hi, ya," Roach said to them, holding up his palm.

"I hear it's hard to find a really choice bag of weed in these parts," Jared said to Roach. "I think it's because all the best fertilizer is taken up to produce the finest potatoes in the world. You know: Famous Potatoes. The license plates. Most states have a state bird. Us, we have the potato. It's our state bird, or state tuber, I guess."

Roach looked blankly at Jared and turned to Jerusha. "Need some help?" he asked.

"I got it," she said. "A guy who sells marijuana instead of going to school sounds like a scumbag to me."

"I understand how you could reach that conclusion," he said. "But what's the point of school, really?" He looked at the Basermans one at a time. "Learn a trade, make a life for yourself and your family. I'm already doing that right now. I cleared $2K last month."

Nephi paused in thought, as though he was doing some mental math.

"Hey, Dad, you should sell marijuana!" Jared said.

"I have one gin and tonic a week, on Saturdays, and that's all the altered consciousness I need," Nephi said. He started up the stairs carefully with his box. "That same day, I buy one lottery ticket. That's the only high I need."

Jerusha headed up the stairs with a box. Roach followed her, trying to strike up a conversation. Jared watched them ascend and smirked.

"He wasn't staring at me," he said to himself.

⸻

AS THE DAYS WENT BY, Roach spent as much time around the Basermans—that is, Jerusha—as he could, considering his busy business schedule. Jerusha was off-putting at first but soon warmed up to him. One day when Nephi was out, Roach was sitting around their apartment with the twins. He turned to Jerusha.

"So, you guys have never smoked pot?"

"I get high on life," Jared said, deadpan.

Jerusha looked at Jared and then at Roach. "We might be open to that," she said. "What do you have in mind?"

"Well, your dad's gone right now. Why don't we head over to my apartment and I'll stoke us a couple bowls. We'll listen to some tunes, have some munchies."

Jerusha glanced at her brother. Jared looked back at her apprehensively.

"Why not?" asked Jerusha. "Come on, Jared."

Jared pushed himself up. "Why do I think I'm going to be telling a psychiatrist about this day twenty years from now?" he asked.

"Don't worry, man," Roach said. "This is going to be great. Trust me."

They walked to Roach's apartment and he offered seats on his shabby couch to Jared and Jerusha. He turned and rummaged through his stash box. "I had an idea you guys might agree to this, so I've been saving some real nasty shit for you all," he said.

"You save your shit?" Jared asked.

"I like you, man," Roach said, stopping his rummaging and looking over at Jared. "You don't quit."

"Yeah, he's too much," Jerusha said, eyeing her brother with a sly smile.

The way Roach told me the story later, he set up all his accoutrements—a pipe in the shape of a skull, a mini blowtorch for a lighter, a kitchen strainer, and a large transparent blue bowl that held a half an ounce of pot—and sat down and rubbed his hands together quickly. (There's a story about the bowl. It was actually the casing of a police car's siren light. On a dare, trying to impress an inarguable fox, Roach had nicked it, three sheets to the wind.) "Let's do it!" he said. Roach took a pinch of pot from his blue bowl and packed it into the pipe's bowl. "Ladies first," he said, handing the skull pipe to Jerusha. Jerusha put the pipe to her mouth and Roach held the lit blowtorch to the bowl. "Take it easy on your first hit," he said. "Just a little bit."

Jerusha inhaled and sat back, her eyes wide.

"Hold it in your lungs as long as you can," Roach said. "That's what gets you high."

"What's it like, Jerusha?" Jared asked. She looked at her brother and nodded her head.

"She's a natural," Roach exclaimed. "Now your turn, Jared." He took the pipe from Jerusha, who was still holding her breath. He packed the bowl and held it out to Jared.

Jared took a timid draw on the pipe and sat back, his eyes watering.

Jerusha exhaled her hit a moment later. "Woo! That was intense," she said. "Jared, hold it in as long as you can."

Jared gave her a thumbs-up sign as smoke escaped from his mouth in two furtive bursts.

"You can do it, man," Roach said. "Hang in there."

At that instant, Jared burst into a fit of coughing and he expelled a cloud of smoke.

"That's cool," Roach said. "It's your first time. You'll get used to it."

The smoke session proceeded from there. Jerusha took bigger and bigger hits, and Jared tried heroically to keep from coughing after each hit. Eventually, he seemed to get the hang of it.

"I think I'm stoned," Jerusha said with a lazy smile. "This is great, Jared, isn't it?"

"Jared's not here," Jared said. "He's gone down some rabbit hole. Please leave a message."

"Man, you're too much," Roach said with a hearty laugh.

At first, they just smoked with Roach in his apartment. Then they started smoking in the Baserman's when Nephi was out selling. Soon Jerusha went out and bought her own bong. Then she bought a bigger bong. When she got to a bong that attached to a gasmask, she figured that was about it. That is, until she saw a pipe at a head shop in the shape of a penis, veined and swarthy and menacing. Jared drew the line at the Wondrous Wang, as it came to be called. He'd smoke from the gasmask bong but not from the Wondrous Wang.

"Man, you need to be comfortable with sexuality, man," Roach said to Jared once when he and Jerusha were smoking out of the penis pipe.

Jerusha took a big draw from the pipe, held her breath, and looked at Jared. "Yeah, Jared. I think there's fellatio in the Book of Mormon somewhere." She eked out the words under the strain of the marijuana.

"Fellatio," Roach said lazily. "That's really a bizarre word, when you think about it."

"What about cunnilingus? Cunnilingus," Jerusha said, exhaling. "Cun-i-ling-gus."

"Or dingus. What's up with that word? Have you ever noticed how many different ways we can speak of a man's private parts? Dingus. Gizmo. Trouser snake. I heard the Eskimos have 25 different words for penis. You know, frozen penis, a penis inside an igloo, a penis outside an igloo, a polar bear's penis."

"That's so high," Jerusha said. She erupted into laughter, followed by Roach.

"I'm leaving," Jared said. "It's not fun being the non-high person around two high people. I think I'll go be non-high somewhere else."

————————

JARED AND JERUSHA told their father they were partaking soon after they started. He looked at them skeptically.

"Okay, look, just don't do it when I'm here and don't do it at school. If you don't have an education, you don't have anything. If I hear you're cutting classes and stuff, then it's all over. No more pot. And don't leave any of your pot-smoking . . . equipment . . . lying around. This isn't an opium den or something. As long as you're treating other people the way you want to be treated, I'm cool with this." He made air quotes at the word cool. "And this isn't going to get in the way of our community service. If it does, you're done. No argument."

One thing I was going to learn about the Basermans was that Nephi actually had high standards for his kids. First off, he insisted on good grades, and the twins effortlessly obliged him. He had never been much of a student himself. He had quit high school to take a job as a night watchman at a spud silo. But if he suspected their pot smoking was getting in the way of their studies, he would have put a stop to it, no argument. Meanwhile, he made a point of having his kids go to community service projects—park plantings, food bank crews, and such—on a regular basis. When I asked him why once, Nephi said, "You learn by doing. It was up to me to give my kids these lessons." He also dragged them to civil disobedience actions on a regular basis. Each of them had been arrested more than once.

"It's not for me, this weed you smoke. But that's me," Nephi told Jared and Jerusha. "I'll tell you though, if Jo finds out, she'll drop us like a rock. No argument."

"So she won't find out," Jerusha said.

So it went. Jared would only smoke with Roach and Jerusha, or just with Jerusha. Never alone. As the months passed, he found that he was becoming more and more jumpy while high, scared of his own shadow. He started finding excuses to beg off when Jerusha would suggest a session with her gasmask bong. One time, he and his sister went to a movie high and Jared couldn't concentrate on the show because he was so sure some toughs behind them were taunting him and suggesting they were going to mangle him in various ways. He couldn't really make out what they were saying. But he knew that it was menacing. He was too afraid to look around and see if they were really there. At the end of the movie, Jared hid in his aisle until he was sure the theater was clear. Jerusha eventually gave up on him and walked home, and then he cautiously followed her.

It was this growing paranoia that led Jared to steadfastly stay away from anything harder. But Jerusha began experimenting with LSD soon thereafter, and she raved about her trips to Jared. He always tried to change the subject.

Eventually, pot stopped being fun for Jared, so he quit.

Several months later, Jared walked into the kitchen, where his father was buttering toast, and suddenly the room around him became warped, as he later put it. That's the word he used. "It was warped," he said. "I wondered if I was disintegrating. I thought, 'Make it stop!'"

"Something wrong, Jared?" Nephi asked. Jared sat down.

"Just feel dizzy," he said. "I don't know."

Soon enough, the warped reality passed, but Jared knew right then—in the hollow of his gut—that this was something he needed to keep from his sister and father. At the time, he attributed it to the lasting effects of marijuana. The thing he knew, though, was that something was wrong with him.

Thus began Jared's secrets.

Another time, months later, when they were in yet another apartment, Jared was in bed and he thought he heard someone at his bedroom window. He could hear the person running back and forth on the gravel driveway and pausing stealthily under Jared's bedroom window and whispering. But to whom?

This, too, Jared kept from his family.

Things went on pretty much in this manner for several months. Likewise, the pattern of Nephi regularly limping to Jo and asking for financial help, that continued, too. The new twist was that Jo would increasingly point out that the time for Jared's mission was approaching. She'd usually make a little speech about the importance of the mission before she would hand the cash to Nephi.

"I don't want to go on a mission, Dad," Jared said once when they were out eating. "I mean, I believe in the gospel but, you know, it's not like we've been super religious or anything."

"Yeah," said Jerusha. "What the hell?"

"Jared, son, I want you to do what you want to do," Nephi said. "But, you know, I went on a mission and it was okay."

"But, Dad, you don't even believe," Jerusha said.

"I believe, Jerusha," Nephi said. "You can believe and still not be all religious and all that. When have you ever heard me say I don't believe in the gospel?"

"Dad, you say it by the fact that we only go to church every now and then," Jerusha said. "You say it by the fact that you let us smoke pot. You don't even pay tithing, Dad."

"I believe by how I live," Nephi said. "I try to love my fellow man. God wants us to look out for one another because life's hard. I try to treat people the way I want to be treated. That's the Golden Rule, kids. That's how I live, and that's how I want you to live. Religion, strictly speaking, it's not really that important, I think."

It was true. Nephi had a kind heart. In fact, one of the reasons he was such a crappy salesman is he was too softhearted. The sleazy salesman type of guy, he'll tell you whatever he has to tell you to get you to buy, even if you don't need it. But Nephi would often queer the deal by talking a prospect right out of the picture, even after they had decided to buy. "This probably isn't right for you," he would say. "You know, you really don't need this." He was at heart a do-gooder, and the only registered Democrat in his entire extended family (though he usually forgot to vote). More than once, he would blow off an important meeting with a big prospect to attend one of his pickets/sit-ins, leading to the loss of the prospect and a swift kick out the door from his boss. On the occasions when Nephi and his kids would go to church—say, every third week or so —he would belt out his favorite hymns with gusto in an off-key tenor, his eyes tearing up.

In sum, Nephi led with his heart in all matters, and often only used his brain when the time came to explain or rationalize his actions.

Nephi's one real vice—other than his weekly gin and tonic and lottery ticket—was sugar, and Sugar Daddies in particular. Just about the only times he wasn't nursing a Sugar Daddy was when he was in church, in a sales presentation, or asleep. However, he often fell asleep with a Sugar Daddy in his mouth and he would wake up with the candy stuck to his clothes, the couch, or his shaggy mop of hair. Jerusha would end up having to cut out the Sugar Daddy, leaving an uneven pattern on the side of his head. He took seven sugars in his convenience store coffee.

Anyway, every time Nephi and the twins would show up at Jo's office to get cash, she would launch into her campaign to get Jared on a mission. Then, this one time, she threw him a curve:

"Nephi, the Senator wants to bury the hatchet," she said. "He wants to bring you back into the good graces of the family."

"He said that?" Nephi said, looking penitent.

"He wants to say all is forgiven, come back."

"What do I do, Jo?"

"Nephi, the annual family reunion is next week."

"Jo, I can't go to that."

"Nephi, be a man. Now's the time to step up. You'll come to the reunion and you'll make your peace with the Senator."

"But–"

"No more of your buts, Nephi. Next Saturday, Thompson Park, noon. You and the kids will be welcomed with open arms. Now, take this." She held out a wad of cash for Nephi. When Nephi grabbed the bills, she maintained her grip. "Nephi," she said, looking him square in the eye, "don't you let me down on this. It's time to show your son what a man is."

Jo released the money and Nephi watched her climb into her car and speed away.

The twins walked up to their father. "We have a family reunion?" Jared asked.

"I haven't been in more than fifteen years," Nephi said, watching his sister drive away.

"Your dad wants to bury the hatchet?" Jerusha said. "What happened fifteen years ago that you stopped going?"

Nephi watched his sister's car fade from view. "We're going to need to cook something, or bake something," he said. "And it can't be from a box. It has to be from scratch. Well, maybe Bisquick is okay."

"Don't look at me," Jerusha said. "I'm not baking anything."

"I'll do it," Jared said, smiling deviously at his sister and placing one hand's fingertips delicately on his chest. "*I'm* in touch with my feminine side."

CHAPTER THREE

On the morning of the Reunion—the fateful meeting between Nephi and his estranged father—Nephi and the twins piled into the Gremlin and began the journey to Ervin "Cyclone" Thompson Memorial Park on the ragweed outskirts of town. Jerusha sat in the back, tapping her feet on the back of the front seat. Jared sat in the front with his dad. Between Jared and his dad was the Impossibly Easy Lasagna Pie that Jared had concocted from the directions on the side of the Bisquick box.

The family reunion was a co-production of Jo and Nita, the only female children in Nephi's immediate family. Jo paid for it glumly and Nita produced it with the verve of a Broadway up-and-comer. This year's theme was "Our Pioneer Past." Nita created a homespun extravaganza to commemorate the day in 1847 when Brigham Young and his bedraggled followers crested the Wasatch and saw for the first time the Salt Lake Valley: Zion in America, of all places. Nita planned pioneer games, a best pioneer costume contest, and a pioneer playland for the kids—even a real Dutch oven! The reunion was the only time each year when Jo and Nita would get within spitting distance of one another. It's worth noting that Nita was the only member of the family who could get close to actually accusing Jo of being a degenerate. She would always couch her allegations behind certain niceties, never come right out and say it. For some reason, Nita was the one sibling who Jo wouldn't push around. When Nita would call Jo to ask for money for the reunion decorations, Jo would cut her a check with all due haste just to get the conversation over with.

As Nephi drove to the fateful reunion, he filled in the twins on all his immediate family members and their quirks. It became clear to Jared and Jerusha that their father had a mole somewhere in the superstructure of the family. He seemed to know all the dirt. The factoids that had apparently sifted down to him were notable for their strategic cruelty. Every revelation was intended precisely to injure the reputation of the subject mentioned, or to confirm the reputation, depending on the case.

In sum, these far-flung Basermans were all at each other's throats, yet smiling toothfully. Not surprisingly, the annual family reunion was a kettle of slow boiling malice, the attendees called hither solely by the devotion to the Mormon ideal of Perfect Families.

Years later, Jerusha told me, "I thought, 'Supposedly, these people want to spend eternity together on each patriarch's personal planet. Good God, they'll kill each other!'"

When Nephi and the twins pulled up to Thompson Park, late, the parking lot was jam-packed—so much so that they had to park out on the road. Over the entrance to the park hung a vast butcher paper sign that read: This is the Place! The welcoming message was to commemorate Brigham Young's first words upon looking down into the Salt Lake Valley, his fellow believers craning their necks over his outstretched arms.

As they walked toward the park entrance, Nephi, Jared, and Jerusha could see that the assembled Basermans were milling around, chatting with one another. Apparently, the reunion hadn't officially started. As they entered the park and started walking among people, everyone greeted them in a cheerful manner, as if they were chums. They were happy to see Nephi and the twins, militantly.

Suddenly, Nephi stopped in his tracks. The twins stopped a few paces ahead and turned back to see what was up. "There he is," Nephi said, squinting into the distance.

Jared and Jerusha followed his gaze. "Who?" they said together.

"My father," Nephi said.

"Which one is he?" Jared asked.

"He's the one that looks like he's giving a sermon. It's probably just a conversation, but with my father even conversations are sermons. Well, might as well get this over with. Time to man up, like Jo said." Nephi took a deep breath and shook his arms as if he was preparing for prizefight.

"Well, what's a family reunion without a sermon?" Jared said as he walked next to his dad.

Nephi's father, Marcus Baserman, The Senator, was a hardbitten old badger who had the build, and all the charm, of a refrigerator box. As Nephi and the twins approached, he caught sight of Nephi and stopped his conversation/sermon.

"He didn't smile. He didn't frown," Jared told me later. "I mean, he was always sort of frowning, like the edges of his mouth were melting into his neck. And he had these huge glasses, black and square-framed glasses, with real thick lenses. You really couldn't make out what his eyes looked like. You didn't know if he was looking at you or through you. The other thing I remember was that he was wearing a belt and suspenders. A belt and suspenders!"

"Well," the Senator said, staring at or through Nephi.

Nephi stood silent, assuming some more words would be forthcoming from the Senator, but there was nothing.

"It was like a contest or something," Jared whispered to me years later.

"Father, sir. Jo told me to come," Nephi said.

"I'd say you were the prodigal son, except I don't think your return is significant of a repentant heart. Most people, when they've been out engaging in riotous living with the publicans and the sinners, they would eventually see the error of their ways, after filling their belly with the husks that the swine did eat. You, you probably want something."

He remained as impassive as a toad. "I couldn't even tell if he was alive, or just standing there dead," Jared told me later.

"Sir?" Nephi began.

"You put me in the mind of Gadianton, the apostate from the Book of Mormon, the founder and first leader of the robber bands that bore his name," the Senator said. "He was a flatterer and expert in many words. And Gadianton betrayed King Helaman, and 'The land was filled with robbers and Lamanites . . . therefore there was blood and carnage spread throughout all the face of the land . . . no man could keep that which was his own, for the thieves, and the robbers and the murderers, and the magic art, and their witchcraft which was in the land . . . and every heart was hardened.' Unless you're here to repent. Are you here to repent?"

"Sir, I haven't done anything," Nephi began.

"Depart!" he said and actually turned his back on them all.

"But Jo said–" Nephi started and then, seeing his father's back, turned and began walking away

As Nephi walked away, he shook his head and said, "I don't understand. Jo said–"

"I smell a rat," Jerusha said. "Something's up."

"Dad," Jared said, looking around nervously. "I feel like, like everyone's watching us. Let's go."

"I've got to find Jo," Nephi said, apparently not hearing anything Jared or Jerusha said.

As they navigated their way through the crowd, Nephi's much-tattooed brother, Hiram, emerged from the side and blocked their path.

"Jo told me you were going to show up," he said, his arms outstretched. "You have the bravery of Ammon. I admire you."

Hiram wrapped his arms around Nephi and gave him a bear hug.

"Hiram," Nephi said, clearly at a loss.

"Little brother, wonderful to see you," Hiram said, keeping his hands clasped on Nephi's upper arms and pulling back a bit for a better look at him. "The question is, are you committed to returning to worthiness? Have you really looked deep down inside yourself and found that part of you that says, 'Yes, I will do whatever it takes to follow the Savior?'"

"Hiram, I came here to–" Nephi began.

"I was like you, little brother. I was never really converted in the first place. A social conversion to Mormonism is not good enough to endure a lifetime. You need to know that it's true. You cannot know that it's false, but you can know it's true. Because it is true. Me, I have an unshakable testimony."

"Hiram, this is Jared and–"

"My point, Nephi, is that, really, your only hope is that you were never really converted in the first place," Hiram said, returning his gaze to Nephi. "When you're really in a fix is when you did convert—you did taste of Heavenly Father's goodness, did have the heavens opened unto you—and then you turned your back on all that, turned your back on Him. No hope remains for such a person."

Jo barged into the circle at that instant. "Jared, I've been looking for you," she said, taking hold of Jared by the arm.

"Jo. There you are. Are you sure the Senator –" Nephi began.

"Nephi, please," Jo said with exasperation. "I have a word for the boy." She pulled Jared from the group and led him away.

Hiram put his hand on Nephi's shoulder when he tried to follow them.

"We're all family here, Nephi," Hiram said.

"I'll be right back, Dad," Jared called over his shoulder.

JO GUIDED JARED through the crowd and turned to Jared. "This is the day, son. This is your day of decision. The day of decision." She maneuvered Jared behind the park's bathrooms and sat him at a picnic table.

"Now," she said, crossing her arms on her chest. "What are your plans for after graduation?"

Jared looked up at her. "Well, I don't really know, Aunt Jo."

"That's your father talking," she said, motioning vaguely across the campground to where Nephi stood. "He's aimless. Do you think he's been leading you and your family anywhere?"

"I–"

"He has no destination planned. He's in limbo. The only reason he's not in the poor house—that you're not all in the poor house—is me. I keep him afloat. And I'm reaching the end of my patience, son."

Jared raised his finger. "The poor house is underrated."

"Now's not the time for any of your jokes, son." She poked her finger into Jared's chest. "Why do you think I'm coming to you? Why aren't I talking to your father or your sister? Why is that?"

"Well . . . "

"I'm coming to you because you are your family's only hope. Do you want to spend eternity with your family in Heavenly Father's presence? Is your family worthy of entering the Celestial Kingdom, son? Is your father the priesthood leader in your home? Someone needs to get this family on the path to righteousness. Your father can't do that and the girl won't. You are the only one, Jared."

"Aunt Jo . . ."

"Here's my deal for you. You go on your mission. You return with honor. You return with honor and you know what I'll do? Return with honor and I'll give your father a job for life running my laundries. A job for life. When's the last time your father had a real job? A job he couldn't lose due to his irresponsibility."

"Aunt Jo, I know my father's not a big success. But he's a good man."

"He's an idiot, and he'll keep being an idiot unless you do something. There's more, though. Return with honor and your father gets a job for life, and you get a new sports car."

"A sports car?"

"A brand new sports car. Your choice. And your father gets a job for life. All you have to do, all you have to do is go on your mission, return with honor, and everything changes for your family. But if you don't accept this deal, know now that I'm through floating your family. No more money from sister Jo." She paused for a moment to let this sink in. "What's more, if you decide not to go on a mission, your family is cut off financially from this minute forward. And if you tell your dad about this offer I'm making to you, your family is cut off immediately as well. You have only one option if you want to maintain my financial support of your father in the near-term and hold out a possibility of financial rescue for your father two years from now. Go on your mission."

"All I have to do is go on my mission and you'll take care of my dad and my sister?"

"Well, go on your mission and I'll continue supporting your father and sister while you're away. However, if you return without honor, the deal is off and your family is cast off from my pocketbook. The only way this really works for your family is for you to both go on your mission and return with honor. Look at it this way: The full blessing is dependent on your obedience. That's the way Heavenly Father works. He only blesses those who obey Him. If you and your family had been going to church—or at least paying attention those few times you did go to church—you might have learned that."

Jared took deep breath. "Looks like I have no choice," he said.

"You always have a choice, son. That's what I'm trying to teach you. Heavenly Father never takes away our free agency. Everything is left up to us to decide: right or wrong, good or evil. Every day, all day, you will be confronted with choices small and large. Do I cheat on this school test? Do I laugh at that improper joke? Do I watch this R-rated movie? Do I drink that cup of coffee? The natural man will tell you, 'Go on. Do it! Everyone else is doing it. You don't want to seem different, do you?'"

"I guess not," Jared offered.

"That's the point, son. You are different. There is a reason that Heavenly Father held you back in the spirit world until this exact moment in history. He wants the fittest soldiers in His army in these latter days. He could have sent you down to a family of Mexicans or Hindus or Catholics, or He could have put you in a handicapped person's body."

"What about handicapped Mormon kids?"

"No jokes!" she said, wagging her finger at Jared and pointing the same finger skyward. "Are you going to ever get in line with the gospel? The point is, nothing good is ever going to happen to you unless you start living obediently. And you can start right now by deciding to go on your mission. And you can keep it up by following all God's commandments on your mission. That's how you're going to make sure you return with honor."

"Choose the right," Jared said dubiously.

"No time like the present, boy, for starting a good habit."

"All right, I'll do it. I mean, I'll go on my mission. I don't know if I can return with honor."

"You can do all things through Christ which strengthens you, Jared," she said, reaching out her hand as if she were going to place it on his shoulder but stopping short.

With the deal finalized, Jo and Jared were rescued from this awkward moment by a voice that suddenly boomed over the PA system: "Okay, all you Basermans. I hate to break up all your catching up and all, but it's time for you to all gather round the stage for the opening prayer."

"It's Nita," Jo said, looking in the direction of the voice. "Let's go."

Jared and Jo followed the crowd as it converged on the stage.

Jared could see his father and sister to one side and he found his way over to them.

"Everything okay, son?" Nephi asked.

"Yeah, Dad. It's great."

All present bowed their heads as the Senator offered the invocation. Then Nita held up an air horn, blasted it, and said over the loudspeaker, "Let the reunion begin!" adding with a giggle, "Commence reunification!"

The women at the reunion brought out trays of food—fried chicken, barbecued chicken, potato salad, macaroni salad, molded gelatin with marshmallows, corn on the cob, hotdogs, hamburgers, and on and on—as the sounds of the Mormon Tabernacle Choir were piped over the PA. Nephi, Jared, and Jerusha loaded up their plates and took a seat at a table far from the stage. They could see the Senator wandering from table to table to welcome different family members. Though he slapped backs and shook hands, he never seemed pleased to see anyone. Or maybe he did. Again and again, he bared his teeth as if he was evacuating his breakfast from his bowels. Jared and Jerusha took this as his attempt at a smile.

The entertainment was a number of musical performances and dance routines. People clapped and laughed. When the performances were over, the area buzzed with friendly conversation. Nephi, of course, had engaged the people around him in chit chat. Jared and Jerusha joined in. Everything was free and easy—until a familiar, stern voice over the PA system caught their attention.

"I have something to share, everyone."

At once, Nephi and the twins recognized Jo's voice echoing over the loudspeakers and turned toward the stage.

"I want to testify that Heavenly Father still works in our lives in this day and age. He'll work in your life if you follow all the commandments. Obedience is the key to blessing," Jo said. "Look at my life. Heavenly Father has blessed me financially because I stay on the straight and narrow. It's not easy living the gospel—really living it—but I testify to you that it pays off, both on this side of the veil and in the world to come." The crowd mumbled its approval.

"But that's not why I'm speaking here," Jo continued. "I'm really here to let somebody else bear their testimony. Jared?" Jo tilted her head back and scanned the crowd for Jared. He stood up without pausing and started walking toward the stage.

"What the hell?" Jerusha said under her breath.

"I helped Jared make a big decision today, and he wants to tell us all about it." Jared climbed the stairs and crossed the stage to her. "Jared, tell your family and all of us. Tell us what you and I talked about."

Jared looked at her, apparently unsure what to say.

"What we talked about," Jo prompted him. "About obedience, and you?"

"Yeah," Jared said, slipping his hands into his pockets and inching up to the microphone. "Well, Aunt Jo, she explained to me that God wasn't going to bless me and stuff until I shaped up and began following Him."

Jo shifted herself closer to the microphone. "I told him that Nephi . . . Nephi? Wave your hand. Yes, my long-lost little brother is here, if you didn't know it. I told Jared that his father wasn't acting as the priesthood head in their home. We're all family here. I can share hard truths of love like that, don't you agree? 'Your father isn't leading your family in the gospel, so you have to take a stand.' That's what I told Jared. And?" Here she looked at Jared.

"And I've decided to go on my mission."

The crowd erupted into applause.

"What the hell?" Jerusha exclaimed.

Nephi was stunned.

Jo closed her eyes and rested her hands on Jared's shoulder. "Heavenly Father, we thank Thee for Thy son, Jared. We thank Thee that Jared has returned unto Thee, like a prodigal son, and we ask Thee to pour out Thy blessing on Jared."

At that exact instant—as best as I can make out—at that exact instant, Jared was, well, *enraptured*, I guess you'd say. He told me later that everything—the trees, the people, the banners, the transportable latrines, the teens necking furtively in the outskirts of the park—they all seemed to be giving off light, throbbing with the light, and humming, too. This all grew until the coalesced light and hum grew so intense that it was all Jared could perceive.

To the onlookers at the reunion, Jared held up his hands as if to shield his eyes. A look of bafflement came over his face and he called out, "Oh, God!" Then he fell to his knees and crumpled to his side. The crowd uttered a collective gasp.

"My son!" Nephi called out and bolted for the stage. Jerusha followed after him. When Nephi reached Jared, he went down on one knee and put his hands cautiously on Jared, who, apparently, was out cold.

"Jo, what happened?" Nephi cried.

"It was the power of God," she said.

"Holy hell!" Jerusha said.

"Jerusha, get a glass of water. Get a glass of water!" Nephi said wildly.

Jared's eyes fluttered open. "It's okay, Dad. I'm okay."

"What in the hell happened to you?" Jerusha asked.

"I don't know," Jared said, looking up into the sky. "Everything was light."

"It was the power of God," Jo said.

Nephi and Jerusha helped Jared to his feet. Jared waved vaguely to the stunned crowd. Polite, baffled applause emerged from the onlookers as Nephi and Jerusha escorted Jared to a park bench. They sat down and Jared looked at his dad.

"It's not like Aunt Jo said. I don't think you're a bad father. I think you're great. But maybe it's what God wants, going on my mission and stuff."

"No, Jared," his father said, tearing up. "I'm not a good father. I've done a terrible job of bringing you up in the gospel." At this moment, Jo walked up. "Jo, thank you so much for what you've done," Nephi said. By now, tears were streaming down Nephi's face.

At this moment, the Senator waddled up, looking as ill-tempered as a hungry goat.

"Father, look," Jo said.

The Senator glared at his children and grandchildren. "Hmmph," he said. Then he looked down and scratched his head with both hands. "Congratulations, boy," he grunted to Jared. "Jo," he said, looking at his daughter.

"Yes, father?"

"Follow me," he said, motioning for Jo to follow him.

As they walked away, Jerusha said, "Holy hell, Jared!"

"Dad, I don't know what happened, but I think I need to go on a mission," Jared said.

CHAPTER FOUR

Back to Sedro-Woolley, 1979. As Jared and I walked back to the apartment, a primitive part of me—my reptilian brain, perhaps?—wired urgent wordless telegrams to my soul. It was insisting that Jared was sent by God, for me. Jared would explain it all. Now, looking back, I can hear the messages loud and clear. They were so obvious. However, at the time, my higher self, the foremost ledge of my brain, epic achievement of human evolution, couldn't be bothered. I only understood the primal gruntings to the extent that I was overcome with a boundless sense of release. Suddenly, all my tension was gone. Twenty months of frustration. Everything was going to be alright, and it was because of Jared, somehow. God was acting.

"Man, I'm beat," I said. "I think I'm just going to crash when we get back."

But Jared was chatty as a Temple Square tour guide.

"I've never done that before, you know, born my testimony like that," he said as we walked to our apartment. "I mean, I've born my testimony when I was a little kid, in Primary and stuff. But that doesn't count. Today, it just seemed to force its way out. It was like

I really meant it. I think it started at the family reunion. God is going to help me return with honor."

"That's how it's supposed to work, I guess," I said. "My stepfather says God takes over after you do all you can do, 110 percent."

"The way they talk at the MTC, this kind of thing should be happening every day on a mission," said Jared. "You know, visions and stuff, seeing angels. When I was at the MTC, they told us not to be surprised if we saw an angel during our missions. They told us all sorts of stories about that very thing, a shitload of them."

"Yeah, I heard those stories too," I said wearily as we walked. I thought about my time at the MTC, the Missionary Training Center in Provo, Utah. It was where every young Mormon man went after being called to a mission. We went for several weeks of hard-core instruction, eight for anyone who had to share the gospel in a foreign language.

"Did you notice," Jared said, "that the missionaries in those stories, their exact names and where they were from, you didn't hear that?"

This alarmed me. Never had any of my companions and I talked about anything that wasn't Party Line. Doubts didn't exist.

"Yeah . . . that made me wonder too," I said, starting slowly and picking up speed. "The way they talk, though. All sorts of spiritual stuff is supposed to happen."

"Yeah. If you're in tune with the spirit."

"They told me, 'You hold more power in your little finger than the Pope does in his entire body,'" I said.

I was referring to the power and authority of the Melchizedek Priesthood—a power we were authorized to use as missionaries, but only in necessary and fitting ways. Performing Priesthood Blessings on people who were sick, stuff like that. It was the very power of God, funneled through men, like chain lightning through a frosting gun. The Melchizedek "offices" are apostles, high priests, patriarch, Seventy, and, bringing up the rear, elders—schlubs like Jared and me. (Women can no more hold the Melchizedek Priesthood than they can pee their name in the snow. And, as Daryl pointed out, until 1978, blacks couldn't hold the priesthood, either.) Any Mormon male can bless a meal, but a Melchizedek Priesthood holder—real spiritual giants like Jared and me—was required to bless a baby or a sick or troubled person by using the Big Guns.

"The priesthood," Jared said. "Lots of power, they say. You can't play with it. They told us about this one missionary who was struck by lightning for anointing and blessing a dog. Kaboom! Nothing left but a grease spot and a name badge."

"Man, until I met you, I didn't know things like that, spiritual things, could actually happen to, you know, people. I mean, people at church talked about 'promptings' and such, but nothing really so —what?—specific."

"I think you have to be in tune with the spirit."

We walked into our apartment and dropped our backpacks by the front door.

"That's the thing. No way you're in tune with the Spirit," I said, collapsing on the couch. "No offense, but you're just a guy, a goofball, truth be told."

"A truer word was never spoken." He sat on the arm of the over-stuffed chair across from the couch. "I'm nothing special when it comes to religion and stuff. I don't really pray, unless I'm in a pinch, and maybe not even then. And I've never even cracked the Book of Mormon."

I craned my neck up from my prone position on the couch. "How in the hell did you get on a mission without reading the Book of Mormon and, you know, receiving a testimony of its truthfulness?"

"Well, my grandfather, who I don't really know, he's a pretty big wheel. He used to be a patriarch and stuff. I think maybe he influenced things. I think God is behind this, really. I have to return with honor, and Heavenly Father's going to make sure that happens. If I don't return with honor, my family's going to be screwed. If I return with honor they're set for life."

"I didn't know the process could be influenced," I said, stretching myself and suddenly feeling a second wind. "Hey, man. Do you know how to play backgammon?"

"I didn't bring my, you know, athletic supporter," he said. "Got to protect the family jewels."

"You don't need it," I said. I got up and went to the bookshelf where I kept the backgammon board.

"When I said 'family jewels,' you knew I was really taking about my, you know, *rocky mountain oysters*, didn't you?"

"It's easy to learn and impossible to master," I said as I brought the board back to where we were sitting and dragged over the coffee table.

"Like choking the gopher!" he said. "God knows I've tried!"

That stopped me. "Holy shit," I said. "You'll talk about anything, won't you?"

"Hey, you're the one who wants to play with shuttle-cocks," he said.

"That's badminton, stupid," I said. "Not backgammon."

"I always get them mixed up," he said.

As we played game after game, the conversation meandered into our recollections of growing up Mormon. My previous companions and I had shared such stories, obviously, but never with such . . . *munificence*.

"Since you mentioned choking the gopher, my first meeting with the bishop when I was 12 was freaky," I said. "My mom, she tells me going in, 'You can't lie to the bishop. You wouldn't lie to God, would you? Well, even if you would, it wouldn't work. God would see right through you, and so will the bishop. Bishops carry the gift of discernment from the Holy Ghost and they're entitled to revelation.' Blah, blah, blah. So I go in there, and I'm scared to death. I'm sure he's going to blurt out all my secret sins. He gets around to: 'Kenny, do you ever abuse yourself?' I had no idea what the hell he meant. Abusing myself? Is that like hitting myself with a baseball bat or something? You could tell it made him uncomfortable. He said something like, 'Kenny, do you ever touch your private areas to feel pleasure?'"

"Ah, yes!"

"Yeah, well, I told him I hadn't, which was a lie. And he said, 'Kenny, I perceive that you are diligent in living the gospel. Heavenly Father is pleased with your diligence,' or something like that. It was total bullshit. Gift of discernment, huh?"

"Yeah, like every kid in these United States of America doesn't yank himself," Jared said. "I was talking to my dad once—"

"Wait a second," I said. "You talk to your dad about, you know, jerking off?"

"Yeah, sure," Jared said. "My sister has a vibrator."

"Holy shit!" I said. "That blows my mind! I can't even imagine saying the word penis to my stepdad or my Mom. They'd spontaneously combust."

"What about dingus?"

"I don't think so," I laughed. "That's nuts, man. Your family's nuts."

"Yeah. They're great."

We sat in silent reverie for a number of moments.

"Have you noticed all the inconsistencies in what we believe?" he said.

'What do you mean?" I asked.

"Well, the way the Plan of Happiness is supposed to work. We start out as spirit children of Heavenly Father in the pre-mortal existence, and then we're sent down to Earth to be tested and see if we'll be faithful enough to make it back to Celestial Kingdom. Then you turn into a God and you get your own planet and you produce your own spirit children and the cycle begins again."

"Yeah, what about it?" I asked.

"The inconsistencies—like, why doesn't the Holy Ghost get a body? Certainly he was worthy enough. Why is He just a tabernacle of spirit? And why doesn't Jesus have his own planet and get to be a Heavenly Father to his own spirit children?"

Good question. Why hadn't I thought of that? Looking back, it's amazing to me now that I could have sat through all those years and years of Primary and Sunday school and the ham-handed talks by members at the pulpit—all of it!—that I could have sat through it and not see all the un-sanded edges and misshapen pieces, the comical incongruity of it all. Comical! I can laugh now. Maybe all the well-intentioned droning lulled me into a stupor of thought back then. (I became suddenly alert, though, should a well-formed girl attain the stage.)

"I don't know," I said to Jared. "Did you ask them at the MTC?"

"Yeah, I did. They said, 'This is one of those things we just have to take on faith. Just focus on teaching the Plan of Happiness and leave the mysteries alone.'"

Jared jutted out his chin and scratched it with his knuckles. "Here's my question: Why doesn't the Prophet give us the answers? What's the point of having a Prophet if he doesn't help us solve life's, you know, mysteries?"

"What do you mean?" I said. I couldn't believe we were having this conversation.

"When's the last time you heard the prophet actually prophesy?" he asked.

"What do you mean?" I asked.

"You know, say, 'Thus sayeth the Lord' or explain shit," he said.

"Wow, man," I said.

"Well, maybe we're all supposed to find our own way," he said. "Maybe we're each supposed to be our own Prophet."

"Oh, that's deep," I said. "I think I need to be stoned to understand that."

"Yeah. I don't get stoned, though, anymore," he said. "It kind of freaks me out. And certainly not during the mission, unless there's some mission rule you haven't told me about yet."

"They didn't tell you?" I asked with pseudo-sobriety.

"I think I was in the can during that."

So it went. Game after game. Mind-blowing conversations. A friendship formed. I finally looked up at the clock. It was 1 a.m.

"Wow," I said. "Let's hit the hay."

We got into our pajamas

"Church tomorrow—or today, I guess," I said. "You get to meet everyone."

"Yeah," he said, as I switched off the light.

"Kenny?"

"What?"

"Just remember this: There are things that are true even if you can't understand them."

I stared up at the black ceiling.

What the hell was that supposed to mean?

CHAPTER FIVE

W hat follows here is the story of how I ended up on my mission—my first mission and, I guess, by extension, the three missions that followed it. That is, if I hadn't gone on that first mission—my two-year Mormon mission—none of those other missions would have fallen upon me as duties. It's a story that begs the belief of everyday folks, rising, as it does, from the loam of Mormon daily life and practice. Breathe deeply the fumes. It's intoxicating, both strange and bland. Still to this day, when I try to explain my upbringing to people I meet, they respond with some version of, "You're kidding, right?"

Let me set the scene:

Me, I'd always known I would get serious when the time came for my mission. From the age of 3, I would sing the hymn in primary, *I Hope They Call Me On a Mission*. Now, when I say that I always knew I would get serious about Mormonism when the time came for my mission, I'm not saying I was one of those kids who was "foreordained," as the church says. In fact, my mission was pretty much the first time in my life I had done something that didn't come naturally. I always operated on instinct, I guess you could say. The part of my brain that weighed options, that considered—it was switched off. I thought as the current pressed me forward and thither, like an amoeba.

In high school, I was a popular kid in my stoner clique—lead dog, really. Looking back, though, I see I really had no true friends. I had associates who were always more than willing to get wasted with me and blow away useless hours. I don't want to make myself out to be some kind of victim. I was just as self-absorbed as they were. I don't remember ever going out of my way for any of my friends. I didn't see that I needed them, or that they needed me— anything past "light the bong" or "pass me a beer." And that was the boys. The girls, they were disposable, interchangeable—serving one purpose.

Academically, I was no scholar. Not that I was a *dullard*. I always liked to read—mainly thick histories. When I was fifteen, I decided to find a new "word of the day" every day and graft it into my working vocabulary. But I don't recall ever doing a second of homework. That I was able to graduate from high school was a testament to the school district's lax standards.

Church, the whole religion thing, though—that was a whole different type of education. From birth until my mission, my indoctrination was slow drip. I mainly just kept quiet at church and didn't make a stink. I wasn't hostile toward the religious instruction, but neither was I warm to it. So, at home and at church, which in faithful Mormon households is a three- to four-day-a-week occurrence, I was thoroughly imbued. It had sunk in, without me really being aware of it. I took it as self-evident that the reformed gospel was laid at the feet of young Joseph Smith whole and intact. The truth, I've come to see, was that Smith's theology was stitched together over the years, taking parts from various worldviews, whatever suited Smith's needs at the time. For example, Smith starts sleeping with various women who weren't his wife and suddenly— huzzah!—he is granted a revelation of the "new and everlasting covenant": plural marriage. Polygamy.

Smith's theology evolved opportunistically. When he wrote the Book of Mormon, his views on Christian doctrine pretty much matched that of the 19th century camp revival meetings he was familiar with. That was enough at the time. As Smith's fame, wealth, and power grew, he became more adventurous, eventually arriving at the conclusion that God the Father and Jesus Christ were men of flesh and bone, just like you and me. Check it out: God could get a hard-on. God could be influenced—swayed. Titillated. Think of the cosmic implications. Smith said Heavenly Father, Jesus Christ and the Holy Ghost, they lived on a planet near the dead center of the universe, near a sun known as Kolob. That's right. Kolob. Further, Smith went on to say that we could all become god-men like Heavenly Father were we to live with sufficient *worthiness*. We, each worthy man, could rule over our own planet. (Women get into heaven as they are pulled in by the husband-god.) The Holy Spirit, Smith explained, was a "personage of spirit." That's what he said.

Anyway, I emerged into young adulthood with an unexamined Mormon worldview and, mostly, an unremitting erection. I assumed that, come adulthood, I would become religious, as that was what being an adult meant, after all. And the only true religion, after all, was Mormonism—a truth as plain as plain can be. At nineteen, I didn't utter a peep when the time came to go on a mission. Of *course*, I was going to go on a mission. How else could I advance into Mormon Manhood? That was the whole point, in my mind. And in the mind of my stepfather, the bishop. His was an ingenious plan, when you think about it. You see, he had pretty much abdicated his stepfatherly role with me, but he knew that I'd get fixed, begin my journey to Mormon Manhood, when the time came for my mission. And it would require no effort on his part. Perfect for the disregarded stepchild.

Shortly before my mission, my stepfather set an Appointment with me. I was to meet him in his bishop's office at the meeting house—2 p.m. sharp (though he made me wait in the vestibule for

20 minutes). Eventually, his assistant came out and told me, "Your father the bishop will see you now."

When I entered the room, my stepdad was at his desk, head down, with the scriptures opened in front of him. Above him was a gilded painting depicting the scene in the Sacred Grove where Joseph Smith is thumped off his feet by the appearance of Heavenly Father and Jesus Christ. According to the Official Account, Smith had been distressed by the religious disharmony in his town and he read James 1:5: "If any of you lack wisdom, let him ask of God, that giveth to all men liberally, and upbraideth not; and it shall be given him." Then he went into the woods to pray about which church was the true church. Then—wham!—the epiphany. In the painting, a wholesome light radiated down on young Joseph. He shielded his eyes from the holiness emanating from Heavenly Father and Jesus as they levitated above him, unaware of the sacred charge that was being given him.

"Have you committed adultery, son?" my stepfather asked, keeping his head down.

"What? Have I what?" I stammered, sitting on the other side of his desk. "Don't you have to be married to commit adultery? What do you mean?"

"'Ye have heard that it was said by them of old time, Thou shalt not commit adultery,'" he read from the pages before him. "'But I say unto you, that whosoever looketh on a woman to lust after her hath committed adultery with her already in his heart. And if thy right eye offend thee, pluck it out, and cast it from thee: for it is profitable for thee that one of thy members should perish, and not that thy whole body should be cast into hell! And if thy right hand offend thee, cut it off, and cast it from thee: for it is profitable for thee that one of thy members should perish, and not that thy whole body should be cast into hell.'"

At this, he looked up at me. "The world has one standard. The Savior has another. Now, have you murdered anyone?"

"What?"

Here he read from the scripture in front of him: "'Ye have heard that it was said of them of old time, thou shalt not kill; and whosoever shall kill shall be in danger of the judgment: But I say unto you, That whosoever is angry with his brother without a cause shall be in danger of the judgment; and whosoever shall say to his brother, Raca, shall be in danger of the council; but whosoever shall say, thou fool, shall be in danger of hell fire!'"

"Well, yes, I've gotten angry with my brothers," adding, with a hopeful laugh, "more than once."

"I think you're angry with me right now, son," he said smoothly. "Are you murdering me in your heart?"

"No, sir, I'm not angry with you."

"I'm trying to set you on the right path, son. You're about to find out just what kind of hard work is required of a man who is committed to live the gospel. It's hard work, hard, thankless work. The Prophet Joseph Smith taught that we are saved by grace after all we can do. That means that you have to give it 110 percent, and only when you've given it your all will God's power kick in and take you over the goal line. God does what we can't. No one's going to thank you for doing the right thing. Is God going to thank you? No. If you're in the army, your commanding officer doesn't thank you when you follow his orders. Are you going to thank me, son? Look at all I've done as your father. Have you ever thanked me for everything I've done for you? I rescued you and your mother, didn't I? Where would you and your mother be if I hadn't rescued you?"

"Sir, I was too young. I don't remember—"

"There's always an excuse with you, isn't there? You'd be up the creek without me. That's where you'd be without me—up the creek."

"Sir, I'm thankful—"

"Do you think you can qualify for the Celestial Kingdom?"

I was at a loss for words at this question. After a few moments, my stepdad continued.

"I do. I believe in you, son. I'm your biggest fan. But you should know now that it's going to take everything you have. Like I said, the hard work, the thankless work, starts now. When you're following the Savior and you feel like giving up, that's exactly the moment you have to depend on God's strength. If you do all you can do—and only if you do all you can do—His grace will kick in, like I said."

"I'm willing to work hard."

"Bear me your testimony, son!" he barked.

I began slowly. "That's what I've been meaning to talk to you about, sir. I'm not sure if I have a testimony. I've asked and asked. I don't think I'm going to get one. Is it really that important that I have a testimony?"

"Son, men can deceive and science can be wrong, but a true testimony is undeniable. No one can contradict your testimony. My testimony is the bedrock of my faith."

"So there should be no mistaking it. When you receive it, I mean? I was thinking maybe I got my testimony but didn't know it."

"There's no mistaking it, son."

"But I don't feel anything."

"It sounds like you're trying to pull the train of your spiritual life with your feelings. That's backwards. Your feelings are the caboose. The engine is fact, the facts of what God's word says and His prophets have said. Commit yourself to the truthfulness of the facts and your feelings will follow, by and by."

"Is your testimony some kind of voice you hear?"

"You don't hear the voice of God. The only person who actually hears the voice of God in person, face to face, is the prophet. The rest of us rely on what scripture calls the 'still, small voice.' It's not really a voice, though."

"What is it then?"

"It's a feeling."

That stopped me. After a few uncomfortable moments, I said, "So what should I do, sir?"

"Son, the gift of the Holy Ghost is a privilege, given to people who have been baptized into the LDS church and who abide the precepts set forth by the church. The Holy Ghost can provide a witness that the Book of Mormon is true, that Joseph Smith was a prophet, and that LDS Church is God's one, true church."

"I know I received the Holy Ghost, but I don't feel anything, about the church and stuff."

"A testimony is received in the bearing of it," he said

"What?"

"I said, a testimony is received in the bearing of it. That means, you'll receive your testimony when you go out there in the mission field and bear your testimony to the people who need the gospel. Your testimony's going to be found on your feet, not on your knees. As you go out and bear your testimony of the truthfulness of the gospel, the more likely you are to gain a testimony."

"Can't I just say, 'I believe the church is true' or something like 'I think I know'?"

"No, you can't. You have to know the truth. Truth is known."

"But that kind of sounds like lying."

"But it's not a lie."

"It's not?"

"No, because the church *is* true."

I didn't know how to respond. My head was spinning. I was slightly nauseated. I had to fart. My stepdad was quiet for a few more moments.

"So, bear me your testimony, son," he said.

"I know the church is true. I know the Book of Mormon is true. I know Joseph Smith was a prophet of God. I knew Spencer W. Kimball is a prophet of God. But–"

"But what? But what? Do your buts bring you any closer to Heavenly Father?"

"But–"

"I say, get off your 'buts,' son. And get off your butt and get to the serious work of the gospel. I testify to you that everything I've said is true. End of story."

After that, my stepfather laid hands on my head and pronounced a blessing over me. Slam-bang.

And that's how I ended up going on my mission without a testimony. Certainly, I'm not the first Mormon missionary to go on a mission without a testimony. Happens with each rising sun, I'm sure. But, at the time, I felt isolated and inadequate. It didn't help that, as my mission proceeded, I just didn't feel a connection with any of my companions, to the extent that I could share my feelings with them. If anything, I felt I was in competition with them. In fact, missionaries are encouraged to report any serious infraction by their companion to the mission president as an act of love. It wasn't until I met Jared and things went nuts that I no longer felt the need to fake a testimony. I had eyes in my head, after all. Miracles were real.

CHAPTER SIX

B efore I go any further—I suppose you're wondering what in the hell a "testimony" is. It's important to understand the concept of a testimony if you're going to get within spitting distance of appreciating Latter-day Saints. A devout Mormon won't tell you, "I believe Mormonism is the truth. " They'll say, "I *know* the church is true." When a Mormon tells you, "I know that the church is true," the testimony is the "knowing" he's talking about. It's supposed to be "beyond human reasoning." The variations on bearing one's testimony are endless, I can tell you, but they all tend to follow this structure:

I KNOW THAT . . .

. . . Joseph Smith was a prophet of God and restored the gospel upon the earth in 1830 after the gospel was lost shortly after the death of the last apostle in the first century.

. . . the Church of Jesus Christ of Latter-day Saints is the One True Church on the Earth today.

. . . this Church is led by a living prophet who receives revelation by speaking directly to God.

AND ALL THIS IS KNOWN, not just believed. The essence of a testimony is that it's a statement of certainty. Mormons who testify to their religion's validity claim to know these matters as they know the blueness of the sky or the fact that their heart is flinching in their chest. A strong testimony is seen as a reliable method for discerning truth. Not a two-plus-two truth, but meaning-of-life type truth. A testimony is often likened to a "burning in the bosom," something un-ignorable. In fact, it's seen as the only truly reliable method for discerning truth.

It's the main tactic missionaries use to drum up converts. They advise people interested in the religion to read the Book of Mormon—all of it, preferably, or at least some of its choicest selections—and then ask Heavenly Father to convey to them a testimony of its truthfulness. This is based on the Book of Mormon citation Moroni 10:3-5, where nonbelievers are instructed to read the Book of Mormon and entreat God to show them the truthfulness of what they've read. And, the verse promises, "if ye shall ask with a sincere heart, with real intent, having faith in Christ, he will manifest the truth of it unto you, by the power of the Holy Ghost." It's actually a great tactic in that it always works, if you're the missionary. That is, if the investigator does receive an inner glow, then, wham, you can wrench him into the boat. And if he doesn't feel that warm feeling, well, it's just an indicator that he wasn't sincere enough or that his real intent wasn't real enough. Try again. The answer is never no. The technique was part of an overall emphasis on feelings. We were taught at the Missionary

Training Center to always ask people how they *felt* about the truths we would impart to them. Any positive feelings they had we were to attribute to the Holy Ghost validating the truth. You weren't going to conclusively prove the truthfulness of Mormonism by thinking it through. Pray about it, we'd always tell people. Read the Book of Mormon and then pray about it. Is Mormonism true? Pray about it. Any warm feelings that visited you were an answer to prayer. "Mr. and Mrs. Brown," our memorized script read, "what you are feeling right now is the Spirit of the Lord testifying to you that we are teaching you the truth. You are beginning to receive your own testimony of the truthfulness of this message."

BACK TO SEDRO-WOOLLEY, 1979. When Jared and I showed up for Sunday service at the ward the morning after our run-in with Lisa P. and Daryl, we were met by Artis Watson, president of the Mt. Vernon Stake, glowering on the front steps of the meeting house like a Turkish prison guard. Normally, from what I've been able to piece together, he was a real jovial guy. He died before I could interview him, as you'll learn. Those who knew him, when I interviewed them, they painted a glowing picture. Across the board, they said he was in love with the Savior and in love with the Church—protective as a nursing mother. Mainly, that meant he was a furious advocate of doctrinal purity. He was immediately suspicious of anything that had even a faint smell of "false teaching." He saw himself as Christlike in that way—Jesus upending the money changers' tables and such.

That, it turns out, was why he was waiting for Jared and myself —mainly, Jared.

As Watson watched us walk up the stairs, he groused to himself and grimaced. I saw him reach into his vest pocket and get one of the nitroglycerin pills he took for his angina. The matter at hand was Jared. Turns out, Watson had it in for Jared. He'd clearly been warned—but by whom?

As we climbed the stairs to the ward's front door, Watson stepped into our path as he inserted his pills back into his pocket.

He smiled at us and his face easily creased into well-worn laugh lines. Then he sombered up, which didn't suit him, if you want my opinion.

"Elders," he said. "I was hoping to meet you and introduce myself to Elder Baserman." He held out his hand for Jared, smiled and then immediately turned grave. Jared was no laughing matter. "Son, I heard about your act at the family reunion. I want you to know that that type of nonsense won't play here. God speaks through the prophet and scripture, and the prophet tells us how to interpret scripture."

I decided to keep mum about our altercation with Lisa P. and Daryl. The better part of valor. What would Jared say next, though? Little did I know how much I would be asking myself that very question in the coming weeks.

"The wind blows where it wishes," Jared said as he shook Watson's hand.

What the hell was that supposed to mean?

"What in the wide world is that supposed to mean, elder?" Watson said, squinting at Jared.

At that second, a couple members interrupted us on an urgent matter for Watson. Watson immediately attended to them and forgot all about us. So we moved on.

Whom should we bump into right when we came through the front door but Algernon Briskey, who had been bishop of the ward until he was released, just recently, from his calling by President Watson. Evil Briskey, I think. Jury's out. Briskey's fatal mistake had been openly and loudly criticizing The Brethren for reversing the priesthood ban. Consequently, Watson gave Briskey the hook.

"Elder Baserman," I said to Jared awkwardly. "This is Brother Briskey. He, uh, used to be our bishop."

Briskey stuck out his hand. "The reason I'm no longer bishop is I stood up for the truth. The Brethren erred when they reversed the priesthood ban. I don't have a racist bone in my body, but I can see what's plain as day: The Brethren knuckled under to political pressure. It's not up to us to say who gets the priesthood and who doesn't."

"So, you're saying. . ." Jared began.

"I think an example will help here," Briskey said. "Let's say you had a fourteen-year-old son and he came to you and asked for the keys to the family car. Any responsible father would say, 'No way, Jose!' He would know the kid would have ended up wrapping the car around a telephone pole or something. The same's the way for Heavenly Father. The Lord had determined that blacks were not ready for the priesthood. They would have just abused the power of the priesthood and done themselves harm. That's not discrimination. Discrimination is keeping something from somebody that would be a benefit for them, right? The denial of the priesthood to blacks protected them from the lowest depths of Hell reserved for people who abuse their priesthood powers. So, in reality, it was a great blessing not to give blacks the priesthood. It was an act of love. Remember that Heavenly Father loves his children."

Jared jumped right in. "Maybe blacks couldn't have the priesthood because God knew that whites weren't ready—morally and spiritually, I mean—ready to accept blacks into, you know, full fellowship," he said. "In fact, you could say that black Mormons were demonstrating superior moral strength through their patience."

That got Briskey's attention.

"That's weak-minded waffling," Briskey said. "I've been resolute. It's not up to us who gets the priesthood. It's up to Heavenly Father. I've always said the Brethren made a mistake when they gave black men the priesthood. That's what got me removed as bishop. I'm a man of my convictions. I suppose you'll be happy, elder, to hear that President Watson wasted no time in replacing me with our only black member."

As if on cue, that very black member, Demetrius Bloodworth, emerged from his office immediately to our right, looking fairly wrung-out. I was to learn later that he had just had a knock-down-drag-out with the Lord in his office. His crisis of faith had been brewing for months. Only he didn't use that term, crisis of faith. He called it his disturbance. He had reached the point at which Heavenly Father needed to intervene—to give him some kind of sign—or, he had determined, he would have to give up his faith, the worldview he constructed brick by brick over the previous ten years.

Bloodworth didn't appear to know where he was or what he was about. He stared at the three of us for a bit—me, Jared, and Briskey—before our identities seemed to register in his simmering brain.

"Brother Briskey, and . . . boys," he said. "Where do you want?"

Before being called as bishop, Bloodworth had never held a calling higher than ward membership clerk. But Watson had always been impressed with his kindness and compassion. Watson was particularly impressed that Bloodworth never uttered a single complaint about not being allowed to hold the priesthood. Consequently, Watson had felt Bloodworth was an inspired choice to be the ward's next bishop. He *knew* Bloodworth was meant to be the next bishop, I assume. The church had a policy that widowers couldn't be bishops—unless they could receive say-so from the First Presidency. In this case, they were happy to oblige, but they didn't make a fuss about it, the fact that he was a black bishop. The less said about blacks and the priesthood, the better, like Daryl said.

Bloodworth accepted the call to bishop out of a sense of duty to the Church, though he felt unprepared to say the least. The bishop of a Mormon ward is an unpaid, volunteer job that requires a lot of time and work, and holds a huge deal of status in the ward. A bishop is called The Father of the Ward. It's assumed that anyone who was called to be bishop in a ward was, one, chosen by inspired leaders and, two, received the mantle of leadership upon taking the role. This would equip him with special revelatory abilities and wisdom. After a bishop stepped down, the Holy Ghost retracted the mantle from him and he returned to being just a member.

Here's where we get to Bloodworth's crisis of faith.

As it turned out, Bloodworth had impressed more than a few members with his wise, gentle guidance as bishop. But Bloodworth felt in over his head in terms of counseling members. So he asked President Watson if the stake would pay to get him some training in counseling/psychology. Watson poopooed this. He stood on doctrine, I guess. "You have the mantle of leadership," he told Bloodworth. "And with that comes special discernment."

"I said I didn't feel any special discernment. In fact, I felt lost,'" Bloodworth told me later.

Several months after Bloodworth met with Watson, Bloodworth was approached at the grocery store by a local black pastor.

"Brother," he said to Bloodworth. "You are my brother, aren't you?"

"Sir?" Bloodworth asked.

"How can you be part of that church?" he asked, motioning vaguely in the direction of the meeting house. "It's racist."

"That's in the past, I think."

"Is it?" the black pastor asked. "Your church didn't really mean it when it gave black men the priesthood."

"What? What do you mean?"

"Your church, its leaders, they were being insincere. Its heart wasn't really in it when they reversed the priesthood ban. Same thing with polygamy. Study it out. The church caved in because the government was holding its feet to the fire. So the church stopped practicing polygamy. However, polygamy is still doctrine. They just don't require it anymore on earth."

"What do you mean?"

"Don't you know that Mormon men take multiple wives in heaven? Your Heavenly Father, for goodness sake, He has multiple wives. The Mormon Jesus has multiple wives. The practice of polygamy on Earth was only suspended and could be restored at any time when it is no longer politically explosive. Couldn't the same happen with the priesthood and blacks? Study it out. You have nothing to fear from the truth."

This alarmed Bloodworth, so he decided to study polygamy. What he found was that Joseph Smith had married upward of thirty women. This surprised Bloodworth because he had never heard the names of any of Smith's wives except Emma, his first wife. He saw where Smith lied to the church and to the press about these clandestine marital relationships. Also, Smith married at least eleven women who were already married. He married women who were pregnant with their husband's child. He married a number of teenagers. And when I say "married," I mean, meshed the flesh. Some parents acknowledged receiving a promise from Smith guaranteeing them a special place in heaven if they allowed Smith to wed their daughter.

What a dingus.

Bloodworth's research branched out from there, slowly and painfully. Bloodworth couldn't find a single prophecy of Joseph Smith that came true. However, he did see that Joseph Smith and his cronies changed prophecies de facto to make them appear fulfilled. Each new discovery was crushing to poor Bloodworth.

Long story short, Bloodworth ended up arriving at the conclusion that Joseph Smith was a con man. Perhaps he was a well-intentioned con man, but a con man nonetheless. The Mormon Church had made Smith money and given him power, which he had abused to the fullest. At best, a pious fraud.

Bloodworth was at the end of his tether by then. He was actually considering the option of leaving the church. Then, on the Sunday Jared and I showed up at the meeting house, Bloodworth made his final plea to Heavenly Father.

"I got on my very knees in my office," he told me later. "I said, 'Heavenly Father, please show me the way to go. I want to believe in your church, but I just don't know. Please give me a sign which way to go.'"

When I saw Bloodworth emerge from his office on that Sunday, he had just made this plea to Heavenly Father. I don't think he was fully registering what we were all saying. Right then, bidding some ungiven call, people began flowing into the chapel. We found a spot in the front pew, as if it had been saved for us by God, I guess.

Bloodworth offered a stumbling intro and we sang a hymn: *We Thank Thee, O God, For a Prophet*. When we finished, Bloodworth took the lectern as if in a daze. He scanned the congregation doubtfully. When his eyes landed on Jared and me, something seemed to register.

"Oh. . . ," Bloodworth stammered, grasping both sides of the lectern. "Uh, today I'm pleased to announce that we have a new missionary in our congregation. Uh, please stand up, son, and introduce yourself," he said. "Or maybe Elder Feller should introduce his junior companion."

Jared and I looked at one another, wondering who was going to stand up and do the introductions. We did one of those little dances where one of us would begin to stand and hesitate to see if the other person actually was going to go first. We went back and forth like that for a few seconds. Finally, Jared stood all the way up, moved into the aisle, and cleared his throat.

"Brothers and sisters," he called out, looking around the chapel. *What now?*

He was obviously quite nervous—no surprise, that, standing in front all these people he hardly knew. "Brothers and sisters in the Lord?" he said again, now in a questioning tone, as if he were searching for us all like a mason jar in a shadowy root cellar. He looked toward the ceiling and held his hand in front of his eyes, as if he were blocking a light. I saw his eyes were now darting from one point to another on the ceiling. From here, it's probably best that I relate how Jared explained it when we got back to our apartment later that morning:

"First off, the room filled up with reddish light. I think it was red. It might have been a new primary color, and it was coming from the ceiling. In that way, it was like the time at the family reunion. And like at the family reunion, I felt a warmth over my whole body. Then, clear as a bell, I started hearing this voice. It was like it was at the back of the church or something. I turned in that direction and saw this personage of light walking down the aisle. I could tell it wasn't The Furthering. It was The Hallowedness—it was him—walking down the aisle toward the front of the church. As The Hallowedness walked down the aisle, flowers and vines and shit would burst forth on the pews he would pass, like he was causing a garden or jungle to bloom right there in the chapel. He stopped a ways from me and he spoke. He said, 'You are the answer.' Then the red light took over everything and I don't remember anything until you shook me awake in the aisle. I guess I fainted, huh?"

Indeed, from my perspective, I watched Jared peer down the aisle with a stupefied look on his face. Then he said, "What? What?" and collapsed on the aisle rug. At this, a communal gasp went up from the members. Bloodworth, ever helpful, rushed from the stage and knelt beside Jared.

"What is it, son?" he asked.

I shook Jared back to reality and he looked up at us. "A personage of light," he said.

"What did he say?" Bloodworth asked breathlessly.

"He said he saw a person made out of light. It was a vision," I said. "He's done this before."

"No, not a person," Jared said, waving away the mistake, "a personage."

"A vision?" Bloodworth burst forth.

"Yeah," I said, looking at Jared. "Did the personage say anything?"

"Yes," Jared said, the back of his hand on his forehead.

At this, the members around the periphery pushed close. "What did he say?" Bloodworth asked. "What did he say?"

"Jared," I said. "What did the personage of light say to you?"

"He said," he began. "He said. . . 'You are the answer.'"

"Wow," I said.

"Who?" Bloodworth said.

"'You,'" Jared said.

"Me?" Bloodworth said.

"No, me," Jared said. "I'm the answer."

"What?" Bloodworth gasped.

At this point, President Watson pushed his way through the growing crowd and into the group. "What in the wide world's going on?" he demanded.

"He had a vision," Bloodworth said.

"A vision?" Watson said. "In church?"

"It was like in the Sacred Grove," a woman said.

"Preposterous," Watson said.

"No, it was a vision," Bloodworth said.

"Were you scared?" another member asked.

Jared looked up at him as if he didn't understand the question.

Bloodworth later told me he quickly put two and two together and realized that Jared's message was for him. "I was sure that Heavenly Father would speak to and through Elder Baserman," Bloodworth told me months and months later. "I knew Heavenly Father was going to make a way where there was none. I knew that once I heard the answer from Jared, it would seem simple, beautiful and obvious. 'Why hadn't I thought of that?' I would ask. But I was too frail. The 'arm of the flesh is weak,' but with God all things are possible."

On this Sunday, Bloodworth gathered up Jared and ushered him into his office. I followed and right behind me was Watson.

"What in the wide world's going on here?" Watson asked over my shoulder. We all got into Bloodworth's office and put Jared on the couch. The rest of us pulled up chairs next to the couch and looked at Jared expectantly.

"Someone better tell me what in the wide world's going on," Watson demanded.

Bloodworth and I looked at Jared, who looked back at us.

"Holy shit," Jared said.

CHAPTER SEVEN

If you swallow the party line from Salt Lake City, Mormonism began—that is, the unadulterated gospel was restored to planet Earth—after Joseph Smith withstood a number of heavenly visitations and went on to tell the tale in reverent tones to an ever-widening group of neighbors and passersby. So, early on, the precedent was set—the permission was given—for adherents of the Restored Gospel to be attuned to vibrations uncommon to the common man. God still speaks! To Mormons! It's no shock then that early Mormonism had a definite holy-roller feel to it. For example, when Smith and his followers dedicated their first temple, in Kirtland, Ohio, in 1836, the service turned into a Pentecostal hoedown. Reportedly, people were discharging messages in tongues, singing in tongues, seeing visions, hearing angels sing, swaying back and forth, everything short of foaming at the mouth. Joseph Smith himself testified to seeing angels storm into the hall like starving cats.

The vibrations didn't last, though. Or, if they did, it became imprudent to act upon those vibrations, lest you incur the wrath of church leaders. Such undignified exhibitions were not befitting of

the children of God. At the close of the 19th century, the Pentecostal gusto began leaching from Mormonism. Church members
were energized less and less by the unfiltered whisperings of the
Holy Ghost. All words and actions had to be approved by the panel
of crusty white guys running the church. By 1979, Mormonism
had long since ossified into a corporation. Everything was stipu-
lated, regulated, and homogenized, particularly the worship
services. One didn't go to a Mormon Sunday service to be rattled. If
one word summed up Mormon Church services of the time—and
they were all the same, still are, like something mass-produced—it
would be predictability. Everything in its place. All very calm and
solemn, as flavorless as a form letter from the DMV. The hymns
were extruded like fix-it caulk. They even used water instead of
wine during communion, for crap's sake. Still do. I think Jerusha
put it best when she told me later, "The thing about Mormonism is
it's so uptight that you couldn't pull a needle from its ass crack with
a tractor."

That's why Bloodworth, Watson and I looked so shocked as we
sat around Jared in Bloodworth's office. Well, not me so much.
Truth be told, I was expecting something like this out of Jared,
crazy fucker.

Sitting there in the office, we had Jared recount his vision to us
in detail, and I could tell we all were struck with how plainspoken
he was. I mean, he didn't use any religious boilerplate. He wasn't
working to make it sound spiritual. It wasn't like he was trying to
convince anyone of anything. He just told us what he had
witnessed.

"That's some crazy shit, huh?" he said to us when he finished.

"Yes, well, it certainly was unexpected, Elder Baserman,"
Watson said. "That I'll grant you. Watch the sailor mouth, though."

"I think God was speaking to him," Bloodworth said. "To us!"

"God speaks to us through the prophet," Watson said with a
warm smile. "He's the one who talks to Christ. We have no need for
missionaries to bring forth signs and wonders. If we had people

firing off visions at every service, there would be pandemonium. We stay true to the gospel by following the prophet."

"But if it's the same God speaking through everyone, it won't matter, will it?" Bloodworth asked. "God will say the same things to everyone, won't He? The Prophet and us. I mean, Brother Watson, we have nothing to fear from the truth, do we?"

"Subjectivity," Watson said with an even warmer smile. "Even if such visions happened all the time, and even if it was always God speaking through church members, how a member interpreted each event would be gingered by his own biases and imperfections. It's too open to abuse. That's why God has a prophet. The prophet even tells us how to interpret scripture. The prophet will never lead the church astray."

"Pardon me, but this isn't the first time he's done something like this," I said. "He had a religious experience at a family reunion. God told him to go on his mission, and he prophesied when we were out door knocking one day and he foretold about how some people were out to get us. There's no way he could have known that on his own. I mean, it was his first day on the mission, even. They had a gun. There was no way he could have known that."

"There's no way I could have known that, President Watson," Jared said.

"Bishop Bloodworth, you need to go back out there and reassure your flock," Watson said. "You need to take control and explain to them Heavenly Father's in control."

"Yes, sir," Bloodworth said and got up.

"You boys," Watson said, taking in Jared and me. "None of this happened. You're going to go out there and, should anyone come up to you, you're going to change the topic. Please, boys. Say it was all a misunderstanding."

Jared and I looked at each other and said nothing.

"None of this happened," Watson repeated, looking around at all assembled in a friendly manner. He stood up. "Now, let's all head back out there and get on with this service."

When we emerged into the chapel, Bloodworth was at the lectern talking to the congregation.

"Let's not us prejudge what we have seen here today. Let's stay open to where the Holy Ghost may be taking us. Who are we to discount the very whisperings of the Lord that He comes to whisper to us?"

I could tell people had their eyes trained on Jared and me. At least on Jared. After the service, as we were bustling about on our way to Sunday School, some members were overly polite to us. Many glared. They clearly hadn't appreciated the diversion from the normal service. One man grabbed Jared by the elbow and said, "Watch what you say, son. People look up to you missionaries."

Bloodworth approached us during Sunday School with his jaw set. "Boys, I'm not going to keep quiet about this like President Watson said. Judge for yourself whether it's right for me to obey men or God. Besides, President Watson won't be back to the ward for weeks. What I think is God is telling me to stick close to you. Elder Baserman, if it's alright with you, I'd like to go out with you when you do your door knocking tomorrow. I've got a lot of over-time built up at work, so my boss won't mind if I take a day off. That's what I'm hearing God say to me, boys." He looked around the classroom. "But let's just keep this to ourselves for now."

ON TUESDAY, Jared and I met up with Bloodworth and started knocking on doors. I could tell immediately that Bloodworth was eager to hear whether Jared had experienced any new "visitations." It also was clear that people didn't know what to make of us when they opened their doors. Jared and I, obviously, we were Mormon missionaries. The suits. The hair. The nametags. But why was that black guy hanging around?

As we walked from door to door that day, Bloodworth told us his story. He had come to the Mormon Church ten years ago after his wife, Denise, had died. He had met her in the Army. When his stint was over, he moved to her hometown, Sedro-Woolley, Washington, and began a career as a bricklayer. He and his wife lived in her childhood home. Also, she insisted that they attend the Nazarene church she grew up in. At the time, Bloodworth wasn't religious but he went along with her and was surprised to find he actually liked it.

To me, I think that comes from the fact the character traits they promoted were the very ones that he naturally exhibited. He was unfailingly kind. Christlike, I guess. A role model for me, really.

One night while attending her church, he had a dream in which a white-robed angel, hair combed back like a shoe salesman, told him that God was calling him.

"He told me, 'Demetrius, God is calling you from the very throne of God,'" Bloodworth said. "He said, 'Will you answer His call? He is calling you but it is not to this church.'"

After his wife's death from ovarian cancer, Bloodworth began a search for the truth. Why had God given him a mission and then taken his wife? Where was the point in all this? Eventually, he reached the end of his tether and cried out, "God, if You're there, please show me the way to go."

At that exact instant, not a second to either side—no shit—two Mormon missionaries knocked on his door. They did so by accident, hapless boobs. They thought it was an investigator's house and were showing up for the First Discussion. It took me a while, but I chased down those two missionaries. These two jokers, there they had been, staring at the black guy who opened the door. Their reflex, I bet, had been to launch into their script: "Hello, sir. We're out telling people about Jesus Christ and we were wondering if we could take a few minutes to speak with you about this message." But there had to have been a moment of hesitation. This guy's black. Remember, at this time, the priesthood ban against blacks was in full force and hotly defended as God's will.

"We didn't know what exactly to do," said one of those missionaries, a man named Todd, then referred to as Elder Horus. We spoke over lunch at Popeye's Chicken in Riverside, California, where he was the dayshift manager.

"Blacks couldn't hold the priesthood," he told me. "I mean, how do you tell someone, 'You should join our religion, but, just so you know, you can't get into heaven in our religion? Well, maybe as a servant, you know, like a butler.' But Demetrius wouldn't let us leave. So we had to come inside. Once we were in there, we kind of looked at each other and shrugged our shoulders and launched into the First Discussion. He hung on our every word."

Bloodworth probed the missionaries to answer his questions about why God took his wife. The missionaries didn't have any answers back then. Instead, they kept turning around the conversation to get back to their Discussion, as they and I were trained at the MTC. "There are many things we don't know," they told him. "But there are certain things we know as truth for a surety. We know that's God's Plan of Happiness is true."

Bloodworth was spellbound. The missionaries told him that burning he was feeling in his soul was the Holy Ghost confirming to him the truth of what they were telling him. They gave him a copy of the Book of Mormon and encouraged him to read it and pray to God to show him whether it was true. They said they would return in a few days. After the missionaries left his house, Bloodworth began thumbing through the first pages of the Book of Mormon and came across a painting of the angel Moroni visiting the Prophet Joseph Smith in his log cabin bedroom. He immediately recognized Moroni as the angel from his Nazarene dream.

When the missionaries returned a few days later, they found Bloodworth all ablaze for the restored gospel. The missionaries then began meeting with Bloodworth to take him through the rest of the seven Official Discussions. He was baptized in short order. He became a steady, if unspectacular, member of the Sedro-Woolley ward of the Church of Jesus Christ of Latter-day Saints. He had been content in the church, until he was called as bishop.

"Certain facts came to my attention," Bloodworth told Jared and me as we walked down the street. "I don't want to burden you, boys. But certain facts. I was kind of at the end of my rope. I don't want to burden you, but I cried out to God. I cried out to God and He brought me to you. Or brought you to me. It's a certitude."

Right there, on the spot, I made *certitude* my word of the day. Wasn't too sure if it was a real word.

"Me?" Jared said.

"You're an answer to prayer, son," Bloodworth said. "I believe it. You're the very answer to my prayer of desperation to Heavenly Father."

"What am I supposed to do?" Jared said.

"Well," Bloodworth said. "I'm just waiting on God. I have a sure knowledge He will speak through you."

"I think God does speak to him," I said. "I really do."

Bloodworth stopped on the sidewalk and we turned toward him. "Yes," he said, motioning for us to come close. We approached and he put a hand on each of our shoulders. "It's a certitude. Everything's going to work out for our good. Let's enter into prayer."

We bowed our heads. "Heavenly Father, we thank Thee for Thy loving-kindness," Bloodworth said. "We ask Thee now to bless us, we who are but Thy willing servants. We don't deserve anything from Thy hand, Heavenly Father, but we know that Thou art merciful. In that merciful blessedness, guide us today as we share the gospel of Jesus Christ, and bring us to meet the people Thou want us to meet and experience the things Thou want us to experience."

When lunchtime rolled around, Bloodworth said he'd like to take us out "for something nice." So we walked downtown. "I'll take you boys to the café that my wife and I used to like to go to," he said. "It was our place." The name of the restaurant was The San'wich Nook.

As we walked on, it just so happened that three friends—Mavis Spender, Patsy Ablemire and Sunshine Toledo—were busy visiting at the café, or so I learned later. Sunshine was leading a discussion about what their next "ministry focus" would be. The three women were members of First Hill Evangelical Church and not infrequently seen together. They had gravitated toward each other because they each had the common experience of having a supposedly devout husband who cheated on her.

Now, Mavis, she grew up attending First Hill Evangelical, an overly shy black girl always on the outside of the youth clique. She was a sad girl and her family had to send her away several times to some sanitarium of sorts downriver. She ended up marrying Pete Spender, who became the church's assistant pastor. Parishioners were happy that Mavis might finally find happiness. However, Mavis was barren, which led to all sorts of marital discord, shouting matches and thrown knick-knacks, as Pete was determined to raise a godly family.

Mavis was so ashamed that she couldn't conceive. I mean, no one in the church supposedly knew she was infertile, but her childlessness was conspicuous. To Mavis, her barrenness finally provided the grounds for the sadness she had experienced her whole life: She was defective.

Eventually, Pete had an affair with the church's choirmistress and the pair left the church in disgrace. When her husband left Mavis, she had to live with the shame of that, too. A double failure.

The church rallied around poor Mavis and she found a sense of purpose, it appeared. She compensated for her childlessness with furious activity on committees and volunteer events. She also got a job. She had always been good with numbers, so she found a job as bookkeeper's assistant at a cannery in Anacortes. She performed so well that she eventually became supervisor of the Cannery's small bookkeeping department. Mavis was no natural leader, but everyone was fond of her and she never made mistakes, so she was promoted.

Truth was, she had had several more visits to psychiatric wards in her adulthood. *Episodes* was the word she used with me. In fact, the day I first met her in the San'wich Nook, she had just returned from a brief stay at Northern State. She kept all these hospital visits as secret from everyone as she could, although Sunshine seemed to know about them somehow. She would subtly needle Mavis about her emotional wherewithal when she felt the need to assert her authority. Here's the kicker: When Mavis was married to Spender, she also was Bloodworth's sister-in-law, as she was married to the brother of Bloodworth's wife. Gets confusing, I know. Just trust me. Bloodworth was always kind and gentle with Mavis, as was his general disposition. And she felt she had helped him cope with the death of his wife. Maybe even some kind of a bond was formed. However, when Bloodworth converted to Mormonism, Mavis lost contact with him.

The three women—Mavis, Sunshine and Patsy—had been friends, or at least associates, for a fair number of years. They comprised a Ministry Team under Sunshine's headship. They would become involved in various initiatives—"as the Spirit led us," Sunshine would explain—becoming the church's official experts on whatever the topic of their ministry was. Together, with Sunshine as their "servant leader," they had promoted Deliverance, Cults Awareness, Inner Healing, and Curse Removal in the church.

On this day, the three women had decided to meet for lunch to discuss what their next Focus Area would be. As usual, Patsy was trying to encourage Mavis to find a man, and Sunshine was insisting that Mavis' neediness was a sign of a weakness that, frankly, "needed to be put at the foot of the cross." At the time, Patsy was encouraging Mavis to show some interest in one of the church's several bachelors.

"Mavis," Patsy told her that afternoon, "they are all godly men who could give you a good life. For goodness sake, Mavis, their child-rearing years are far gone anyway."

As always, Mavis looked down and shook her head. "No, no, they wouldn't want me," she said. "Nobody would want me."

"Mavis, you talk as if having a husband was some sort of prize,"

Sunshine said. "It's not a prize. It's a hindrance. I know and you know, and Patsy knows, that when we have to watch over a man—and you all know, girls, that when the men aren't watched over, they tend to stray—when we have to watch over a man, well, we're really of little use to the Lord. As Paul says, 'the unmarried woman or girl is anxious about the affairs of the Lord, how to be holy in body and spirit; but the married woman is anxious about worldly affairs, how to please her husband.'"

Finally, Patsy asked, "Mavis, isn't there anyone in this whole world you would be interested in?"

"Well," Mavis said, still looking down, "the only man I've ever met that I might think could maybe love me is my former brother-in-law. He was so kind."

At that exact instant, Bloodworth, Jared, and I walked into the San'wich Nook. A coincidence? It *must* have been Heavenly Father.

"My stars!" Mavis said. "There he is right now. Oh, my goodness."

Sunshine, ever on guard for heterodoxy, looked suspiciously at us. "Why is he with those . . . Mormons?"

"Well, he is a Mormon, a Latter-day Saint," Mavis said. "He left Christianity."

"Ladies," Sunshine said. "I think this is the Lord telling us something. We need to do Cults Awareness again, with an emphasis on Mormonism. In fact, let's start by inviting them to have lunch with us."

"We can re-convert him to the true gospel and then Mavis will be able to marry him," said Patsy, who was always good for a joke.

"Oh, Patsy, please," Mavis said.

"What's his name, Mavis?" Sunshine asked.

"Demetrius. Demetrius Bloodworth," Mavis said. "But what are you going to do, Sunshine?"

"Mr. Bloodworm," Sunshine called to us, standing up and

waiving. "Please join us, Mr. Bloodworm. We're here with Mavis Spender."

"Well, I'll be," Bloodworth said, looking over at the three women. "It's my former sister-in-law. It's been years and years."

"Mr. Bloodworm!" Sunshine called out to us again. "Won't you and your friends the missionaries join us for lunch?"

"What do you think, Bishop?" I asked.

"Well, I think it would be rude to decline the invitation," Bloodworth said. "She's a good woman."

"Is she a member?" I said.

"No," Bloodworth said. "But she's a good woman."

"She could be Cruella De Vil, as long as she's paying," Jared said. He walked toward the three women. "I'm starving."

Bloodworth and I looked at each other. I shrugged and followed Jared. Bloodworth followed me.

"Ladies," Jared said as he got to the table. "Good afternoon to you."

"Oh, so polite," Sunshine said. "Why am I not surprised?"

"Perhaps because word of our politeness has reached your ears. It's been getting around. May I?" Jared motioned toward a chair and received a nod from Sunshine to sit down. "This is my senior companion, Elder Feller. You can call him Kenny. His first name's not really Elder. It's Kenny. That's what his mother calls him—that and 'sweetums.' I gather you already know Bishop Bloodworm."

"Bishop," Sunshine said with a smile. "We feel so honored."

"I'm just a man," Bloodworth said. "Just a man. Thank you for the invitation. Mavis, it's nice to see you. Been a long time."

"Yes," Mavis said meekly. "Demetrius, nice to see you, too."

Sunshine introduced everyone in her group. Bloodworth, Jared and I all looked at the menus, placed our orders, and tried to engage in small talk as we waited for our food. When things became particularly strained at the table, Bloodworth turned to Mavis.

"So, Mavis, how's the world been treating you?"

"Oh, things have been great," Mavis said without looking

Bloodworth in the eye. "I'm part of First Hill's Ministry Team. We just finished a focus on Curse Removal. Sunshine here is the real leader."

"You mean curses like 'The Wicked Witch put a curse on me and I turned into a donkey?'" Jared quipped.

Sunshine disregarded the one-liner and looked me in the eye, erroneously coming to the conclusion I was in charge. "Let me ask you this. What would you gentlemen say the Biblical definition of sin is?"

At this, I took stock of everyone at the table. Mavis was looking into her lap, apparently folding and refolding a napkin nervously, trying to block out what was happening, I assume. Patsy was looking into her coffee cup with a pained expression. Bloodworth glanced at me with a frown and a furrowed brow that asked if there was a way to make this stop. And Jared, he was now looking directly at Mavis like he was about to cry.

What now?

"Well," I said. "We don't want to argue."

"Nobody's arguing with anybody, elder," Sunshine said. "I'm just asking you some questions, trying to understand where you're coming from. Everything must be measured against the Word of God."

The waitress arrived with our food. When she put Jared's plate in front of him, he didn't look at it or acknowledge the waitress in any way. He just kept looking at Mavis sadly.

"I'll say the blessing," Bloodworth said and immediately bowed his head and began before anyone could suggest anything contrary, keeping his voice low and meek, almost a whisper, lest anyone nearby be offended. "Heavenly Father, thank you for this nourishment for our bodies. Please help us to have a peaceful lunch. Help us to love one another and to be kind to one another and to have a good lunch. Amen."

When I looked up, Sunshine was staring directly at me. It was plain she hadn't participated in the prayer of blessing. I suppose she considered it blasphemous to participate in a prayer to Our Man on Kolob.

"So," she said. "What would you men say is the Biblical definition of sin?"

"Well," said Bloodworth, "I would say sin is anything that is contrary to the very commands of God. I mean, we sin when we don't do what God wants us to do, or when we do something that God doesn't want us to do."

"You speak correctly," Sunshine said. "Let me ask you: Do you men think that you have sinned?"

"You mean since we sat down at this table?" I asked with a smile and a look at Jared, thinking he'd be impressed by my quip. But he continued staring sadly at Mavis. "I mean, of course. Yes. We all make mistakes."

"Mistakes?" Sunshine said. "'We all make mistakes,' you say. The Bible doesn't say we are mistakers. It says we are sinners. 'Jesus Christ died for sinners.'"

"Well–" I said.

"The plain truth," she continued, "is you have chosen to rebel against God and love yourself and hate God. The only deciding factor in whether you sin or not is your own willful choice. A sin is a choice, not a mistake."

"That's why we need the atonement," I said, launching out with the gusto infused into me at the MTC, and yet immediately realizing I had no idea where to go from there. "Uh, God can help us get better. As we grow in obedience and faith and we, uh, take advantage of the, ordinances of the gospel, He helps us get better if we try with all our heart. God kicks in after all we can do—110 percent."

It occurred to me right then, again—for about the thousandth time on my mission, for fuck's sake—that I was woefully ill-equipped for this undertaking. I knew how to regurgitate about God and the gospel, but I really didn't know how to have a real conversation with someone about it.

I was at a loss. A gigantic game-show wheel of prizes spun in my head. Rakata, rakata, rakata. It slowed and finally came to rest with the arrow pointing at my answer:

Ding!

"Ma'am," I said, "have you ever prayed about this?"

Sunshine recoiled in her seat, looking satisfied. "Elder, are you referring to James 1:5, which says 'If any of you is lacking in wisdom, let him keep on asking God, for he gives generously to all and without reproaching; and it will be given him'?"

"I think so," I answered.

"Elder, in this matter I don't need to ask God about it, because I don't lack wisdom. I know what the word of God says about it and that's that."

"And that's that," I said, realizing the argument was over before it had begun and I had lost.

"You're sad," Jared said right then.

"What?" Sunshine said, turning toward Jared.

"She's sad," Jared said, pointing at Mavis.

Mavis blushed. "Oh, no," she said. "My life's very full."

"It's worse," Jared continued. "You're desolate."

"Oh!" Mavis said, clearly shocked.

"What did you say?" Sunshine said with eyes narrowing.

"She's desolate," Jared said and turned back to Mavis. "But don't worry. Heavenly Father loves you. He'll make it better."

"She'll be healed?" Bloodworth asked.

"Demetrius!" Mavis gasped.

"Mavis, he gets words from the Lord," Bloodworth said.

"He gets nothing," Sunshine said.

"It's true," I said.

"How'd he know, Sunshine?" Mavis said, tears coming to her eyes.

"It was Satan masquerading as an angel of light," Sunshine said. "He does that."

"Satan?" Bloodworth asked. "He said she'd be healed."

"It's Satan," Sunshine said. "The Prince of the Air. I can discern the spirit of falsehood from the spirit of truth, and this is the spirit of falsehood."

"It's one of her spiritual gifts from God," Patsy interjected.

"How could Satan do that?" Bloodworth asked.

"Oh, Demetrius," Mavis said, covering her face with her hands and beginning to sob. Jared, too, began to cry.

Bloodworth bolted to his feet. His napkin was still stuck into his belt, looking like a loin cloth. He reminded me of Tarzan. "Mavis," he said. "Take heart. He said Heavenly Father will make it better."

"Demetrius, those days are long past." Mavis sobbed as Bloodworth walked around the table and put his arm around her shoulder.

"Is there a problem?" It was a guy from the café, the manager presumably, a spindly suggestion of a man.

"No, no problem," said Bloodworth, comforting Mavis. "No problem at all. Everything's good."

"Perhaps everyone needs to calm down," the manager said. "Or else I may have to ask you to leave."

"We were just leaving," I said, standing up. "Come on, elder. Bishop?"

"Yes, maybe that's best," Bloodworth said, now with both hands on Mavis' shoulders. "Mavis, I'm sorry. I think we need to leave. But, remember, Heavenly Father will make it all better."

"Your God is a false God," Sunshine barked. "He can do nothing. You're no better off than praying to a wooden idol."

"Now I'm really going to have to ask you to leave," the manager said.

"Come on, Elder Baserman," I said to Jared, who looked at me as if he didn't recognize me for a moment.

"She's desolate," he said.

"Yeah," I said. "I heard. Let's go, man! Bishop, I think we should go now."

"Yes, go. You lose," Sunshine barked as Bloodworth patted Mavis on the shoulder.

"Ma'am, this is really inappropriate for a public establishment," the manager said to Sunshine.

"Sir, they're leaving," Sunshine said to the manager. "We were peaceable before they came and we'll be peaceable now that they're leaving. Scurry away. Hide under your rock," she said to Bloodworth, Jared and me, waving at us dismissively before sitting back down. "We're fine now, sir."

Outside the café, Bloodworth put his arm around Jared's shoulders. "Elder, how'd you know that, what you said in there? How'd you know she couldn't have babies?"

"What?" Jared said. "I knew what?"

"Mavis, she's barren, and you said so. Nobody knows about it, except Mavis, me and, I guess, God," Bloodworth said. "How'd you know?"

"What do you mean?" I asked.

"She isn't able to have children," Bloodworth said. "She never could have children. Still can't, I guess. But you said Heavenly Father would fix her."

"Wow, man," I said to Jared.

"I didn't know that," Jared said. "I don't know that."

Bloodworth put his arm around Jared. "Son, it was God speaking through you without you even realizing it. The flesh is weak but the spirit is strong."

"I don't feel so good," Jared said. "I'm doing this but I don't know I'm doing this. What if I can't control what goes in and out of my brain. What is God doing to my brain?"

"Elder Baserman," Bloodworth said to Jared, giving his shoulders an affectionate squeeze. "The time has come to take your gift to the church."

CHAPTER EIGHT

J ared and I hit the streets. Jared seemed out of sorts since our disastrous—yet prophetic!—meeting with Sunshine, Patsy and, most of all, Mavis. He was clearly not in the mood to talk to gentiles about God's One True Church. Providentially, he didn't get the chance, as all we got were doors shut in our faces. These were neighborhoods I had already tracted, at least twice before. I tried to encourage him. "It's okay to knock on a person's door more than once. Remember, only one out of every 1,000 doors knocked on results in a baptized member, according to Dewey."

"Easy for him to say," Jared said, adjusting his backpack with a shrug. "He's driving around in his air-conditioned Cadillac."

"Yeah," I said. "No shit."

Wednesday night, the Sedro-Woolley ward hosted the Young Men's and Young Women's groups, as it did every Wednesday night. These were opportunities for growth in the gospel. For the young men, it was a chance to hear some lesson on a spiritual topic or talk about their role as priesthood leaders in the ward and their families. For the Young Women it was usually a teaching or activity related to modesty or homemaking and crafts. Girl stuff. Normally, it would just be another night of tracting for Jared and me, but this night we found ourselves walking to the meeting house after dinner. Bloodworth had called a special, secret meeting of the Melchizedek Priesthood. He wouldn't say what the topic was about but he said it was "of special importance to the ward and our walk with Christ." It was indicative of his sway in the congregation that few men heeded his call. Bloodworth had specifically asked us to attend. We certainly didn't look forward to fossilizing for two hours in a boring meeting, but just about anything was a preferred alternative to door knocking on a sticky-hot August night in our monkey suits. Just about. For my part, it was clearly the lesser of two evils. But Jared still seemed gloomy.

"Come on, man. A night off from door knocking," I said, trying to cheer him up.

He looked over at me and attempted a weak smile.

"How can I help you, man? Come on."

"I've just been, I don't know. Stuff on my mind, I guess."

"Like what?"

"Believe me, you don't want to know."

Melchizedek Priesthood holders immediately approached us as we walked through the door. It was clear that Bloodworth had leaked the news of Jared's word for the unnamed "desolate" woman —and they were either intrigued or pissed.

"Watch your step, son," a man scolded Jared. "You're a representative of the gospel."

Another man nudged Jared and whispered with a smile, "I think you just might have a something, son."

"I agree!" another man said, insinuating himself between Jared and myself. "A something!"

Bloodworth emerged from his office, beaming. "Boys! Let's go to meeting," he said. "Big things tonight."

We all filed into the meeting room. It looked like about twelve men had been willing to leave their homes on Wednesday for a meeting of ambiguous purpose. It's worth noting the class of member who attended Bloodworth's meeting. They were not among the ward's stars. They were the outsiders. They had little to lose and they liked the idea of being called hither by the bishop, I suspect.

Bloodworth walked to the head of the room and nodded over at Jared and me with a smile. Jared was looking at the ground, so he didn't notice.

"Thank you for coming, everyone," Bloodworth called out. "This is a meeting of special importance. I felt impressed to call this meeting. Seeing as how we've been seeing God move in our very midst lately, I thought it would be good for us to have our own little testimony meeting here so we can share with one another how God has been speaking into our lives as we strive to live the gospel.

"So, I'll go first," he continued, smiling shyly. "I'll start by confessing to you, my brothers, that my testimony has been weakening lately. I admit I've been reading materials critical of the church and Joseph Smith." Here a slight buzz, a *murmuration*, flowed around the room. "I prayed out to God in despair, and Heavenly Father answered my prayer by sending this young man." Here he motioned to Jared and his voice cracked. "Sending this young man into my life, into all our lives. This young man, the young man is a young man who God speaks through. I've seen it. I believe that Heavenly Father will speak to me, that he'll show me the answers to my questions. What's more, I believe Heavenly Father can speak to all of us through this young man, this young man right here."

Bloodworth sat down. "Now, my brothers, please bear your testimonies of Heavenly Father's faithfulness."

A period of silence followed and then eventually a rotund man stood up and cleared his throat.

"Bishop," he said, "I must start by asking for your forgiveness. In my heart, I haven't loved you as I should have. Yes, I've heard others that said that black men were . . . black . . . because they had been less valiant in the pre-mortal existence, and, yes, I must admit

I bought into that reasoning. When the Brethren decided to let black men hold the priesthood, I thought, 'well, they're the Brethren. I guess they know better,' and I sustained them in their decision. Yet my heart was still sinful."

The rotund man began dabbing his eyes with his wienerwurst knuckles.

"But the Holy Ghost just . . . fell upon me, just now," he continued, "and all my ill-will was laid bare in my eyes. I realized at that time that I had treated you—in my heart—I've treated you in my heart like I was looking down on you. All this time, I've looked down on you!"

The rotund man walked over to Bloodworth and hugged him and the other men in attendance clapped in well-mannered mystification. I could see Bloodworth was crying and the hug went on for what to me was an embarrassingly long time. Eventually, Bloodworth put his hands on the man's shoulder and pulled himself back to look in the man's face.

"Brother," Bloodworth said, his voice cracking, "you're my brother."

And—what else?—they re-hugged. Eventually the rotund man took his seat, Bloodworth wiped his eye and looked at the assembled men. "Well, my brothers," he said, "who would like to speak next?"

The men present all looked uncomfortably at one another and no one said anything. After a few awkward moments, Bloodworth said, "Elder Baserman, I call upon you to share your gift with the brothers here so assemblized."

"I believe in this boy," someone said.

Jared looked at a loss. I admit, I thought Bloodworth was out of line. I mean, I know he meant well. But I didn't think at the time that Jared could just turn on and off his gift on command, like flipping the switch on a mail-order marital aid or something.

"I can't," Jared whispered to me.

"What's up?" I asked.

"Elder Baserman, don't be shy, son," Bloodworth said.

"Man, you've got to give me a priesthood blessing," Jared said to me. "And quick."

"Okay," I said, placing my hands on his head.

"Not on my head, man," he said. "People will see you. Just do it on my arm or something."

"Heavenly Father," I said, "in the name of the Melchizedek priesthood, I ask Thou to give brother Jared power from on high to share Thy will unto these men."

As I prayed, Jared was muttering to himself, no doubt sending a supplication straight up the pneumatic tube to Kolob.

"Amen," I said and looked up. "Well, go for it, man."

Jared exhaled. "Oh, man," he whispered, as he stood up and cleared his throat.

"Well," Jared said to all before closing his eyes. He opened them and briefly scanned the room. "Now–" He closed his eyes again and placed the thumb and middle finger of one hand on either side of his forehead, each on a temple. He held out his other hand in front of himself. He looked like a sideshow psychic. The Amazing Kreskin or something. I had to suppress a guffaw. Everyone else, they all looked at Jared expectantly. And when, after a few seconds, he didn't deliver some kind of punch line, I knew something was up. Jared's timing was just too good to delay this long for the laugh.

"I see," he began. "I see...a...thing...of light."

The men in the room murmured uncertainly.

"The light, it's getting brighter," Jared said. "It's . . . getting brighter. Brighter."

"Here it comes, brothers," Bloodworth said in a hush.

"Now," Jared continued. "I see . . . a . . . being."

"Is it Heavenly Father? Is it the Savior?" someone called out somewhere in the room.

"Uh," Jared said. "I–"

"Is it Joseph Smith?" another voice called out.

"It's unclear exactly who the being is," Jared said.

"Praise God," someone said somewhere.

"The being has something he wants to say," Jared said.

"Is it Heavenly Father?" someone called out.

"His," Jared said slowly. "His name . . . is . . . unknowable."

"Is it the Savior?" someone asked.

"His name is unknowable," Jared repeated.

"Ask him his name," someone said helpfully.

Jared took a deep breath. "He won't say," he said. "But he knows what God thinks."

"What does He think?" Bloodworth asked desperately.

Jared was silent for the longest time. A few people coughed. An unnamed brother failed at his honorable attempt to suppress a fart.

"He thinks . . . " Jared stammered. "He is displeased with many in this room."

"What did we do?" someone called out.

Jared continued. "Too many of us have secrets. Secrets we try to keep from everyone. Even from God, if that were possible."

A man in a cardigan bolted upright. "It's me! He's talking about me!" He put his face in his hands and began to cry, as Mormon men are wont to do at such times. "I'm so sorry, everyone! My brothers! When I was on my mission in the '50s, in Missoula, I slept with someone. A woman. I slept with her, in sin. I did it. I've kept this secret all those years. It's been terrible. I should have been sent home. Instead, I pretended I was worthy. Can I be forgiven? I don't think I can be forgiven."

"My brothers," Bloodworth called out. "I told you. This Elder is a gift to us. God will use him."

Another man stood up, cleared his throat and said. "I have lied every time I've stood at Fast and Testimony Meeting and said that I knew the Church was true. I've never known. I think I may only believe or hope. But all those testimony meetings, I've stood up and testified. Can a man know that the church is true? I don't know anymore."

Bloodworth walked over to the man and put his hand on his shoulder. "The life of faith is a difficult one," Bloodworth said.

"But can you know?" the man said, his eyes tearing up.

Bloodworth looked him in eye. "I don't know, brother," he said.

Another man raised his hand, as if he were in a grade school classroom. "Can I say something?" he asked.

Bloodworth looked at him. "What is it, my brother?"

"It's the Law of Chastity," he said. "I think I've broken it, again and again. I know I've broken it again and again. It's not that I've been unfaithful to Cora . . . in deed. But my thoughts. Brothers, I have to admit . . . well, you all know I'm a truck driver by trade. Brothers, I can't keep myself from looking down at the cars that pass me, with the women. They show you their breasts! I mean, not most of them. But every now and then, a woman does it. And it happens often enough—well, it doesn't really happen that often—but it happens, so I'm always looking . . . and thinking. I want to serve God but I feel so . . . broken."

"I think we're all broken," another man said from the rear. "I think that's why we need the church. It's all about repentance. God looks favorably upon a repentant heart."

"Marcus!" a man shot up across the room. "Please forgive me. I've lusted after Cora—time and time again. She's a fine woman!"

The truck driver/cardigan man looked at the man with no emotion on his face for a few moments. Then he buried his face in his hands.

"Dear God," he said. "What are we going to do?"

Another man cried out, "I envy other men's callings!"

"Brothers!" Bloodworth called out, "Let us not have any secrets from God!"

By this time, Jared had returned to his seat next to me, clearly distressed. He leaned over to me and whispered, "I made it up. What's God going to do to me?"

"You faked it?" I whispered. "How? What do you mean, man?"

"I just made it up," Jared whispered. "Shit, man."

"Shit!" I said.

"I'm in the shit," Jared said, burying his face in his hands.

"Brothers!" Bloodworth called out, "Let us not have any secrets from God!"

"I've got to get out of here," Jared whispered, learning into me. He rose and bee-lined for the door. I followed him out to the front steps of the church.

"I had no choice! The bishop put on me the spot," he said. "I faked it. And now God is fucking with my brain. Heavenly Father bent me over and fucked me in the ass!"

"Man!" I said. "Don't talk like that about Heavenly Father!" I guided him toward a seat on the concrete steps that led to the church's front door. "So you faked that whole thing. The whole 'His name is unknowable' stuff? Why'd you do that?"

"I don't know, man. I don't know anything. This could fuck up everything."

"Wow, man."

"How come, when I don't ask for God to give me a prophecy, in the sandwich shop, He gives me one without me even knowing it or feeling it? But when I need a prophecy from Him and desperately pray for it, I get nothing from Him? What the hell?"

Bloodworth emerged from the front doors at that moment.

"Jared! Elder Baserman. Are you alright?" Bloodworth asked. "You looked like something was bothering you."

"Uh–" Jared responded.

"He said he faked that prophecy," I told Bloodworth.

"What?" Bloodworth said, shocked.

Jared looked up wearily at Bloodworth. "You put me on the spot," he said.

At this, Bloodworth sat down on the steps with an "Uff!" He looked out on the horizon for several moments, lost in thought.

"Elder Baserman. Here's what I think. God used your lie. Now, listen. Don't say anything. Just listen for a second. God can use the foolishment of the world to confound the wise. You said you faked the revelation, and you think that's a sin? I'm not going to say what's a sin and what's not a sin. I mean, I know lying's a sin, boys. My point is, there are men in there who are being reconciled to Heavenly Father. And to one another. Boys, the Holy Ghost is ministering to men in there. Hearts are being healed by the very love of God. You saw it, boys! So maybe you made it all up. Or maybe you thought you made it up. Who's to say how Heavenly Father works? God's more powerful than any lie. God can use things that we think are of no account and use them for His glory."

"God . . . used his lie?" I asked.

Bloodworth paused, then added, "I don't understand it but I accept it."

Jared and I looked at Bloodworth, unable to speak.

"Jared," Bloodworth said. "There's a movement of the Spirit going on here, and it all revolves around your gift."

And that's how Jared took upon himself, uncomprehendingly, as if in a Talent Show Trance, the mantle of Instrument in The Hands of Heavenly Father for the Sedro-Woolley Ward of the Church of Jesus Christ of Latter day Saints. Amen.

CHAPTER NINE

Now, Algernon Briskey, erstwhile bishop of the Sedro-Woolley ward, had been among those called to Bloodworth's special meeting of the Melchizedek Priesthood. But since Jared's first vision at the Sunday service, which Briskey witnessed, a hunch had begun to form in his brain like a pearl in the soft folds of an oyster's knife pocket. It was an uneducated hunch, though, as he had no experience with visions and such—miracles—so he determined to learn all he could. He began on Tuesday—while Jared and Bloodworth and I were out tracting—as would anyone raised in the Mormon Church, with the Book of Mormon. Somewhere in there, there was the answer to how he could return to power in the ward. He found that the book was lousy with people succumbing to visions, giving prophecies, and healing people.

How had he never seen that before?

Are we missing something the early Mormon Church had? And if we are, could that my opening? What if the church wasn't energized the way God wanted it to be? Not that Briskey gave a shit necessarily. At the time, he was pure Evil Briskey, to hear him tell it. Then he thought of the *History of the Church.* Somewhere in his house, he had all seven volumes of the official *History of the Church*. Briskey felt he was being led to look at those volumes. The answer would surely be in there. When he found it in a closet under some photo albums, he sat down right on the carpet next to the closet like a teeny bopper and searched through it. Turned out that signs and wonders were commonplace in the days of Joseph Smith.

His un-regenerated brain coughed up this treacherous morsel:

I think I can use this somehow.

And then:

I've got to see this with my own two eyes.

He opened the yellow pages and looked through the listings for churches. When he hit *The North Cascade Tabernacle of Pentecostal Full Gospel Fellowship*, he knew he had struck paydirt. The tagline in the church's yellow pages ad declared, *Come as You Are, but Be Prepared to Be Changed by the Fire of the Holy Spirit's Power!* So the next day, the same Wednesday Jared was fitted with the dubious mantle of prophecy, Briskey showed up at the North Cascade Tabernacle of Pentecostal Full Gospel Fellowship for what turned out to be their Summer revival, in the place of their regular midweek service. The place was jumping. Even the greeters standing on the front stoop, they were shimmying to the music pouring forth from inside the church. Inside, everyone was standing, arms raised, swaying back and forth like seagrass. On the stage, Pastor J.R. Coldiron bounded from side to side yelling, "You don't need a *religion*! You need a *relationship*!" Briskey had never heard music this loud, let alone music this loud *in a church*! Behind the pastor on the stage, a number of women ran around waiving large banners on poles. The banners proclaimed things such as "Our God Reigns!" and "Jesus is Lord!"

Pastor Coldiron came to the front of the stage, motioned for the band to stop playing, and grabbed the microphone. "Brothers and sisters. Brothers and sisters. And all our guests. Why are we here? Why are we here?"

The parishioners shouted in unison: "To Give Glory!"

"Yes, to give glory to the one and only, the matchless Jesus of Nazareth," the pastor responded. "I would ask anyone here tonight from another church: Does your church look like the church of the first century, the church you read about in the *Acts of the Apostles*? Have you ever seen any church that looks like the New Testament church? Probably not. Why is that? It's because too many of us have believed a lie. We've believed that we have to settle for our infirmities. We believed that God doesn't move today as He did in the olden days. Let me ask you a question. Can I ask you a question? If Jesus were to walk into this building right at this moment and were to see any one of us with any kind of illness or infirmity, what would he do? You know what he'd do? He'd heal that person. The reason we don't see God moving in our churches and in our lives—it's not because God has checked out. No! The reason we don't see God moving is we don't *believe* He can. I'm here to tell you tonight that God can move, that He still does move, and that He can move in *your* life . . . tonight!"

Coldiron went on in this manner for a while, strutting back and forth on the stage in the bombastic style of a banana barker.

"God has a wondrous gift for you," he concluded. "Are you ready to open your arms and receive it? If so, we're ready to help usher you in. Let me have my assistant pastor, Marcus Mungus, explain what we're going to do here."

Mungus, a dirigible of a human, waddled to the front of the stage pushing an overhead projector, as one of the banner-waving women carted a screen on to the back of the stage and set it up. Mungus flipped on the overhead and put up a transparency that showed the "Steps to a New Life."

Mungus explained the two necessary steps over the next 45 minutes, impassioned and covered with a veneer of perspiration. First off was to "accept Jesus Christ as your personal savior." In such a way, one would be born again and the Holy Spirit would take up residence in one's meaty being. Second, once one had the "indwelling of the Holy Spirit," he or she was duty-bound to release the Spirit out of his life, "to bless the world around you." This was known as the "baptism in the Holy Spirit," and it was always accompanied by the sign of speaking in tongues. Always.

Now we're talking!

Here Pastor Coldiron bowed his head and spoke into the microphone: "Father God, we know that no man comes to You unless he is first called by You. So we ask you to work in the hearts of the people in this room tonight and open them to the full gospel. Put a burning into the hearts of our unsaved friends here tonight. Give them the courage to stand up! Yes, stand up. 'I don't care what the world thinks! I don't care if I look like a fool! I'm going to stand up and stand in that line and go down into the waters of baptism and arise a new creation!' Then, once you arise, you will release the power of the Holy Spirit in your life, with the evidence of speaking in other tongues. Amen and amen! Brother Thomzak, if you please."

As the band started playing, levitating hypnotically between a major and minor chord, people immediately began rising and walking over to the side aisle to get in line for the advertised new life. Briskey knew he would be standing up and getting in that line.

I must!

So he stood and walked past the swaying parishioners and got in line. Some of the people in the line were crying. Others looked utterly confused. Briskey was resolute and purposeful, although he tried to affect the dejected bearing of the penitent.

Don't overdo it!

The first person in line, a modestly dressed woman, was ushered into the font and into the welcoming arms of Pastor Coldiron. She answered in the affirmative to all the questions he posed. Then she was dunked and remained under for one, two, three seconds—Briskey actually counted out loud to himself—and when Coldiron pulled her up, the congregation, which was already rumbling with parishioners praising God, erupted into shouts. She held her arms over her head and let loose with a "Yeah!" Then she hugged Coldiron close, rocking back and forth as they stood in the font.

"Now, you have been reborn, born from above," Coldiron said. "And, as promised in the Word, you now have the indwelling Holy Spirit living inside of you. Now, you must let that Spirit flow out of you. You must release the Holy Spirit. Follow me in prayer," Coldiron said, bowing his head. The woman, likewise, bowed her head. As Coldiron spoke the prayer, Briskey could see the woman muttering back the exact words she heard. Coldiron continued. "Father, I believe I'm truly saved and born again. I believe that all of my sins have now been fully forgiven and washed clean under the Blood of Your Son, Jesus Christ. Father, I now, by an act of my free will, turn my entire life over to You. I now place my body, my soul, my spirit, and my entire life into Your hands. I now ask that You enter me into Your perfect will for my life. I now ask that You set me up on the perfect plan and destiny You've set up for my life. Your perfect plan for my life. So in the Name of Jesus Christ, my Lord, I am asking You to fill me to overflowing with Your precious Holy Spirit. Jesus, baptize me in the Holy Spirit. Because of Your Word, I believe that I now receive and I thank You for it. Holy Spirit, rise up within me as I praise God. I fully expect to speak with other tongues, as You give me utterance."

Coldiron and the woman remained with their heads bowed for a moment, and then Pastor Coldiron looked up and said, "Now, speak forth! Just say whatever nonsense syllables come to your mouth. Just let it flow. When you let go, God will take over. You must take that step of faith, though. You must begin to speak!"

Coldiron raised his hands, each thumb and forefinger on each hand connected in a small circle and the other fingers fanned out, looking like a street corner magician about to pronounce the moment of prestidigitation. "Now!" he commanded. The woman, her hands palm upward in front of herself, delayed, understandably nervous about being on performance front of all these people.

"Speak forth!" Coldiron commanded again. "Just trust!" ("Come on, come on," Briskey muttered to himself. He realized his hands and teeth were clenched in anticipation.) The woman winced and spoke quietly. Or at least Briskey assumed she was because he could see her lips moving.

"No!" Pastor Coldiron said. "Take the step of faith. Speak out! The Spirit will give you utterance!"

The woman took a deep breath and blasted out. *"La-ba-la-ba—la-la-ma-machooey!"*

"Praise God!" Pastor Coldiron responded, slapping the woman on the back and joining her in the stream of tongues. The banner ladies ran up and down the center aisle waving their banners and shouting praises to the Lord Jesus Christ.

When Briskey first got in the line, he didn't really know what he was going to do. But he trusted in his diabolical brain to come up with something. First, as regard to the first part of this process—the whole "accepting Jesus Christ as your personal Lord and Savior"—he was surprised to find that he didn't have any problem with it. To the extent he had a personal doctrine, it lined up pretty well with what was being said: Jesus was God's son, he came to Earth, died on the cross for your sins, etc. The second part of this prospect, though—the whole "baptism in the Holy Spirit" part of what he was about to go through—was a bit more problematic. It actually required something from him. He needed to *execute*. He couldn't be the only one for whom this process didn't take. One by one, the converts to be, the prospective vessels for the Holy Spirit, went into the font and emerged exulting and jabbering—and Briskey started to prime himself for his performance. Soon enough, he was standing at the lip of the font and Coldiron was calling him into said font. He entered the waters cautiously, and Pastor Coldiron leaned into him conspiratorially and whispered, "Don't worry, my son. Nothing to it."

"There's nothing to it," Briskey repeated back to him. "There's nothing to it. I agree."

"So," Pastor Coldiron said, "ready to join the family of God?"

Briskey looked at him. "Always ready to do God's will, sir," he said.

"That's the spirit," Pastor Coldiron said, catching himself: "'That's the spirit'? Hey, that's funny. Get it?"

"Less jokes, more jabbering," said Briskey. "Let's do it."

"I like that," Pastor Coldiron said. "All business. Well, let's do it." He placed a hand on Briskey's shoulder and called out to the congregation. "This gentleman, he's all business. 'Put me under!' he says. I've got a feeling he's going to be a doer of the Word, a real soldier for the Lord." He turned to Briskey. "Okay, my friend. Here we go. Next thing you know, you're going to be a child of God."

Briskey responded matter-of-factly, "Heavenly Father *is* my father. I testify to you of that." He couldn't tell if what he had said had registered with Coldiron, who was leaning into Briskey, presumably focusing on the task at hand.

"Do you renounce sin and Satan?" Coldiron asked Briskey.

"I do."

"Do you believe that God the Father sent his only begotten Son into the world in the flesh as Jesus Christ of Nazareth and had him die on the cross to pay the penalty for your sins?"

"I do."

"Do you believe that Jesus of Nazareth defeated death when He rose bodily on the third day after His crucifixion?"

"I do."

"Well, then, all I have left to ask you, my son, is do you accept Jesus Christ as your own personal Lord and Savior and promise to follow Him henceforth in your life?"

"I do."

"Then I baptize you in the name of the Father, of the Son, and of the Holy Spirit," Coldiron said.

He lowered Briskey into the water. While Briskey was under, he started devising his subterfuge for speaking in tongues. He had picked up the gist of it from watching the people baptized before him. *Shamma-lamma-ding-dong.* These people will accept anything I do. Just jabber.

Pastor Coldiron lifted Briskey out of the water and shouted, "You are born again!"

Briskey sucked in air and blinked the water out of his eyes. "That's good news," he said. "Let's get to the Holy Spirit part."

"See?" Coldiron said, turning to the congregation. "All business! I love the way you think about things, brother. Well, let's be about it then. Repeat after me: Heavenly Father, I thank you that I am under the protection of the precious Blood of Jesus, which has cleansed me from all sin. Dear Lord Jesus, please baptize me in the Holy Spirit and let me praise God in a new language beyond the limitations of my intellect. Thank you, Lord. I believe that you're doing this right now. In Jesus' name, I pray."

When Briskey had repeated everything, Pastor Coldiron placed his hands on Briskey's head and shouted, "Now!"

Briskey inhaled deeply and then belted out: *"Shabba-labba-babba-lo Bom-bom-bow-cholabba-labba-lo!"*

"Praise the Lord!" Coldiron shouted. "Freedom in the Spirit!"

Briskey kept going: *"Labba-babba-lo, chum-chee-babba-lo. Bum-chum-chum-chee-babba-labba . . ."* And he found to his surprise that he was enjoying this experience. It was so . . .freeing.

"Like riding a bike!" Pastor Coldiron shouted and slapped Briskey on the back. "Like riding a bike! Taking your bike for a spin in the park."

"As I went on," Pious Briskey told me months and months later in the food court, "part of my brain said, 'Maybe this *is* from God.' You see, my experience was the reverse of what most people experience when they first receive their spiritual language. They think, 'Maybe this is just *me* talking. Maybe this isn't God.' Me, I was saying, 'Maybe this *is* God. Maybe it isn't just me talking.' What I've come to learn, as I've become more and more spiritual, you see, is that the answer is yes to both concerns. It *is* you, and it *is* God. Life in the Spirit is like a dance: He leads but you choose to follow.

'The spirit of the prophet is subject to the prophet.' So it says in I Corinthians chapter 14, verse 32. It's not like you're going to be in the line at the Piggy Wiggly and suddenly be overtaken by the Spirit and start spouting forth in tongues at the top of your lungs. You *choose* to let the Spirit flow out of your mouth and out of your life. You're in control, but you're not in control. It's a mystery. It can't be explained. There's no compulsion involved in speaking in tongues. God does not compel His people to do this. He *inspires* them. It's Our Great Enemy of Old who possesses and compels people against their will. Whenever anyone says, *I do this because God makes me do it*, referring to any physical manifestation, it is likely that it is not God at all, but either his own psychological nature that is acting or, worse yet, an alien spirit that is oppressing him. Of course, I didn't understand any of that back them. I hadn't progressed spiritually enough."

Back on the stage at the North Cascade Tabernacle of Pentecostal Full Gospel Fellowship, Briskey went on: "*Labba-babba-babba Shamma-lamma-namma-namma!*" The banner women waved their banners back and forth as they ran up and down the center aisle. The congregation swayed and rolled. The band searched for the Lost Chord of Blessedness. Mungus paraded across the stage like a professional wrestler. Pastor Coldiron exulted in God's goodness. And, Briskey—still Evil Briskey at the time, mostly—didn't have the first clue what had just happened.

"That was the beginning. The beginning of my release in the Spirit," Pious Briskey told me later in the food court. "Right there, Heavenly Father planted the seed that would grow into the Restored Church of the Restoration Gospel and into my deliverance from carnality. I was still lost at the time, but the change had begun."

And that's how Algernon Briskey, erstwhile bishop of the Sedro-Woolley ward of the Church of Jesus Christ of Latter-day Saints, first tasted of the myrrh that issues from the throne of heaven. More's the pity.

CHAPTER TEN

J ared and I continued tracting for the next two weeks. Jared was out of sorts at first, still worried that his fake prophecy had fouled his chances of pleasing heavenly Father and, thereby, returning with honor. Here's how a By The Book day penciled out for us:

6:30-9:30—Wake up, mandatory calisthenics, shower and dress, eat breakfast, read scriptures.
9:30-12:30—Proselytize
12:30-1:30—Eat lunch
1:30-5:30—Proselytize
5:30-6:30—Eat dinner
6:30-9:30—Proselytize
9:30-10:30—Unwind, tell jokes, jabber about life back home, go to bed.

IT WAS MIND-NUMBING, no argument, Novocain for the brain. No wonder our thoughts wandered.

"Check out those girls over there," I said one day while we were out tracting, leaning into Jared and talking out of the side of my mouth. I nodded toward a pair of girls walking in the opposite direction, breasts toward us, across the street. "Check out the rack on that one."

"My concern is only for her soul," Jared said.

"You're full of it, man," I said, elbowing him. "I heard you in the shower this morning. Man, you *saw* her."

"Yes, it's true," he said, shaking his head in an exaggerated, rueful motion. "I'm more animal than missionary. A burr in the saddle of the General Authorities if there ever was one."

"Man, you got a girl back home?" I asked.

"Well, there's my sister," he said.

"Your sister?" I said. "Man, you know what I mean."

He looked at me. "I'm not really what you call a ladies' man," he said. "What about you?"

"Hey, man," I said. "There are some babes in the stoner crowd, hippie goddesses some of them. Some don't shave their pits, I'm telling you. This one girl, I'm, like, doing it to her and I stick my head in her pit, her left pit. She's more hairy than a hobo. *Hirsute.* But you know what?" I nudged him with my elbow again.

"Does hirsute mean infectious?"

"No, man," I said, laughing. "I liked it! Got me off."

"The throes of love will do strange things to a young man."

"Man, I've done it more than once," I said, sounding authoritative, God's Gift To Doing It. "Five times. Check it out: five times. The secret is to bide your time. Laugh at her jokes, if she tells them. If not, tell a few of your own, progressively more suggestive as the kegger progresses."

"I've never been to a kegger," he said.

"Man, a perfect place to score if there ever was one," I said.

"Score?" he said.

"Us," I continued, as if I hadn't heard him, "we would classify the girls by how . . . sexually compelling they were. Babe to stone fox. The rest, the ones that would only do, you know, in a pinch, were listed as a single bagger, a girl who was so ugly one was required to place a grocery bag over her head—a double-bagger, a girl who was so ugly that one was required to place a bag over her head and over one's own head—and a triple-bagger, a girl who was so remarkably unsightly that a third bag was necessary to have on standby, lest anyone wander into the room. Man, it's funny."

Jared smiled at me. "Man, my sister would tear you a new bilge pipe if she heard you talk like that."

"A bilge pipe?" I said. "Come on, man. Don't be so serious."

"Hey, man," he said, "I dig girls. I don't know how many times I'm in class and I'm looking at this girl and, of course, Little Jared comes to life. So class ends and I'm like, 'I can't stand up, lest my shame be revealed.' You know what I mean. So I sit there and go over the notes I was supposedly taking as the teacher went on and on, which I wasn't. You can't stay there long enough, though. So you have to, like, walk out with your books over your man zone."

"Yeah, man," I said. "And then you go to the can to pee and—no way—you can't pee with a hard on."

"Only straight up," Jared said. "You think they'd take into account when they're designing high school urinals."

"And junior high, man," I said. "I lost my virginity when I was 14. I don't remember her name."

"I think I had a model train set when I was 14," he said.

"That's funny!" I laughed.

We walked on in silence for a bit.

"Nothing like a good-looking girl," I said.

"I vote yes," he said. "The way you talk, that's how all the boys treat my sister—at least at first."

"This is the sister with the vibrator?" I said.

"Only one I've got."

"So what does she say?" I said.

"I know for a fact she looks at guys . . . hungrily," he said. "She's got a pot pipe in the shape of a dick, man. She doesn't let any guy push her around, though."

"Man, no girl's going to change me, man," I said.

"You better hope you never meet my sister," he said. "She'd change you up."

"Not likely," I said. "Anyway, that kind of stuff is over now that I've done my mission. Straight and narrow. I'll probably get married soon, good Mormon girl. And then once I'm married, I'm the priesthood holder for my family, the man of the house. Nothing but a steady girlfriend, a good girl, and no funny stuff until I'm married. No more fooling around with girls. It's against God."

"He must really be pissed with all the, you know, fornicating on this planet. Funny thing is, He invented it. Fornication. Or maybe that's from Satan. I keep getting them mixed up."

So it went.

During these two weeks of tracting, Jared didn't burst forth with any more messages from heaven. However, we were far more successful tracting than I had been my entire mission, which I suppose is a miracle of sorts. During those two weeks, Jared and I, we must have knocked on, I don't know, 1,000 doors. A shitload. We would be invited inside into three or four homes a day—a major moral victory! Like all door-to-door salesmen, we had a routine, exactly prepared and tirelessly rehearsed. Once we were sitting inside people's homes, we would engage the earthlings in a bit of purposeless chatter. After five or ten minutes of such small talk, we would then remind them, nonchalantly and courteously, of the message we were there to share—The Plan of Happiness. That is when we would take our flipchart out and begin presenting the First Discussion, the gist of which was that God had shown His love for mankind by appearing to the Prophet Joseph Smith, a wondrous guy. Not only did he miraculously translate the Book of Mormon from golden plates written in Reformed Egyptian but he also reinstituted the true church on the planet Earth, having been deputized to do such by God Himself. And here's the kicker: You, we would tell the people, you can know the truth of all these facts by reading the Book of Mormon and praying sincerely for God to manifest said truth to your woebegone soul.

All the Discussions, One through Seven, were to be memorized, presumably during one's spare hours at the MTC. We were *not* to ad lib. We even memorized, presumptuously, the sections where we were told to say "I testify to you that I know these things are true."

My role, as senior companion, was to lead the discussion. At certain junctures, Jared, as junior companion, was directed to chime in, usually to the effect of bearing his own testimony of the truth of what I had just shared. A one-two punch.

"I know you will feel the truth of our message if you will make the effort to ponder these things and will seek the Lord in sincere prayer," the memorized spiel we were to give to people read. "How do you feel about the truths we've shared with you?"

Anyone willing to talk to us more than once was called an investigator.

By now, I'm sure you've seen the chink in this strategy, the turd in the tapioca, as my mother would say. Jared was liable to say just about anything.

For example: I was up to Concept Three in Discussion One. "By the gift and power of God, Joseph Smith translated the record from the gold plates and called it the Book of Mormon. The book takes its name from an ancient prophet named Mormon who lived in the Americas and was one of the last prophets to write in the record." (Here I was instructed to *Hold up a copy of the Book of Mormon.*) "This is where you can read about the Savior's visit and teachings to the ancient inhabitants of the Americas. The Book of Mormon is the story of the Lord's dealings with the people the ancient Americas. . . I know that this book is the word of God. I testify that Joseph Smith translated it by the power and gift of God."

Here, the junior companion was instructed to interpose his testimony regarding the Book of Mormon. So the first time I did this, I looked over at Jared. He looked dispassionately at the person. "All the kids are talking about it," he said.

The next time we finagled our way into a house and we came upon this section of the discussion, I offered Jared the prompt—his straight line, I see now—and he said, "He sounds like he really means it . . . this time."

And then, in another house, Jared expounded thusly: "Your results may vary, however."

Each time, when we'd get back out on the streets, I'd give him the business, first with an affected gravity—reminding him that he was the one who said he so desperately needed to return honor, not me—then with affection. "Every day's a new adventure with you, man!" I'd say, or something like that.

"You're right, though, man," he said. "I've got to serious up."

Anyway, when we would finish the First Discussion, on those rare occasions we would finish the First Discussion, we would challenge the person to read Joseph Smith's hand-written account of meeting Heavenly Father and Jesus Christ, both beings of flesh and bone (and, therefore, as hopelessly prone to hard-ons as you or me) and then to read some selected sections from the Book of Mormon and pray sincerely For God to manifest the truth of what they read to them. We wouldn't leave without a scheduled appointment for two or three days hence to come back and check in on their headway toward the Truth and take them into the Second Discussion, which included the all-important Baptismal Challenge.

During those two weeks of tracting, we never made it all the way through the Second Discussion. In fact, we usually never made it back inside the house. Often the person would open the door and beg off in some way, usually something like, "I've come down with something, boys. We'll have to reschedule," to which we'd respond, "That would be great. How about tomorrow at . . . 2 p.m.?" to which they'd say some version of, "why don't I call you when I'm better?" Or, we'd knock at the appointed time and . . . nothing. More than once, we'd hear some clandestine shuffling of feet on the other side of the door and then the peephole would darken as the person, clearly, was checking who was knocking. *Quiet! It's those Mormons.* On the few times we'd actually get inside, almost always the Joseph Smith pamphlet and the assigned sections from the Book of Mormon had not been read or prayed over. In such cases, we'd read the passages with them aloud, asking them to focus on their feelings as we read. Once again, Jared wasn't much help. One time, when I was reading aloud Joseph Smith's testimony, I got to the part where Joseph described his befuddlement over the religious landscape of his day, all those warring denominations in his village, each "zealous in endeavoring to establish their own tenets and disprove all others." I went on and read where young Joseph stumbled upon James 1:5—"If any of you lack wisdom, let him ask of God, that giveth to all men liberally, and upbraideth not; and it shall be given him"—and walked out to what would later be termed "The Sacred Grove" to put God's word to the test. Heavenly Father and Jesus Christ hovered above him in radiance and told him, essentially, all the bickering churches were full of shit and that he should start his own church, which would be "the one true church on the face of the earth." Truth is stranger than fiction, I guess.

I followed my memorized lines from there: "We testify that God the Father and his Son Jesus Christ appeared to Joseph Smith and spoke to him. In fact, the purpose of our visit is to deliver to you this wonderful message and explain how you can know that it is true." The book reads, *Companion adds his testimony here.*

"What?" Jared said with exaggerated alarm. "I thought we were selling encyclopedias!" and, that time, I had to guffaw—and thus was our chance to "plant a seed" for the Kingdom of God dispatched down the crapper like Sunday's family dinner.

"Man, I thought you were going to 'serious up,'" I told him when we were outside, affectionately punching him in the shoulder when I said "you." I shifted my backpack on my back. "If you're going to return with honor, you've got to be more Party Line. What would the prophet say?"

"I think he'd be cool with it," he said flatly. "Hey, man. Don't tell me. Tell the Spirit that constraineth me."

"Seriously, man," I told him, stopping in the street. He walked a few paces and then turned to face me. "I think God's going to use you to talk to people, to talk to, you know, me. Maybe. C'mon, man. This could be something we remember forever. "

I paused. You never knew, with Jared, if you were walking, unwittingly, into a punch line.

This time, though, nothing. He smiled. "That'd be cool," he said.

CHAPTER ELEVEN

W hen I interviewed Algernon Briskey and his ex-wife, Lydia Kay, separately—they couldn't be in the same room with one another—the one point they could agree on was that Algernon had been a "good Mormon boy." That is, Algernon was always consumed by the need to do as he was told. That is, as he was told by his mother, whom he apparently worshipped.

Others weren't so sure. What they saw was a conniving little grasper who twisted the knife on anyone who got in his way. Like this one time: This fellow Boy Scout shows up Algernon in a knot-tying competition, and Algernon pops a gasket on him when they're alone and the kid is admiring his blue ribbon, or whatever it was. I mean, Algernon, he puts the kid in a literal stranglehold. I met the kid later. His name was Bill Grout. When I met him, he was a chemical engineering professor at Utah State. But back when he was getting his neck wrung by Algernon, young Billy was just a timid kid who was fond of puzzles. So there's Algernon astride Billy, choking the life out of him, and Billy's mom comes through the door. Of course, she yanks Algernon off Billy with no lack of will and begins castigating him for the demonstrable deviant he is.

Who should come through the door at that time but Mother Briskey? She sees Mrs. Grout shaking her Pride and Joy like a Doberman with a gopher and she launches herself—launches!—into Mrs. Grout.

"Get your fucking hands off my son, you cunt!" she screams.

Now, granted, Professor Grout may have embellished the expletive a bit when he recounted this scene to me, considering the passage of years and all. But clearly Mrs. Briskey was miffed. She laid into Mother Grout and smote her two front teeth from their God-given roost. It was a big hubbub and a lawsuit, not the last surrounding the troubled, angry boy.

Young Algernon had few friends.

In 1953, when he was eighteen, Algernon entered BYU with an eye toward majoring in engineering. His Gateway to Success, he thought. It was in his freshman Geology class that he first laid eyes on Lydia Kay Starling. She was born and raised in Sedro-Woolley, Washington, eleventh child in a family of seven sons and four daughters, all born In the Covenant, meaning that their parents had achieved a temple marriage. Algernon was smitten. She was quite a catch: darkly beautiful and well-formed—smart as whip, too. She was always top student in her class. Her goal was to be married in the temple and sealed to a valiant man for time and eternity, thereby making it into the Celestial Kingdom as a goddess. Algernon made a vow to Heavenly Father that she would be his. However, it soon became clear that she vigorously ignored Algernon's existence and, as a matter of fact, had targeted another young Mormon man—a chisel-chinned and virtuous pre-med student. After this young man's sophomore year, he went on his mission. Lydia Kay pined and prayed for him while he was gone. That same year, Algernon went on his mission to France, determined to best his pre-med rival through his righteous performance.

But there was a hitch, as there always seemed to be with Briskey. A turd in the tapioca.

"Story of his life," Lydia Kay told me years later when I interviewed her in her sewing store. She had set up shop to make ends meet. "His bright designs always seemed to come to ruin, and he'd have to come up with Plan B. That's the story of his life. Plan A fails so he goes to Plan B. He's a Plan B Man, and nothing has ever come of Plan B except mediocrity. Plan A Men get it right the first time."

To wit: When Algernon was on his mission in Paris, he began suffering migraines that would keep him off the mission trail for days at a time. He tried staying in a darkened room and taking massive numbers of painkillers. He even was given double-secret clearance by his mission president to try stiff black coffee. Coffee! But nothing worked. It was baffling to Algernon, he told me, that Heavenly Father would keep a zealous infantryman of the gospel from his sacred duties because He wouldn't heal simple headaches. Headaches! Eventually, there was no recourse for the mission president but to send Algernon home, after twelve months in the mission field. Being medically discharged from a mission didn't carry the stigma that Returning Without Honor did, or so it was said. But Algernon was consumed with shame nonetheless. He started missing meetings, which distressed his mother to no end. What I think really devastated Algernon, though, was he thought his lackluster mission performance destroyed any chance he had of wresting Lydia Kay from the grip of her beau, Mr. Dimpled Pre-Med.

His headaches, though, abated.

Lydia Kay barely took notice of Algernon when he returned from his mission, so much did she ache for her Departed Missionary. Any number of suitors approached her but she was steadfast. She was saving herself for Him. What's more, she "felt led of God" to give herself to him sexually when he returned.

"She . . . had . . . it . . . all . . . worked . . . out . . . in . . . her . . . tiny . . . brain," Algernon told me later in the food court, punctuating each word with a stab of his French fry into the air between us. He munched for a bit, picked some detritus from a canine tooth.

"The way she had it figured was that, after all, she was going to be sealed to this boy for time and eternity, for goodness sake. So it didn't really matter when she lost her virginity to him, did it? After all, what is time?" He popped another fry into his fry hole. "What a pea brain."

When Lydia Kay's Pre-Med Prince returned from his mission, he was put off by her sexual advances. He broke it off, and suddenly she was 22 and without marital prospects: an old maid in Mormondom. She worried that no worthy priesthood holder would want to marry her. She became desperate. And into that gloom inelegantly walked Briskey. He confessed his infatuation for Lydia Kay, and she saw him as her only option.

"In my mind, I was damaged goods," Lydia Kay told me.

Soon enough, though, it became apparent to Lydia Kay that she had made a tactical error in marrying Algernon. He was verbally abusive. He threw furniture. All because things weren't panning out at work. He was hired with the implicit understanding, in his mind, that he was the engineering firm's Young Turk. However, his early efforts were flops, and soon after that the firm hired a single-minded achiever named Artis Watson. He was a real find by the firm's managing partner, it seems. First in his class at Stanford and a returned missionary to boot. It agitated Algernon all the more than he had to see Watson at church on Sundays, valiant son of a bitch.

What made things worse was that the Briskeys couldn't conceive. It turned out that Algernon had "lazy sperm."

Once again, Heavenly Father had let Algernon down.

Soon enough, it was apparent to Briskey that he wasn't advancing in his firm. He would never make it above the status of senior draftsman. When he was thirty, Algernon was passed over for a promotion at work in favor of that latecomer, the hated Artis Watson. He would be the next managing partner instead of overly-deserving Algernon.

"I was so focused on material success at that time," Pious or

Evil Briskey told me in the food court. "But remember, that was before I was regenerated."

Lydia Kay simply rolls her eyes at this. "When Algernon was passed over for promotion, the seeds for all this nonsense with this new church were planted," she told me months later. "He realized he would have to start making up for God's shortcomings in his life. Algernon would create his own blessing. Years later, he came up with the idea for the church after your missionary companion showed up with all his . . . powers. He saw an opening to use all this charismatic nonsense to gain status. Make no mistake. Algernon's a conniver. His church is a total fraud."

Algernon agreed with Lydia Kay's assessment, to a point. He admitted to me that he fomented the charismatic revival at the Sedro-Woolley ward out of dark desires. However, sometime early on, God got a hold of him and converted him to Pious Briskey. Try as I might, I couldn't get him to pinpoint that moment he wriggled from the chrysalis.

"God is good," Briskey said in the food court. "I was bad."

"Algernon doesn't give a rip for God," Lydia Kay told me.

Anyway, after Briskey was passed up for the promotion, he started working late every night. I mean, 9 or 10 p.m. late. And he'd always conspicuously walk past the big boss's office.

"You're still here, Algernon?" he would ask.

"I don't know," Briskey would say. "I just get into a groove after everyone else calls it quits."

Five, six years went by, and no promotion was forthcoming for Briskey. Eventually, he succumbed to a moldering depression that insinuated itself into his brain like water rot. He stopped staying late at work and, with nothing better to do, would come home and find fault with Lydia Kay.

When Algernon was 37, Watson was called as bishop of the Sedro-Woolley ward. It was an easy call for the stake president: Everyone was impressed with Watson's warm uprightness— everyone except Briskey. He hated Watson's fucking guts.

"I was full of malevolence," Briskey told me in the food court.

After Watson served four years as bishop, he stepped down and, in due course, was called as stake president. This meant he oversaw all the bishops in the stake's ten wards, one of which was the Sedro-Woolley ward. Then, in a spasm of unmerited charity, Watson called on Briskey to serve as bishop.

I'm sure Watson's motives were pure, but what Watson didn't know yet was that Briskey had a habit of crapping in his happiness.

To wit: a year into his calling, Briskey was discovered "in the act" with pornography by Lydia Kay. This led to the discovery of his large cache of hidden pornography.

"I had been lured in by Satan's schemes," Pious Briskey told me in the food court. "I admit it. But, in retrospect, it was a good thing. God had to bring me low to raise me up, and raise up this new church."

"Algernon's full of bupkis," Lydia Kay told me in her sewing shop.

Lydia Kay had been deeply unhappy with the course her marriage had taken, and with the type of man her husband had proven to be. She wasted no time in ratting out Briskey to Briskey's boss, Stake President Watson. But Watson wasn't inclined to fire Briskey as bishop, if that's the right word. Watson was a model of forbearance. Everything was forgivable except false teaching, I guess.

However, when Briskey was 43, in the third year of his calling as bishop, he began openly criticizing the Brethren for reversing the priesthood ban on black men. Watson's boss, Regional Rep Evans Pearsley, demanded that Watson sack Briskey and install in his place the most unlikely of choices, a mild-mannered black member named Demetrius Bloodworth. This was humiliating for Briskey, being replaced by a "coon."

After he was sacked by Watson, Briskey began concocting a plan to return to power—or at least respectability. (I mean, he may have been Evil Briskey, but he certainly wasn't Stupid Briskey. He must have known he had a snowball's chance in hell of being called as bishop again. Or maybe he just chose to ignore that blatant fact. I don't know.) He called it Plan Delta Sigma. Plan Delta Sigma, though, was notable for its impotence. Another Plan B, it turned out. It was the diabolical scheme equivalent of lazy sperm. He was about to ashcan the whole plan when, suddenly, he was given a cryptic glimmer of hope with the appearance on the scene of Jared and his giftings. Like the other members of the Sedro-Woolley ward, Algernon had been baffled, and perhaps even scared, by Jared's manifestations. But Evil Briskey knew there was some use he could make of Jared and his powers.

This is what was on Evil Briskey's mind as he drove to church silently with Lydia Kay Sunday, two weeks since Jared's vision of the Hallowedness walking down the church aisle and producing the erupting jungle—making some use of Jared to get back into power, or respectability. Or something. I don't know. The church was still buzzing about Jared's first vision at the past Sunday's service, and then his second (fake) prophecy in the Wednesday Priesthood meeting. Buzzing! When he parked the car, Lydia Kay cleared her throat.

"Algernon?" Lydia Kay said.

Briskey stared straight forward, as though he hadn't registered her voice.

"Algernon?" she repeated. "Algernon?"

"What, woman?" he said, hitting the steering wheel with the heel of his hand. "Can't you see I'm busy thinking?"

"Algernon, I have something," she said meekly.

"You what?" he said.

"Here," she said, passing across some papers she had twisted into a cone. "Read them."

"What are they?" he snarled.

"They're divorce papers, Algernon. I'm presenting you with divorce papers."

"You're what?"

"Divorce papers, Algernon. I want out. No more."

Lydia Kay had thought long and hard about this. Divorce was no piddling matter in the Church of Jesus Christ of Latter-day Saints. But she had learned that she could achieve a Temple Divorce with the approval of the leadership in Salt Lake. Then she could enter in to a Celestial Remarriage with a worthy man, one who could get her into the Celestial Kingdom. This was the best of her limited options, she felt. (She had learned that if she died unmarried she could be sealed to a worthy Mormon man in proxy as one of his polygamous wives, but she did not like the idea that she wouldn't get to choose that man.) She would get the Temple Divorce and find some righteous man, an older gentleman, well-heeled, no kids, whom she could be sealed to. Heavenly Father would pave the way.

She knew the divorce papers would be a blow to Algernon. She knew he wanted the reins of power again. And she knew he knew he had absolutely no chance of achieving such a feat as a divorcee, none. The Scarlet Letter D.

Briskey looked at the papers in disbelief.

"You did what?" he asked.

"Divorce, Algernon. The church will bless it. I'll explain about your issues, and the church will bless it. Algernon?"

"Get out," he said quietly.

"It's for the best, Algernon. For everyone."

"Get out," he repeated. "Out!"

"I'm going to leave now, Algernon, and I hope you'll give this some deep thought." She opened the car door and got out before sticking her head back in. "It's for the best."

When Lydia Kay came through the door of the meeting house, a fellow Relief Society member, brimming with cheerful suspicion, asked, "Where's that husband of yours?"

"He's thinking," she said. "I think."

Off to one side of the foyer, President Watson had cornered

Bloodworth. He was reading him the Riot Act, as my mother used to say.

"Listen here," he told Bloodworth, wagging a finger at his chest. "No funny business. I want a solemn, dignified assembly. None of your holy roller hocus-pocus."

Lydia Kay sat down by herself in a row in the chapel, and everyone immediately took note of her solitude. Women buzzed in the ears of their husbands or Beauty Parlor Buddies. Jared and I noticed. He was glum again, like right after his fake prophecy. Clearly, something was on his mind. The congregation finished the opening hymn . . . and still no Briskey. He was back in the car, gripping the steering wheel in both hands and starting intently . . . at nothing. In the Funny Pages, he would have had little squiggly lines radiating off the top of his head: Smoldering Man. He was scrambling for Plan C, to hear Lydia Kay tell it.

Meanwhile, back inside, we were having Fast and Testimony meeting, and Bloodworth had just stood at the lectern and encouraged any members who were so touched to approach the dais and bear their testimony. The first testifier was a girl, ten or so, who addressed the crowd on the topic of Meekness and how Heavenly Father had revealed to her the importance of said character jewel in these Final Days. A thickset woman, clearly the girl's mother, beamed from the third pew from the front.

This girl, she went on for ten minutes. It was a sermon, for gosh sakes! I wasn't in the mood. ("Somebody plug her up," I said, leaning into Jared in the pew. Jared looked back at me blankly.) She obviously had been coached by her mother. You could even see her mother mouthing the words of the monologue along with the girl at certain particularly stirring—and instructive!—stretches.

More testimonies followed. Finally, Briskey strode into the chapel.

He marched down the center aisle, staring straight ahead, unblinking as a hired gun, and took an empty spot in the front row. As he did, Bloodworth rose and approached the pulpit. "My

brothers and sisters in Christ," he said. "I'm inspired by the heart-
felt testimonies we've heard. Heavenly Father is here amongst us,
brothers and sisters. I'm sure you've heard of the miraculous occurrences happening in our very midst of late."

Watson shot up in his pew. "Don't do it!" he barked, wagging
his finger at Bloodworth.

People were shocked, no doubt, by this exchange. But they
were, I don't know, *flummoxed* by what happened next. Briskey
shot up and said at the top of his lungs, "Glory! Help me, Jesus!"
and collapsed into the aisle. The congregation let out a collective
gasp. And a number of people rushed to Briskey, lying prostrate.
One man, an optometrist, took Briskey's head into his hands and
slapped him helpfully on the cheeks. "My heavens, I think he's
dead!" the man cried.

"Somebody get the first aid kit!" a woman near Briskey yelled,
all but running around in circles. "Where's the first aid kit?"

"Holy shit!" I offered from my pew.

Adults rushed every which way. Children were bawling.
Suddenly, Briskey came to with a loud, moist "Paw!"

"Give him air! Give him air!" the optometrist insisted.

"Our God reigns!" Briskey yelled and got to his feet. Immediately, he began processing toward the dais, expounding as he went.
"Brothers and Sisters! It's true. I died. I was transported to the
Celestial Kingdom. Whether it was in the spirit or in the body, I
don't know. God knows. The Celestial Kingdom, I tell you!" By
this point, he had achieved the platform and he nudged Bloodworth
aside. "I died! I was gone. But the things I saw . . . and heard. I met
the Savior. I tell you, I was shaking in my boots. The Savior! I was
given a message by the Savior Himself!"

"You!" Watson yelled. "Stop this now!"

The congregation glanced at once at Watson and slowly turned
toward Briskey to see what was next. What a show!

Briskey continued, "The Savior said this boy"—here he pointed
at Jared—"this boy has a gift for us all. We are missing the blessings

God has for us. The Savior, he asked me, 'Does your church look like the New Testament church?' I said, 'What do you mean, Jesus?' He said, 'Too many of your brothers and sisters have been lulled to sleep by a lie!'"

As Briskey went on, Watson tried, again and again, unsuccessfully, to interrupt him.

"These poor people have fallen for the lie that they had to lead lives without power—lives of defeat, at every turn," he continued. "They believe that the Holy Ghost doesn't still move as He did in the days of yore." He grasped both sides of the lectern. "Brothers and sisters, if Jesus were to walk into this building right at this moment and were to see any one of us with any kind of illness or infirmity, what would he do? You know what he'd do! He'd heal that person. The reason we don't see God moving in our churches and in our lives—it's not because God has checked out. No! The reason we don't see God moving is we don't believe He can."

He bowed his head momentarily. "It's this boy here, Elder Baserman, who has the gift for us all. And the Savior told me we are called to nurture his gift!"

"Wow!" Jared whispered in the pew next to me.

"This is false teaching!" Watson yelled, standing and looking around the congregation, pleadingly. I wondered if he was about to cry.

"And I don't deserve this and I'm certainly unworthy of such a visitation, but Heavenly Father has appointed me to mentor the boy," Briskey announced.

"Holy shit!" I said.

Watson reclaimed the lectern and pleaded for sanity. Looking around, I could tell most members were hostile to what was happening and weren't buying. Others didn't know what to think.

"You two," Watson whispered harshly, getting as loud as he could, I suppose, without causing a ruckus, and pointing his finger at Briskey and Bloodworth. "This is your fault! Now I have to clean up your mess. Take a seat."

Bloodworth looked shocked. Briskey stood erect and said, "I must follow God."

"I mean now!" Watson growled at him. Bloodworth wasn't one to get into a pissing match with someone, so he sat obediently in the bishop's seat.

There was still a vigorous murmur floating about the room as Watson smoothed back his hair and took a deep breath. "Brothers and sisters, please," he called out. I could tell that he could tell he had lost the crowd, like a magician caught with his rabbit showing. "Please."

He set his jaw and breathed deeply.

"What is needed now is the steadying influence of the Word of God," he said. "All of you. We will now dismiss for Sunday School. Leave this distraction behind."

Lydia Kay was unmoved when I interviewed her. "Algernon's evil brain came up with the near death experience nonsense because he felt cornered. He had no other options. He was desperate. What a, what a . . . jerk!"

The congregation obeyed, haltingly, but if Watson thought his strategy would put an end to the clamor, he was wrong. It just moved it into several rooms, like coals kicked from a campfire. If anything, it picked up steam as it abandoned the moderating influence of the chapel.

"It might be a move of God," someone said.

Others were unimpressed to hostile. "What a bunch of hooey!" I heard a bald man say as we passed him.

Of course, all sorts of people came up to Jared—the Anointed One, as it were. They wanted to know what his take was on all that happened. Others clearly wanted to know if he had been "in on it." Most everyone felt the need to touch him physically in some way. When we were finally in the Sunday School room, the teacher gained some semblance of control.

"Members," he called out. "I hope you don't mind if we stray from the lesson manual this morning. I think we are duty-bound to weigh this experience against the scriptures. In fact, I feel that the Holy Ghost is leading us to do just that very thing this morning. I feel led."

"It was hooey!" the bald man said gruffly, his arms folded across his chest.

"What do we do?" someone asked the teacher.

"Well, let's just see where God takes us," the teacher offered helpfully.

As the teacher said this, Briskey walked in and stood at the back of the room, leaning against the wall.

"I think," said ardent longtime member Billie Fisher, rising to her feet, "that what we're forgetting here is that Heavenly Father speaks to us through the Prophet and the Apostles—the Brethren—not through someone who has had an experience. That is one of the ways He has given us to discern whether or not something is from Him. The Lord does nothing except through His prophets. Amos 3:7."

Some people seemed to be attracted by her tight-fisted logic and they looked at her thoughtfully.

"Also," Billie continued, "an experience as sacred as seeing the Savior would not be appropriate to share with the public. That's the same way we don't speak of our experiences inside the temple. They're sacred."

"He didn't have any experience!" the bald man groused. "He's full of it!"

At this, Bloodworth stood up and addressed the group. "Maybe it's that very type of an experience that must be shared. Maybe that's the way it is."

"Bishop," Billie said. "We are in danger of being deceived. Nothing good is going to come of this."

"Hooey!" the bald man said.

"Certainly, it's a wise course to action to see what the scriptures have to say about these visions," the teacher offered.

"The index. Let's go to the index!" an honest-to-goodness little old lady called out.

So they did. The whole room echoed with sacred pages being flipped and fingered.

"I don't even have to look. Lehi's dream," a man burst out. "It's one of my fondest gospel memories from my youngster days. Father Lehi had a vision, an important vision, and he shared it with those he loved and felt needed to hear it. Why would God expect us to do otherwise today?"

"That's compelling evidence," the teacher said, nodding thoughtfully.

"Hmph!" the bald man said.

Briskey leaned off the wall and spoke up. "It's not just visions," he said. "That's just the tip of the iceberg. It's about spiritual gifts from the Holy Spirit—revelations, visions, tongues, healings, special guidance and direction, evil spirits cast out. Look that up. Signs and wonders!"

Once again, the room echoed with the sound of flipping pages.

"Look at this," a man said. "This is Helaman 14:28. 'And the angel said unto me that many shall see greater things than these, to the intent that they might believe that these signs and these wonders should come to pass upon all the face of this land, to the intent that there should be no cause for unbelief among the children of men. . .' That seems to be saying that special signs and wonders are meant to keep us from unbelief."

"Well, listen to this," another man said as he stood up, with the Book of Mormon opened in one hand. "3 Nephi 2:3. 'And it came to pass that the people began to wax strong in wickedness and abominations; and they did not believe that there should be any more signs or wonders given.' This says that it's a sign of unbelief—a sign of wickedness—to say that signs and wonders should not be . . . given."

This caused quite a stir in the room.

"Listen to this, everyone," said an older gentleman as he stood up. "'And these signs shall follow them that believe—in my name shall they cast out devils; they shall speak with new tongues; they shall take up serpents; and if they drink any deadly thing it shall not hurt them; they shall lay hands on the sick and they shall recover.' That's Mormon 9:24. 'These signs shall follow them that believe.'"

"Yes, signs follow believers," Billie called out, trying to restore order, "but seeking them is the mark of a wicked and adulterous generation."

"We didn't seek them," a man said, pointing toward Jared. "They just . . . fell upon us."

"What I'm hearing is that we shouldn't be bound by our human reasoning," Briskey said. "We just have to accept it. Experience it!"

"God does nothing unless he speaks it first through His prophet," Billie called out. Others agreed with her.

As Briskey spoke, Watson entered the room and sat against the wall for a few minutes, listening. Eventually he stood with his hackles raised and addressed the room.

"This must stop!" he barked, elbowing himself into the conversation. "You and you," he said, pointing to Briskey and Bloodworth. He was tearing up, his chin quivering. Such an affront to the holy gospel! "This is your fault."

Watson tried to speak sense to the assembled members.

I looked over at Jared. He had a Funny Pages light bulb above his head. He leaned into me. "This is what God thinks of this. He thinks that this is okay. It's okay."

"God thinks that?" I asked as Watson was dressing down Briskey and Bloodworth in the front of the room.

"God thinks about stuff," he said, seeming somewhat put off. "Just like you or me, as he walks around the Celestial Kingdom doing stuff. He thinks about all sorts of shit. And here's what he thinks about this: He thinks it's okay."

"How do you know that?"

"I think I hear God's thoughts. Most of them, at least."

Right then, Briskey walked up to us as Watson railed on from the other side of the room.

"Boys, what's the good word?" he whispered before continuing without waiting for answer. "Boys, I have an inspiration. God is moving. I've already had people come up to me expressing interest in our ministry."

"Our ministry?" I asked.

"Our ministry," Briskey said. "Elder Baserman and myself. People are hungry for the power of God in their lives. God wants what you have for the rest of his children. You are a new breed of Mormon. No, not a new breed. You are what God intended from the beginning of Mormonism."

"Him?" I asked.

"Yes!" Briskey said excitedly, my sarcasm obviously not hitting home. "It all has to do with the concept of prophecy. Everyone should be a prophet. That's how the Mormon Church began. The Prophet Joseph Smith squelched it himself. He said only he could prophesy, after numerous members were following his lead and receiving words from the Lord. It was pride that did it, his pride. He wanted all the glory for himself. There was never meant to be just one prophet, seer, and revelator."

"I hear God's thoughts," Jared said.

"Like you hear me right now?" I asked.

"Well, like it, very much like it," he said. "Different. But more real, if you want to know."

"More real?" I asked. "What does that mean?"

"God is the really real," Briskey whispered. "All this is ephemeral, a mere shadow. Spiritual reality, that's the real reality. What you need to do, Elder Baserman, is to start writing down your revelations. Use your missionary journal. That's what Doctrine and Covenants is. It's just record of the revelations God gave to the Prophet Joseph Smith. It's scripture. You can receive your own scriptures from God."

At that moment, Watson barked at Briskey. "You! Brother Briskey! Come in here!" he said.

Briskey pulled us aside. "This is important. You're important to Heavenly Father's plan, Elder Baserman. And, that being the case, you can be sure the devil has taken notice. The people who are caught in sin, the devil doesn't have to worry about them. He leaves them to their own devices. But the people who are of use to Heavenly Father, those ones catch Satan's attention. He has schemes for you, no doubt. Your best bet is to stick close to me, Elder Baserman."

"Come here now, Brother Briskey!" Watson yelled.

"Satan has schemes about me?" Jared asked.

"I'm certain of it," Briskey said. "I testify to it."

"Well," Jared said, "if you testify to it." Briskey couldn't tell Jared was making fun of him. Or was he?

Thus it was that the foundation was laid for the ministry of Algernon Briskey and Jared Baserman.

How could the devil *not* notice?

CHAPTER TWELVE

And it came to pass that Jared and I found ourselves walking to Briskey's house for the first meeting of the Holy Ghost Society, so called. We walked on in silence until we came around a bend and saw Briskey's house. We saw Bloodworth standing nearby. Briskey's house looked deserted. You could discern no movement inside and there were no cars in the driveway. Lydia Kay, it seemed, had moved back to her parents' house. And Briskey insisted that all the attendees of the Holy Ghost Society park at least five blocks away, which didn't apply to us because we walked. "And not in suspicious clumps," he added.

"Don't knock on the door yet, boys," Bloodworth told us. "I'm expecting someone."

"Who?" I said.

Bloodworth looked at me and smiled deviously. "Someone," he said.

Briskey had told us that the purpose of the Holy Ghost Society was to "learn more about the historic roots of the Spirit-led lifestyle in the Mormon Church, and to experience the movement of the Holy Ghost in our collective lives in new and revitalizing ways."

Pious Briskey—or maybe he was still Evil Briskey at this point; I don't know—he talked like that. I mean, going to the Celestial Kingdom, if he went, that would kind of make an impression on a guy, I suppose.

Jared, he had his nose in his journal, God's girl Friday.

"Here she is," Bloodworth said.

As I looked in the direction Bloodworth was looking, I saw Mavis come around a hedge a block or so away.

"Oh," I said. "I get it. You like her, Bishop. And vice-versa, I think."

"Hush now, son," Bloodworth said with a scowl.

"Gotcha," I said, making an exaggerated zipping motion across my lips.

"Mavis, lovely to see you," Bloodworth said as she neared. "Glad you could make it. I think this will be instructional."

I wagged my eyebrows at Jared but he wasn't looking.

Bloodworth shook Mavis' hand vigorously as she came up. "Hi ya, ma'am," I said. "Good to see you again." Jared didn't even look up.

"Let's head in," Bloodworth said, arching out his arms to usher us toward Briskey's door.

We rang the doorbell and Briskey opened it. "Everyone else is already here," he whispered. "We're ready to get started." We walked into his drawing room. There, sitting in a circle in an assortment of home chairs and church folding chairs were five women:

Marcia Berg, 35, homemaker, mother of six, including her youngest, the ankle-biter Jerome, who played with his toy cars at her feet.

Penny Arbogast, 52, homemaker, mother of five grown children and 33 grandchildren.

Lee Dublin, 38, homemaker, mother of nine boys and, consequently, prematurely and totally grey.

Sally Hill, 29, homemaker, mother of five children and possessor of a singing voice noted for its warble.

Renee Skeemer, 37, homemaker, mother of but three children.

They looked at us with self-conscious smiles and shy darting of the eyes. They all knew we were about something unauthorized.

Months and months later, Briskey explained to me that he sought out these five women because he discerned that they had a "special sensitivity to the Holy Ghost."

Jerusha thinks he's full of shit. She says he used the women's sincerity against them. Briskey needed people on his team and he could tell he could play on these women's devotion to Heavenly Father. At least that's what Jerusha thought. Celestial Kingdom, her ass.

Jared, Bloodworth, Mavis, and I found seats. Bloodworth sat next to Mavis and immediately introduced her to everyone present.

"She's not a member," he explained, "but she loves the Savior with her whole heart." All welcomed her gushingly.

Briskey gave his introductions, told us why we were there. It was a divine appointment!

"The Spirit-led life was the life of Jesus and his disciples. And then it left the Earth after the Great Apostasy. It died away. The Holy Ghost was hamstrung until the Restoration of the true gospel by the Prophet Joseph Smith. In those early days of the Restoration, the Holy Ghost was a fire among the people of God. Visions! Tongues, and interpretation of tongues! Prophecies! Miracles! Miraculous healings! Then, soon after the martyrdom of the Prophet Joseph Smith, the fire of the Holy Ghost began to dwindle, until it died out. The people of God had a relationship, and they settled for a religion. I'm guessing each of you wants a relationship, not a religion. Am I right?"

What a question. Here polite, befuddled murmurings of agreement gurgled up around the circle.

"In this church, the very church that was inaugurated with a mighty move of the Holy Ghost, we have come to expect profound spiritual experiences and miracles to only be visited upon to The

Brethren. We have turned the Holy Ghost into part of the church bureaucracy."

He went on to explain that the Holy Ghost wasn't for "a select few." Rather, "personal revelation" was a cornerstone of the true church. And when he said "personal revelation," he said, he wasn't talking about the things you hear mostly at Testimony Meeting, things like *impressions* or *feelings*. No. We could all prophesy. The whole enchilada.

We all, we looked around at one another for a clue as to how to respond to Brother Briskey.

Briskey—presumably somewhere en route between Evil Briskey and Pious Briskey—then went on for 45 minutes outlining the scriptural underpinnings—both the Bible and the Book of Mormon—of his new. . . what? . . . sect. Clearly, he'd been doing his homework.

"Yes, you may not believe it, but God has seen fit to . . . revitalize. . . the Restoration—to restore the Restoration—here in sleepy Sedro-Woolley, Washington," he told us. "I don't blame you if you wouldn't believe it. But it's the truth. I testify to it."

At this point, Sister Arbogast raised her hand and Briskey nodded toward her with a smile.

"Yes, I'm excited about the possibilities. Yes. But I'm a little concerned that we're not going through the proper . . . channels. If this restoration of the Restoration was to be accomplished, wouldn't Heavenly Father use the Prophet to accomplish it?"

"I'm glad you asked that," Briskey said, looking at Sister Arbogast. "I've already told the elders this, but it was revealed to me that God's will is that we all should prophesy, man and woman. God has been disappointed that members of the true church have neglected their responsibility to prophesy and receive spiritual gifts."

Here, Briskey paused, presumably to let that settle into each brain in the circle.

"To be more specific, Heavenly Father has seen fit to kick off this new outpouring of the Holy Ghost"—at this he motioned to Jared as he scribbled in his notebook—"through this boy. Just a boy! Just like the Prophet Joseph Smith. Take note of that."

We all turned toward Jared and, sensing that, he looked up. He folded his journal in his lap, drew a deep breath, and said, "I'm sure you're all wondering. Well, in case you're wondering, what I'm doing is I'm recording my revelations. Just like the Prophet Joseph Smith did in the 1800s. I figured that, you know, my memory isn't perfect and I might forget some of His thoughts that I hear."

"Heavenly Father's been speaking to you as you've been sitting here?" Sister Skeemer asked.

"I didn't say that. I said I hear His thoughts, like I'm listening in, in secret. I hear what He's thinking as He's going about His day, what he thinks about stuff, you know, that's happening down here."

"I think," Briskey broke in, "I think Elder Baserman here is an example to all of us. We can all be talking with Heavenly Father all day, every day. And what happens when you're always listening? He changes your life. He changes you. I think it's fair to say that Heavenly Father has brought Elder Baserman into our midst to show us what can happen when you lead a Spirit-led life. He is an example to all of us. An example."

"That's not what I said," Jared said. "Weren't you listening? I'm not talking about the poison of corpses. I'm talking about the blistering rays that come from the heart of Kolob. There are things that are true, although no one can understand them."

"I would point out that Heavenly Father doesn't always act in ways we would expect, through people we would expect," Briskey said. "Look at Joseph Smith."

"Yes, indeed," Bloodworth said.

"I don't think he was listening to me," Jared said of Briskey as he looked over at me.

"Well, Elder Baserman," Sister Skeemer said, leaning forward in her seat. "Just what is Heavenly Father thinking?"

"Finally!" Jared said. "The Divine Opinion. Yes, it's a weighty matter. Having lived for many moons among miracles, I can say that the spread of these opinions will revolutionize sacred thought. You see, there are innumerable misunderstandings on God's part."

I whispered to him, "Man, watch the jokes!"

"I'm not joking!" he replied, which I thought was a joke.

"I'd love to know God's thoughts," Sister Skeemer said. "I wish Heavenly Father would speak to me all the time. I'm always so full of questions. That's why I'm here. I just want to hear from Heavenly Father. Life's so hard, and I just want to serve Him. But I don't always know how."

"Me too," Sister Arbogast said. "That's why I'm here. I want more of God."

At this moment we all heard the squeak of a car pulling up out front and engaging its parking brake.

"Hold," Briskey yelped. "Everyone, freeze! Someone just pulled up out front." We all looked at one another. "Everyone," Briskey shouted, "On the floor. On the floor!"

He went prostrate on the carpet, and—wouldn't you know it?—we all complied, obedient Mormons that we were. Even Mavis. She wasn't a Mormon, but she wasn't one to rock the boat. Little Jerome, rump on the floor, just kept playing with his toy cars, making motor noises and not skipping a beat.

"It's President Watson," said Briskey. "I know it's President Watson. Somebody go to the window and peek through the curtains."

I don't know why, really, but I complied. I elbow-crawled over to the window like a corn-fed farmboy at basic training and peeked through the small slit between the two drapes.

"It's President Watson, all right," I said. "And he looks angry. Here he comes."

I ducked back down to the floor, and you could see Watson's body block the light through the slit in the curtains as he put his hand on the window to peer in. The window squeaked all but noiselessly when he pulled his hand and head back. His shadow stopped blocking the light through the slit so I dared a second look. This time, I even pulled back the drapes ever so slightly.

"He's looking through the other windows," I hissed. As I turned to say this to the group, I noticed Jared was furiously scribbling in his notebook as he lay on the floor. I looked back through the crack in the drapes. "Now he's going around to the side of the house."

"Everyone, stay down," Briskey ordered. "He's not through with us yet."

We lay there silent for a few moments and eventually Briskey said, "Well, as long as we're all lying here, I might as well proceed with the agenda I put together for this gathering. As I'm lying here, I feel inspired to produce a message in tongues." He stopped, I suppose, to let that sink in, and we all were quiet as a bucket of mussels.

"A what?" Sister Hill eventually asked.

"A message in tongues," Briskey said. "It's a gift you receive when you receive the baptism in the Holy Spirit."

As he said this, we could hear Watson crunching through the underbrush in the back of the house.

"The what?" Sister Arbogast asked.

"The baptism in the Holy Spirit," Briskey said. "It's when the Holy Ghost, who came inside of you at your baptism, starts flowing out of you, changing the world around you for Christ." Briskey'd clearly been boning up on Pentecostal theology.

"It's negative tremors," Jared said, not looking up from his notebook as he kept writing. "When God gets to you, you'll drop like a cartload of crap."

"Man!" I whispered to him. I looked over at Bloodworth and he had this alarmed look on his face

"I have received this baptism in the Holy Spirit and my resulting prayer language, and I testify to you that it is true," Briskey said. "It is a true and holy thing."

Here Briskey went into a long treatise on the baptism in the Holy Spirit, everything he heard from the North Cascade Tabernacle of Pentecostal Full Gospel Fellowship, and everything he read subsequently on his own.

Near the end of his explanation, he said, "and the initial evidence of receiving the baptism in the Holy Ghost is speaking in tongues."

"But isn't speaking in tongues . . . wicked?" Sister Arbogast asked.

"You are just like the Brethren, saying it's God's will to keep the priesthood from women when in actual fact they're just repeating back what they've been told to believe. You're just repeating back lies you've heard. I say this in love."

It occurred to me, and it must have occurred to others: This is the same guy that didn't want blacks to have the priesthood.

Everyone was silent for a moment before Briskey continued. "As I explained, I'm feeling inspired to deliver a message in tongues, but—and this I must stress—someone must provide the interpretation. That's the rules from the Bible. That's the rules they followed in the early Mormon Church: 'Always there must be an interpretation.'"

We could hear Watson rustling around the final side of the house, bumping into things on the ground. A hose and stuff, I guess.

"Okay, here I go," Briskey said. Everyone was silent as he began. "Shamma lamma damma damma, do bamma. Fa-sa la-la, do bamma, mamma."

I swear, he went on for a good five minutes and no one uttered a peep. When he finished, he paused for a second and said, "Amen and amen."

We could all hear Watson getting in his car, starting it up, and driving away.

"Great!" I said and began getting up.

"No. Stay down, all!" Briskey said. "The Holy Ghost is in this moment. It's a holy thing."

So I lay down again and we all waited for the interpretation that Briskey had assured us would come. It was a few minutes later when Briskey said, "Wait on it. Don't lose faith." All you could hear were Jerome's car noises. After a few more minutes, Sister Skeemer said, "I think I may have something."

"Well, go ahead, sister," Briskey said. "We're all ready."

"Well," she began, "I've never done this before, but I think I hear the Holy Spirit. He says, I think he says, that what Brother Briskey said in his spirit language was that we should not be afraid of new revelations from God, things we haven't seen before, things that don't fit our definition of religion. He said that this thing Mr. Briskey spoke about, the baptism in the Holy Ghost, is a good thing. We should all receive the Baptism of fire in the Holy Ghost."

"My spirit confirms that what she has spoken the truth," Briskey said. "It's a true word. We don't want to miss His blessings, do we?"

Jared scribbled away as Briskey spoke.

"What are we to do?" Sister Skeemer asked.

"People, I feel this is our time. I testify to it," Briskey said. "Heavenly Father wants me to lead you all to receive the true baptism in the Holy Spirit. He wants you all to be speaking in heavenly languages as the Holy Ghost gives you utterance."

"Oh, I don't know," Sister Skeemer said.

"Anyone who denies Christ might as well deny his nuts," Jared said.

"Elder!" Bloodworth said.

"Don't be timid, Sister," Briskey said. "God is here. He is smiling on us right now. Repeat after me: Heavenly Father, I place my body, mind, and soul into Your Hands. Please fill me to overflowing with your precious Holy Ghost. Baptize me in the Spirit. Please help me to speak with other tongues as the Holy Ghost gives me utterance."

We all lay in silence for a moment. Then Sister Skeemer said, "Now what?"

"Now, you speak," Briskey said. "Have faith. Let the words flow, whatever words come to your mouth. It will be the Nonsense

of God. The Nonsense of heaven. Just say whatever nonsense syllables come to your mouth. Just let it flow. When you let go, God will
take over. You must take that step of faith, though. You must begin
to speak!"

Believe it or not, they all started in, Briskey leading the way and
the rest of them following timidly. Bloodworth was doing it. Mavis
was doing it. Not Jared, though. He was plugging his ears. So I
shrugged and stepped out . . . in faith, I guess. Nothing to it. Soon
enough, I was moving along at a good clip. It was a rush.

I must admit, for a long moment, it was dazzling. I was carried
along. The melodies and anti-melodies cascaded one over another,
undulating, throbbing. I rode the waves and turned the waves to
new directions. Eventually, all the flowing words died down, seemingly on command. We all lay there, stupefied, as it were. The room
seemed to be hyperventilating, and then, unbidden, came the
thought: That was a bunch of horseshit. I mean, how hard can it be
to be carried along by a flood of nonsense? The brain's a chattering
squirrel. Let lose, it would scrabble up trees, across boughs, in unexpected ways—artful, even if arbitrary—ways you couldn't have
planned, that seemed out of your control. Random beauty. What
was I thinking? Suddenly, the presumption of this whole affair—
speaking for God, bearing the title of elder, vouchsafing a message
from heaven. Me! What a bunch of horseshit. I looked over at
Jared. He was clenching shut his eyes and clamping his palms over
his ears. I looked around the group to see if I could spot signs of
doubt on the others' faces. But they also seemed suffused with
something otherworldly—if it weren't so unseemly, I'd say orgas-
mic. Except Bloodworth. He looked like he had caught the faintest
whiff of horseshit as well and he couldn't tell if it was sweet or sour
or simply horseshit. I looked over. Jared still had his ears stopped up
with the heels of his hands.

"That was wonderful," Briskey said. "A new thing has begun at
the Sedro-Woolley ward of the Church of Jesus Christ of Latter-
day Saints."

"A new outpouring," Sister Skeemer said.

"Yes," Briskey agreed. "A new outpouring of God's spirit. Now, listen to this." He began singing in tongues. Singing! "Shamala-mama dodoso so-tocootoo lamama da-pa-eee!" he sang. Briskey went on for a good two or three minutes before pausing. "Heavenly Father has given me the interpretation of all the messages in tongues we were giving. All of it was a declaration of thanksgiving unto Heavenly Father for his gracious gift of tongues."

"Praise God!" Sister Skeemer said, sounding for all the world like a card-carrying, Kool-aid-drinking Revival Tent Holy Roller.

(Years later, I would have someone say to me that anyone could speak in tongues if they just repeated, "She bought a Honda, she bought a Honda, she bought a Honda." It's pretty spot on. Reminds me of when Jared told me that the music that accompanies every porno film can be mimicked by quickly repeating the phrase, "Brown chicken brown cow." Once again, pretty spot on.)

Briskey got to his feet and dusted himself off. We all followed his example and took our seats. Sister Hill raised her hand like a shill and Briskey smiled toward her.

"Yes, sister?" Briskey said.

"I think they mean well," she said, "the Brethren, I mean."

"Yes, no doubt," Briskey said, shaking his head sadly. "It's true, they love Heavenly Father. That's why it's just a shame." Here he raised a finger: "But, let's be careful. We don't want to freak out anyone," he said, making air quotes. "For now, let's keep this hush-hush," Briskey said. "God moves in mysterious ways. Now, what's say we have some refreshments? I've set some things out in the next room."

We all meandered to Briskey's family room and began mingling. Eventually, Mavis and Jared pulled away from the group and went to one corner of the large room. Of course, I was curious, but soon enough I was caught up in another conversation with Bloodworth, a conversation about everything except the very thing we desperately wanted to discuss—which was what we just experienced, the whole baptism in the Holy Ghost thing and Jared's strange behavior. Bloodworth talked to me about tracting, but he kept looking over my shoulder in the direction of Jared and Mavis. When his eyes narrowed and his brow furrowed, I turned around and looked. There was Jared and Mavis. They were leaning into one another, their foreheads touching. Jared had his hands on the sides of Mavis' head. Something like this was never done in public. They were clearly in a deep discussion. What was Jared doing? What was he *capable* of doing? In the margins of my vision, I could discern Bloodworth staring like myself. Everyone else, too. As if aware he was the center of attention, Jared pulled up from Mavis and called out to Bloodworth and myself.

"Hey, guys, c'mere," he said with an excited smile.

Everyone else, they strenuously ignored the spectacle.

"C'mon, bishop," I whispered to Bloodworth. When we came up to Jared and Mavis, I whispered again. "What's up, man?"

"Holy business," Jared said.

"What do you mean? What happened?"

"A voice told me what to say to Mavis."

"Whose voice?"

"God's voice, I think. It was from Kolob, by way of Cassiopeia, if you must know the truth. It ricocheted. It said that I need to open up Mavis' womb," Jared continued. "So we have to give her a priesthood blessing."

"What?"

"You heard me," he said. "A priesthood blessing."

I looked at Bloodworth. He returned a helpless, defeated stare.

"Well," Bloodworth said, appearing unsure. "It appears God is moving in new ways."

"I wouldn't have believed it myself just a few days ago," Mavis said excitedly, placing one hand on her chest as if trying to still her racing heart. "But so much has changed."

"So," Jared said. "Let's do it. C'mon, guys. God's holy business."

Bloodworth and I looked at one another. If I didn't know better, I'd swear that Bloodworth gave the slightest shrug.

"C'mon, guys," Jared said. 'This is cool shit."

We all placed our hands on Mavis' head. She closed her eyes and held her arms slightly out to her side, palms up, as if catching rain.

"Heavenly Father," Jared began, "Never fear. Bear to share. Here we go. Open this womb from the tomb of childlessness—distress. Your daughter is in distress. We're under duress. Look under her dress and restore her womanly functions. Solid unction."

Here, Jared began muttering under his breath. I couldn't make out what he was saying. Then we all stood silent, until Jared pronounced, "It is finished."

"So!" Jared said, pulling his hands from the top of Mavis' head. "That's that. God has spoken! In Jesus' name, amen."

Briskey rescued us by walking up and inserting himself into our little group.

"Well, boys," he said. "I feel inspired. I'm going to come out tracting with you tomorrow, if you'll have me."

"Sure," Jared said. "God thinks that's a good idea."

"I'm coming too," Bloodworth burst out. I learned later that he was starting to mistrust Briskey and his designs for Jared. At the time, he didn't even recognize it as mistrust, only as a certain unsettled feeling, maybe the warnings of the Spirit, maybe.

"I don't know what God thinks about that," Jared said. "Maybe He's busy right at this moment. Cleaning his apartment."

"God is busy," Briskey said. "He's busy through us. These are great days."

"And at night we sleep the slumber of the righteous, little darlings that we are," Jared said.

"Truer words were never spoken," Briskey said judiciously, pointing at Jared and nodding his head. "Never."

CHAPTER THIRTEEN

That night, when we had gone to bed, Jared started getting out of bed and looking across the field upon hearing one of the cryptic PA announcements from the loading dock.

What now?

"That was a message for me," he said.

"You're nuts, man."

"No, really. I heard it. It said something like, 'Call for Edgerman Collins. Edgerman Collins!'"

"Edgerman Collins?"

"They don't use my real name, obviously," he said, rolling his eyes—a joke? "They have to use code. But I think I may be able to crack it."

"Man, go to sleep."

He was up and down all night, looking out the window when he'd hear a message from the PA. Eventually, he said he was going to go over to the loading dock and talk to someone.

"Come on, man," he said. "You have to come with me. Mission rules."

"Man, there's no way in hell I'm going across that field with you."

"Desperate times call for desperate measures."

"Just try not to get beat up," I said, turning over in my bed.

He went out, pajamas, temple garments and all—just asking to be beat up, as he was wont. I have to admit, I had to get out of bed and watch his progress across the field to the loading dock. He scrambled over like an infantryman at Normandy, taking cover every few seconds. An infantryman in pajamas and a stupid hair-cut. Bit by bit, he made it to the hedge that bordered the loading dock facility. I could see him peeking through the hedge. Eventually, he walked over to two beefy guys standing by the loading dock and engaged them in an energetic conversation. Soon, the men who were talking to Jared were gesticulating animatedly. Jared pointed an accusing finger at them.

"The guy is fucking nuts," I mumbled into the bedroom window.

The two guys he was talking to pointed back at Jared. Jared held his arms over his head, as if he were signaling a touchdown. Like he knew how to signal a touchdown. Then he bolted. The two guys stood frozen and watched him run away. Their disbelief was discernible from my vantage point, even though their faces were nothing but fleshy smudges. I lay back in bed and expected Jared to burst through the door at any moment. I decided I would pretend I was asleep. Five minutes went by, though, then ten and then fifteen. After thirty minutes, I stood up and looked out the window again. I could see the two guys who had confronted Jared milling about, conspicuously indolent. Another 15 minutes went by and I wondered what to do. The clock radio said it was midnight. I wondered if I should call Mission President Dewey. Probably not—but maybe Bloodworth. I decided I'd wait another half hour. When that time was up, I got up and phoned Bloodworth.

"Yes?" Bloodworth said groggily when he picked up the phone.

"Bishop, this is Elder Feller."

"What happened to Elder Baserman?" he immediately asked.

"Well, he went out to talk to the PA guys at the loading dock and now I don't know where he is. It's been a long time."

Bloodworth was silent on the line for a moment. "That's concerning," he said.

"Should we pray?"

Bloodworth was silent again for a moment. "I suppose so," he said. "Lead on, Elder."

"Heavenly Father," I began. "We don't know where Jared is, Elder Baserman. He could be anywhere. Keep him safe by Your power. Bring him back here in one piece. Amen."

"Amen," Bloodworth repeated.

"Bishop?" I said.

"Yes, son."

"Can I ask you a question, about the Holy Ghost Society?"

"Certainly, son."

"What did you think about that whole thing, the baptism in the Holy Spirit and speaking in tongues and stuff?"

There was silence on the line for a few moments, and then Bloodworth said, "Well . . ."

"'Cause I'm not too sure what to make of it," I said. "I mean, I did it, but I think it was just, you know, me, my brain."

"I did it, too, son," Bloodworth said. "I've got to admit, I'm not too sure what to make of it, either. I mean, it was wonderful—but it was also so strange. It occurred to me, too—that maybe it was just me talking away."

"Yeah!"

At this, I heard the front door open and close and saw Jared walk in. "He's here!" I said. "I'll get back to you. Thanks, Bishop. I'll let you know what I find out about where he's been."

I sat up and looked at Jared. He was breathing heavily. "Man, you freaked me out. One of these days your crazy jokes are going to get you killed," I said.

"You're probably right," he said, falling into the overstuffed chair. "Whew. You have no idea what I've been through."

THE NEXT MORNING, Jared and I walked out of our apartment to wait for Briskey and Bloodworth. Briskey pulled up. We watched him park his car and walk up to us, a smile of what seemed like sincerity stretching across his Evil/Pious face. Perhaps it was malevolence or dark glee? Or maybe imbecilic joy or simple, garden-variety courtesy. When Bloodworth arrived—Briskey had suggested leaving without him—we piled into Briskey's car and drove to today's neighborhood, out past Northern State, where, Jerusha was later to inform me, magic mushrooms litter the damp pastures like wedding confetti, strewn by the calloused hand of Jah.

As we drove, Briskey went on about the re-restored gospel he had re-recovered. Jared didn't seem to be paying attention, and me, I didn't know what to think.

When we pulled into the subdivision and began walking door to door, Briskey kept up his patter. The Prophet Joseph Smith said this and The Prophet Joseph Smith did that and The Prophet Joseph Smith brought forth miracle after miraculous miracle. The guy was all atwitter for Joseph Smith, at least to the extent that the prophet could illustrate some point Briskey needed to make about the re-restored gospel.

Elderly black lady opens door: "Good evening, ma'am, I'm Elder Feller, and this is Elder Baserman, and this is Brother Briskey, and Brother Bloodworth. We're here with a message about Jesus Christ." The black lady squinted at us. "Jesus Christ?" she asked. "I've seen the Jesus Christ you all talk about, white as the whitest white bread. I've seen it on your billboard. Jesus was a black man, you all. I'm telling you. At least, he wasn't white like that. Take your white-boy Jesus Christ somewhere else." At this, she shut the door in our faces.

"The problem with her schism is that she doesn't see cosmic reality vis-à-vis race relations," said Jared.

I wondered what *that* was supposed to mean.

Woman taking her dog for a walk: "Don't say it! Don't say it!" the lady said, holding up her hand. "Don't even start."

"But, ma'am, please," Briskey began.

"I said don't even start." Her little dog turned toward us and yipped murderously. "That's right, Pistol."

As we kept on walking, Jared said, "Dogs are known to have a different dictum than you or I due to their idealized trample orbs."

I looked over at Bloodworth with a "What the hell?" look on my face, but he was staring into the ground.

Man in a Woody Woodpecker T-shirt comes to his front door: "Yeah?" he said gruffly. "What?"

"Sir, we have a message about Jesus Christ we'd like to share with you," Briskey said.

"Already heard it. Not buying," the man said.

"There's no way you could have heard this message, as it was only just recently re-revealed in this dispensation," Briskey said.

"I heard it enough," the man said.

"If we could just have a few minutes of your time, I'm sure we could tell you something new," Briskey said.

"Here's something new: Kiss my ass," he said and slammed the door.

We stood staring at the door. Jared said, "My alter ego's negative brain waves are going to put an end to his misshapen sensibility."

Bloodworth and I looked at one another with wide eyes. As we walked away, Briskey said, "Satan is alive and well on the planet Earth. Little wonder people are hostile to the gospel. It's self-evident."

"Yeah?" Jared said.

"It's a certainty," Briskey said. "He has demons spread across the face of the Earth, reporting things back to him."

At this second, as we walked down the sidewalk, who should pull up alongside us in his sedan than Artis Watson, Tool of the Devil. He leaned across his bench seat and rolled down his passenger-side window.

"I told you to desist, Brother Briskey!" he yelled. "Why aren't you obeying me?"

Briskey kept his gaze in front of him and responded, "I must obey God."

"God has placed me in leadership over you!" Watson yelled.

"Rules promulgated by men!" Briskey said, staring ahead.

"These are rules sent directly from the throne of heaven, through our appointed prophets, as you know!"

Briskey took a deep breath. "Come, boys," he said, and pulled us in the opposite direction.

"You can't run away from me!" Watson yelled. You could hear him shifting his sedan into reverse and then the delicate whine as he drove backward to keep up with us. "This is false teaching, and false teaching will not stand!"

Jared leaned across the sidewalk and called out to Watson, "Your sensibility is misshapen!"

"Young man, you will not talk to me that way!" Watson yelled, still backing up as we walked.

"Misshapen!" Jared repeated, leaning across the sidewalk again.

"Careful, man!" I whispered to him.

"Tell him!" Jared said, pointing to Watson.

"Man, watch it!" I whispered again forcefully.

Right then, who should pull up behind Watson's sedan than the testosterone torpedo from our first day of tracting, the sounds of Creedence Clearwater's *Heard It Through the Grapevine* issuing from its insides. The driver honked at Watson and leaned out his window.

"You're going to wrong way, man!" he called to Watson.

Watson slammed on his brakes and yelled out his window. "This is church business!"

We stopped in our tracks and watched this interaction unfold before us. Watson appeared to be heroically stifling a purple string of crudities, fit to be tied and egged on by the torpedo pilot's sage observations of "fuck you!" and "up yours!" All this stress had to be shit bad for President Watson's angina.

"Church business!" Watson yelled back to his antagonist.

The torpedo pilot yelled back, "Man, you're full of shit!"

It was a spectacle, no argument. We could see Watson gripping his steering wheel with both hands and staring out his windshield in righteous humiliation. For all I knew, he was crying, at least on the inside. The torpedo pilot kept honking.

"Shall we pick up the pace, gentlemen?" Briskey said and motioned us to follow him to the end of the block. When we got there, we turned back and saw that Watson had given in, ruefully, no doubt, and was moving ahead. The torpedo pilot congratulated him with a hearty, "'Bout fucking time!"

As we watched him drive away, Jared said, "I don't want Satan chasing after me. You know, he has demons spread across the face of the Earth."

"That wasn't Satan, man," I said. "That was President Watson."

Jared looked at me like I was The King of The Dumbshits. "Of course it was President Watson." he said. "What the hell are you talking about, man?"

"Well, I don't know the particulars of how Satan goes about his business," Briskey interrupted before I could respond. "But I do know this: He knows a threat when he sees it, and that threat is you, Elder Baserman."

Jared stopped and checked his fly surreptitiously. "He's threatened by me?" Jared said. "What did I ever do to him? I don't think I want the devil mad at me."

"You should count it as a privilege, Elder," Briskey said.

"Like hell!" Jared said. "I don't want him doing his shit to me."

"Elder, you have nothing to fear," Briskey said, his eyes fluttering. "You hold the power of the Holy Melchizedek Priesthood, as do we all. But you, you have that power at full strength. You alone have been given the ability to use the full power of the priesthood. You are the man through whom Heavenly Father is re-inaugurating the Restoration of the gospel."

Jared gave us all a pained look, squinting his eyes and frowning.

"Brother Briskey, I think you're scaring the boy," Bloodworth said.

"Yeah," I said. "That's not cool, man."

Briskey closed his eyes, breathed deeply, and held palms up to us. He smiled. "You'll have to forgive me, brothers," he said. "I'm just so excited about what Heavenly Father is doing through this boy. You'll have to forgive me. And Elder Baserman?" he said, turning to Jared, "you'll have to pardon my enthusiasm as well. I've told you how you fit into Heavenly Father's plans, haven't I?"

Jared was still squinting and frowning. "Yeah, I guess," he said.

"Then it's settled," Briskey said, clapping his hands. "God is on our side. I testify to it."

"But how in the hell do we know we're on God's side?" Jared said.

AFTER THE FIRST meeting of the Holy Ghost Society, the sisters couldn't wait to get on the phone and start buzzing about the experience with their fellow female ward members. They said things like, "The peace I felt!" and "You have to experience it!" And, of course, each woman who received a call from Sisters Berg, Arbogast, Dublin, Hill or Skeemer, in turn, called four or five friends, who went on to tell their priesthood leaders. And so on. A ward is nothing if not a hive for gossip. Eventually, Sisters Berg, Arbogast, Dublin, Hill and Skeemer agreed they all needed to invite that lovely gentile from the Holy Ghost meeting out to lunch. Sister Berg was deputized to call Mavis. She repeatedly called Bloodworth in hopes of learning Mavis' last name.

Mavis shot up with excitement at the call from Sister Berg. "Oh, I'm so glad you called. I was wondering if we could all go out for a cup of coffee."

"Well, probably not coffee," Sister Berg said. "But we could go out for a lemonade. Coffee is forbidden by the Word of Wisdom, or at least strongly discouraged, I think."

"Well, that would be lovely," Mavis said. "I have so much to learn from you all."

"We all feel the same way about you," Sister Berg said.

They all went out together and ended up at a local park the same day we were out tracting with Bloodworth and Briskey. The women, indeed, all politely purchased lemonades from a vendor with a cart and sat themselves down by a pond.

"Ladies, I must tell you how taken aback I am with all you," Mavis started off after they sat down. "You really love Jesus. I don't mind telling you that my church says that you Mormons don't love Jesus or love the wrong Jesus."

The sisters said they were likewise taken by Mavis. "You're such a dear," Sister Skeemer said, patting Mavis on her thigh. "I don't have to tell you that our Church says you are mistaken. Well, I say they're mistaken. You're a dear."

But what they really wanted to talk about was the Holy Ghost meeting, and their suspicion that Bloodworth was sweet on Mavis.

"I never knew they spoke in tongues in the Book or Mormon. I mean, I guess I knew, but I thought it was just for, you know, the olden days," Sister Dublin said. "And the Prophet Joseph Smith. Why weren't we told about this before?"

"I think it's what Brother Briskey said," said Sister Berg. "Joseph Smith, what he brought through the Restored Gospel was a relationship. But the people—or at least the men in the high spots— they wanted a religion instead. It was all about control."

"All I know is I had a shiver go up my spine like I never had before when Brother Briskey began singing in tongues," Sister Hill said. "It was miraculous"

"But what about that Elder?" Sister Arbogast asked. "Brother Briskey said Heavenly Father was going to use him to bring forth this new move of the Holy Ghost. Can that be true?"

"He's a good boy," Mavis said. "And I've seen his gift in action. He told me something about myself that he in nowise could have known on his own. God told him. That's the only way it could have happened. He has power. He gave me a priesthood blessing."

"I felt it," Sister Dublin said matter-of-factly. "I felt it while he was sitting there."

"But wasn't he a bit strange?" Sister Arbogast asked.

"They said the same thing about the Prophet Joseph Smith, remember?" Sister Hill said. "For good golly, they ended up shooting him dead."

"Tarred and feathered him once," Sister Arbogast said.

"My goodness," Mavis said.

"I think you're right," Sister Skeemer said. "People who are touched by God always are picked on. They just don't fit in with the rest of us. I'm not surprised that Elder should seem strange to us. Me, I expect big things from him."

"And from us," Sister Berg said. "The Holy Ghost will use us, all of us. Priesthood or no."

"Remember," Sister Skeemer said, raising a finger, "God moves in mysterious ways."

"There is neither Jew nor Greek, there is neither bond nor free, there is neither male nor female: for you are all one in Christ Jesus," Mavis said.

"That was wonderful," Sister Skeemer said. "Did you just prophesy that?

"No," Mavis said. "That's from the Bible."

"That's another thing. We don't read enough from the Bible," Sister Berg said. "Why don't we know more from the Bible? I think the men in power don't want us to read the Bible because we'd read things like that."

"Let's not start a Conspiracy Theory, girls," Sister Arbogast said. "I don't think the men are that clever."

This broke them all up. "I can't believe I said that," Sister Arbogast said, touching her chest.

"Mavis, you should come to church on Sunday morning," Sister Skeemer said. "We've all got something planned, something that will knock the church's socks off."

"Ladies," Mavis said in mock horror. "It sounds like you have some sort of conspiracy in mind yourselves. I'll definitely be there."

––––––––

AFTER OUR DAY of tracting with Bloodworth and Briskey, Bloodworth felt he needed answers, something conclusive, not just something to believe in. He needed knowledge. So he found his reading glasses and headed to the Sedro-Woolley Public Library. He asked the helpful librarian to point him toward the books on mental illness. Even in the backwater of Sedro-Woolley, there were a truckload of them. So he sighed and began at one end. Took him several hours, but eventually, book in hand, he stared at nothing and said, "Psychosis. Jared is sick." He released one hand's hold on the book and let drop to his side. He bowed his head and supported himself against the shelves with his free hand.

"Where is God?" he said.

CHAPTER FOURTEEN

When Sunday came, Jared and I went to church for service. Who knew what in the hell was going to happen now? When we arrived, right off the bat, members began coming up to Jared. What I didn't know was that word of the Holy Ghost Society had spread throughout the congregation like a shitfire at a dump, along with the mention of Jared's purported special role in "restoring the Restoration," as Briskey put it. Some were plainly warm to the idea, others righteously indignant, and rightly so, I suppose. Really, it all sounded like horseshit, I can see now, with the benefit of years. When we got in, I saw Mavis standing with the sisters in a throng by the door to Primary. Suddenly, the name came to me: The Mothers of Invention.

"Elders," I heard Bloodworth call out to us. I turned and smiled in greeting and held out the hand of fellowship, as they say. "I was hoping I'd see you before church," Bloodworth said. He came up to us—or to me, as at that moment I noticed that Jared wasn't beside me anymore. I looked around and saw him over talking to Mavis, whom he apparently had pulled away from the sisters.

"That's good," Bloodworth said, pulling me close. "I wanted to talk to you about him, and it's hard to get the two of you apart. I'm concerned about him."

"You and me both," I said.

"I went to the library," Bloodworth said.

"The library?"

"Yes, and I researched Elder Baserman's . . . symptoms, I guess you'd say."

"His symptoms?" I said. "Like of a disease? Shit."

"That's the very thing I'm wondering," Bloodworth said. "The truth is I'm wondering if he has a disease of the brain of some kind."

"A disease of the brain? Shit, man."

"Yes."

Jared and Mavis came up to us. "Man, I left my journal at the apartment," Jared complained. "What am I going to do if I get a revelation?" We stood there uncomfortably for a few moments. Then Mavis turned to Bloodworth. "Demetrius, could I speak with you?" She pulled Bloodworth to the side.

"Demetrius," she said when she had him alone, "I just wanted to thank you for introducing me to the women at this church. They're just lovely."

"Uhh," Bloodworth said.

"Now, Demetrius, I have one more thing to say," Mavis told Bloodworth, moving closer to him. "Demetrius, when I'm with you I feel warm."

"Uhh," Bloodworth said again.

"Now," Mavis said, "shall we go to service?"

"Uhh," Bloodworth said as she clutched his elbow and led him toward the chapel. As they proceeded, President Watson blocked their path. You could see he was already about to cry.

"I felt Heavenly Father calling you. I prayed for you," Watson said, clasping his hands as Jared and I looked on. "Was I wrong? I guess so."

"I may have been wrong," Bloodworth replied dejectedly.

"Darn tootin', you may have been wrong," Watson barked. "What in the wide world did you think you were doing?"

"I was listening for God," Bloodworth said.

"And you weren't listening to me," Watson said. "How do you think God speaks to the bishop? Through the Stake President, that's how. Why didn't you come to me and discuss this? When Brother Briskey presented you his harebrained plan, why didn't you come to me?"

"I, uh—"

"I'll tell you why," Watson said and a single tear crested the faint gully circumscribing his eye. "Pride. Pride is the universal sin, the great vice. It's a, a . . . me-first philosophy. So you began to follow false and vain and foolish doctrines—the precepts of men! Now I have to relieve you of your bishop duties."

"It's probably for the best," Bloodworth said. "My faith isn't good."

"Darn tootin'," Watson said then closed his eyes and breathed a deep breath of righteous exhaustion. He looked at Bloodworth wistfully. "Well," he said, "I suppose I should pray for you."

"Yes, sir," Bloodworth said.

Watson closed his eyes and placed his hands on Bloodworth's shoulders. "Heavenly Father, we know Thou lovest Brother Bloodworth. Heavenly Father . . . I love him. Please show him the error of his ways. Please show him the sure path back to your arms of love. Heavenly Father, I will be waiting for him when he doth return, as I'm sure he will. I pray this is in the name of Jesus Christ. Amen."

"Amen," Bloodworth said.

Watson looked at Bloodworth. "I'll be praying for you, my brother," he said. Here Jared and I came into his field of recognition and he wiped his eyes clumsily with the back of his hand. "Excuse me, brother," he told Bloodworth and here he grabbed his belt on both sides of his waist and adjusted his trousers, ready to tear Jared and me new bilge pipes. My bowels clenched defensively, like a cornered badger.

"You!" he said, coming nearly nose-to-nose with Jared. "You better keep your nose clean. One more disrespectful peep from you, missionary, and you're gone! And you!" he added, turning toward me. "You're the senior companion here. Why are you allowing this rogue behavior?"

Jared opened his mouth to respond to Watson but I took over. No telling what in the hell was coming out of Jared's mouth!

"So sorry, President Watson," I said, pushing Jared gently away. "You never know what he's going to say next. Real strange sense of humor. Won't happen again, sir. I'll be more watchful in my duties as senior companion."

Watson looked at us as I pushed Jared away. He didn't seem convinced. But he watched us and shook his head slowly, closed his eyes and seemed to emit a long breath from his nose. Then he turned around and went into the chapel.

When everyone had filed into the chapel and sat down, Watson surmounted the pulpit and cleared his throat clumsily.

"Brothers and Sisters. It is a pleasure to be with you this evening," Watson said with a smile and then, instantly, a frown of regret. "However, I'm troubled in my spirit. There have been rumblings of evil in this body. False teaching has taken root, and it's my job, as your shepherd, to, well, nip it in the bud—the bud. It's up to me to expose it. There has been some talk, some mischievous talk, about the tenor of the early days of the Restoration. Yes, brothers and sisters, it's true, there were any number of signs and wonders in those early days. Some of it genuine, no doubt. However, many, many members, as well as members of other Christian groups, sometimes acted upon influences from evil or false spirits, believing they were under the influence of the Holy Ghost.'"

Watson looked down at some papers on the lectern. "Joseph

Smith said, 'Nothing is a greater injury to the children of men than to be under the influence of a false spirit when they think they have the Spirit of God. Thousands have felt the influence of its terrible power and baneful effects.'"

He looked up from his papers. "Not all so-called manifestations are of God. Some are of hellish origin." He looked around the sanctuary meaningfully, clearly wanting his point to hit home. Then he looked around some more, with silence descending upon the congregation. Seemingly satisfied, he returned to his book.

He looked across the room. "I am your leader, people, my brothers and sisters, and I am telling you that I discern that the recent occurrences in our body have been inspired not by the Holy Ghost but by false spirits." Murmuring flowed throughout the sanctuary like thin water over rocks. "Brothers and sisters, you have been deceived by people who are twisting scripture and the history of the church."

At this, the Mothers of Invention stood up in unison and Sister Berg turned to face the chapel.

"Brothers and Sisters, we are here to testify of the power of the Holy Ghost in our lives."

Watson looked like he had swallowed a beetle, butt-first. He knew these women were the very women who attended Briskey's clandestine meeting.

"Oh, man," I said to Jared. "Something bad's about to happen."

"We're here to share the power of the Holy Ghost," Sister Arbogast said.

At this, Watson barked, "Enough of that, sisters! You're out of order!"

"Judge for yourself whether it is right for us to obey you, a mere man, or to obey God," Sister Arbogast said, pointing angrily at Watson.

Jared leaned into me. "We're in the Devil's Scullery."

"We have something to share," Sister Berg cried, lifting her arms. She looked at the other Mothers of Invention. "Now!" she said.

With this, they began singing in tongues. No shit. Right in the meeting house during Sacrament Meeting. A Mormon Sacrament Meeting. It was as improbable as a flying pig and immediately gorgeous. As it rose, Watson yelled, "This is of the devil!" as well he might. He was in charge, after all, supposedly.

Watson's outcry didn't cause a hitch in the Mothers' song. They went on, dazzlingly, even though Watson continued to shout over them and pound the lectern.

"Stop this devilry," Watson shouted.

"Stop it! Stop it!" Jared cried, putting his hands over his ears. He turned to me. "It's the voice of Satan. He found a way to get his thoughts into my head!"

The members in the pews looked back and forth between Watson and the Mothers of Invention. What a scene! They look thunderstruck, like a streaker had just shot through the service, his various nasties wobbling hatefully.

Soon enough, the Mothers ended their song and sat down as placid as can be. You could have heard a pin drop, just an anonymous ticking and tapping sound. The sound of the universe imploding on itself. Watson was stunned silent.

Sister Berg shot back up. "There must be an interpretation!" she shouted.

"There will be no interpretation this day!" Watson yelled.

At that, Billie Fisher shot up: "President Watson is most correct!" she shouted. "We need no Holy Ghost singing. We have a modern-day prophet. He speaks with Heavenly Father for us."

At this, Mavis did something so unlike herself, so out of character, that the only explanations for it could be divine intervention or demonic possession. Or perhaps a discharge of excess infatuation, like when one of your kitchen appliances, a blender, say, kicks in during an electrical storm.

"I have the interpretation," she announced, looking around, petrified, and smiling shyly to Bloodworth.

"This interpretation is that we need to be kind to one another and to bear with each others' faults patiently, and look out for one another. We need each other. We're like Jesus to one another. And we shouldn't shout at one another, and that God doesn't like it when we argue back and forth. Amen."

"No," Watson shouted. "That's false teaching! There is no interpretation. It was gibberish. The work of Satan."

"Let's hear from the boy," someone yelled in the room.

"Yes," someone agreed. "Let's hear from the boy."

"Satan, you're a fuck," Jared cried out, bolting for the door.

"Hold on, man," I said and rushed after him.

I could hear the members gasping as we ran out the door. I caught up to him in the *narthex*.

"Hey, man. Hold on!" I said, taking hold of his arm. "What is it? Are you hearing Satan's thoughts?"

"Yeah," he stammered. "I'm hearing them."

"Well, hold on, man," I said. "Let's figure out what to do next." When I said this, Bloodworth came running out of the chapel.

"What's wrong?" he asked.

"I'm wrong," Jared said. "Now get away from me." He pushed me hard and I stumbled back and bumped into Bloodworth. We hit the floor as we heard the front door of the church swing open.

"Shit," I said. Bloodworth and I struggled to get to our feet, getting our legs tangled up with one another comically. When I finally got outside, Jared was nowhere to be seen. Bloodworth came and stood next to me.

"Where'd he go?" he asked.

"I don't know, Bishop," I said.

"Um, I'm not a bishop any more, son," he said.

"Huh?"

"As of about fifteen minutes ago, I'm just a regular man. Good thing, too, I think."

"Was it President Watson?"

"Yes. Him."

"That sucks," I said. "I thought you were the best bishop I've ever known, for what it's worth."

"I'm better as just a man, really," he said. "Now what are we going to do about Elder Baserman?"

Good fucking question.

CHAPTER FIFTEEN

I ran straight to the apartment after the blow-up at the Sunday service, hoping I'd find Jared there, perhaps squirreled away in fright. The apartment was empty as a cup. I plopped on to the couch and said a little prayer. "Heavenly Father, please help us find Jared." I looked over on the side table and saw Jared's journal. I picked it up and opened to a random page.

Whispered suspicions are being secreted into my ears. Devil! I'm trying to work out what exactly the fuck they're saying. It's hard to hear here. I think this is the place where spirits go to die. How the fuck did I get here? Whirlwind of hateful beauties. I think if I just had one congregation of lightning, that's all that would be needed to teach somebody about my humanoid singularity. What people don't understand is that shit has self-contained energy. It has a healthy smell that swells the air. The truth is that I'm made out of shit. I can say that because I can see the relationship to infinity.

I flipped a few pages and read. More of the same. And again. Complete gibberish. It was crap. Gabble. Nonsense. At least forty *parsecs* away from numinous.

Now, for most missionaries, should something like this happen, they would have immediately contacted their mission president. The protocol had been drilled into us. But I immediately called the Sedro-Woolley PD and reported Jared as a Missing Person.

"You can't report someone as a Missing Person until that person's been gone for 24 hours," the dispatcher told me.

"We think he's sick," I said.

"24 hours," she said.

I slammed down the phone. Immediately, the phone rang. It was Bloodworth.

"I called directory assistance—easy enough—and I got the number for Jared's family in Idaho. I got it. I'll come over. We can call together. Won't take me much time to drive over."

Soon enough, Bloodworth arrived. It was just after 11 a.m. on Sunday when we called the Basermans in Boise.

"Yeah?" Jerusha said when she answered the phone.

"Hello, is this the Basermans?" I asked.

"Yeah, it's us," Jerusha said.

"This is Elder Feller. Kenny. I'm Jared's senior companion here in Sedro-Woolley," I said. "I need to tell you about Jared."

"What happened?" Jerusha asked.

"Well, he kind of . . . lost it," I said.

"Lost it? What are you talking about? Who is this?"

Bloodworth came over. "Excuse me, son. Let me talk to them. I'm the one who went to the library. Hello? This is Demetrius Bloodworth. I used to be Jared's bishop."

"What happened to Jared?" Jerusha asked.

"Well, we're not too sure," Bloodworth said. "But we think he has a disease of the brain."

"A disease of the brain? Dad, something's happened to Jared!"

There was a commotion on the line and Nephi's voice came on.

"What happened to Jared? This is his father."

"Well, sir, this is Demetrius Bloodworth, and . . ."

"What happened to my son?" Nephi cut in, his voice cracking.

"Well, sir, we're not too sure. But we think there's something wrong with his mental faculties. I think it's best if you're able to come out here."

"His mental faculties?" Nephi said. "Are you saying he's stupid?"

"No. Excuse me. I misdirected you. He has a sickness . . . in his brain. At least, that's what we think. I went to the library."

"His brain? What do you mean?"

"It's a psychosis."

"A psychosis?"

"There's a lot of them, and we think Jared has one of them. It makes him have hallucinations and delusions."

"Delusions?"

"Those are a belief you have and no matter how much someone tells you the thing you believe in doesn't exist, you keep believing it."

"What are you saying?" Nephi asked.

"He's sick and we don't know where he is. He could get hurt, or hurt himself, I suppose. People can kill themselves when they have psychoses."

"Jerusha!" Nephi cried, his voice cracking. "Jared's sick. He could hurt himself."

There was another commotion on the line for a few moments, and Jerusha's voice returned. "We're coming out there. We'll be there as quickly as we can."

When they hung up, Nephi and Jerusha immediately called Jo and asked her for money for plane fare to Seattle and money for a rental car from the airport back and forth to Sedro-Woolley. Of course, she wanted to know why.

"Jo, I can't tell you," Nephi said. "I can't tell anyone."

"You better if you want the money, Nephi," Jo said.

"Jo, don't you have some secrets you don't tell anyone?"

There was a pause on the line. "What are you saying, Nephi?"

"Jo, I'm saying this is something I can't tell you," Nephi said. "Can't you see that?"

There was another pause, this one long. "Alright, Nephi. You're lucky you have a sister like me. I'll give you the money. You and the girl come by my office in about an hour."

Nephi and Jerusha packed in a hurry and by 7 p.m. they were on a flight to Seattle. By 9 p.m. they were in their rental car driving north to Sedro-Woolley, resplendent tapestry of magic mushrooms and moisture.

After the phone call with the Basermans, Bloodworth and I went out looking for Jared in his car. When I went to the passenger seat, I had to remove a pile of books. I picked up a couple and looked at them. Among the titles were *Mormonism-Shadow or Reality?*, *The Golden Bible*, *No Man Knows My History*, *Under the Prophet in Utah*, *Mountain Meadows Massacre*, and *Isn't One Wife Enough? The Story of Mormon Polygamy*.

"What are these?" I asked.

Bloodworth looked at me with shame. "I met this brother in the supermarket. I mean, he wasn't a brother. He was a brother. A black man. He challenged me. He told me the Brethren weren't serious when they removed the priesthood ban, and that they could bring it back, just like they could with polygamy."

"What do you mean?"

Bloodworth pulled out of the parking lot and continued: "The Brethren didn't really get rid of polygamy. They just suspended it. There's still polygamy in the Celestial Kingdom. And the reason they suspended it, it wasn't a word from the Lord. The US government was harassing them. So they relented."

"Relented?"

"Well," he said, nodding toward the book, "I didn't believe it at first, so I read a lot. And it seemed like the brother was right, the black man."

"He was right?"

"There's more. The black brother said the Brethren was doing the exact same thing, caving in to pressure, when it came to black men and the priesthood. He said they didn't mean it, that they could go back on it."

"So what did you do?"

"Well, I read a lot of books, like I said. And what I read was disturbing, about the church and the Prophet Joseph Smith. So I went to President Watson and asked him. I said, 'Do you know about this?' And do you know what he said?"

"What did he say?"

"He said, 'I don't care about any of that. I have an unshakeable testimony in the truthfulness of the Church'. So I went to Mission President Dewey, and you know what?"

"What?"

"Well, he told me, he told me basically that it was a lie."

"He said what he was saying was a lie?"

"No, he said it was a lie. The Church. The whole thing."

"What?"

"He said the Church was just a . . . a placebo?"

"A what?" I said.

"I don't know. A placebo. He said, people have to believe in something. He said, 'Human beings need religious myths.' That's what he said. 'Religious myths.' He said the Church really didn't have any power, just like a placebo. But placebos can do a lot of good. He said, 'without religious myths we must brave a pointless life with no hope of an afterlife. No glory. Just dirt, dust and bones.' I remember his exact words. 'Dust and bones.'"

"He said the Church is a . . . placebo? I can't fucking believe that! Dewey, the guy who would chew out our ass to spread the gospel. He thought it was all crap? I'm not too sure how to process this."

"Well, I wasn't supposed to tell you, I'm afraid. I guess this is an emergency, so it's alright, though," Bloodworth said. "I just can't believe that Mission President Dewey was right, that there is nothing. It just doesn't make sense. There has to be a God Who loves us and talks to us, and Who ministers His power unto us. If there is a God, would He want to leave us in the dark? Wouldn't He want to show Himself? That's pretty much what led to my disturbance. That's when I broke down and pleaded with Heavenly Father to show me the way, and that's when He brought Elder Baserman into my life. Or, at least, that's what I thought. But Elder Baserman isn't touched by God. He's just sick. I called out to God and He allowed me to believe in a sick boy. Why doesn't God intervene?"

Bloodworth began to cry quietly.

I had no idea what to say. I didn't know whether to comfort him, criticize him, or, as they said at the MTC, exhort him. "Exhort one another to be firm in the gospel," they told us—admonished us —at the MTC.

"There is a God," I told him, at a loss.

He looked at me. "Yes, there is a God, but why does He hide from us?"

"Yeah. I've wondered pretty much the same thing," I said. "It seems the answer we've been told to give people is this life is a test. We're being tested to see whether we will have faith so that we can live with Heavenly Father in the next life. The Plan of Happiness."

"The Plan of Happiness," Bloodworth said.

"That's what we say."

"So He's testing us. But why does He stay invisible and silent? We could use some help with the test."

"Yeah," I said. "Help."

We went on looking. Eventually, the sun set. We didn't say much.

"There he is," I said, lurching forward in the seat and pointing out the window. "There's Jared!"

Indeed, there he was, running across the road. He looked into the glare of our headlights, shielding his eyes with his forearm. He bolted into the woods and we screeched to a halt.

"Jared, brother!" I called out as I leapt from the car. I could hear Bloodworth calling after me as I ran into the woods after Jared.

"Hey, man," I called out. "Don't run away! We called your family, man! We want to help you, man!"

It was black as Satan's Sunday shoes and hopeless, but I clambered on. I could hear the brambles crackle ahead as Jared ran through the woods. After a hundred yards I tripped and fell face first into some blackberry vines.

"Shit," I said. It hurt like a bitch. "Fuck!"

I could hear Bloodworth crunching toward me on the undergrowth, panting like a Labrador.

"He's gone," he huffed.

"No shit," I barked at Bloodworth.

I could hear Bloodworth pause next to me. His breath was heavy

"I'm sorry, bishop," I said. "I fell into some thorns, I think. Fuck."

"Let me help you, son," Bloodworth said, bending down to lift me to my feet. The woods were soundless but for the creaking of the plants and thorns as they strained longingly toward the moonlight. We breathed into the dark air.

"I think we lost him," I said.

"Come on. Let's go back to the car," Bloodworth said. "We're not going to find him in these woods. Let's circle around."

So we did, over and over, fruitlessly. We didn't say much, just "turn down there" or "let's try over there" every now and then. Eventually, we gave up and limped back to the apartment like a pair of truants. When we got inside, we both collapsed into chairs. No conversation passed between us for fifteen minutes.

"Hey, Bishop," I said eventually. "Do you know how to play backgammon?"

"Never even heard of it, to tell you the honest truth," he said.

"Come on. I'll teach you."

I spent ten minutes teaching him how to play and we played for a while, chatting about nothing much. I think we were just liking the company, and the distraction. Eventually, we tried to hit the sack around 11 pm. I offered Bloodworth Jared's bed, but he wouldn't take it.

"I'll just sleep out here on the couch," he said.

However, as I was in bed, I could hear him pacing about. Clearly, he wasn't sleeping. Neither was I. I tossed and turned and flipped my pillow over again and again, but I was too worried about Jared to fall asleep, I guess. At midnight, there was a rap on the door and when I came out of the bedroom, Bloodworth was standing there talking to two people who could only be Nephi and Jerusha Baserman. When I walked up to them, Nephi reached out and gave me a bear hug.

"Thank you so much for what you've done for Jared," he said.

Then I noticed Jerusha.

Looking back, I think the first—what?—image, word, feeling that I experienced upon seeing Jerusha was *Autumn In the Sunlight and Strong Wind.* I know that sounds screwy, but that's what it was. That and *Muscle of Desire.*

When I saw her face, I couldn't help but immediately think of her piloting her vibrator to the Land of Vast Rapture. I wanted to see her naked, her thin waist, her smallish firm breasts, her vulgar flower. No big surprise. I wanted to see most girls my age naked, all except the triple-baggers. This was different. I didn't want to see her naked so I could . . . consume her. I realized that was what I had done, maybe, with all those girls I had cajoled into fornication: I consumed them. I ingested them until they were nothing. And then I was done with them and I shit them into a pot. Conquest completed. I could tell right there that this was one girl who wouldn't be consumed. She owned herself. I had been attracted to any number of girls in my life, but I realized now that, really, I had been impelled toward them. I was the driving force. I pushed my way in rather than being pulled. Those girls, they were something to be dominated. But, as I said, this was a girl who was different. It was she who was pulling me toward her. I was in danger of being conquered, and I'd only been around her for all of two minutes.

We all sat down and Bloodworth and I brought them up to speed on everything that happened with Jared, starting with his prophecy about Daryl and Lisa P. and their Spirit of Contention.

As I heard myself saying these things, I was struck how stupid it all sounded.

"I thought he was an answer to prayer," Bloodworth said. "I think it was because I was so focused on myself. I couldn't even see that he was sick. I'm so ashamed."

Nephi, who had then known Bloodworth for all of fifteen minutes, stood up, walked over to Bloodworth, and held out his arms in an obvious invitation to a hug. Bloodworth stood up and allowed himself to be embraced by Nephi.

"You're a good man," Nephi said to him. Bloodworth cried into his shoulder.

"So, what should we do?" Jerusha asked, looking around them at me.

"I tried to file a Missing Person report about him but they said he has to be gone 24 hours—which is actually coming up," I said, realizing that I was glad for the chance for a conversation with Jerusha.

"I'd say we should pray about this, but I'm not too sure anymore," Bloodworth said.

"God knows Jared's in trouble," Jerusha said. "Let's just try to send out positive vibrations to Jared."

"Vibrations," I said. "Yeah, that'll do it."

"Positive," Jerusha said, giving me a smile, which sent a spasm of youthful enthusiasm through my Trouser Snake.

"I thought God had a special purpose for Jared after what He did for him at the reunion," Nephi said.

"It got to me," Jerusha said. "That's what started me thinking it might just be possible to connect with God in some way."

"So what'd you do?" I asked, realizing I was sincerely interested, not just trying to "move the discussion toward spiritual topics," as I had been trained at the MTC.

"I became a Rastafari. Did you see my start on my dreads?" I swore this sounded like a flirt.

"Yeah, great," I said hopefully, completely unsure what she was talking about.

"I wanted to choose a religion as far away from Mormonism as possible, so I ended up a Rastafari. That's what we say. We don't say Rastafarian or Rastafarianism, because we don't believe in -ians or -isms."

"I see," I said.

"With all the ruckus about blacks and the priesthood, I figured why not find a religion for black people. So I found Rastafari."

"Rastafari," I said slowly, liking the sound of it on my lips.

"I like that we're all about defending the oppressed. The down-pressed. That's what we say. Down-pressed."

"She says *we* but she hasn't found any other Rastafari in Boise," Nephi said, adding with a smile and a wink toward Jerusha. "She's hopeful, though."

"I'm always looking for potential converts," she said with a smile my way. "We're opposed to Babylon, which is Western commercialism and consumerism. Like I said, I wanted something as far from Mormonism as I could get and still be connected with Jah in some way. That's what we call God. Jah."

"What do you mean?" Bloodworth asked.

"The Mormon Church is all about down-pression. I hate the way the church down-presses women. It down-presses everyone. Rastafari strongly oppose any type of chauvinism or down-pression."

"Down-pression?" I asked.

"That's what we say, Rastafari. We don't say oppressed. We say down-pressed."

"The Mormon Church doesn't hurt women, does it, Jerusha?" Nephi asked.

"Dad, a woman can't get into heaven unless she's pulled in by her husband-God, and once she's there, her only role is to produce spirit children for him—for eternity. That's what Heavenly Mother does."

"Oh, that," Nephi said.

"The Mormon Church is totally corrupt. Like how they tell members they can't drink soda pop and then they own 43 percent of the Coca-Cola Company. They're no better than the IMF. The Church isn't a church. It's a fucking billion-dollar corporation, funded through tithing money and run by a bunch of old white geezers. Totally corrupt."

"Six months ago, I probably would have taken exception to you there," Bloodworth said. "But I just don't have it in me anymore."

"And the ganja use," Jerusha said. "I like the use of ganja."

"The what?" Bloodworth asked.

"Don't ask," Nephi said with an exaggerated rolling of his eyes.

"I believe in living without wickedness," Jerusha said.

"Me, too," said Bloodworth.

"Our dreads are a distinct expression of our complete disdain for egotism and the significance of superficial good looks," she said.

"Yeah," I said.

"It's not like I buy everything about Rastafari. There are still some screwy things," she said. "I don't believe some dead Ethiopian king was God incarnate. Not because I don't believe God could do something like that. God can do anything."

"You can't choose what parts of your religion you like and don't like, can you?" Bloodworth asked. "I mean, you don't choose your religion. It chooses you, doesn't it?"

"I'm taking what I like and throwing away what I don't like," Jerusha said.

"Can we pick and choose?" Bloodworth asked.

"Why not? It's not like He or She is giving us clear directions. Who can understand Jah, anyway? Is He going to be offended because we misunderstand Him? Is He going to punish us for having an inadequate conception of the unconceivable? We should be able to expect God to be at least as understanding—or over-standing—as we expect ourselves to be, it seems to me anyway."

"Over-standing," I said.

"But what if you're wrong?" Bloodworth asked.

"What if? Jah's going to punish me because I don't think about Him in the right way?" she asked. "Besides, there are parts of Rastafari that don't come natural to me. It's not like I'm rejecting things just because they're hard for me. Rastafari believe in being humble and walking away from arguments and conflict. I want to do that. So I'm not just doing what comes naturally."

"Are you a Latter-day Saint in any way anymore?" Bloodworth asked.

"Well, I do believe like Mormons that families are crucial," she said. "I mean, God sets us down here naked and confused with no instructions. All He gives us is our family. Family is the source of all the joy and horror in our life. There's always bad with the good."

"And you can be happy?" Bloodworth asked.

"Yeah, I can be happy. And I can be sad. And I can be mad. All of them."

Around 3 a.m., Nephi stood up and said, "I suppose we should go to bed. We've got a busy day tomorrow, I guess. Although I don't know what we're supposed to do. Maybe Jared'll come back by morning."

"You can sleep in Jared's bed," I said. "And Bishop, I mean, Mr. Bloodworth, you can sleep in my bed."

"But where will you sleep?" Nephi asked.

"Well, Jerusha can sack out on the couch and I'll just sleep in the chair, I guess. I'm not too sure I'll sleep much anyway."

"Yeah, we can do that," Jerusha said.

"Come on, Demetrius," Nephi said. "You need some rest. Let's leave the youngsters out here and we'll get some shuteye. A few hours at least."

Bloodworth and Nephi went to the bedroom and within twenty minutes I could hear dueling snores from that direction.

Jerusha and me, we stayed up talking. It was clear—to me, at least—that we clicked. As I said, I was drawn to her. I've since learned that she was feeling warm toward me, as well. Warm for my form, as Jared would say. We talked until daylight, mostly about growing up, more or less, in the Mormon Church. About the ways our families didn't work, in my case, or did, in her case. It was clear that Jared and Nephi were precious to Jerusha. We talked about God and trying to find Him, or Her, as Jerusha suggested.

Bloodworth and Nephi walked out of the bedroom at 6 a.m. the next morning, rubbing their eyes and yawning. Bloodworth and Nephi splashed water from the sink in their faces. The front door opened and in walked Jared.

"I've got to pee," he said. "Bad."

CHAPTER SIXTEEN

At the time, we couldn't get a straight answer out of Jared about where he had been, what he had done, and who he had seen. He looked like hell, his tie askew and his shirt untucked, a walking, talking Fuck You to the missionary rules. A blackberry bramble stuck out of his vest pocket like a boutonniere. He didn't seem to remember running from Bloodworth and me. He smelled funny. What we could piece together is he had spent a certain amount of time at Briskey's house "being ministered to by Brother Briskey."

"Who is this Briskey asshole?" Jerusha asked. "What was he doing with Jared and why didn't he call us?"

"He used to be the bishop at the ward," I said. "He was relieved of his call shortly after I arrived, mainly because he wouldn't stop blasting the Brethren for removing the priesthood ban on blacks. Also, he had a porn problem," I said, making air quotes. "No one's supposed to know about it. But everyone does. And then Mr. Bloodworth here was called as bishop."

"That's about it, I guess" Bloodworth said. "I was a mistake, though."

"You were great," I said. "Best bishop I've ever had, and my stepdad was a bishop."

"Well, this Briskey sounds like an asshole," Jerusha said. "What was he doing with you, Jared?"

Jared looked at all of us nervously, licking his lips. "Why are you guys here?" he said to his father and sister.

"Jared, son, we came when we heard you were in trouble," Nephi said. "We think we need to take you to a doctor."

"I came back because Brother Briskey told me to come back," Jared said.

"You should have called here, man," I said.

"This Briskey guy sounds like an asshole," Jerusha said.

"That's what Brother Briskey said you'd say," Jared said. "Well, he didn't say asshole. He's helping me train my gifting, although he may be an asshole. I don't know. I'm hearing Satan's thoughts now, along with God's thoughts. I had to figure it out. Brother Briskey says I have nothing to fear from Satan, but I'm not too sure. What are you guys doing here?"

"Jared, have you slept at all? You need some rest," Nephi said. "Have you slept at all since you've been gone?"

"Sleep becomes impossible for me when Kolob is in its fifth ascension," he said.

"See? That's what I'm talking about," I said to Jerusha. "Crazy crap like that."

"You're talking stupid, Jared," Jerusha said. "We've got to get you to the doctor today. For now, you need to rest."

"What does the doctor want with me?" he asked. "How do I know he's not working for Satan? I think he'll try to plant some memories. In here," he said, tapping his head. "They can get into your thought regions like that. Whamo!"

"Come on, Jared," Jerusha said, helping Jared to his feet. "Let's get you in bed."

"I don't sleep anymore," he said. "Weren't you listening, Sister of Fire?"

"You'll sleep," Jerusha said, shepherding him to the bedroom.

She was right. Jared lay in the bedroom, rambling intermittent nonsense for fifteen minutes or so and then . . . quiet. I checked on him and he was out. With Jared home, I think we all felt like a burden had been lifted. Bloodworth returned to his house, stopping first at Mavis' to fill her in.

"We should get a motel, I suppose," Nephi said. "But I'd feel better if we could just stay here right now. You know, now that he's come back. I'd feel better about it."

"That's cool," I said. "You didn't get much sleep. Why don't you sack out in my bed?"

"Yeah," Jerusha said. "It's okay, Dad."

Jerusha and I sat and talked while Nephi and Jared slept. Eventually, we fell asleep too around 11 a.m. It was 1 p.m. when we woke up and Jared was standing on a chair between us, fiddling with the ceiling light and murmuring.

"Something's cooking here," he said to himself. "Something."

I sat up and rubbed my eyes. "What's up, man?"

"Yeah," Jerusha said from the couch. "What's up, Jared?"

"I'm sure there's something somewhere," he said, turning his attention back to the ceiling. "Maybe not here, but somewhere. I think the people at the loading dock put it here somewhere. They're working for Satan."

"What are you talking about?" Jerusha asked

"Cameras," he said with exasperation. "I told you the loading dock people have put cameras in here somewhere. To watch me, it seems. They're in league with Satan, I'm pretty sure."

"Shit, Jared. No one's watching you with cameras," Jerusha said. "You're talking nonsense."

"That's what they said to Copernicus," Jared said.

"That's what I mean," I said. "Sometimes, with Jared, you don't know if he's jerking your chain or if he's just being crazy. The guy never stops joking. You say, 'Is he joking or is he just strange?'"

"He's strange, all right," Jerusha said. "Come on, Jared. Let's eat."

"Eating?" he said.

"Yeah, eating. Food," Jerusha said. "Kenny, can you make him something?"

It was the first time she had used my name. It sounded warm, like a baby's laugh.

"We usually eat oatmeal for breakfast," I said. "What time is it? What day is it?"

"About 2," Jerusha said.

"Well, Mission President Dewey says oatmeal 'sticks to the bones' and 'keeps us up and going.' He's full of shit like that."

"That'll work," she said. "Jared, how about some oatmeal?"

"Does it have any tenuous energy?"

"Shit, Jared," she said. "I don't know. Just come on down and have some oatmeal. Kenny, can you make him some oatmeal, please?"

"Yeah, I can do that," I said, and, in no time at all had three bowls of steaming oatmeal in front of us on the table.

"How is everyone?" Nephi asked, walking out from the bedroom and stretching his arms over his head with a yawn.

"Here, Dad. You can have my oatmeal," Jerusha said. "I'm not really hungry."

Jared eyed his oatmeal suspiciously and pushed it around his bowl with his spoon. "Are you sure this has tenuous energy?"

"What'd he say?" Nephi asked.

"Don't worry about it, Dad," Jerusha said. "We'll take him to the doctor."

"I already told you what I think about going to a doctor," Jared said, cautiously touching his tongue to a spoonful of oatmeal before returning it in disgust to the bowl. "No memories put into my head, please."

"You're going to see a doctor today," Jerusha said. "Or else."

"Well, someone's trying to get me," Jared said to Jerusha. "For all I know, this oatmeal is poisoned."

"By who?" I asked.

Jared narrowed his eyes and looked at his bowl of oatmeal.

"Interests," he said. "Various . . . interests."

"Jared, son, this is why we need to take you to the doctor," Nephi said. "Well people don't think folks are trying to poison them with oatmeal."

"Satan is a roaring lion. That's what Brother Briskey says," Jared said.

"Who is the Briskey asshole?" Jerusha asked again.

We took Jared to the emergency room at 3 p.m., which turned out to be just a few blocks away, so we walked, Jared straggling behind us and murmuring.

As we waited—and waited—in the reception area of the emergency room, Jared paced around, muttering to himself. Jerusha and I sat and watched him.

"This is creepy," Jerusha said, leaning into me. "Something is wrong with his brain, for sure. Jared's always been weird and a big joker, but this is too strange. What did your old bishop say he thought this was?"

"He didn't say, specifically," I said. "He said it's a psychosis. He said he believes things that are stupid to other people."

"Sounds like your average Mormon, to me," she said.

"He's supposed to have hallucinations, which is when he's thought he's seen angels and stuff, and delusions, which are the things that no one else believes, like Satan has poisoned your oatmeal, I guess. Stuff like that."

"How have you two gotten along?" Jerusha asked. "You seem to get along okay. I mean, for a normal person and a not normal person."

"We get along great," I said. "Yeah, we really click, if you want to know the truth."

"He doesn't have many friends," she said, watching Jared pace.

"We get along maybe better than anyone I've ever known."

She watched Jared some more. "I don't know what I'd do if anything ever happened to him," she said, blinking back tears.

"Yeah," I said.

Jared stopped his pacing to look up at a ventilation grate on the wall near the ceiling. He looked around as if he was cogitating and then pulled a side table underneath the grate. He stood on the table and looked in the grate.

"He's probably looking for cameras or microphones," I said.

Jerusha sighed and called out to Jared. "Jared, come on. They don't want you standing on their furniture."

Jared looked at Jerusha and then down at his feet on the table. He shrugged.

"I have a duty to my posterity," he said.

"See that?" I said.

"Yeah," Jerusha said. "I see." Then she called out to Jared, "Come on, Jared. Get off the people's furniture."

Jared looked at Jerusha. "I'm blaming you if something gets planted," he said.

"Jah, give me strength," Jerusha said to no one in particular.

Jared resumed his pacing. Nephi stood up and began pacing with him and talking. They did this for a while. Then Jared stopped and hung his head. Nephi hugged him. Jared began crying —and then sobbing—into his father's shoulder. Soon enough, Nephi was obviously crying, too.

"Shit," Jerusha said. She stood up and went over to them. She engulfed them in her arms and began crying as well. They were all they had, each of them. Except for me, I guess. I was new to the mix. I felt no choice but to walk over to the Basermans and put my arms around as many of them as I could and—miracle of miracles!— I started crying. We would have kept this up for a while, I suppose, if the woman behind the counter hadn't called out to us, "Mr. Baserman. Excuse me, Mr. Baserman. May I talk to you?"

Nephi pulled himself away and took Jared and set him down in a nearby chair. Then Nephi walked over to the woman and talked to her about whatever paperwork he had to fill out. We sat on either side of Jared and he immediately stood up and began pacing again.

We waited in that room for another 45 minutes before a nurse stuck her head out a door and called us back. They weighed and measured Jared, took his vitals, and put all four of us in a small room. "Why do doctors do this kind of shit to you?" Jerusha asked. "Just be glad you're not a woman."

There was only one chair in the exam room, and the examination table, and we gave those seats to Nephi and Jared, respectively. Eventually, Jared stood and tried to pace in this little space.

"I need to take a dump," he said.

"Okay," Jerusha said. "But I'm waiting outside for you."

They walked out the room, and about five minutes later Jerusha burst through the door.

"He bolted!" she cried. "Come on!"

"How'd he get out?" I asked.

"There's a little window in the can," she said. "I don't know how he squeezed through. See?"

I looked up at the tiny window. "Yeah," I said and whistled. "He's a slippery devil."

"Enough jokes," Jerusha said. "We know where he went. He went to the asshole Briskey's house." She turned to me. "Take me there."

We jogged back to the apartment, where we got into the Baserman's car and drove to Briskey's. It was shut up tight. No car in the driveway. We decided that Jerusha would stay and wait to see if anybody returned. I wouldn't want to be Briskey if he were to arrive home and find Jerusha. Nephi and I went to the Sedro-Woolley Police Department to fill out a Missing Person report. We drove to Briskey's house when we finished. Jerusha was sitting on the front stoop.

"No one ever showed," she said.

We spent the rest of the day cruising around Sedro-Woolley

looking for Jared, even calling out for him like a lost dog. Now and then we would stop and get out—for example, we thought he might be inside the San'wich Nook for some reason. We even drove over to Lisa P. and Daryl's house. Nothing. We made sure to loop back past Briskey's several times. Back at the apartment, I made us some sandwiches and we sat around and talked about Jared. The next day came and we searched more. After dinner, when we were quietly sitting around the apartment, the phone rang. It was Bloodworth.

"I just got a call from Mavis at the church, and she said Briskey is having some kind of meeting at the church. What day is it? Jared is there. In fact, he and Briskey are kind of running the show."

"That Briskey asshole!" Jerusha said.

When we got to the church, we saw a smattering of cars in the parking lot. Bloodworth and Mavis met us in front of the church.

"I think Brother Briskey is using Jared," she said in a rush of words. "I don't think it's good."

We entered the chapel at the exact moment Briskey said from the lectern, "Let's bow our heads and Elder Baserman will lead us in prayer." Believe it or not, we all stopped, including Jerusha, and waited for Jared to finish.

"Well, it stinks of copulation in here, that's for sure," he said. "Everyone in this room got here thanks to an orgasm."

I didn't bow my head, so I could see that everyone else kept their heads bowed in the silence that followed Jared's benediction. They stayed that way for a few moments, until Jared said, "And I say this in the name of Jesus Christ. Amen."

"Amen," the congregation agreed.

Briskey looked up and gave a sideways glance at Jared, but Jared looked as if nothing was amiss. Briskey stood at the lectern with Jared by his side. The Mothers of Invention were all seated in the front pew. The others there were dotted around the chapel. Jerusha and I have talked about it since, and we decided each person was sitting in his or her regular spot.

Briskey cleared his throat. "Today we're going to talk about the reason you don't see Heavenly Father acting in your life. The reason you don't see God act in your life is you don't believe He can."

"Son!" Nephi called out to Jared.

"Jared!" Jerusha called out.

"Hey, guys!" Jared responded with a friendly smile. "Kenny? How'd you get here, man?"

"What the hell are you doing with my brother, you asshole?" Jerusha said as she rushed to the front of the church.

"Briskey!" a voice shouted from behind us. Jerusha stopped in her tracks. It was President Watson. He was madder than a sack of cats, striding toward the podium and jabbing his finger toward Briskey. "What the hell are you doing, you pervert? I told you to desist!"

"You don't own me!" Briskey shouted back at him. "I'm leading these goodly believers!"

"Like heck, you are," Watson shouted back and jumped onto the dais. He followed his finger straight to Briskey and jabbed him in the chest. "Desist," Watson said.

"You're nothing," Briskey barked back at him as he swiped away Watson's hand. "This boy is touched of God and Heavenly Father has put me in headship over him."

"You're not really alive," Jared cried out. "It's the scooped-out machines in you that are talking."

"Jared, stop this craziness," Jerusha cried out.

"You started all this," Watson shouted at Jared.

"I call down the power of Kolob's Mighty Army on your head!" Jared shouted at Watson.

"You're done, boy," Watson shouted back.

"Now!" Jared roared, as if a command, and threw his hands out toward Watson.

Watson clutched his chest and gasped. He went to one knee

and touched his other hand to the carpet on the dais. "Dear God. .
." he said and collapsed on the floor.

Everyone gasped at once and many of the people, including
myself, rushed up to Watson on the floor.

"Sir? Sir? What's the matter?" I cried.

Watson looked up at me with fluttering eyelids and gurgled,
"The birds . . . they're gone." He expelled a rush of air and lay still.

A man kneeled down and put his fingers to Watson's jugular.
"Good gracious," he said. "He's dead."

"Holy shit!" I said.

"Elder," an older woman next to me scolded me. "Watch your
language."

"Sorry, ma'am," I said.

Briskey walked over to the corpse with a vindictive look on his
face. What he couldn't see, that I could see, was coming up fast
behind him was Jerusha, virtuously incensed.

"Hey, asshole!" she called out.

Briskey turned toward her and she pulled back and put every
ounce of her fiery, righteous frame into her fist and connected it
with Briskey's nose. You could hear the crack. It sounded like somebody stepped on a seashell with a knobby jackboot.

"Holy fuck!" Briskey yelled as blood poured from his nose.
"What the hell did you do?"

"That's for screwing with my brother, asshole!"

CHAPTER SEVENTEEN

I t was pandemonium inside the meeting house until the cops arrived—people going every which way, exclaiming this and that and exhorting one another to Stay Firm, Heavenly Father Was In Control. Amidst all of this, Jared was going off on rants about the government implanting thoughts in his head and shit. It quickly became clear to the two cops who arrived that Jared was the Person of Interest, and they sat him down in a front pew

"You can't interview him alone," Jerusha said.

"Who the hell are you?" one officer said.

"He's sick," she barked.

"He's a suspect," the other cop said.

"Shit, Jerry. He's not a suspect," the first cop said. "He didn't kill the pastor guy. But we got to start with him."

"It's not totally accurate to say it was me who killed President Watson. Not totally accurate," Jared said. "It was the influences from Satan, or the government. They're putting magical thoughts into my head."

"You didn't kill anyone, son," the second cop said. "We just need to talk to you."

"You can't interview him without us there," Jerusha repeated.

The second cop looked at Jerusha. I think he could instantly see this was a battle not worth having, especially considering that this interview was just a formality.

"Fine," he said. "Sit down."

He flipped open his notepad. "Now, let's talk about what happened."

"I didn't know I could kill him," Jared said. "I was just as not un-surprised as anyone. It wasn't me. It was Satan, or the government!"

"You didn't kill him," the second cop said.

"If you can't believe your own eyes, what can you believe?" Jared asked. "Do you have eyes yet see not? Are you stupid?"

"Watch the tone, boy," the first cop said, pointing the eraser end of his pencil toward Jared. "Now, where do you think you got this power? What was going through your mind at the moment this happened?"

"Shit, Jerry," the second cop said. "I told you that's crap."

"Hey, we have to explore every option," the first cop said.

"Some options aren't options," the second cop said.

"Look," said the first cop, asserting himself. "When you assume things, you miss things. We do this by the book or we just don't do it."

"Fine," the second cop said, waiving both hands in front of himself in defeat. "Just do it."

"So," the first cop said, "explain what happened. Every detail, from the start. What happened when you shouted at the pastor?"

"I don't have to sit here and endure this questioning," Jared exclaimed. "I'll tell you once, you ignoramus, so pay attention. President Watson was trying to corner Brother Briskey—put him in a corner. I couldn't abide by that. Abide. Imbibe. I certainly wouldn't have imbibed at a time like that."

"What?" the first cop asked.

"I'm telling you. Weren't you listening? I was mad at President

Watson, so the government spoke through me and vindicated itself against President Watson. Or maybe it was Heavenly Father."

"The government?" the first cop asked.

"Or Satan," Jared added.

"Jerry, this little shit is yanking your chain," the second cop said. "Stop yanking his chain, you little shit."

"Are you yanking my chain?" the first cop asked Jared.

"Chain. Brain. A chain in your brain," Jared said. "That was the start of my problems: the chain in the brain. But I'm telling you it came from Satan or Heavenly Father. Or both. I don't know. Aren't you listening?"

"Listen, you," the first cop said.

"Look, dingus. He's sick," Jerusha said, tapping the side of her head. "He's got a sickness in here. He needs to go to the doctor, but you're keeping him here asking stupid questions."

"You watch your mouth, missy," the second cop said.

"Missy?" Jerusha said.

Nephi patted Jerusha's thigh to calm her. "Officers, we're here to cooperate with you," he said. "I'm just not too sure this is going to get us anywhere. My son, we think he needs to see a doctor. He didn't kill anybody. Heavenly Father wouldn't kill that man like that."

"Don't be too sure," Jared said. "The government's into all sorts of weird shit."

"Why does he keep talking about the government?" the first cop asked.

"He doesn't know what he's talking about, you dipshit!" Jerusha said.

"Girl, you're about this far from getting arrested for obstructing an investigation," the second cop said, holding his thumb and forefinger a half-inch apart.

I jumped in and patted Jerusha's other thigh, feeling elated that I felt I had the freedom to do that. "Jerusha, remember what Jah's trying to teach you," I said.

"Shit," Jerusha said and folded her arms in front of herself in a huff.

The first cop gave her a glare and returned his attention to Jared. "So, where'd you get this power?" he asked.

"Where I got the power is irrelevant," Jared cried. "Either I had the power or I didn't. Don't be stupid."

"This is bullshit, Jerry," the second cop said. "I think this kid is sick in the head."

"I told you," Jared said. "It was Heavenly Father or Satan or the government."

"This is stupid," the second cop said. "Jerry, we need to talk to who's in charge here. Who's in charge here?"

"You want to talk to the bishop," a helpful female member who had been snooping from the periphery chimed in. "You want to talk to Bishop Bloodworth."

"He's not bishop anymore," her companion chided her. "He was released by President Watson."

"Well, President Watson's dead, if you haven't noticed, Deborah," the helpful woman said, pointing toward the room-temperature corpse of Watson, which by that time had been covered with a cloth. "He's right there, if you haven't noticed. The elder killed him. Honestly."

"He didn't kill shit," the second cop said. By this time, he clearly was at the end of his tether. "Where are we going to find this bishop?"

"He's around here somewhere," the helpful female offered, tittering, "with his girlfriend."

"I'll go find him," I said, standing up, maybe wanting to appear helpful to the frustrated cops. "He's here somewhere, I'm sure."

I went down one hallway, checking in every room. But I didn't find Bloodworth. I cut through the gym—all Mormon Churches feature a basketball court that doubles as a large gathering space for Boy Scout pack meetings and chaste LDS singles dances—and went to the other side of the meeting house. As I walked down the second hallway, I could hear muffled voices coming from some-where. I checked each door in sequence, the voices becoming more distinct as I went on. As I approached the last door, it was clear the voices were coming from inside that room. I could see the door was ajar. I recognized the voices of Bloodworth and Mavis. When I turned toward the door, I could see in, and there was Bloodworth, standing in front of Mavis in his temple garments. Mavis was in front of Bloodworth, on her back on several desks in the Primary Room.

"Those are some undergarments you're wearing, Demetrius," Mavis said, craning her neck over her prone form.

"They're my temple garments. They're supposed to protect me from Satan," he said, pulling them off. "They don't work."

Holy shit!

I froze at the door. Whatever this was that was transpiring in this Primary room, it was personal—I mean, Bloodworth in his temple garments and all—and I was interrupting. What to do? Should I have just gone away? No, the cops wanted Bloodworth. Should I have just barged right in? That would be uncomfortable in the extreme. Should I have cleared my throat or coughed to give them some warning?

Instead, I just stood there, and watched and listened. As I watched, Bloodworth stepped out of his temple garments and stood there, at full Army salute, if you will.

"Oh, Demetrius," Mavis said, craning her neck up with diffi-culty. "You're a fine figure of a man."

"I do know that lying is a sin," he said, as he climbed upon her. "But love covers over a multitude of sins, and I do think I love you."

"Oh, Demetrius!" she said. "I love you!"

———————————

WHEN I LEFT the chapel to look for Bloodworth, the two cops started conferring with each other.

"You're all in danger," Jared cried. "Back off, I tell you!"

"Are you threatening us?" the second cop asked, leaning toward Jared.

"This is a Level-3 threat," Jared said. "Man the battleships. Call the General Authorities!"

"You," the second cop said, pointing menacingly at Jared. "You will settle, right now, or you will be arrested." He turned to the first cop. "Where the hell is that other kid with the bishop? Jerry, you take care of this. I'm going to find that other kid and the bishop."

As the second cop walked out to find me and Bloodworth, the first cop turned to all assembled. "No more nonsense. Everyone's about this far from a whole hell of a lot of trouble."

MEANWHILE, outside the primary room, I watched in horror as Bloodworth and Mavis came to know each other in a Biblical manner. Of course, months and months later, I did ask Bloodworth about the situation, and here's what he told me, after much prodding:

"Well, Mavis was really shook up about what happened with President Watson. 'Elder Baserman killed your president,' she said. 'My gracious, Demetrius!' I could see I needed to be more . . . involved, so I kneeled next to her and embraced her, I guess. First time in my life. I put my arm around her shoulders and pulled her close. That was my first mistake. 'There, there,' I said. I really didn't know what to say.

"So Mavis leaned her head into my chest and kept crying. I didn't know what to do, so I began rubbing her shoulder with my right hand. That was my second mistake. Right there, all sorts of kinds of thoughts came to my mind. Remember now, I hadn't been with a woman for years and years. My desires were at war inside of me. I took my left hand and began patting her gently, consoling-like, on her thigh. When she didn't protest, well, all sorts of cravings rushed through my body. I wondered what to do. Should I choose the right? I knew that stopping right there would be the godly thing to do. But then I told myself, 'Where has being godly gotten you, Demetrius? You are still essentially an outsider at the church you have attended for ten years, even though you're bishop.' Used to be bishop. I had failed as a believer. Jared was sick, not inspired. And me? I was left alone. Except for Mavis. Hadn't Heavenly Father brought her into my life? Would Heavenly Father do that? Looking back, I think I was trying to confuse myself, to be frank for you. I knew what I wanted at that moment, and it was the closeness of this particular woman. And then—like it was a sign from God—she takes her hand and places it on top of my hand and begins to caress it. 'Oh, Demetrius!' she said. And my brain, filled with animal lust, was playing games with me. Is Heavenly Father speaking through Mavis? Would God tell me to do something like this? How do I know that God wouldn't tell me to do something like this? I know because the Book of Mormon told me so.

"'Why would God do that to your poor president?' she says to me, and I say, 'I'm not too sure that was Heavenly Father doing that to President Watson. I don't think He does things like that.' And she said something like, 'How do you know? He did things like that in Bible.' So I say, 'That's a good point,' and I kept on patting her hand. She kept crying and put her face into my chest. At this, I brought my left hand from her thigh to her shoulder. Now I was essentially hugging her. 'I need to stop this silliness,' she said or something like that and tried to pull away, and what did I do? I said something like, 'No, no, this is good. You just let it out.' You see, I was aflame with passion at that point. Right then, I tilted down my head and kissed Mavis on the forehead. 'There, there,' I said or something like that. She said, 'Oh, Demetrius!' or something and— well, let's just say one thing led to another.

"Remember now, I hadn't been with a woman for years and years. She tried to stop me. She said, 'Demetrius, is this sin?' And you know what I said? I said, 'Let me think.' Then after a moment I said, 'I don't discern it as such,' if you can believe that. 'I don't discern it as such.'"

Basically, Bloodworth's desire emerged from its crevasse, where it had been sleeping like an eel, and climbed. Hello, you old villain! Where had it been all these many sad years? Bloodworth immediately realized a moment of delicious indecision. Do I go on like this or do I . . . choose the right? The very possibility of choosing the wrong was exhilarating for poor Bloodworth. Stopping, right now, would be the godly thing to do. But then where would he be? Still alone. Alone with God. He had been alone for so long. And this was now, and she—her!—she was here.

I watched as Bloodworth introduced his personage into Mavis and said, "Oh, Lord! It's been so long!"

"Oh, Demetrius!" she said.

Down the hallway, I could hear a door opening and I saw one of the cops headed toward me.

Oh shit.

"Did you find him yet, kid? What's taking you?" he asked.

As he approached, I could hear the flimsy Primary desks squeaking furiously as Bloodworth and Mavis were reaching terminal velocity.

Now what do I do?

As the cop strode toward me, I could hear the couple's labored breathing. Just before the cop got to me, Bloodworth and Mavis hit their stride and bucked and rolled like a washer with a sideways load. Bloodworth said, "Oh, Oh, Oh. Oooh!"

"What the hell is taking you?" the cop asked. He pushed past me, right as Bloodworth collapsed on top of Mavis and the desks groaned under their weight.

"Holy shit," the cop cried. "Bishop, is that you?"

"I'm not a bishop anymore," Bloodworth said, panting and nearly crushing Mavis. "I'm just a man."

MEANWHILE, back in the chapel, the other cop's hold on his investigation was growing ever more tenuous.

"Everyone, settle!" the first cop barked. "Or else I'll drag you all in. Each and every last one."

"I told you, he's sick," Jerusha said.

"I don't have to stand for this," Jared said. "Watch out or you may get something from me, too."

"Was that a threat?" the first cop growled.

"I make no threats. Only assertions of cosmic power," Jared said. "You're within striking distance of the armies of Kolob."

"That's it," the cop barked. He reached into the back of his belt and grabbed his handcuffs. "I'm taking you in for obstructing an investigation."

"He's sick!" Jerusha cried.

"And you might just join him, missy," the cop said through gritted teeth.

The cop grabbed Jared by the arms, spun him around, and handcuffed him.

"Kenny," Jared cried out. "Kenny, help me!"

Outside the primary room, I could faintly hear Jared calling out for me. I was grateful for an excuse to quit this embarrassing scene. "I've got to go," I said and ran toward the chapel. As I ran, I called out over my shoulder, "Bishop, I've got to run. I think Jared needs me." I could hear Jared: "Kenny! Where's Kenny?"

As I ran into the chapel, the cop was escorting Jared down the center aisle as he struggled. "Jared, man!" I called out.

"Kenny, help!" Jared cried.

Near the front of the aisle, Nephi was restraining Jerusha from going after Jared. Actually, more than going after him, really, truth be told. She was liable to *interpose*, and Nephi knew that could quickly lead to both of his children ending up in the hoosegow.

"Jerusha, he's not going to hurt Jared," he was saying to his daughter. "He's an officer of the law."

"Hey, man!" I called out to the cop, immediately realizing I was in over my head and probably shouldn't be getting in the way of an arresting officer. I ran up to Nephi and Jerusha. "What the hell happened?" I asked breathlessly.

"He's sick!" Jerusha cried.

"Jared angered the officer, I'm afraid," Nephi said. "He went too far."

"Yeah, he'll do that," I said.

"He didn't know what the hell he was doing," Jerusha said. "It wasn't him."

"Kenny!" Jared cried.

Jerusha and Nephi continued talking to me, but, suddenly, I wasn't hearing them. It occurred to me suddenly, right there, that no one had ever expressed a need for me. Sure, people had asked for my help—light the bong, pass the beer, gimme one, sure. But they didn't really need me. They wanted something from me. I had served an end. This, though, with Jared—I was the thing being sought. I was needed. Me.

"Jared's in trouble," I said out loud to myself, stunned.

"Come on," Nephi said. "Let's go to the police station."

BACK OUTSIDE THE PRIMARY ROOM, you can imagine how awkward the whole situation was when the cop walked in on Bloodworth and Mavis. Bloodworth clambered off Mavis and stood there before the officer, naked except for his black socks.

"Oh my, oh my, oh my!" Mavis said as she got up from the desks, grabbed her panties from the floor, and used them to cover her face as she ran out the door past the cop. Bloodworth stood frozen, making no attempt to hide his shame, and watched her run out.

"What have I done?" he said to no one.

"Well, this is a new one," the cop said to himself.

"Please forgive me," Bloodworth pleaded.

"Bishop, we would like to talk to you, out in the church meeting area, where the pews are."

"Yes, of course. Of course," Bloodworth said and began walking for the door. "Of course."

"Uh, Bishop. You're probably going to want to put some clothes on," the cop said.

"Yes, yes," Bloodworth said, in a fog.

When Bloodworth finally got out to the chapel and spoke to the cop, he didn't have much to offer. What did he really know? He could only say what he witnessed. He answered in short, miserable sentences. When the cop realized they weren't going to get much of anything from him, he cut him loose. After all, the way the cops saw it, this was all just some freaky accident.

Bloodworth staggered home with the lifeless gait of a soldier separated from his troop by ill fortune. At home, he took off his temple garments, wadded them up, doused them in lighter fluid, and burned them to ashes in his back yard. As he watched them burn, he remembered the vows he took in the temple when he received his garments. They were vows to always maintain his temple covenants and to never tell any gentile about those sacred covenants, and to never take off his temple garments. As he stood watching the smoke snake up before him, he prayed, "Heavenly Father, if you're really there, please forgive me for breaking my temple covenants. Please don't cast me into outer darkness. If I'm denying the Holy Ghost, I'm sorry. But I just don't even know if You're there."

CHAPTER EIGHTEEN

W e saw the cop inserting, brusquely, Jared into his squad car as we exited the church. We all stopped, perhaps in disbelief. It was one of those "this can't really be happening" moments. Jared arrested, the most harmless guy on the planet. The cop turned from the rear door of the squad car and stared at us blankly. Perhaps his lack of emotion was the most powerful emotion of all. He grabbed hold of his belt to adjust his pants authoritatively. Hmmph, he seemed to be saying to us with his swagger.

"I've got to be with Jared," I said.

"We all do," Jerusha said.

We parked out front of the police station—there were plenty of open spots—and dashed inside. There, a receptionist in cat's-eye glasses viewed us with alarming suspicion. It was her job, I guess. Gatemistress to the Halls of Justice.

"Yes?" she asked in a superior, nasally tone, as if we were asking a question by our very entrance. I didn't blame her for being jaded. I couldn't imagine having her job.

"We're here to see Jared Baserman," I said in a formal manner and realized immediately how stupid it sounded, like we were showing up to pay a visit to a long-neglected grandparent.

"Yes?" the gatemistress repeated. Her nametag said her name was Ardith.

"My son," Nephi said. "You arrested my son."

"Falsely," Jerusha interjected.

The receptionist didn't twitch a facial muscle. Instead she reached to scratch her ass and sniffed her fingers. "What the hell are you nitwits talking about?" she asked, looking down at her desk.

"Jared Baserman. My son, the missionary," Nephi said. "You just arrested him at the church, the Mormon church."

"Have a seat," she said.

"Listen," Jerusha said, wedging herself between us. "Get off your fat, smelly behind and find my brother."

The receptionist glared at us emotionlessly. "Take a seat," she said and pulled shut the glass partition between us.

"Who's the old hag?" Jerusha asked, looking from her father to me and pointing over her shoulder at the glowering gatemistress.

"By the book," the ever understanding Nephi said. "We have to do this by the book, I guess."

"Someone should shove the book up her ass," Jerusha grumbled, taking her seat. She folded her arms in a huff. "Do her some good, old bat."

The receptionist continued with her work as though we didn't exist. Eventually, the first cop emerged from a door to the side and favored us with a look of Grudging Due Process.

"His lawyer can see him, not you," he said.

"Lawyer? Who the hell do you think we are?" Jerusha asked.

Nephi held out a hand toward Jerusha and patted the air. "Sir, we're simple people," he said to the cop. "We don't have money for a lawyer."

"In that case, one will be appointed to him at the public's cost," the cop said flatly. "So your business here is complete." He turned on his heel.

"Sir," Nephi said, standing up and motioning imploringly to the officer, "we appeal to your familial instincts. Have mercy. My son, her brother"—here he motioned toward Jerusha—"and his . . . dear friend has been incarcerated."

"Falsely," Jerusha interrupted, leaning toward the cop abruptly as she sat with arms folded.

"I need to go in," I said.

"Are you a family member?" he asked dryly.

"No," I stammered.

"Then fuck you," he said.

"Let me in," Jerusha said. "I'm his sister."

"And you, you mouthy bitch? Go fuck yourself as well," he said. "Now," he said, looking toward Nephi, "who are you?"

"I'm the boy's father," Nephi stammered.

"You'll do," he said, reaching out to usher Nephi into the inner sanctum. "Come on." The receptionist looked up and sniffed.

"Yes, yes," Nephi said, tamping all his pockets as if he were looking for his car keys. "Yes, yes." He followed the cop's invitation and stepped through the door.

THE NEXT MORNING, I awoke after a fitful night in the Chair of Ass Agony and found Jerusha leaning against my chest, asleep. She was muttering, fetchingly. I dared not move. I stayed put and counted the ceiling tiles and read the corkboard. The local Rotarians were all agog about Berry-Dairy Days, it seemed. Eventually, Jerusha groaned and lifted her head from my chest, stretching out a spider-thread of drool. "Ugh," she said, moving her hand to her forehead. "What a night."

"Yeah," I said.

"Did you sleep?" she asked.

"I think so," I said. "Some."

"Ugh," she repeated, stretching her arms and twisting her back.

"Where's your dad?" I asked.

She stared at the light fixture. "I guess he spent the night in there," she said eventually.

"Good for him," I said.

"He's a good man," she said, leaning over her knees and regarding the checkered floor tile. "Ugh. What a night."

At this, Nephi emerged from the side door, as if beckoned. "You stayed here," he said. He scratched his stomach. "Jared finally fell asleep. Quite a night."

"Is he okay?" Jerusha asked.

"He had a rough night," Nephi said. "Lots of nonsense talk. God's thought's or Satan's thoughts, or he is God or Satan." Here he sat down next to us. "He's sick. I asked the officer and he said he'd have the local doctor connected to the jail come look at Jared. Sort of a volunteer, I guess." He exhaled and put the heels of his hands against his eye sockets. "He had a rough night."

"The fuckers," Jerusha muttered.

"When's the doctor coming?" I asked.

"Don't know," Nephi said. "Sometime." He pulled his hands from his eyes and turned his head toward Jerusha and me. "You two need some sleep. You need to go home. I mean, not home, but you need to go and get some sleep. Some peace."

Jerusha looked at me and then turned to face her father. "Dad, you need rest, not us."

"I'm okay," Nephi said. "I'm going to wait for the doctor and help him if I can. Whether you stay or you go, I'm staying. So you might as well leave. Don't be silly. No need to be a martyr. You can't do Jared any good. I'll be here. This is my fault."

"You're a good man," I said suddenly.

Nephi smiled at me weakly and sighed. He tilted his head back so it rested on the wall behind him and deeply exhaled with exhaustion. He rubbed the bridge of his nose between his eyes slowly. Jerusha stood up and stretched with a groan. She looked down at her father tenderly.

"Are you sure you're alright staying here? Did you get any sleep last night?" she asked.

Nephi, his head still resting against the wall, closed his eyes and was silent for a moment.

"No, I didn't," he said. "But Jared needs me here. I'm the reason Jared's here."

"Dad, Jared would have gotten sick whether he went on his mission or not," she said.

"It was God's will," I said hurriedly. I immediately regretted it.

Nephi, his eyes still closed, said, "I know that." I don't think he heard what I said, thankfully. "But it's time to start being a decent father to the boy."

Tears took the course of least resistance down Jerusha's cheeks. She reached out and grabbed my hand. This was alarming, but, through superhuman effort, I moved not a muscle. "Dad, you're all we've ever needed," she said. "God gave you to us." She reached over with her other hand and grabbed me by the arm, seemingly steadying herself. Seemingly.

Nephi opened his eyes and looked over us, as best he could without taking the back of his head from the wall behind him. He paused a moment. "Help each other." Then he closed his eyes again.

When we got out to the street, Jerusha turned to me. "Why is God doing this?" she asked.

"He can't possibly approve of this," I said.

She looked at me blankly as if she hadn't registered what I had said and then stared up at the sun. "I need a Sugar Daddy," she said, opening the driver's side door. "Let's find a convenience store."

When I got into the car, Jerusha leaned her head against the steering wheel. I dared not say a word. At least, that's what I thought. She pulled her head back and said, "Let's go."

When we stopped into a convenience store, we bumped into a

dentist member who, oddly enough, was buying an armload of candy. He was all abuzz about Watson's miraculous death.

"I heard about things like this when I was on my mission," he said, "but I've never seen anything like it. Straight out of the Book of Mormon!" He lowered his voice, put his hand to the side of his mouth, and added conspiratorially, "What's more, the news is all over the ward that Bishop Bloodworth was discovered having relations with a gentile in the church. Same day! Right after President Watson died. In the meeting house!"

"Oh, man," I said bleakly.

"I know!" the dentist said, leaning in toward us. "You know, I never thought he fit in with the rest of the members, right from day one. He just wouldn't let himself be one of us."

As the dentist walked away, Jerusha said, "Wow. Just . . . wow."

"Yeah, that sucks."

Of course, the ward grapevine was crackling with discussion of Watson's death. But Bloodworth's fornication was a close second. In the process, the story was embellished and mis-told. Bloodworth was even called. The member who called him said, "Bishop, this is terrible. Some Jehovah's Witnesses came into our meeting house, right when members were in worship, and had intercourse in there. Imagine that, if you will. First President Watson dies, then there's sex right in the meeting house. And speaking in tongues. I think we're under demonic attack."

"You should pray for that person," Bloodworth told the woman.

"Yes, yes. Of course, Bishop Bloodworth," she said. "That's the Christ-like thing to do. But what kind of person does that? Walks right into a church and copulates, right when God's family is worshipping their Heavenly Father?"

"A desperate person, I suppose," he said. "You should pray for him."

"Yes, of course," she said. "But what kind of person would do such a thing?"

"Sister, I'm going to go now," Bloodworth said wearily.

"Yes, yes. I'm sorry I bothered you, Bishop. Goodbye."

In the coming days, the story of Bloodworth's horizontal mambo was told and retold, debated endlessly. The not-infrequent opinion was that it just went show to you. Blacks shouldn't have been given the priesthood. Evil Briskey had hit it dead square.

CHAPTER NINETEEN

Jerusha and I pulled up to the apartment. I wandered over to the couch and sat down once we got inside. Jerusha wandered around the room a bit, talking aimlessly, before sitting down awful close to me.

"So, what should we do?" she asked.

I've got to admit, I wasn't use to putting my moves on a girl without a beer or a bong in my hand. This type of thing usually happened at a kegger, and when the time came to make my move, my inhibitions had already been transformed into exhibitions by pot and/or beer. And, of course, the girl was always similarly slackened. Point was, I wasn't really too sure what to do when Jerusha sat so close to me, after she had been dropping hints, I think, all day. But it wasn't up to me to "make my move." Jerusha wasn't a girl—a woman—to be moved upon.

"Do you know how to play backgammon?" I asked.

It didn't take me long to get the basics of backgammon across to Jerusha. She was gifted, after all. Pretty soon, she was beating me, as we played game after game. I was sitting on the couch with my knees pointed out, twisting my torso to play the game. Jerusha sat cross-legged facing me.

As we played, we got to know each other better, I guess you could say.

"So why'd you go on your mission?" she asked. "You seem like a normal person."

"Well, I look back now and I see I had my head up my ass."

"You did?"

"Yeah, but I felt I should go on my mission."

"Where'd that should come from?"

"God?"

A faraway look came over her face. "There was a time I thought Jared went on his mission because of his spiritual experience at the family reunion. But I think he really did it for my dad. I think he would have gone, sooner or later, with or without the experience."

"He told me so."

"Yeah?" she said, looking out the window for several moments. She sighed then turned her attention back to me. She sighed again. "You know, this is getting boring."

"Yeah?"

"Yeah," she said. "Why don't we liven it up some?"

"What do you propose?" I squeaked.

"I think we should play . . . strip backgammon."

Holy shit!

"Come again?"

"Exactly," she said. "Now, each game a person loses, they have to take off an article of clothing, of the other player's choosing."

"That could work," I said, gulping a gulp.

"So, let's do it." She uncrossed her legs and re-crossed them in the opposite position.

First game, she dispatched me pretty quickly and eyed me appraisingly. "I think, your pants."

She watched me de-trouser myself. "By the way, the magic underwear comes off all at once," she said. "You'd never walk around with just a top or bottom on. You wouldn't be protected from Satan then. The spiritual power doesn't kick in until they're both being worn. They're a set. All or nothing."

The next game came down to the wire, but I pulled it out—miraculously?—with a string of improbable rolls of the dice. Or did she let it happen?

"So the shoe is on the other foot," I said. "And by that, I'm not asking you to take off your shoe."

"You've been around Jared too long," she said. "Just make your choice, Mr. Lucky Roller."

I have to admit, were Jerusha to win the next game and were to go for the fatal stroke—no pun unintended, as Jared would say—she would discover me at full-mast. This was exquisitely arousing, far better than anything that ever transpired at a kegger. And I was as sober as a census taker, yet never more debilitated. She did something powerful to me, left me not knowing myself for who I had thought myself to be.

"Tit for tat. Pants off," I said.

"If it's tit for tat, you'd have me take off my shirt," she said. "For all you know, I'm not wearing a bra."

"Actually, I'm counting on it," I said, getting bolder. "All part of my master plan. I like the suspense, though. It's titillating."

"There you go with tit again," she said as she stood up and took off her jeans and held them aloft with pinkie extended and dropped them with a *poof!* Her panties were alarmingly green and bore the words One Love right over the crotch.

Look at the record, the lore. Survey my associates. With any other girl, my history proved I would never wait for desire to ripen. I'd jump her bones at the first suggestive word from her mouth, or the first sign her defenses were adequately undermined. In this case, I knew I couldn't proceed without Jerusha's say-so. It's not that I didn't want to jump her bones. Like I said, she called me hither from someplace I never knew existed on this side of the veil. In fact, she was in control and she was toying

with me. I mean, I was fully lengthened and pulsating with exis-
tential hunger—with the boomba-dee, boomba-dee, boombadee-
boom. But I had to abstain, being at her mercy as I was, a waif,
really

"Let's set them up," she said, using the backgammon jargon and
—right then, that second—it occurred to me that she may have
hustled me, reeled me in with the pretense of inexperience.

What was it about this chick?

She dispatched me quickly the next game, which confirmed to
me my theory that she was a hustler. She told me to just take my
shirt off, having mercy. This was awesome—all but unendurable.
My boner was *obdurate.*

"You're hurtin' for certain, Elder Feller," she said.

"No kidding," I said, throwing my shirt on top of her pants.
"However, just watch me and learn, missy," I said, shaking the dice.

"Missy?" she said with a mischievous smile. "That does it.
You're going down."

Well, she pounded me and then leaned back and looked at me
appraisingly. "Well, well, well," she said. "What's my next move?"

I mean, I looked like some kind of sideshow attraction there in
my magic underwear. *Is it* supposed *to look like that, mommy?* Ah,
yes. I was a victim of my baser instincts, more animal than missionary. A burr in the saddle of the General Authorities, if there ever
was one.

"What am I going to do with you?" she asked.

"Or to me," I ventured boldly.

"Effrontery is the imprudence of the ungodly."

"I'll have to take your word for that."

"Look, I'll take mercy on you. Just take off the top half off your
magic underwear."

I did as I was told, inartfully yet strategically, playing my cards
with my fingers crossed.

"So," she said, holding up her cupped palm and shaking her
dice deliciously. "Do you dare?"

"Never dare a man wearing magic underwear. We have powers from On High."

So we set them up again and played, and she let think me I was going to win for a turn or two. Then she brought the hammer down.

"So, it's come to this," she said.

"Apparently."

She leaned across the board and flicked my chest. "You've been spending too much time with Jared. So do it."

I stood up—intoxicated by the moment, inebriated by my desire —and stepped out of the lower half of my magic underwear. I took a deep breath and stood erect, as it were, and hoped to Heavenly Father she'd accept me as I was, so pitiful and needy.

"Well, I've never been good with peer pressure," she said and stood up and took off all her remaining clothes with one magical swoop, as far as I could tell.

"I suppose it would be foolish to hope that a Mormon missionary was packing protection on his mission," she said.

"Well," I said, taking a deep breath. "I've already taken off my temple garments. So no."

"Well, that sucks," she said, pointing toward the couch. "So lay down."

I obeyed.

"So, we'll do the 69," she said.

"The 69?"

"Yes, the 69. Didn't they teach you anything at the MTC?"

"Is it in the Doctrine and Covenants?" I was still totally in the dark, but sure that she was talking about something electrifyingly carnal.

"Haven't you heard of the Kama Sutra?"

"Ah, no."

"Your mouth goes there and my mouth goes there," she said.

"So my face is in your–"

"Don't get squeamish on me now, underwear boy."

"I've never–"

"Well, then, this will be something to tell your grandchildren about. Precious memories."

"I don't know—"

"Look, doofus. What's your wang except a hungry mouth on a pole? Any place you're willing to stick the latter you should be willing to encounter with the former."

"What?"

"Just do it."

"So you want me to . . . consume you?"

"That's the general idea," she said. "Just improvise. I'm sure it'll work out."

"And you'll—"

"Enough talk, Mr. Magic Underwear. More love."

"Love?" I said, but by that time Jerusha already had her hindquarters next to my topmost quarters. She extended herself toward me with, I thought at the time, surprising delicacy. (It shouldn't have been a surprise. For all her chutzpah, Jerusha was at heart a gentle person. She just never had patience for people she thought were stupid.) "You okay?" she asked.

"Yes," I said obediently.

Then I felt it.

To say that it was an utterly new experience is a falsity. It was a lot like intercourse, which I'd accomplished—what?—five times, thank you. But this was different. She was in control more. Now, I'm sure girls can manipulate their private parts . . . to an extent. But only so much. The mouth is different, though. I mean, I was at this party once where this chick—this young woman—she put a matchbook in her mouth and struck a match with her tongue and teeth. No shit. Try doing that with your private parts. Maybe I was drunk and/or stoned. I don't know. Anyway, Jerusha was making full use of her faculties.

Then I entered the zone of increase, of mounting tumult. I was oh-so-close, and I assumed, by her rhythmic ministrations, she was likewise.

Then, at that exact instant, in an apparent frat-house joke from Heavenly Father, Mission President Dewey walked through our front door.

"Good God!" he cried.

"Wha?" Jerusha jerked her head upward, away from my manhood, and, at that exact instance, I issued forth, in *profundity*, as they say in early morning seminary. (The first early morning I heard it in seminary, I made it my word of the day. Hadn't used it until just now.)

"My hands are tied, boy," Dewey cried. Jerusha and I tumbled off the couch and on to the carpet comically.

"My hands are tied, boy," Dewey said. "You're gone."

I stumbled to my feet and said, perhaps, the most stupid thing I had said in my twenty years up to that point. The stupidest.

"I can explain," I said.

"There's nothing to explain!" Dewey cried.

"Who the hell are you?" Jerusha asked, standing up and facing Dewey without an iota of shame. In fact, she put her hands on her waist and cocked her hips to the side.

"I am his head," Dewey proclaimed.

"That's what she said," Jerusha countered.

I fumbled for my clothes, found my temple garments and began inserting my legs until I fell on my side. Sitting prone and three-quarters naked, I uttered the second stupidest thing I ever said in my life.

"It's not what it looks like," I cried.

"It looks like your ticket back to wherever you came from, which I'm not grasping at this moment." Dewey said.

"Piss off," Jerusha said as she scanned the room for her clothes.

"You are but a harlot," Dewey cried.

"Hey," Jerusha said, turning toward Dewey with her panties in her hand and an evil look on her face. "Piss off!"

Dewey covered his eyes with both hands. "Boy!" he shouted. "Meet me outside!"

"Yes, sir," I said.

"Hey," Jerusha said, grabbing my arm. "Don't let that asshole jerk you around. Tell him to piss off."

"Yes, ma'am," I said all but unconsciously.

"Look," she said, bending down to put on her panties. "This guy's a dipshit. Don't let him fuck with you. Tell him to piss off and let's go somewhere."

"Like where?"

"Hell bells," she said. "Anywhere but here."

"Okay," I said. "But I've got to talk to Mission President Dewey first."

"Like hell," she said.

"No, I think he's serious," I said.

"Go do it, Underwear Boy. Then come back." She gave me a peck on the cheek.

"Okay," I said, stepping into my pants as I stumbled toward the door. "Just give me a minute here. I think President Dewey wants to talk to me."

When I got outside, Dewey was on me like ugly on ape, as my mother would say.

"This is your fault, plain and simple. Led away by your own selfish desires. When you decide to break the rules, you take it to the limit. You're drunk with sin."

"Yes, sir. It's true," I said, feeling tears well in my eyes. "I'm sorry. Please don't kick me off the mission."

A change seemed to come over Dewey's face. He closed his eyes, pushed his thumb and forefinger up under his glasses to pinch the bridge of his nose, and sighed. He looked off into the distance for a moment and turned back to me. "My hands are tied, elder," he said.

"You don't have to mention it," I said.

"Son, that's something I can't do," he said. "By the book. We have to do this by book. First thing is we need to convene a Church Court."

I knew what that was. A Church Court is the disciplinary council called when charges are brought against a member, missionary or otherwise—equivalent of a court martial for missionaries.

"If you're lucky, you'll just be dis-fellowshipped," Dewey continued.

"Sir, I mean it. I'll never do it again. I've learned my lesson."

Dewey looked into the horizon, like he was tracking a falcon. "No need to go there, son. We both know you'll do it again.

"Yes, sir."

He turned to face me. "Look, son. If you had come to me and reported you had engaged in such a sin, I could have asked you, 'Are you sure? Are you sure it wasn't just a bad dream?' And you could have said, 'Yes, Mission President Dewey, now that you mention it I think it was all a bad dream.' It could have been that easy. But what am I supposed to do when I see your transgression with my own two eyes?"

"Sir . . . could I ask you something?"

"What is it, missionary?"

"Is it true you think the church is a crock of crap?"

He looked at me meaningfully before looking off into the distance for several moments.

"Sir?"

"The Church is not what it claims to be, son," he said then breathed heavily. "Now I suppose there are two broad responses to that realization. Firstly, one could rail against the dishonesty, seek to uncover the truth for all to see, all in a very self-righteous way. But why would I want to tear down the Church? Consider the philanthropy, the boundless selfless acts. What about the youth programs that teach our young people to be earnest, hard-working, honest? Look at yourself—look at the missionary program: thousands of young men becoming highly employable contributors. You're given challenges to overcome and become better people. The whole church is about building better people—

making people more moral, more like the Savior. So why tear it down?"

He smoothed out his lapels and seemed to settle in.

"Elder Feller, I'm a wealthy man. I haven't been gainfully employed for years and years. That being the case, I have a lot of free time on my hands. Because I, for years, have been a church-going man, I have no vices that could occupy my time. I don't smoke. I don't drink. I don't"—here he nodded toward the door and, by extension, Jerusha—"chase women. Instead, I attend church functions. What's more, thanks to my status in the Church, I am called to calling after calling, each one a challenge I eagerly engage in. My current calling as mission president brings me untold hours of enjoyment."

"Holy shit, sir."

"Humans need religion, son, and that being the case, why not choose the best from all the man-made religions? Man's been clambering up the hill of religion, starting with the pagans and their insensible polytheism. The Jews rose up from the sea of paganism around them. Then Christianity came and did Judaism one better. Catholicism had its heyday, but Protestantism was an improvement on Catholicism. And, last of all—or the latest so far—is Mormonism, the most improved religion. It's the only religion that simply explains the eternal questions. Where we came from. Why we're here. Where we're going. What more could you want from a religion?"

"Holy shit, sir."

"I tell you all this because I know that you're leaving the mission field and, I assume, leaving Mormonism in general. Your heart was obviously never in it, son. I could see that from Day One. Frankly, I saw this coming. It's not for you. Now, if you divulge any of what I have just told you, I will simply deny it," he said, fluffing his hands in a dismissive way. "Who are they going to believe? A mission president or a rogue missionary caught with his pants down?"

"Yeah."

Right then, Jerusha came out the front door.

"I have to have a Church Court," I told her.

"A Church Court? I don't even know what that is but I know it's bullshit," she said. "I told you to tell this dipshit to piss off. A Church Court?"

Dewey offered an indulgent smile.

"I don't think I have a choice," I said.

"Like hell," she said. "You have a choice. Use your free agency, for Christ's sake. Be over with all this down-pression. What right does this tool have to tell you what you can do with your body, or with whom?"

"What is my stepdad going to say?"

"Kenny," she said, putting both hands on my shoulders, "you're a man now."

I stood silent for a moment while that permeated my brain.

"Yeah, but my stepfather. He won't let me live in his house. He won't give me any money at all. I'll be screwed. I'll be an outcast."

"I think you're screwed if you stay in this crazy church. You'll find a way to make it."

"What should I do, sir?" I said, turning to Dewey.

"She said it, son. Use your free agency."

"Should I pray about it, sir?"

Dewey sighed. "Just consider your options, son. Is there a utility, for you, to stay in the Church of Jesus Christ of Latter day Saints? You've got to believe in something, you know?"

"You can believe in something without being an idiot, Kenny," Jerusha said. "Look at me. Look at my dad. Hell, look at Jared."

"Jared," I said and looked off to the horizon.

"Yeah," she said.

I took a deep breath and looked at Dewey. "Mission President Dewey?" I said.

"What is it, missionary?"

"I know I can't be a missionary anymore, but I also know I need to stay here, for now. So I'm going to stay, but I don't think I'm coming to a Church Court." I looked over at Jerusha. "I think I'm done with the Church."

Dewey put his hand on my shoulder. "It's not for everyone, son. That is one thing of which I am sure. It's not for everyone." Here he leaned his head, closed his eyes and exhaled deeply.

"Those of us in the Church could learn a thing or two from you unbelievers," he said, digging his car keys from his pocket and getting into his air-conditioned Cadillac. "It takes courage to find your own way."

Jerusha and I watched him drive off.

"What did he say to you out here?" she asked.

"He said the Church is a crock of crap."

"I could've told you that."

CHAPTER TWENTY

After Dewey left, Jerusha instructed me to run—run!—to the nearby convenience store and buy a pack of condoms. When I returned to the apartment, Jerusha was asleep in my bed, slack-jawed and snoring like a goddess. Then the thought hit me: I started this day a Mormon and now I'm not a Mormon. Then, just as quickly, I thought, I'm not sure I ever was a Mormon. I still don't know. Shit.

Since I left the Church, I've met many people like myself and, without exception, they all say "I'm a Mormon" when introducing themselves. Not that they believe any of it anymore. They don't. But being a Mormon is weird, I found, unlike any other religion, with the exception, I think, of Judaism. Mormonism isn't just a religion. It's a way of being. Like alcoholism, I guess. Alcoholics say they never stop being alcoholics, don't they? They're always recovering alcoholics. Same thing with Mormonism. It's a culture. If you're born a Mormon, you're always a Mormon—more so if you were actually raised in the church. So even if you leave the church, like I did, you still consider yourself a Mormon. I've heard many refer to themselves as ex-Mormon or post-Mormon or New Order

Mormon. Or Recovering Mormons. You never hear that with any other religion. Hi, I'm Joe. I'm a Recovering Buddhist. At best, you might get: I used to be a Buddhist or I was into Buddhism once.

But then you move on.

Not so with Mormonism. Post-Mormons, ex-Mormons, New Order Mormons—they just can't stop pounding on Mormonism. In fact, it's one of the common criticisms Mormons make of ex-Mormons. *They left the church but they just can't leave it alone.* That is, so many ex-Mormons are dedicated to debunking Mormonism or finding fault, trashing the whole scam. It comes from the fact they feel they were lied to. Bamboozled. I can't blame them. I mean, the leaders of the church in Salt Lake—the prophet, in particular—he knows he doesn't speak to Jesus Christ face-to-face. He knows he can't predict the future. He knows he can't read ancient languages. He knows he's just a guy. But he sits there and lets the rest of the Mormons believe all his . . . bullshit. You can't help but want to shove a banana up his tailpipe. It's righteous indignation, I think. If this story has a villain, it's the Brethren generally and the Prophet in particular, I guess. Not Briskey. Not the disease. Not God. The Brethren.

Not me, though. I mean, I know The Church Jesus Christ of Latter-day Saints is a house of lies, tottering toward destruction, one hopes. But I had no interest in exposing the church. Back then, on that crazy day in 1979, I just wanted to get on with my life.

So leaving Mormonism—if, in fact, I ever was a Mormon—was simple. I didn't feel like I was losing anything. On the contrary, I felt I was entering a whole new world of possibilities. I mean, how was it Jared, Jerusha and Nephi were so in love with each other and weren't true-blue Mormons, whereas my family members were all dyed-in-the-wool Latter-day Saints and they could barely stand to be in the same area code with one another? I wanted what Jared, Jerusha and Nephi had, and it wasn't religion. Or at least religion as I had ever thought of it. I mean, I believed in God, in the fact that He existed in some way. But Jerusha was right. If He was so concerned that we think about Him in only a certain way, He did an awful crappy job of being clear about it. If mean, why not just come right out and say it? Why all the hide-and-seek?

I began undressing and then stood up and took stock of myself in my temple garments. My magic underwear. When we were given the garments at the endowment ceremony at the temple, we were told to be rarely without them—without their protection. (The official wording is "it will be a shield and a protection to you inasmuch as you do not defile it and if you are true and faithful to your covenants." The blessing depends on the obedience, in other words, as my stepfather told me.) I've heard of Mormons who would make sure they keep contact with their garments while they were showering. I mean, they'd take them off, but they'd make sure to keep one hand on them outside the shower, as they were showering. And, yes, many Mormons have sex with their temple garments on. Truth is stranger than fiction. Those post-Mormons/ex-Mormons I talked about earlier—I know a ton of them who still wear their garments. The garments have just become part of who they are, even though they don't believe any of the bullshit. Nephi still wears his garments and he still believes some of the bullshit, at least tangentially, at least.

Not me. They had to go. I wasn't angry. I just wanted them off. So I slid them down my legs and kicked them to the corner of the room. Then the tops. I climbed into bed naked next to Jerusha. I wrapped my arms around her. Within minutes, I was asleep.

When I awoke, Jerusha was gone. I heard muffled talking from the front room. I put on my clothes and walked out. Bloodworth was staring out the window. Nephi was asleep on the couch. Jerusha was at the kitchen table, reading Jared's journal.

"There's some crazy shit in here," Jerusha said, looking up and pointing at Jared's journal.

"Yeah," I said and walked over to her. I sat down and leaned into her. "Were we in bed together when they showed up?" I whispered. She looked over at her dad on the couch.

"My dad was here. He was exhausted. Shortly after I got up, he fell asleep there on the couch," she said. "The bishop just showed up. I think he just needs people to be around."

"So he didn't care about . . . us?"

"Who?"

"Your dad. He didn't care we were . . . together?"

"Of course he cared," she said. "But he didn't say anything. Kenny, we're grown ups."

"So . . . what do we do now? I have to leave this apartment and we can't stay in your motel."

Bloodworth turned from the window. "My house is plenty big for everyone. I have three bedrooms. I'd be honored to have you stay with me, for as long as you want."

Nephi opened one eye from the couch and said hesitantly, "Demetrius, we couldn't impose like that."

"No imposition whatsoever," Bloodworth said. "It's a big house."

"We'll pitch in," Nephi said. "When we can."

"You'll find employment soon enough," Bloodworth said. "No hurry. I don't want your money. The important thing is that you'll be able to help your son. Besides, it's a big house, plenty of room for you to stay with me. I'm all by myself."

"Well, that would work, I guess—one bedroom for you, one for me and one for the young people here," Nephi said. "Thank you so much, bishop."

"Yeah, that'll work," Jerusha said, winking at me.

JERUSHA and I made our way to the jail. We had to force Nephi to stay home and rest. Jerusha and I stayed in that Police Department waiting room for hours. On two occasions we gave one another a breather, letting the other person walk around the block or something, browse the five-and-dime purposelessly. Whatever.

Me, I sat in a nearby park and considered thoughts about God that were amazing and scary to me.

Back in the waiting room, Jerusha and I sat for another hour or so and then, who should walk in but a dour gentleman carrying a fat black satchel. He had doctor written all over himself, and, indeed, his name was Robert Ray Simpson, M.D., according to his flat black satchel. It was his misfortune to draw the shift at the Sedro-Woolley jail among all the emergency room physicians at United General Hospital. Whenever someone needed medical examination at the jail, it would fall to the on-call doctor to come hither, grudgingly. He did not look happy to be there, and who could blame him? He could be at home, feet propped luxuriantly, as befitting his station in life. But, no. He had to do his jail work, and this time for some recalcitrant nutso who believed he was God. Or Satan. Or the Republican Party. As he passed Jerusha and me, he favored us with a grimace befitting his predicament. Jerusha wasn't paying attention.

"You need to let me back there," Jerusha cried to the reception- ist. "My brother is in trouble."

"Sit back down, girl," the receptionist barked, actually rising from her seat, miracle of miracles. Thus erect, she nodded sweetly to Dr. Simpson. "Afternoon, Doctor," she said. "Perfect timing. Our boy's acting up."

"That boy is my brother, you crone," Jerusha yelled.

"You!" the receptionist spat, pointing menacingly at Jerusha with one hand while she gingerly motioned the doctor past her into the inner sanctum with the other. "Sit down or else."

"Fuck you," Jerusha said, "and your beehive hairdo."

"Little missy, I can have you escorted from the premises," the receptionist said.

"Go ahead," Jerusha said.

The receptionist puckered sourly at Jerusha. "I will," she said, and true to her word, moments later a razor-burned deputy emerged to escort us from the premises.

"Shit," Jerusha said when we were on the street.

"I think that guy was a doctor," I said to her, looking toward the building and pointing. "I think he was a doctor."

"Well, good," Jerusha said, lowering herself to the curb with a huff. "It's about time. What a fucking backwater. This place is worse than Boise."

"Worse than Boise?" I said, putting my hands to my cheeks.

She looked over at me and rested her head against my shoulder. "Well, maybe now they'll send him to the hospital."

We sat like that for a long time. Two hours, maybe. I don't know. Other people came in and out of the police department. To pass the time, we shared stories from growing up Mormon, more or less. Eventually, an ambulance sped up to the curb, red lights afire. The paramedics rushed out and scrambled to the rear of the vehicle. They pulled a gurney out, its wheels folding open automatically underneath.

"Oh, shit," Jerusha said as the paramedics hoisted the gurney up the jailhouse steps. "They've come for Jared. Here we go. Let's pray." She lowered her head and muttered. I lowered my head next to her. "Jah, help us figure out what happens now," she said. "Show us how we can help Jared. We don't know what to do. We hope You do."

We stood like that, holding hands with our heads down for a moment. "Amen," I said. Jerusha looked up at me. "Amen," she said with a smile. "Here we go. Are you ready?"

"Yes," I said automatically, unaware what I was agreeing to but, by God, willing to do whatever it was Jerusha was referring to. Especially since it was for Jared. Mainly for Jared.

We watched the paramedics bumble through the door. Shortly after this, the doctor emerged with his black satchel.

"Excuse me, sir," I said. "We're friends of Jared Baserman. And family. She's family."

The doctor stopped and looked at us. "You're family?" he said to Jerusha.

"He's my brother," she said. "He's my twin."

"Well," he said, pulling off his spectacles and cleaning them with his necktie. He held the glasses skyward and squinted through. Satisfied, he looked at Jerusha, "Your brother is suffering from a psychosis. Probably schizophrenia. His condition is grave."

"Schizophrenia?" Jerusha asked.

"No one's really sure what causes schizophrenia, but it clearly is an illness of the brain. And there's no cure. It generally appears in late adolescence or early adulthood, someone your brother's age."

"Enough with the encyclopedia," Jerusha said, her voice cracking. "What does all that mean?"

"Well," the doctor said, "schizophrenia involves a breakdown in the relation between thought, emotion and behavior. It leads to faulty perceptions. An inability to perceive reality as it really is. People suffering from schizophrenia will hear things, usually voices. They will perceive things that are not existing as being in reality. They can even *smell* things that don't exist. Schizophrenia makes it hard to tell the difference between what is real and unreal —to think clearly, to have normal emotional responses, to act . . . like normal people . . . in social situations."

"Yeah," I said. "That pretty well sums it up."

"Your brother is going to withdraw from reality and from personal relationships. He's going to live in a world of unreality. Your brother is being separated from reality by his sick brain. Your brother will largely lose the ability to care for himself or hold a job. He won't be able to form attachments."

Jerusha's legs buckled from underneath her and she collapsed to the sidewalk. I kneeled beside her, my hand on her back. The doctor didn't seem moved. He just continued his monologue in the same vein.

"Is there a cure?" Jerusha whispered from the sidewalk, staring into the pavement.

The doctor paused, inhaling deeply. "In a word, no. All we can do is manage the disease."

"Manage the disease?" Jerusha said dully.

"The primary treatment of schizophrenia is antipsychotic medications—neuroleptics—often in combination with psychological and social supports. But, really, the medicine is almost worse than the disease, to be frank. All the existing medications carry deleterious side effects. The side effects will render him largely incapable of leading a normal life."

"What kind of fucking world is this? Does Jah have His head up his ass?" Jerusha said. "What did Jared do to deserve this shit?"

I took a leap of faith. "I think God hates this," I said.

"Genetics, most likely," the doctor said. "I've signed a Physician's Emergency Certificate, which allows us to hospitalize your brother for fifteen days. He's dangerous to himself and/or others. Simple as that. During that time, the doctors at the hospital will conduct further tests and determine the best course of action."

At this, the door to the jail opened and the paramedics struggled to remove the gurney. The doctor looked over. "They'll tell you everything you need to know at the hospital. Now if you'll excuse me."

"Why are you doing this to me?" Jared howled, for, yes, Jared was on the gurney. Strapped down, in fact.

Jerusha bolted to her feet and rushed toward the gurney, dragging me with her. "Jared!" she said.

"Why are they doing this to me?" he screamed, looking into Jerusha's face, although it was clear that he had no idea who she was.

"Why is he strapped down?" Jerusha yelled. "He's not some fucking animal."

"Miss, if you'll excuse us," the closest paramedic said as he maneuvered the gurney past us.

"Why is he strapped down?" she repeated.

The nearest paramedic stopped abruptly and faced Jerusha.

"See this?" he said, pointing at a shiner beneath his eye. "This is why he's strapped down. The poor fucker keeps going on about Satan. He thought I was in league with Satan, so he did this."

"It's for his protection, miss," the other paramedic said.

I put my hands on her shoulders and leaned toward her head. "They're taking him to the hospital, Jerusha. This is what we want."

"For his protection?" Jerusha cried, tears snaking down her face.

As they inserted the gurney into the ambulance, Jared cried out, "Kenny, help me. For God's sake!"

I rushed toward the ambulance as the paramedic was backing out of it. "Steady, boy," he said, putting a hand on my chest. "Steady." He shut the back doors to the ambulance. "You can follow us. We're taking him to Northern State."

"Northern State?"

"It's the nuthouse," he said. "Now, back up. We're leaving."

He went around the ambulance to the passenger's door. "They're taking him to the nuthouse," I said to no one. "This isn't happening."

Jerusha grabbed me by my shoulder. "We need to go get my dad," she said, wiping her face and pulling me toward her. "Come on."

We ran to the apartment. "This is going to be hard on my dad," she said as we ran.

"He already knew something was up. You know, medically," I said. "He knew Jared was sick."

"This is going to be hard on my dad," Jerusha repeated. "What kind of fucking world is this?"

CHAPTER TWENTY-ONE

Back in the ambulance, as the paramedics tried to take Jared's vitals, Satan was talking to Jared. Satan leaned against the back door of the ambulance as it rumbled down the road and picked at his jagged, knife-edged teeth with a claw. He was a large salamander, as best as Jared could make out.

"You're in the shit now," Satan said.

"Get away from me!" Jared yelled. He turned to the paramedic, who was struggling to get a blood pressure cuff around Jared's arm. "Get him out of here!"

"Look, I'm not one to burst a man's bubble, but it's best you realize that you're fucked," Satan said. Satan pulled his pocket watch from his vest and checked the time. He looked surprised. "We're ahead of schedule. That's good. Boy, Heavenly Father bent you over and fucked you in the ass, and now you're on my team. Welcome aboard, you poor fucker."

He laughed a laugh from the pit of hell, most likely, a laugh full of *schadenfreude*, which was once one of my words of the day. The ambulance darkened as Satan laughed. Black smoke emanated from, well, everything, obscuring Jared's vision. He could still see

Satan's eyes, though, glowing a grievous orange through the dark. His teeth also glowed and they were caked with crud, vicious wreckage, the blood of his victims. For all that Jared knew, he was next.

"Let me out!" Jared shrieked.

"Steady, son," the paramedic said, looking Jared square in the face. Satan's eyes glowed orange and his breath put a hurt on Jared's nose.

"Let me out!" Jared shrieked again.

It was a quick ride to Northern State Hospital, nestled in the undulating ecosystem of Magic Mushrooms like a canker, the site of the first frontal lobotomy in the US.

When the ambulance pulled up to the hospital, the paramedics hustled Jared inside. Satan followed. His footprints left burning tattoos on the pavement. Once inside, the paramedics removed the straps pinning Jared to the gurney and escorted him roughly to an examination room, as he was trying to use any opening to flee. They shoved him into the room and locked the door. Jared could see Satan smiling at him through the chicken-wire-reinforced window in the door, his caldron breath fogging up the glass. Satan tapped on the glass gently, mockingly. Jared was freaked, as he told the story, and understandably so—Satan tormenting him in a nuthouse and all. Who knew how long Jared paced in that room? Could have been hours, each one a Spring Break on the River Styx. Eventually, Jared's Screening Team arrived: a dour Indian psychiatrist, another psychiatrist of indeterminate ethnicity, a psychiatric nurse, and a therapy aid. The latter was there for no diagnostic purpose, but rather to provide muscle should Jared act up.

When the door was opened, Satan sneaked in, too, slippery devil.

The first psychiatrist asked Jared to count backward by sevens, starting at 100. The first psychiatrist wrote in his notes that Jared was disoriented in all three spheres. That is, he wasn't sure who he was, where he was, and what day it was. The second doctor found

Jared's memory for recent and remote events difficult to assess, as he "displayed marked loosening of associations." That is, his thoughts kept jumping tracks like a snowmobile. Also, Jared exhibited circumstantiality, or getting bogged down in a tangle of trivial details that impede communication on the main topic. In short, he was crazy as a blistered pimp, and Satan pacing back and forth behind the Screening Team, clasping his bejeweled hands behind his back and chortling, that couldn't have helped. Understandably, Jared grew more and more agitated. (*Labile* was the word noted on his chart.) At some point, Jared grabbed a fountain pen sticking out of one of the doctor's vest pockets and an altercation ensued. Jared was forced to the ground and the doctor ordered him to be injected in the dimple of his thigh with 100 mgs of Trilafon, a neuroleptic—that is, an anti-psychosis medicine. As they injected Jared with the medicine, Satan taunted him.

"They're shooting you with demon juices, my fleshy friend," he said. "Turn you into a demon. And you thought you heard God's thoughts."

"Somebody help me!" Jared yelled. "They're turning me into a demon!"

"You're headed for the devil's corkscrew, you little shit!" Jared remembers the beefy therapy aid as saying. I doubt that really happened. Who's to say?

Satan's laughter echoed in the small room.

At that time, we were coming through the front entrance of the hospital, and I thought I might have heard the Devil's mocking laughter. But it was probably just something that could be easily explained, a woodland animal caught in the electric fence that circled the hospital grounds like a deadly necklace, perhaps. We had awakened Nephi back at the apartment and bundled him into the car, calling Bloodworth first to tell him what had happened. The entire ride to the hospital, Nephi sat in the backseat, crying and moaning things like "This is my fault! My fault!"

"Dad, how could you possibly be at fault?" Jerusha asked.

"Would you say that if Jared had cancer? It's just a disease. It just happens to be above his neck. No difference."

"I brought this on the family because I wasn't raising you in the gospel," Nephi said.

"Excuse me, sir, Mr. Baserman, but that's bullshit," I said, looking over at Jerusha for validation. "Right?"

"Positive," Jerusha said. "The thing about this disease, Dad, I guess, is that there's no cure for it. I mean, it's not fatal, but it's going to make Jared's life miserable."

"I did this," Nephi said softly, looking out the window in the general direction of Kolob, as best as I could figure. "I did this."

When we reached the dingy hospital foyer—the vast checkerboard floor that wouldn't come clean—we saw Bloodworth. When we came up to him, he said, "A disease of the brain."

"Right," I said.

"I told them we're here, though we weren't all here yet," Bloodworth said. "I figured it would take them a long time to do anything and, by that time, I would be a we."

"So what'd they say?" Jerusha asked.

"Not much," Bloodworth said. "Not much. Told me to have a seat."

We all sat on the foyer's vinyl-covered chairs and tried to talk about anything other than Jared. We didn't talk. No word about Jared. After several hours, Jerusha said to me, "You, come here." She pulled on my sleeve and guided me over to the corner of the foyer.

"So, looks like you're my boyfriend," she said.

"I don't think I've ever been anybody's boy . . . friend."

"Jah was saving you for me," she said, leaning over and punching me in the shoulder affectionately.

Was she joking?

Jerusha smiled at me. "What do you think of that?" she asked.

"I like being around you," I said. "I've never had a girl . . . friend."

"You owe me. I rescued you from the Evil Empire."

"For which I'll be eternally grateful."

"Grateful on this side of the veil's good enough. After that, who knows what happens for sure? Me, I plan on having my own planet. You're welcome to visit, of course."

"That's very Christlike of you."

"How'd you ever become a missionary?" she asked sweetly. "You think for yourself."

"Somebody's got to do it."

"That sounded like Jared."

ABOUT 90 MINUTES LATER, as we were all sitting there, Jerusha said, "Bishop, have you seen Mavis at all? I mean, since, you know."

Bloodworth looked at his shoes. "I don't know," he said quietly.

"Bishop, why should you be so ashamed of acting on your desires?" she asked.

"My desires?" Bloodworth asked dully.

"I'm not talking about your sexual desires. Well, not primarily. I'm talking about your desire for Mavis. You love her. Everyone can see it."

Bloodworth looked at his shoes. "Yes, it's true," he said. "But what I did to her. Wasn't it sinful?"

"Sinful?" Jerusha asked. "How could it be sinful?"

"Marital relations outside of marriage are, well, I guess that's why they call them marital relations," Bloodworth said. "There's a time and a place for everything. With sex, it's within the confinements of marriage. Inside marriage, it's pure. Outside marriage, it's sin. At least, that's what the church told me. I don't know if I can believe anything the church says though, to be frank for you. I just don't know anymore what's up and what's down."

"Mavis is what's up for you, Bishop," Jerusha said. "That's your up."

"What does your heart tell you, Demetrius?" Nephi interjected.

"I can't hear God anymore that way," Bloodworth said. "Don't know if I ever could, honestly."

"Hells bells!" Jerusha said. "Who knows what the voice of God sounds like? We just do the best we can."

MEANWHILE, Jared had been moved to the Quiet Room, also known as Seclusion. Basically, it was where crazy people went when they acted up. It was pretty much just a small white room that was totally empty except for a soiled mattress on the floor. At first, Jared felt lucky—even blessed. Satan hadn't squeezed in with him.

Soon enough, though, he realized Our Great Enemy of Old in the crawl space behind the walls. First here and then there. Tap, tap, tap. Even worse, he was talking. But Jared couldn't make out what he was saying. Almost, but not quite. Was that a laugh? In some way, this was worse than hearing his voice clearly, his unending fountain of bullshit, like someone opened up a fire hydrant of bullshit on a hot street. Consequently, Jared bellowed. Consequently, the medical staff gave Jared an injection of Valium. Even I know what Valium does, except in this case it didn't. Jared kept bellowing, which inspired the medical staff to administer a higher dose of Trilafon, hoping to douse his white-hot nonsense. Good luck. Jared wasn't one to let the Devil win, evil fucker. So, there was more bellowing, drug-resistant bellowing. If he had known the rules, Jared would have known the quickest way out of the Quiet Room was to be quiet, hence the name.

All told, Jared would be in the Quiet Room for six hours,

according to hospital records. Finally, he fell asleep in a heap, just yards from the soiled mattress.

———————

OUT IN THE FOYER, we hadn't gotten anywhere with the hospital bureaucracy.

"This is bullshit," Jerusha said angrily once again. While we argued with the front desk lady, the white-shirted orderlies standing guard over the doors to the inner sanctum spoke not a word. But this alone spoke volumes: Try to go this way and we'll tear you a new bilge pipe. What are you going to do? The powers of the State were arrayed against us. We were fucked. So, eventually, we slept fitfully, on the vinyl-covered furniture in the visitor's lounge. Every time we moved, the chair or couch beneath us would squeak or fart. As best as I've been able to figure, Jared was asleep along with us, in solidarity—another Baserman family act of civil disobedience.

In the morning, the dour Indian doctor came out to us in his white coat. The thing I remember most about him is that he called everyone sir, whether they were young or old, male or female. I don't think he knew what the word meant.

"Well, sir, the good news," he said, not even stopping to ask if we were Jared's friends and family, "is that he won't hurt himself or anyone else. But we're at the beginning of a long, long road. Long road. I encourage you to think of his hospitalization in terms of, in terms of, well, certainly not days, sir. At least weeks, possibly months. Maybe years."

Nephi fell slowly into the chair behind him and put his head in his hands.

"That is false!" I blurted out for some reason. Inspiration, I guess.

"You doofus," Jerusha said to me, shoving me in the shoulder. "What's next? A priesthood blessing?"

"Sorry," I said, tilting my head down and looking at Jerusha and Bloodworth with my eyes upturned.

"Can't hurt, I suppose," Bloodworth said.

"He is floridly delusional and hallucinated," said the doctor. "He thinks Satan is after him. Floridly. He's miles away from being reasoned with. We will speak to him with medication. That is the ticket, sir. Eventually, we'll suppress the psychosis and the young man you know will emerge, after a fashion."

"After a fashion?" Jerusha asked.

"Well, sir, the young man you all know and, I assume, love, that young man may never emerge again," the doctor said. "Of course, we have to conduct a full evaluation to get an actual diagnosis, but from my experience, your friend is suffering from some sort of schizo-affective disorder, probably garden variety paranoid schizophrenia.

"Yes, well, when we have more to report, we will, sir," the doctor said.

"Why can't we see him?" Jerusha blurted. Once again, she bowed her head and held up her hands. "When can we see him?"

Nephi, who had been holding his head in his hands during the entire encounter stood up. "Yes! When can I see my son, and when can she see her brother, and when can he see his friend—and Demetrius, too, when can he see Jared?" He pointed over to Bloodworth.

"Thank you," Bloodworth said.

Nephi took hold of Jerusha's other hand, the one I wasn't holding, and put his free arm on Bloodworth's shoulder.

"When we have more to report, we'll report it, sir," the doctor said, turning his back to us and walking away. When he was twenty feet away he turned around. "It would do you no good to see him now. I doubt he'd even recognize you. He's floridly delusional. The best thing you can do is go home and rest, sir. Gather your strength. Marshal your forces."

"Yes," Nephi said, standing up abruptly. "That's what we

should do. We have a home now, don't we?" He patted Bloodworth on the shoulder.

"Thank you," Bloodworth said softly.

———

THAT MORNING, more or less, the staff awoke Jared in the Quiet Room, gave him another 100 mgs of Trilafon, and escorted him to the Intensive Care Wing, also known as the back ward. Northern State was comprised of an Intensive Care Wing, a Geriatric Wing, an Adolescent Wing, a Forensic Wing (for those determined criminally insane), a Multiple Disability Wing (for those who were psychotic and, say, mentally retarded), and an Alcoholics Wing. The occasional addict who would succumb to drug-induced psychosis would just be stuffed into the Intensive Care Wing with Jared and the rest of the lost causes, back in the back ward, alone and in the dark, past the reach of reasonable hope.

He remembers being scared shitless. Mostly, he hid under and behind stuff—desks, chairs, beds, and other patients, shivering like a Chihuahua and crying out for a respite from Satan's attacks. Yes, Satan was there too, lost cause that he was. On those days when Jared did have a typical day—that is, typical for the average patient of the back ward—it would go like this:

7 am: Breakfast
8 am: Morning meds
8:30 am: Community meeting
9 am-noon: Empty hours of pacing, muttering and television watching.
Noon: Lunch
12:30 pm: Midday meds
1 pm-6 pm: More empty hours of pacing, muttering and television watching.

6 pm: Dinner

6 pm-9 pm: Two-plus hours of pacing, muttering and television watching.

9 pm: Final meds of the day

10 pm: Lights out.

FOR JARED, most days were spent hiding from Satan, for all the good it did him. It wasn't just hiding under stuff. During the weeks of his first stay at Northern State, Jared would, at times, vanish completely. Just vanish. They'd put the entire hospital on lockdown and search for the crazy Mormon kid. *Yeah, this kid was a Mormon missionary, you know, and he went insane.* They could never find him, though. Eventually, he'd just show up, usually hungry. This presented a problem, as he thought all the hospital's food was poisoned by Satan, slippery fucker. Jared filled me in later. Seemed that during these absences, he was transported to the Celestial Kingdom, whether in the body or out of the body I do not know, where he had his sit-down with Heavenly Father. I was never able to drag the details about these interviews from Jared.

"What did He, you know, look like?" I asked Jared after he was released from the hospital.

He looked up at me blankly, mouth open. "What?" he asked.

"Heavenly Father? What did he look like?"

He stared at me for a full minute. "Did you say something?"

So I never found out what Heavenly Father looked like.

AS THE DAYS DRAGGED ON, Jared didn't get any better. We'd show up every day, always Nephi and Jerusha and I, and often Bloodworth. After ten days—mind you, we still hadn't been let in to actually see him—they switched him from Trilafon to Thorazine and Moban. That was supposed to encourage us, I guess.

When the fifteen days of Jared's Physician's Emergency Certificate lapsed, we were presented with Jared's official diagnosis: chronic paranoid schizophrenic with acute exacerbation. At this point we were presented with three alternatives.

One, the hospital could just let him out. But that wasn't going to happen.

Two, Jared—or us, really—could sign a piece of paper agreeing to stay in the hospital. The piece of paper was called a Voluntary.

Three, at our request, the hospital would hold a Civil Commitment hearing at which a judge would hear the cases in favor of continued hospitalization—the hospital's case—and the case in favor of release. That would be our case.

"Hell, yes! That's what we'll do," Jerusha asserted.

"Look," I said. "I know none of us likes it, but this place, the hospital, it's the best place for Jared now. He needs to stay here."

Jerusha and Nephi looked at me. Eventually, Jerusha said, "You're right."

"Yes, you're right," Nephi said. "Thank you, Kenny."

"Here's what we'll do," I said. "I'll live here in the hospital, all the time, and as soon as he's well enough for us to see him, I'll call you."

"Really?" Jerusha asked.

"Yeah," I said. "I feel called, to be honest for you."

Jerusha tilted down her chin and look up at me with a smirk on her face.

"Really!" I said. "I mean, I don't hear God's voice or anything like Jared. But what else can we do?"

"How are you going to live?" Nephi asked.

"We have all Jared's money from his aunt," I said. "I can live off the vending machines and sleep in the lounge. They don't give a shit."

So that was the plan. It freed up Jerusha and Nephi to find

some employment. Nephi ended up landing a job as a janitor at a crisis counseling agency. Jerusha found a job with the Sedro-Woolley Police Department, believe it or not. She took care of their police dogs, Luke and Arrow, feeding them, taking them for walks, etc. She got them stoned once. They liked it, reportedly.

When Jerusha wasn't at the hospital or working, she visited Mavis. They became fast friends, which, on its face, sounds unlikely, they being about as different as two people could be. Mavis taught Jerusha how to play the card game Spite and Malice, and they'd sit in her parlor playing for hours at a time. Jerusha would tell her about Rastafari without ever pushing. No skin off Jerusha's nose. She liked Mavis, and Mavis liked her. Mavis would tell Jerusha about growing up lonely, which fascinated Jerusha, who, for all I know, had never been lonely a day in her life. And, of course, they'd talk about Bloodworth.

"Does he ever talk about me?" Mavis would ask.

"Not unless we ask him, but he's always thinking about you," Jerusha would answer.

Mavis would look confused. "How do you know he's thinking about me if he doesn't talk about me?" she would ask.

"I discern it," Jerusha would say.

"I think about him," Mavis would say.

Jerusha tried to convince Mavis to come to Bloodworth's house, to ambush him, if you will. But, of course, sweet Mavis would never do such a thing.

FOR MY PART, living at the hospital was no picnic. After a few weeks of sleeping on the waiting room couch, the hospital took mercy on me and gave me a cot in the furnace room. At my request, Bloodworth brought me all his books on Mormonism, the ones that led him to his crisis of faith. After that, Jerusha brought me books on Rastafari. I had no idea how she found them in Sedro-Woolley.

Also, I asked the Indian doctor for every book he had on schizo-phrenia. The hospital hooked up a little reading light for me in the furnace room. It wasn't the Ritz.

It reminds me of a joke Jared told me. This woman was devoted to God and she decided to join the strictest order of nuns there was. In this order, you were allowed only to say two words every year. Well, she strives and prays and, whattaya know, she stays utterly silent for a full year. So she's allowed to come in to see the Reverend Mother, or whatever, to say her two words and the Reverend Mother, she says, "My daughter, you have performed a great service for God over the past 12 months. You can now say your two words."

So she says, "Food bad."

So she leaves and, whattaya know, she goes a whole 'nother year without uttering a word. She comes in front of the Reverend Mother to say her two words and she simply says, "Bed hard."

So she goes out and, would you believe it, she goes a third year without saying a word. She comes before the Reverend Mother and to say her two words and she says. "I quit."

The Reverend Mother says, "It doesn't surprise me. All you've done since you got here is complain."

ONE DAY, Bloodworth and I took a walk around the hospital grounds.

"I'm lost," he confided to me.

"What do you mean?" I asked.

"I don't know what or who to devote my life to. When I met my wife, I devoted my life to her. Then she got me involved in the Church, which seemed fine. I devoted myself to her and the Church. Then she died and the Church was no help. Then God gave me the vision of Moroni and brought the missionaries to my door, or so I thought, and it was clear to me that I needed to devote my life to this Church, the Church of Jesus Christ of Latter-day Saints."

"Yeah," I said.

"The Church made me happy," he said. "That should count for something, shouldn't it?"

"I don't know," I said. "People find a lot of things that make them happy, you know. Like stamp collecting and pornography."

"The Church says those people are deluded. They just think they're happy. They're actually under transgression."

"Yeah, well the Church says a lot of things."

"What do I devote my life to now? God? I don't know if He's worthy of my devotion. I mean, He's powerful and all. He made everything, after all. He's really, really powerful. He just doesn't seem very . . . competent."

Ahead of us, we could see Jerusha sprinting toward us, far away, waving her arms.

"There's Jerusha," Bloodworth said.

"She's on fire about something."

Soon she got close enough to us that we could hear her calling out.

"They're going to let us see Jared!" she called. "They're going to let us see Jared!"

"Let's go!" I said, patting Bloodworth on the back. When we got to the foyer of the hospital, Nephi was standing with the Indian doctor, talking. We all came up to them, Bloodworth last of all, panting.

"Well, now that you're all here," the doctor said, "I think the time has come to let you see the patient."

We leaned toward the doctor expectantly, all at once. "However, I must warn you, sir, that you may be shocked by his condition. He is still symptomatic. That is, he's still delusional. He still suffers from hallucinations. Specifically, he still thinks Satan is hunting him down. But compassion compels me to allow this meeting. He is, after all, dear to you."

I knew Jerusha well enough by then to know that she was being impelled to say something. But she restrained herself.

"So," the doctor said, beckoning us, "follow me."

So we did, down dung-colored halls. As we progressed, we passed a number of disturbing sights. Disheveled old men and women knitted obscure patterns in the air with feverish stick digits. As we walked on—past a person who you would swear was the skinniest person you had ever seen, until you saw the next person—we could hear various cries and laughs. We also heard an occasional scream, desperate and adrift. Everything—counters, desks, and tables—looked state-issued, and, in fact, when you looked closely, you could see N.S.H. stenciled on everything in white paint. That is, on everything except the mismatched plastic chairs. A number of patients sat on the floor rocking back and forth and muttering. About every third fluorescent ceiling light flickered. As we walked past a dayroom, I looked in and saw that the TV the patients were watching was encased in Plexiglas. The picture on the tube quivered and quaked. The air smelled of over-baked coffee, cigarettes, and neuroleptic-infused shit.

"What kind of fucking world is this?" I said to Jerusha.

"No shit," Jerusha said.

"And Jared is stuck here," I said.

"In here, in here, sir," the doctor said, motioning us into a room to the side. "Have a seat. Over there, over there. Yes, please, and I'll go get the patient. Have a seat."

He walked through a door and we sat down on the vinyl-covered furniture. A scruffy woman entered the room without taking her feet from the floor, just inching in on her slippers. It appeared the life had been sucked out of her, slowly, and replaced with pestilential gasses. Her head was tilted forward and she twisted it to the side and lifted it slightly to take us all in, baffled and disgusted. She made exaggerated chewing motions with her lips, and her quivering hand rose.

"The time isn't here for you. I'll destroy you all! Get out!" she said threateningly.

"Easy, grandma," Jerusha said softly.

Just then, the door opened and the doctor escorted Jared out. Jared shambled in like a broken robot operated from some location very far away. It seemed his brain wasn't talking to his arms and legs. I was to later learn the gait is known as the Thorazine Shuffle by those who know. He was wearing a bathrobe, untied.

"Good God," Jerusha said quietly to no one in particular.

Jared looked up at all of us. "Hello, everyone," he croaked.

"Jared!" Nephi said, rising from his chair with a squeak and reaching out to his son.

The doctor directed Jared to a chair. Jared sat unsteadily.

"How are you, son?" Nephi said.

"Jared!" Jerusha said.

When Jared spoke, his voice sounded reconstituted, processed through some *rapacious* machinery. "This place bites," he said.

"Jared, how are you doing, man?" I asked.

"I told them about Satan but they couldn't believe me because they aren't people, really," he said. "They're just husks, inhabited by machinery and various elixirs. Tonics of torture. I told them. I used to be machinery and elixirs, but my guts were returned to me. By someone. I think it's maybe how Satan distinguishes me from the others. The husks. He has some kind of detector, in the walls here."

"Shit," Jerusha said.

"That, too," Jared said. "There's shit in the walls, too." He took us all in. "Kenny, Dad, Jerusha, Bishop. Where have you been?"

"Fuckers wouldn't let us in, Jared!" Jerusha said, crying softly.

Jared looked at his sister for a moment. "I told them about Satan, but they couldn't believe me," he slurred.

"What have you done to him?" Jerusha cried.

"I told you all to be prepared for a shock, sir," the doctor said, holding up his palms. "The medications eventually should reduce the delusions and the hallucinations. They should. But that comes at a cost. The side effects of psychotropic medications are quite debilitating."

"Will he get better?" I asked.

"Well, sooner or later we hope, as I said, his delusions and hallucinations will ebb," the doctor said. "However, psychotropic medications—anti-psychotics, I should say—take a toll on the patient. It's much better than it used to be, say, back in the '50s, years ago. But it's still terrible. More than likely, he will be always dependent."

"He's a zombie!" Jerusha said. "Give me back my brother!"

"The disease, schizophrenia, has taken hold of your brother. I'd give him back to you whole and fine if I could, but no one can."

"When can we take him home?" Nephi asked.

"Let's not be in any kind of a hurry here, sir," the doctor said. "Your son, your brother, your friend, he's still very sick. The best place for him is in here where experts can keep a watchful eye on him. He has a full care team: doctors, psychologists, social workers, nurses."

"But, eventually, he'll be able to come home, right?" I asked.

"By state law, the goal of his treatment is to have him in the least restrictive living situation as possible, the least restrictive as possible. So, yes, we can all hope for that outcome."

"You can't keep him here," Jerusha said. "This is America, for godsakes."

"If we determine him to be a danger to himself or others, then, yes, we can keep him here, indefinitely," the doctor said matter-of-factly. "You couldn't care for him in the conditions he's in. This is best now, sir."

"This is the best?" I asked.

"As I said, we're hopeful that the neuroleptics will take effect, eventually, and he will be able to surmount his delusions and hallucinations."

"But he'll always be a zombie?" Jerusha asked.

"You shouldn't be in this time," the disheveled woman barked from the side. "Get out of now."

"They've got me in here with all these nutcases," Jared drawled. "Like her. She's one of them. Batshit crazy."

"You don't know shit," the disheveled woman said.

"Could you leave us alone for a while, doctor?" Nephi asked, ushering Bloodworth and myself close to himself and Jerusha. "We're a family."

"Of course," he said, turning toward the disheveled woman. "Mrs. Scanlon, let's give these people some privacy, shall we?"

"It's not my time," the woman shouted as the doctor escorted her out of the room.

We all turned to Jared and sat around him.

"Is it really terrible here, Jared?" Jerusha asked. "It looks terrible."

"I've had better," Jared said slowly. "The food is poisoned."

"We miss you, son," Nephi said.

"I am a danger to God Himself," Jared said. He sat up in his chair and scanned the room. "Satan appears not to be here right now. If you could get me some place away from that fucker, it would be great. He's a fucker. I think he must be put off by your presence, so that's a good thing."

"We're here for you, man," I said. "Hells bells, I'm living here. I mean, out there," I said, pointing vaguely toward the hospital entrance. "I'm living off Milky Ways and Fantas!" I realized I was trying to give Jared a straight line he could riff off of. But instead he just looked at me in an indefinable manner.

"Where have you guys been?" he asked. "Kenny, why aren't you out tracting?"

"I left, man," I said.

"You left?" he said.

"Yeah, just like that," I said.

"You've got to get me out of this place," he said.

"Son, we're doing all we can," Nephi said. "We won't leave you."

"Man, I'm living here," I said.

"I used to live with you all once," Jared said, looking around at us. "Except you, Bishop. I never lived with you. It's probably for the best."

"We care about you, son," Bloodworth offered. "We won't forsake you."

Jared leaned back in his chair and closed his eyes. "That's good, I guess," he said. "I think Satan's put off by you. That's why he's not here right now."

We sat in that room for ninety minutes, trying to carry on a conversation with Jared, trying to encourage him. Jared kept talking about Satan. Jerusha never stopped softly crying. Eventually, the doctor returned to take Jared to some sort of therapy. When he left, we all sat back down and looked at one another.

"We can do this," I said.

CHAPTER TWENTY-TWO

Mavis began complaining to Jerusha that she was feeling punk—pains in her abdomen and just plain out of gas. She had to pee all the time. She had some odd bleeding. One day while playing Spite and Malice, Mavis barked at Jerusha, which was completely unlike her.

"I'm so sorry, dear," Mavis said. "I don't know what's wrong with me lately."

"Maybe you should see a doctor," Jerusha said. "You haven't been yourself lately."

Of course, Mavis was hesitant to have anyone make a fuss about her, so she demurred. But, of course, Jerusha wasn't one to be put off, so she won, eventually. They went to a doctor, an acidic woman who long ago lost her last ounce of patience, to hear Jerusha tell it. The doctor poked and prodded Mavis, thumping her like a tribal drum, and listened halfheartedly to her complaints. The doctor determined Mavis had a bad pelvic infection and put her on three strong antibiotics. The pain and other symptoms persisted for days, though. Jerusha took her to another doctor and they ran a raft of tests. Eventually, the truth came to light: Mavis was pregnant, which hit Mavis like a thunderstrike. And Bloodworth? He broke down, blubbering like a little baby. He actually fell to the ground right in front of Nephi, Jerusha and me at the hospital. Bloodworth had arrived first and was sitting with me when Jerusha and Nephi arrived. We clearly could tell they were brimming with news.

"Good, you're sitting down," Jerusha said as she and her father came up to us. At this, Bloodworth stood up. "What is it?" he asked desperately.

"Bishop," Jerusha said. "Mavis is pregnant. Mavis is pregnant."

"Holy shit!" I said reflexively.

"What did you just say?" Bloodworth asked Jerusha.

"Mavis, Bishop, the woman you love, she's pregnant," Jerusha said with a laugh of delight. "You know, with child. Your child. And Jared did it! Take that, General Authorities!"

"Holy shit," Bloodworth said. He began blubbering.

Bloodworth fell back down into his seat. From there, he slid off the chair and collapsed on the checkerboard floor. "Bishop!" we all cried and shot to our knees.

As Bloodworth sobbed in a heap, we all patted his back. Nephi laid his hands on the crown of Bloodworth's head and closed his eyes. "In the name of Jesus Christ and in the power of the Holy Melchizedek Priesthood, I anoint Demetrius Bloodworth with oil for the healing of infirmities," he said. He reached into his vest pocket with one hand and pulled out a tiny vial, which he handed to me. "Would you open this, please?" I did so and he said, "Now, put a little bead of the oil on my finger. There. Yes, that's it." He touched the finger with oil on it on the top of Bloodworth's head. Then he placed his other hand there as well. "Please help Demetrius, Heavenly Father. Now," he said, looking toward me, "You have to seal the anointing."

I looked at Bloodworth crumpled on the floor and breathed deeply. I closed my eyes and breathed.

"Demetrius Bloodworth, I am sealing this anointing by the

Authority of the Melchizedek Priesthood. Please help him. God. In Jesus' name, amen."

"Amen," Nephi said.

"Puh," Jerusha said.

Bloodworth looked up at us. "Is God in control?" he asked weakly.

"I don't know, Bishop. I really don't," I said, looking up at Jerusha. "But I think you have something to devote your life to, whoever did it or however it happened. The question of who's in control is irrelevant at this point, seems to me. Here's the question: What are you going to do about it? That's what I want to know."

Suddenly, Bloodworth stopped crying and stared at the ceiling. "Yes," he said firmly. "We must be married now."

"How are we going to do that?" I asked.

"And Jared, he must be at the ceremony," Bloodworth said.

"How are we going to do *that*?" I asked.

"They've got to have some kind of chaplain or something here at the hospital," Jerusha said. "He can do it."

"Perfect!" Bloodworth said. "Nephi, will you find the chaplain, please, and explain the situation to him? Jerusha, will you come with me to get Mavis?"

"Sure, let's do it," she said.

"Can I come?" I asked, somewhat offended.

"Of course, Kenny. Yes, do," Bloodworth said, wiping the tears from his eyes.

As we drove to Mavis', Bloodworth asked, "What if she won't have me?"

"I don't think that's going to be a problem, Bishop," Jerusha said.

We pulled up in front of Mavis' house and Bloodworth put his car into park. We sat in silence for a moment. Bloodworth turned to me. "Kenny, would you give me a priesthood blessing? You know, for courage."

"Uh, sure. I guess," I said, "but I think you need to have two priesthood holders to perform a blessing. Jerusha's a woman."

Jerusha looked at me dubiously. "Really? You're serious? I'll do it with you."

"That'll work," Bloodworth said.

"By the power of the Holy Melchizedek Priesthood, we ask Heavenly Father to give Mr. Bloodworth courage and words, the words to say what he feels," I said when Jerusha and I had placed our hands on Bloodworth's head. "We pray this is the name of Jesus Christ."

"Amen," Jerusha said. "Now, get to it, Bishop! Time's a wasting."

"Do you feel anything from the blessing?" I asked. "Power from God?"

"No, to be frank for you," Bloodworth said and sighed. "Here goes nothing."

When Mavis opened the front door, Bloodworth went to one knee. Mavis covered her mouth with both hands. You could tell she was sobbing. Bloodworth stayed on his knee for a long time, apparently talking to Mavis, who didn't say a word. Eventually, Bloodworth stood up and they embraced.

"Let's go," Jerusha said, getting out of the car.

"Do you think we should?" I asked.

"It's a party," she said.

I shrugged and smiled. "Looks like it's a party," I said. "You first."

When I got to the front porch, Bloodworth was embracing Mavis and talking to Jerusha, who was laughing. "It's a party," I said.

"Well, let's do this," Bloodworth said.

"Now, Demetrius?" Mavis said. "Right away? Who is going to perform the service?"

"The chaplain at the nuthouse," I said. "Come on, let's go!"

"Don't we need a license or a blood test?" Mavis asked.

"We don't have time for that," I said, looking at Bloodworth and winking. "God will use our lie."

"Yes," he said.

"Married at a mental hospital? What next?" Mavis laughed. "Let me get my purse."

When we got back to the hospital, Nephi had roused the chaplain, who appeared none too pleased as he stood next to Nephi. To Nephi's other side stood Jared, bathrobe askew. A hospital orderly stood in the background on the off chance Jared might try to make a break for it, I guess. Jared appeared disinclined. He probably thought Satan was lurking nearby, elusive fucker. Safety in numbers. That's the ticket.

When we had all gathered around the chaplain, he looked at us all skeptically. "So you're a Mormon, and you're something else, and you want me, a Lutheran, a chaplain at a mental hospital, to perform a civil ceremony to unite you in matrimony?" he asked. "Why don't you go to one of your churches?"

"Well, I guess I don't know if we have churches anymore, to be frank for you," Bloodworth said. "But we wanted to do this right away and we wanted Jared here to be at the ceremony."

The chaplain looked over at Jared, who looked blankly at him in return. "Well," he said. "The gang's all here."

"Let's do this thing," Jerusha blurted.

So the Lutheran chaplain took us through a short form of the civil ceremony. When he arrived at the part of the service in which he asked if there was anyone present who objected to the union, Jared spoke up. "We're lucky Satan's not here right now," he said.

The chaplain, who clearly was used to ministering in the midst of crazy loons, looked at Jared and nodded. "Okay, then. Then by the power vested in me, I pronounce you husband and wife. You may kiss the bride."

We all cheered. Mavis and Bloodworth embraced. Nephi cried and Jerusha and I held hands.

"This is good," she said.

"Yeah, they're going to have a rockin' sex life," I whispered to her.

"You're confusing them with us," she said.

"Is that an invitation?" I whispered.

"Right here? Right now? Buck naked in the foyer?" she said, sounding shocked. "Okay, let's do it. It'll be a family home evening to remember." She began unzipping her pants.

"You're so literal," I whispered to her. I turned her away from the others, who were talking together, and put my hand on her zipper hand. "You must be a fundamentalist."

"Fundamentally horny," she said.

"I think I'm going to have to have therapy or something—this having sex with a friend," I said. "I might as well be having sex with Jared."

"Jared doesn't have sex. A new Jared just appears on his back, like a—what was it?—a goiter. And he spontaneously generates a new Jared."

"Trust me," I said. "Jared is as horny as I am, maybe more, if that's possible. I just act on my impulses with you. Him, he just practices on his own."

"I'm well aware of Jared's penchant for spanking the monkey," she said, sounding authoritative. "Remember, we've often slept in the same room. Did you know I have an assortment of vibrators?"

"More than one? I just heard about the one. The famous vibrator."

"I vary between vibrators according to my mood. Fantasies about men. Fantasies about multiple men. Fantasies about women. That kind of thing."

"Okay, this discussion ends now, or else we *will* end up having sex right here in the foyer, friend."

"Your loss. Friend."

Just then we heard Nephi calling to us. "Over here, you two," he said. "We're taking a photo of the wedding party."

"The wedding party," Jerusha said. "My family is nuts."

"And you're the head nut," I said, kissing her on the cheek.

JARED WAS STILL BEING PUT in restraints periodically, when he would get really spooked about Satan. We were allowed to visit with him when he wasn't in restraints. It tore up Nephi and Jerusha to think of Jared in restraints, like some homemade monster. It tore me up, too.

The doctors determined that Thorazine and Moban weren't doing the trick, so they switched Jared to another anti-psychotic, Navane. The doctor explained the deleterious side effects to us. This didn't set well with Jerusha.

"Why did Jah put us down here to have to figure out everything on our own? Would a human parent do that to its offspring? No, the human parent would say, 'You're going to want to watch out for that and you're going to want to use X to cure Y.' If there is a cure for schizophrenia, why doesn't he tell us? Instead we fumble along and Jared suffers. Does Jah have His head up his ass or what?"

"Yeah, easy for him to be glib about it. He's riding around in his air-conditioned Cadillac," I said.

"Yeah, no shit," she said. "That's profound."

"It's from Jared," I said.

"Oh, for a second there I thought you had been profound," she said. "Is my face red."

"I think deeply," I said, pretending I was hurt.

"I know you do," she said, leaning in and kissing my cheek. "That's why Jah saved you for me. Did you know I'm gifted?"

"Yeah, so I heard," I said.

Soon enough, the side effects of the new medicine emerged: tardive dyskiniesia and akathisia. I was sorely tempted to put each of those in the bank as future words of the day, but I realized there would be no way to use those words in day-to-day speech with average folks. Sort of like cheating. Here's the gist. Tardive dyskinesia is involuntary movements of the tongue, lips, face, trunk, and extremities. Basically, Jared was twitching everywhere and everywhen. Akathisia is a syndrome characterized by unpleasant sensations of inner restlessness that manifests itself with an inability to sit still or remain motionless. You could see both of them in full effect whenever you would talk with Jared. He'd flit like a flea. He looked like someone possessed by a demon, not that I've ever seen that, to my knowledge. Jared was a restless corpse. It pissed him off, which I took as a good sign. The old Jared was poking through.

One afternoon, Jared and I took a walk of the hospital grounds, with a minder, a white-shirted orderly following behind at a polite distance.

"This place is the shits," he said. "I don't belong here."

"Yeah, you don't in one way," I said. "But in another way, you do."

"Do you think I'm sick?"

"Yes, but I think you're getting better. I wouldn't lie to you, man."

"Kenny?"

"Yeah, man?"

"You're the only friend I've had in my life, other than my sister and my father. But they don't really count as friends."

"I know what you mean," I said. "Before I met you, when I was back in my real life, my life before my mission, I would have said I had a lot of friends. But since I met you, I think about things differently."

I stopped. Jared went on a few paces and then turned and looked at me. "I think God did this," he said. "You know, brought us together."

I stared at him for a moment. I wasn't too sure what answer to give.

We walked on.

"Kenny?"

"Yeah?"

"I've realized that all I need to do to get out of here is to stop talking about all the crazy shit I talk about," he said. "I mean, I still think those thoughts, though they're starting to not become part of me. I think them, but less and less. They're always a part of me. But I've realized that if I just shut up about all the crazy shit, I can get out of here."

I would look back on this conversation and realize that what was happening was that, after weeks and weeks on anti-psychotics, the neuroleptics were starting to take effect. However, he was still left with all the side effects of the medications.

Praise Jah.

EVENTUALLY, the day came when they let us take Jared home to Bloodworth's house, home for now. He was to see a shrink chosen by the hospital three times a week and to attend group therapy sessions at the Community Mental Health Center twice a week. And stay on his medications—he was to stay on his medications, above all else. I realized that the doctors felt that the group and individual therapy might help some. Who's to say? But the one thing they did know is that the medications, if diligently administered, would prevent Jared from becoming psychotic again, spewing nonsense and fleeing demons. And that, though they didn't come right out and say it flatly, was the best we could hope for. The best.

"Now that I'm out, I can be honest with you all," Jared said slowly one night at the kitchen table. "I don't think I'm sick, really. Thoughts are thoughts. They're not diseases. So I may have had some wrong thoughts."

"Wrong thoughts?" Jerusha asked. "You thought Satan was after you."

Jared looked at his sister for a moment. "How do you know that wasn't the case? I mean, you don't know that wasn't the case. Don't you believe in Satan?"

"Shit, I don't know, Jared," she said. "But you used to say Satan was after you and then you took the medicines and, eventually, when they found the right medicine, you stopped saying those kinds of things. The medicine did it."

"Well," he said, pausing and looking down at his hands on the table, "I feel like shit. At least I could think before the medicine. Now I can't think straight. My face feels like wood. My arms and legs don't feel connected to my body. It feels like my brain is submerged in something."

"But you're better," Jerusha said.

"Better? Maybe I was better without the medicine," Jared said. "Maybe I was seeing things clearly without the medicine. Maybe it was a harsh reality, but it was the real reality. Maybe I have to live with that. Life's harsh. Maybe it's better that I know if Satan's after me, you know, if He really is after me."

"Jared!" Jerusha shouted. "You can't stop taking the medicine. You're going to kill me."

"It's my brain," Jared said slowly.

"I can't lose you," Jerusha said, tears streaming down her cheeks.

Nephi, Bloodworth, and I looked at Jerusha. When we turned back toward Jared, he looked up at us from his tilted head. "It's my brain."

"Jared," Nephi said, "let's do what the doctors say. Let's keep taking the medicine."

"You say let's, but I'm the one taking the medicine," he said groggily. "It makes me feel like shit. I can't think. You say let's like it's all of us, but it's my brain."

"Jared," Nephi said, his eyes tearing up. "Please."

Jared looked at his father for a long time silently. "Okay," he said. "But it's my brain."

ONE DAY there was a knock on the front door and, being closest, I went to answer it, and who should it be but Aunt Jo, which I realized when Nephi put his hand on my shoulder and said, "Jo! What are you doing here?"

At this, Jo stepped to the side and revealed a feather wafting in the wind, a wisp of a woman—a girl, even. A twig in the breeze. Shit, I don't know. Jo looked at her brother apologetically.

Jerusha came around my other side and took in this sight. "Holy shit," she whispered.

"Jo, come in, come in!" Nephi said, waving her inward. "So happy to see you—and shocked. Why in the world are you here? Not that I'm not happy to see you, because I am."

Jo nudged the wispish woman toward the door and followed her. "Thank you, Nephi. I'm sorry to shock you."

The wispish woman smiled shyly and tiptoed into Bloodworth's sizable foyer, Jo gently ushering her onward with small taps on her back. Bloodworth came around the corner.

"Visitors," he said with a smile.

"Bishop," Nephi said, placing a hand on Jo's shoulder. "This is my sister—one of my sisters!"

"Welcome," Bloodworth said.

"Bishop?" Jo said.

"That was before I am what I am now," Bloodworth said. "Welcome, though."

There was an uncomfortable pause and then Jo broke in. "This," she said and breathed deeply, "is Emily."

"Well, welcome, Emily," Bloodworth said.

Nephi paused. "Yes, yes, welcome, welcome!" he said. "Let's go sit in the drawing room."

As we walked toward the drawing room, Jo said, "I've come all this way because I felt I had to. I felt I owed you that."

"You, Jo? You don't owe us anything. It's the other way around," Nephi said. "Have a seat, have a seat."

When we had all sat down, the wispish woman sitting as closely to Jo as possible, Jo smiled at us all nervously and we all smiled back.

"So . . . ?" Jerusha said.

Jo breathed deeply and reached over and patted Emily's thigh. "This is difficult for me," Jo said.

"No shit," Jerusha said.

At this, Jared entered the room and took us all in. "Holy . . . motherfucking . . . shit," he said with overblown deliberation.

"Jared!" Jo said. "I came for you. I came to, to . . . apologize."

Jared poked his finger in his left nostril and fished around hopefully. "Apologize?" he said.

"Yes, apologize," Jo said, adjusting her rump on the divan. "Apologize."

"Well," Jared said, sitting next to his sister and shivering a shiver. "Brrrr! Well, let's hear this apology. Don't keep us in suspense. I have a weak bladder."

"Hey!" I said. "A joke!"

Jared looked at me soberly. "I wasn't joking," he said. "Don't make fun."

"Yeah," Jerusha said, smiling crookedly. "Don't make fun."

Jo cleared her throat. "Yes, well," she said, "I owe you an apology."

"You already said that," Jared said flatly.

"Yeah," Jerusha said, smiling crookedly at her brother. She was clearly enjoying this.

"Jared, I'm cancelling our agreement," Jo said. "I have no claim on you and you have no obligation toward me, toward me for what I insisted upon."

Everyone was quiet and eventually Nephi said with a smile, "Well, I'm lost!"

Jo sighed. "Nephi, it was terrible, what I did, what I did to you."

"Jo, what are you talking about?" Nephi said with a tentative laugh.

Jo closed her eyes. "Any religion," she said, "that won't let me be who I am at my core, is no religion—and, anyway, I think religion comes from humans."

"Will wonders never cease?" Jerusha said.

"Jo, what are you saying?" Nephi said.

"I think I might be an atheist," Jo said.

"Well, Jo," Nephi said, "let's not do anything rash."

"Rash," Jared said.

"Well," Jo said. "I do know this. Material success doesn't bring happiness. There's got to be more."

"Well, of course," Nephi said kindly. "But what are you saying, Jo?"

"Nephi," Jo said, "I blackmailed Jared into going on his mission. Blackmailed."

"Take some cranberry juice for that rash," Jared said.

"This is great," Jerusha said with a crooked smile.

"Nephi," Jo said, "the only reason Jared went on his mission, the only reason is that I told him—I blackmailed him."

"You blackmailed him?" Nephi said.

"I blackmailed him when I told him that if he went on his mission and returned with honor I would set you all up for life . . ." Jo began to cry.

Jerusha stopped smiling. "What did you say?" she said, glaring at Jo. "What did you say?"

"I just wanted to please my father," Jo said. "I'm so, so sorry."

Jerusha shot up. "I can't believe you fucking did that, Jo!"

"Please . . ." Jo said pleadingly.

"Who the fuck do you think you are?" Jerusha cried.

"Jo, what are you saying?" Nephi asked.

"I'll tell you what she's saying," Jerusha cried. "She fucked us over so she could kiss the Senator's big ass. She fucked us over. Jared, why didn't you say something?"

Jared looked at his sister uncomprehendingly, mouth agape.

"I threatened him," Jo said, tears running down her face and her chin quivering. "I told him that if he told you about it, the deal was off and you three wouldn't receive any more money from me."

"You fucking cunt!" Jerusha cried, lunging for Jo. Instinctively, I stood between her and Jo.

"Jerusha!" Nephi cried, shooting up and grabbing his daughter.

"It was probably the stress of this fucking mission that brought on the disease, you fucking cunt!" Jerusha cried as her father pushed her away from Jo. "She fucked us! She fucked Jared!"

"Jerusha, remember Jah," I said.

"Fuck Jah!" she said, flailing against me and striking my nose. "He's the asshole that gave Jared this fucking disease! What kind of fucking world is this?"

"Jerusha, please," Nephi said.

"And fuck you, Jo!" Jerusha said, "and your little . . . bitch!"

Jo had buried her face in her hands. Emily had both arms around her.

"She's saying she's sorry!" Emily cried at Jerusha. "Have mercy."

Jerusha shook off Nephi and me. "Enough! Leave me be," she growled, shaking out her arms and stretching her neck to the side. "I'm fine."

I put both hands up, wanting to embrace her but not sure if she would be willing.

"Mercy?" Jerusha cried at Emily as I put one hand on her shoulder and grabbed her by the arm with my other hand. "Mercy? There is no such thing!"

Nephi placed his hand on her other shoulder. "Jerusha, please," he said.

"Who the fuck do you think you are?" Jerusha cried at Jo.

"Stop it!" Emily cried, rubbing Jo's shoulders. A string of snot hung from Jo's nose like Christmas tinsel. "She wishes she never did it. She's sorry."

"I wish she hadn't fucking done it, either!" Jerusha cried. "But she did and now we're all fucked. So your 'sorry' doesn't amount to shit! 'Sorry' doesn't bring Jared back!"

"I'm right here," Jared said.

Jerusha wiped her eyes and looked down at her brother.

"Shit," she said and actually laughed for the shortest second.

"Jerusha," I said. "Come with me." I guided her toward the entryway. That's when she broke down in tears and collapsed into me. I guided her to the front door and out to the porch.

"Jerusha," I said, facing her with my hands on her shoulders. "Jerusha, Jared had his disease long before Jo blackmailed him. He was born with it. This all would have happened to him, no matter what."

She wiped her nose with the back of her hand. "Why would Heavenly Father do this to us?" she asked. "He could have made Jared different. He can do anything, can't He?"

I looked into her eyes for one . . . two . . . three seconds. "Shit, Jerusha," I said. "I don't fucking know."

She wrapped her arms around my middle and laid her head on my chest.

"I will never be able to forgive her," she said.

"I think she's really sorry," I said. "She knows she made a terrible mistake. A mistake—or maybe it was a sin. Christ didn't die for mistakers, I've been told."

"Doesn't matter," she said, turning her head and resting her other cheek against my chest.

"Jerusha," I said, easing her away from me so I could look her in the face, "listen to me."

She sniffed and looked at me expectantly.

"Are you listening to me?" I said.

"Yes, I'm listening to you."

"Your father just learned that his sister blackmailed Jared. He's going to be devastated. You know your dad. Family's everything to him. He needs your strength now. Jerusha?"

"What?"

"You're a strong person, strongest person I know," I said. "Your dad's going to need that strength."

"Kenny," she said, "I can't forgive her."

"I know," I said. "But keep it to yourself. Help your father forgive her. This will go deep."

She wiped her eye and looked at me. "Keep it to myself?"

I kissed her on the forehead. "Yes, this is just between you and Jah, I think," I said.

"Jah," she said. "Yes, Him. I think I told Him to fuck off—or Her or whatever."

"He'll forgive you, Jerusha," I said. "That's what He does, I think."

"You think?"

I looked at her, and my heart swelled. "I hope," I said, pulling her close to me. "I'm a big-ass sinner—what with the fornicating with you and the jaywalking."

"You've been around Jared too long," she said, hugging me and sniffing.

"He would want you to help your dad," I said. "Jared, I mean. Wouldn't he?"

She was silent for a long moment. "Yes," she said.

"Well, there you go," I said.

She was silent for another long moment. "Kenny?" she asked, muffled against my chest. "Do you think God brought us together, you and me?"

I said nothing for the longest time. "That's what I'm trying to figure out," I said.

JARED KEPT COMPLAINING about the side effects of the medicine. Once, he threw a lamp through a window, screaming, "I can't live like this!" But life went on. One day, we were all in the living room together, even Mavis, and Jared was complaining about the medicine again. There was a pause in the conversation, a weighty pause. Nephi looked at him and said, "Maybe it would be okay to take a little less of the medicine for a bit. Just a little less, for a bit."

"Dad!" Jerusha said.

"I'm not saying stop the medicine entirely," he said. "Just a little. I'm saying just a little. Maybe it would, you know, take the edge off, help Jared think better."

"Think better?" Jerusha asked. "His brain is broken. The medicine is the only thing that keeps him from being crazy. He thought Satan was after him."

"Maybe your Dad's right," I said. "It couldn't hurt to try."

"Yes it could," Jerusha said, starting to cry. "Why am I the only one who is thinking straight? Are you trying to kill Jared?"

"Jerusha!" Nephi yelled, bolting to his feet. "He's my son, too! He's my son, too!"

We all sat stunned. It was the first time I heard Nephi raise his voice. It seemed to be Jerusha's, too, from the look on her face. That's saying something, considering that she lived with her father for twenty years. My stepfather couldn't go half a day without snarling like a mastiff.

Nephi crumpled back into the chair. "I'm sorry," he said softly. "But he's my son, too."

Jared cleared his throat. "It's okay," he said. "I'll keep taking the medicine. I don't want to see you fight."

But he didn't, it turned out.

The signs of a new psychosis were very small at first, barely discernable. Jared would just look around nervously for a few moments. Then he started saying strange things, which, at first made us think the old Jared was coming back, his oddball sense of humor and all. At least, that's what I thought. I was finding that we all found ways not to talk about Jared's condition with one another.

Then Jared started not coming out of his room for long stretches. This went on for weeks. That didn't get us talking about his condition at first, but it did get us sharing barely concerned looks among ourselves. Eventually, one of us would knock on his door and say something like, "Jared, why don't you come out and spend some time with the family?" Sometimes he would. Sometimes he wouldn't. When he wouldn't, that's what got us talking amongst ourselves again.

"Jared's been strange lately," Nephi said one night.

"Well, he does have an incurable disease," I said.

"Yeah," Jerusha said. "But I know what you mean, Dad."

"Yes," Nephi said. "Yes. What do we do?"

We looked at each other. Nobody knew.

Mavis would come into any room with Jared and you could tell —Jared could tell—that she was made uncomfortable by his strangeness. I think Jared scared Mavis with his strange talk and aloofness. I think she was protecting the baby, if you want to know the truth. I've never really asked her about this. Point is, as the months went on and Jared was in and out of the mental hospital, Mavis became sort of a bellwether for us, a canary in the coal mine. When she would start withdrawing from Jared, it was a sign to all of us to release our collective denial. It was when we realized Jared was off his meds and becoming psychotic again.

We went to Jared and confronted him about his medicine when this happened. He swore that he was still taking the neuroleptics religiously.

"But, Jared, you're saying all sorts of strange things. Paranoid things," Jerusha said.

There was a pause as Jared looked at this twin sister. "I have an active imagination," he said. "You know that."

"Yes, I know that, Jared," she said. "I also know you have a disease of the brain."

"I'm not sick," Jared said.

"Man, you're sick," I said. "You have to take your medicine, man."

"You'd talk differently if you were the one who had to take these medicines," Jared said.

"Jerusha, try to look at things from Jared's point of view," Nephi said. "The medicines debilitate him."

"Yeah," Jared said.

"So? So what does that mean?" Jerusha asked heatedly. "It means we should let him kill himself? Dad, he'll die if he stops taking his medicines. He'll hurt someone, or he'll hurt himself."

"The medicines are killing him," Nephi said.

Jerusha stood up angrily. "Shit, Dad. Why do you have to be so stupid about this?"

"I'm your father," Nephi said defensively.

"I can't take this," Jerusha said, throwing her arms up and bolting out of the front of the house and slamming the door. Jared looked after her sadly. He put his head in his hands and shook his head. I sat down next to him and put my arm around him.

AND THEN IT CAME.

It was the middle of the night. By that time, I had the habit of waking up several times each night to check on Jared. Sometimes he was asleep in bed. Sometimes he was pacing around the house. Sometimes he was sitting at the kitchen table in the dark. But he was always there. Then this one time, he was nowhere to be found.

"Shit," I said. I pondered about whether I should wake Jerusha and Nephi. I decided against it. I put on my coat and went outside. I lowered my head and prayed a short prayer. "Which way should I go, Jah?" I asked. I could see my breath. I received no answer, as far as I could tell, so I walked toward downtown. It was colder than a witch's tit. I went on. After about fifteen minutes, I was in the silent downtown core, silent except for an occasional person coming out of Curley's, bundled up against the cold and getting quickly into a car. Then I saw Jared bolt across the street. He was in his pajamas.

"Hey, man!" I called out, running after him. "Hey, man! Stop! It's me, Kenny!"

I turned down an alley to see his lower half hanging out of a window above a back door to an outdoors store. He was going through the window, just like he did that day at the emergency room, I guess. When I got to the door, he was completely inside, slippery devil.

"Hey, man!" I called out. "It's me, Kenny!"

Nothing.

"Shit," I said. I saw the garbage can Jared had used to pull himself up to the door to make it up to the window. What were my options? I could call the police, but that was a bad idea. I could go get Jerusha and Nephi. Also a bad idea. I had to go in after him. "Shit," I said and, somehow, got myself through the window and spilled onto the floor on the other side. As I fell, I slid against a screw that was sticking out and it gouged into my side.

"Shit!" I screamed in a whisper, not sure why I was whispering. I stood up and started calling Jared's name as I walked through the dark outdoors store.

Eventually, I heard Jared call out. "Be quiet, man! Satan will hear you!"

"Oh, shit," I said, moving briskly toward the direction of Jared's voice. "Hey, where are you?"

"Quiet, man," he called out.

Eventually, I found him, huddled behind a tent display. He was freaked out, sincerely, with real intent.

"Hey, man," I said, reaching out toward him. "You stopped taking your medicine, didn't you?"

"Shhh!" he said, urging me toward him.

I scooted next to him. "Man, what's up?" I whispered.

"Satan's been chasing me around town," he answered. "I knew

this might be a safe place because I think the Ark of the Covenant is in here somewhere."

"The Ark of the Covenant?"

"Shhh. Quiet, man," he whispered. "Yes, the Ark of the Covenant. Weren't you listening? The Holy Ghost told me."

"The Holy Ghost?"

"Yes, weren't you listening? Don't you think the Holy Ghost can talk to you?"

I paused. "I don't know."

"Well, I know it," he said.

"Man, I think you need to go back to the hospital."

"The Holy Ghost told me you'd say that."

"Well, what does He say about it? About going back to the hospital."

Jared closed his eyes and was silent for a minute. Finally, he said, "He says I should go."

"He does?"

"But, Kenny, man, I can't do it right now, not with Satan roaming around the streets out there. I can't go out there now. He's a mean fucker. Really bad. I'm scared. Man, can you stay with me?"

"Yeah, man," I said. "I can do that." I scooted in closer to him, wrapped one arm around him and drew him into me. He didn't ask me to hold him, but when I did it, he drew his head into my chest and wrapped his arm around me. Now, I'd hugged many males at church services. It was something that happened, a sign of fellowship. After all, we called each other brother. But that was one-two-three and you were done. You barely had time to congratulate yourself for being such a sensitive man before it was all over. You never really had time to freak over the idea of holding one male's body to your body. So, I wasn't really prepared for this embrace in the dark outdoors store. I'm not going to lie and say it was an easy thing for me to do. It wasn't. It was hard. But I had to do it, for Jared.

He needed me.

"Shit, man," Jared said. "I'm freaked. Satan's out to get me. He wants to plant machinery inside my brain, the better to control my thoughts with. Shit, man. Shit, man."

We sat like that for five minutes. Jared kept saying, "Shit, man. Shit, man. Shit, man."

"It's colder than a witch's tit in here, man," I said. "And you're in your pajamas. Wait, I have an idea." I moved to stand and Jared said, "Man, you said you'd stay with me."

I crouched next to Jared. "Look, man, just stay quiet. I'll be back in just a sec."

"But–"

"Man, it's cool." I patted him on the chest. "I'll just be a second. Stay quiet."

He looked at me and I could tell he was trying to decide whether he could trust me, whether, I guess, I was on his side or Satan's side.

"Okay," he whispered. "But hurry up, man."

I ran down the aisles until I found the sleeping bags and grabbed two identical ones. When I got back to Jared, I unrolled the sleeping bags and zipped them together.

"Come on, man," I said. "Let's get in here. I can hold you in here and we can stay warm."

Jared didn't hesitate about the prospect of holding another man in a sleeping bag. He just climbed in. "Thanks, man. Thanks, man. Thanks, man," he said, repeating it over and over. I didn't have time to freak out. He needed me. I slid into the sleeping bags and Jared immediately glommed on to me. "Shit, man. Shit, man. Shit, man," he kept saying. I wrapped my arms around him. Will miracles never cease.

"It's going to be okay," I said. "Don't worry. I'll protect you from Satan."

"Thanks, man."

As night turned into dawn, Jared shivered now and then and muttered a few words I didn't always get. Even when I could hear him, I usually couldn't understand him. He said things like, "It's the poison of corpses" and "strife in the heavenlies." At one point, he began singing the hymn *If You Could Hie to Kolob*. I'm shocked he knew the words. That said, he couldn't carry a tune in a bucket. We passed the night this way. As it got lighter outside, I'd say, "Come on, man. We can go now." Jared would answer, "No, not yet." Eventually, the owner of the store unlocked the front door and came inside, clearing his throat.

"Come on, man," I whispered. "We've got to go now."

"Okay," Jared said.

As we heard the store owner clomping around, flipping light switches and clearing his throat some more, we snuck down a side aisle. We crouched low even though our heads wouldn't have shown above the shelves if we stood up. Seemed more clandestine this way, I guess. We were just a few feet from the front door, crouching, when we heard a door being opened. I assumed the owner was going into some sort of backroom. "Come on," I said. "Now's our chance."

We bolted into a full sprint, heading down the quiet streets and straight for Bloodworth's house. Jared actually outran me. When we got inside, we immediately bumped into Jerusha.

"Where were you guys?" she cried. "We were freaked out."

"Jared has to go back into the hospital," I said. "He's crazy again."

She didn't look surprised. But she scowled at him, making it obvious she was mad. Jared looked at his sister imploringly, but she wouldn't look at him. "Shit," she said, shaking her head.

We all bundled into the car and drove to Northern State. Jerusha didn't say a word. Nephi kept saying things like, "It will be okay, son." Jared stared out the back windshield, as if someone was following us. Me, I didn't know what to think.

Jared began screaming at the first sight of the hospital. "That's Satan's house! Don't put me in there! Don't put me in there! Kenny, don't let them put me in there!"

I put my hands on him to try and calm him down. As we pulled up to the front door, a team of male orderlies stood with their arms crossed. Next to them was a gurney with leather straps.

"Take it easy, man," I implored Jared. "This is for the best. They can get you back on your medicines. They can get you so you won't be psychotic."

"Man, I'm not sick!" Jared yelled. "This is bullshit. Why are you guys doing this to me? Do you know who's in there?"

"Jesus Christ, Jared," Jerusha exclaimed. "For godsakes, Satan isn't in the hospital. You're sick. You need doctors."

As the orderlies walked toward the car with the gurney, Jared screamed, "I'm not sick! I'm not sick!"

The orderlies wrestled Jared onto the gurney and strapped him down. Jerusha rushed over to me and collapsed into my chest, bawling. I held her tight. Nephi walked alongside the gurney as they wheeled Jared in, trying to reassure his only son. "Your dad's with him," I said. "Look." She turned to look back, and we saw one of the orderlies stand up in front of Nephi and put his hands up to prevent him from going any further as they rolled Jared into the back room.

"Shit," Jerusha said. "It's bad enough they put him in the hospital but they have to keep him all alone? He needs us!"

She turned toward the car and punched the windshield with a loud, "Uhh!" She wailed in pain. She crumpled to her knees and I kneeled down to her.

"My hand!" she wailed. "Ow! Shit! I think I broke my hand!"

"They've got to have a doctor in there that can help us," I said, lifting her up. "Come with me. Let's go see."

Turned out they didn't have a doctor who could set her broken hand, or at least a doctor who was willing to set her broken hand. So Nephi and I took her to the emergency room and they set her hand in a cast. Once that was done, I stood in front of Jerusha and Nephi. "Jerusha, I know you're in pain, and I know I want to be there for you, but I really need to be back at the mental hospital for Jared," I said. "I've got to live there again. I need to be there for him in case he gets well enough to see me. Can you guys take me to Bishop's house so I can grab some stuff and then take me to the hospital?"

Jerusha looked up at me and smiled. "That's fine," she said. "But sign my cast first."

CHAPTER TWENTY-THREE

Jared was in the hospital for two months this time. The neuroleptics kicked in faster. On the plus side, the hospital gave me more access to Jared. They needed to get him calmed down with Valium first, but after four days they said they could let me visit with him once a day, assuming he wanted company. At first, he didn't. But after a couple days he did. We broke no new ground during those visits. When he was symptomatic, it was all bullshit about Satan. But I sat with him and listened to all his crazy ramblings. I'm not going to lie: It wasn't enjoyable. As much as I liked spending time with Jared, listening to him was maddening. And boring. I prayed for strength.

Jerusha and Nephi came every day. Jared seemed not to recognize them at first. One day near the end of this second stay, as we were sitting with Jared, Nephi said, "Well, I've learned my lesson, believe me. Stay on the medications from here on out."

"What do you mean you learned your lesson, Dad?" Jerusha asked.

"I shouldn't have said anything," Nephi said. "I'll stop talking now."

"Dad, did you tell Jared he could stop taking his medications?" Jerusha asked.

"I told him he could just reduce them," Nephi said. "I didn't see how that would make a difference. I was wrong, no argument."

Jerusha leapt from the couch. "Shit, Dad!" she cried. "I can't believe you fucking did that!"

"Jerusha, I love him!"

"Shit," she yelled. "And I don't? God, Dad, I can't believe you fucking did that. God, how are we going to get Jared better if we don't work together as a team?"

"Jerusha, I'm sorry."

"Stop fighting, you two," Jared cried. "Stop fighting."

"Jared, we're fighting because of you," Jerusha said. "Can't you see this is killing us? You're killing us."

"Don't say that," Jared said, putting his hands over his ears. "Don't say that."

"Shit, Jared, can't you see this is killing us?" Jerusha cried.

"Jerusha," I said, leaping up from the couch and pressing myself against her. I began to gently push her toward the door.

"What in the hell are you doing, Kenny?" she cried. "Stop it."

"I need to talk to you," I whispered to her.

"Stop it," she cried.

When I got her on the other side of the door, she pulled back and punched me in the shoulder with her unbroken hand. "What the hell was that for?"

"Jerusha, I love you," I said, taking her face in my hands. "But it doesn't help Jared to hear us talking like that."

Jerusha said nothing. She just cried and stared into my eyes, breathing hard.

"Did you say you love me?" she asked.

"Shit," I said, staring into her face silently for a moment. "I don't know. I think I do. Jerusha, I've never been in love before. Shit, Jerusha. I've never even had a girl as a friend until you. I have no fucking idea what it feels like to be in love." Now *I* was crying.

"I never loved anyone until I met Jared and now I love him, and I'm in love with you."

"I'm in love with you, Kenny," she said, still crying and looking into my eyes.

"Shit, Jerusha," I said, holding her close. "What are we going to do?"

"Just as long as you're not in love with Jared, too," she said against my chest.

"Shit, Jerusha, don't confuse me." I pulled her back and smiled at her.

We kissed.

Nephi came through the door a moment later. "Is everything all right?" he asked.

"Yeah, Dad," she said, smiling.

"Jerusha, I'm sorry I did what I did. I was wrong."

Jerusha released me and walked over to her dad. She wrapped her arms around him. "I understand, Dad," she said. "This is new for all of us. I'm sorry I yelled at you. This is just really hard for me."

"It's hard for all of us," Nephi said. He looked at me and waved me over. When I got there, he enfolded me into his embrace with Jerusha. They were both crying so I started crying too, which, somehow, didn't shock me.

"I love you all," I said as I cried.

Jared walked through the door in his bathrobe. "Are you all crying because of me?" he asked. "I don't want you crying because of me."

Nephi, Jerusha, and I released one another and looked toward Jared. There was no way to answer that question. A long pause ensued.

"Jared," Nephi said, "We love you."

"I know that," Jared said testily.

"Jared, you're the one who is having to live through all this, and we know this is hard, really hard, on you," Jerusha said. "But it's hard for us, too."

"I want to go home," Jared said.

"Boise?" Nephi said.

"No, home here, to Bishop's house," he said.

"The doctor said you're real close to getting out," I told him. "Just hang in there a bit more, man."

"I've got a good feeling that you'll be coming home right away," Nephi said.

"And this time, Jared, please, for godsakes, stay on your medicine," Jerusha said.

He looked at all of us. "I promise," he said.

SOON ENOUGH, Jared was back home, and right away he was complaining about his medications. He complained that he could barely think straight. He complained about "losing words." He complained that everything was "foggy, grey and tasteless." He complained that he couldn't find joy in anything. (The word is *anhedonia*.) He complained that his body "felt erased." He complained about his twitchy arms, legs, and face. All of the lights were too bright. He complained that he couldn't remember anything. (He was forever asking questions that we had just answered.) He complained that he couldn't sleep at night or nap during the day. When he did fall asleep, he later complained of "death-hell" nightmares. He complained that he couldn't get out of bed. He complained that he couldn't read because he couldn't focus. He complained that he couldn't follow television shows. He complained that he couldn't stop complaining.

And each complaint stabbed at our hearts, because we fretted that, as a consequence, Jared would stop taking his medications to be done with the side effects. Jerusha was a wreck. She was always tense. We were hyper-vigilant for any sign of returning psychosis. We fought with one another. Jared would complain and one of us—

it was always someone different—would stress to Jared the importance of staying on his medications. Immediately, one of the other
of us would chastise that person for hounding Jared. You could play
either part on two given days. We didn't have any set of instructions
for how to cope with this. We only knew two things for certain:
Jared had to stay on his medications and Jared hated his
medications.

We kept sharp objects from him.

Jared saw all of this.

The next six months or so are a blur. Jared would go off his
meds and end up in the hospital again. During one of his stays in
NSH, Mavis gave birth to a boy. She and Bloodworth named him
Jared. When Mavis was feeling better, she and Bloodworth brought
the baby out to the hospital to show him to Jared. When they got to
the dayroom, Mavis stayed at the head of the entryway while we all
filed in.

"Come in, dear," Bloodworth urged softly from next to Jared.

Mavis had a worried look on her face. "Here's the baby, Jared,"
she said, looking down at the baby and then pointing him
toward us.

Jared raised from his overstuffed, vinyl-covered chair and, with
that, Mavis withdrew the baby closer to herself. Jared stopped, his
ass in the air and his hands on the arms of the chair. Mavis began
crying.

"This is our boy, Jared," she said and then said nothing for
several moments. "We named him after you. Because we
love you."

Jared remained suspended above the seat of his chair. He stared
at Mavis for a moment, with his mouth slightly open, as if he was
about to say something. Then he slowly sat down. He seemed to
deflate.

"Thank you," he said softly.

We all stood silently, unsure of what to say.

"He's a good boy, Jared," she said. "Just like you."

Jared tilted his head back and exhaled, closing his eyes softly. "That's nice," he said.

Mavis continued to cry. She tried to wipe her tears with the side of her arm while she held the baby. "He's a good boy," she said.

"One big happy family," Jared said.

Once again, who knew what to say? Eventually, Jared said, "Tell the orderly I'm ready to go back."

"Jared," Jerusha said.

"I'm done," Jared said.

THEN JARED CAME home from what would be his last stay at Northern State. As soon as I was alone with him, he began his campaign. "Man, you have to kill me," he said.

"What the fuck?" I asked. "What do you mean?"

Jared exhaled slowly. "What do you think I mean? I need you to stop all this."

"Stop all this?"

"Man, I'm destroying everyone."

"What?"

He exhaled slowly again. "This is going to keep on going on unless you stop it. I'm going to keep going back and forth between crazy and sane. I can't take being sane and you guys can't take it when I'm crazy." He rubbed his eyes with his knuckles. "Actually, being crazy's no picnic for me, and all that happens when I'm sane is that I'm tearing my family to pieces."

"Man, if you're asking me to kill you, no way."

He looked up at me. "I can't do it, Kenny. I'm too scared. I need you."

"No fucking way, man," I said. "Don't ask me that." I stormed out of the room. "You're fucking crazy, man."

"Kenny!" he called out to me.

I turned toward him. "What, man?"

"Don't tell the others."

I looked at him for a moment. "Shit, man."

He didn't let up. The next time he asked me was when we were all together and Nephi and Jerusha began arguing again about Jared's medication. The altercation ended with the two of them storming from the room. Well, not so much storming in Nephi's case. I don't think it's in his power to storm. When they were gone, Jared leaned into me.

"This is what I was talking about," he said. "This is why you need to do it. I know it's a lot to ask. I know that. But I'm killing everyone. And also, I don't want to live like this."

"Man, don't start that shit again," I said.

"Think about what it's like for me," he said slowly, breathing deeply. "I can't keep on living like this. Here at home, on the shit they have me on, I'm a fucking zombie. I can barely think or move. When I'm not on this shit, I'm not myself. I'm never myself. Shit, man, I'm never myself. Can't you see?"

"Shit man, you can't ask me that."

"Hells bells, man, don't be so selfish," he cried. "I'm the one who's suffering!"

"Suffering?" I cried. "We're all suffering."

"That's my fucking point, man!"

"Man, don't ask me this."

At this, Jerusha reentered the room. "Don't ask you what?" she asked. "What is it?"

Jared and I looked at each other, each waiting for the other to speak, I guess. Jared tilted his head down, pursed his lips, and looked up at me.

"It's a temple covenant thing," I said slowly. "We can't divulge it. It's sacred."

"Yeah, right," she said, collapsing into a chair. After a while, she said, "Shit, Jared, I'm sorry we blow up at each other. I know it bothers you." She looked at the floor. "It bothers me, too."

"I know," Jared said, once again looking up at Jerusha.

So it went. It was our secret, Jared's and mine. To me, he was always asking, at least with his eyes. But, eventually, he stopped voicing his request, and I tried not to think of it. We all had our jobs to do now and then. I got a job as a telemarketer for the town's weekly, the *Courier-Times*, pitching subscriptions to locals in their homes. I was good at it, so much so that the publishers offered to let me put together the Police Blotter each week. It's not as impressive as it sounds. It wasn't much of a paper. The job consisted of visiting the SWPD and reading the incident log and pulling out the juiciest bits. I did this under the suspicious eyes of gatemistress of the Hall of Justice. People in town loved reading about the latest locals to run afoul of the law. Talk of the town. Local watering holes tacked copies of it above their urinals.

At home, things were no better. It was hard for us to be in the room all together. Jared would always complain about his medications. Jerusha tried to constrain herself, but more often than not, she'd blow up at Jared, her father, or me. Mavis tended not to come into any room that contained Jared, and she insisted the baby sleep between Bloodworth and herself in their bed. Nephi cried, mainly.

Soon we started insisting that Jared take his medications every day in our presence. This really pissed off Jared. We'd make him open his mouth after he took the pills so we could check. That brought us some comfort, even though Jared complained.

"You're treating me like the baby. I'm the big Jared, not the little Jared," he said. Little did we know that Jared was using a skill he learned in the nuthouse: cheeking. This involved hiding your pills in your cheek or under your tongue. Hey, it fooled the nurses at Northern State more often than not, so it easily fooled us. As the weeks passed, we comforted ourselves with the fact that Jared wasn't talking like a crazy person—just like a depressed person. However, in hindsight, I can see that Jared was applying the lessons he learned at Northern State: If he just kept quiet about his crazy thoughts, no one would hassle him. He grew more reclusive, but we just chalked that up to the depression.

We'd say, "Dinner's ready" or "Jared, come here and watch TV with us" or "Jared, we're going to the grocery store. Wanna go?" and he'd comply wordlessly. Really, we didn't want him out of our sight. There was no telling what he'd do. He stayed in bed a lot. He asked me to sleep with him, so I did. He'd hold me during the night and I wouldn't sleep much. It didn't bother me to hold him like that. Whatever helped Jared, I was happy to do. Well, not happy. It was a pain, really. Now and then, I cast up a prayer to the Celestial Kingdom like tossing a bread crumb to a bird. This went on for weeks and weeks. I wasn't getting much sleep. I was a wreck.

One day, Jared and I were lying in bed together, and I turned Jared.

"This is going to sound weird, but I think there was no reason you got sick," I said.

"No reason?"

"No reason whatsoever. I know that that's what we heard in church—everything that happens happens for some purpose. I'm beginning to think that's bullshit."

"It's bullshit?" he said.

"Yeah," I said. "It's like, God didn't do it to punish you, or punish your father for not raising his kids in the gospel. He didn't do it because you used to smoke pot or because you jerk off. God didn't do it, period."

"Who told you I jerk off?" he said.

"Serious up, man," I said. "I'm imparting truth to you."

"Well, if you're imparting truth. . ." he said slowly.

"Nobody gave you your sickness," I said, spreading my arms wide.

"What do you mean?" he asked.

"I'm not saying there isn't a God. There is. But He has this thing about freedom."

"Freedom? You mean free agency?"

"Yeah, but not just that. The universe is free, everything in it: killer comets, microbes, Mormon missionaries. They're all free.

Uncontrolled. Everything has a degree of freedom to be itself. Rocks have less freedom. We have more. Everything does whatever it is that it does, whether it's smash into planets and kill dinosaurs or whether it's dumbshits like you and me dressing up in a monkey suit and knocking on people's doors."

We lay in silence for a bit.

"Okay. Freedom," he said. "Everything is free to go about its way, and to knock into everything else and cause all sorts of mischief?"

"Yeah," I said.

"Seems like a screwy way to run the universe," he said.

We let that sink in. "Yeah, but maybe—maybe—God's not running the universe."

"That's what you think, huh?" he said.

"I think God's preference," I said, "is that there be fairness and kindness and justice. But he usually doesn't arrange for it. Or can't. Can't. He can't."

"So He doesn't get in the way of the freedom of meteors or bacteria or dumbshit Mormon missionaries. He allows them to be free, to do what they will?"

"That's the thing. He doesn't allow them to be free. He doesn't allow shit to happen. That implies He could intervene if He wanted. He can't. Otherwise, what's the point of making a universe if it's just a little You. It has to be free."

"You've learned your lesson. Okay, but let's see if you've really thought this through. If everything's free, then God's off the hook, isn't He?" Jared said.

"Not really. It's not like God just started the universe—pushed it from the pier—and then stepped away. If that was the case, He could maybe be excused for the state of the universe. But nothing has to be. Nothing is necessary. It only keeps on existing because God gives it its be-ing. Everything's free to do what it does—from cancer cells to killer whales—and it depends on God for its continued existence."

"Wow. Killer whales. Heavy. So what does God . . . do? Does He act in any way?"

"Well, God doesn't orchestrate things, if that's what you mean," I said. "He ad libs."

"Ad libs?"

"Yeah, ad libs. Like He does a guitar solo while this band, the universe, is playing along. I mean, the universe goes one way and He follows along, trying to make the most beautiful sound He can make, realizing the band's going to go in whatever direction it wants to go in. He riffs, just tries to do whatever He can to make the best of a sometimes bad situation. If He's really good, he steers the band in a certain direction."

"God improvises?"

"Yeah, he riffs when He can. Lots of times, the band won't let Him elbow His way in. I don't think God even knows the future. All that prophecy stuff is bullshit. How can God know the future? It doesn't exist yet. It's waiting to take shape based on our decisions and based on the random knocking about of all the things in the universe. God is in control to the extent that He's the one making up the riffs."

"Wow. That's trippy," he said and then stared at the ceiling for several minutes. I dared not continue the conversation. "Let me ask you one last thing: Is God riffing with . . . me?" he asked eventually. "Think carefully before you speak."

"Yeah," I said finally. "He's riffing with you. Is it beautiful?"

"No, man," he said. "It's a pile of shit."

"Positive," I said.

"A truer word has never been spoken," he said. "Now . . . I've had an inspiration!"

"An inspiration?"

"An impression," he said.

"Man, I don't know if you're joking or serious," I said.

"Therein lies my genius," he said.

"So . . . what's your . . . impression?"

"Give me a priesthood blessing," he said.

"Man, I don't think I hold the Melchizedek Priesthood anymore, if I ever did, if that priesthood even exists, which I don't think it does." I looked up at the ceiling.

"I know."

We lay like that for several more minutes.

"It can't hurt, a priesthood blessing," he said.

"Yeah, I suppose you're right." I lifted myself on one elbow and looked at him. "You ready?"

"Yeah, I'm ready. You need oil, man, or it won't work. Consecrated oil. Go get my dad's. Tell him you're giving me a priesthood blessing. He'll like that. But don't let him join us. Tell him I specifically just wanted you to do it."

"We need someone to seal the blessing."

"I'll seal my own blessing."

I did as he said. Nephi did, in fact, ask to join the blessing, but he didn't protest when I told him what Jared said. I think he was out of gas.

Back in the bedroom, I sat on the bed and unscrewed the vial of consecrated oil. I put some oil on the tip of my finger and touched the crown of Jared's head. Then I set my hands on his head and prayed out loud, "Jared Baserman, in the name of Jesus Christ and by the power of the Holy Melchizedek Priesthood, I anoint you with oil and ask Heavenly Father to bless you and give you what you need."

I inhaled deeply. "Do you want to say anything?" I asked Jared.

He opened one eye and looked up at me. "Three things," he said. "Number one: I love you, Kenny. Number two: thank you. Number three: I'm the funniest man in America."

"Amen," I said and closed my eyes. When I opened them, Jared lay still on the bed. He looked so peaceful. Maybe it worked in some way, I thought. "I love you, Jared," I said. I crept out of the room silently and went into the living room where everyone was reading.

"I think the blessing helped Jared," I said, handing Nephi his vial of oil.

"That's good," he said, looking up at me absently from his book and smiling. I saw that he was reading one of Bloodworth's exposés of Mormonism.

I sat down and picked up the library book I was reading: *The Rise and Fall of the Third Reich.* After an hour, Jerusha looked at her watch and said, "It's time for Jared's meds."

"I'll do it," I said and walked to the bedroom.

I went into the bedroom.

Jared lay on the bed.

The air was as still and thick as the pause before the prosecutor's climactic accusation.

"Jared," I said, sitting on the edge of the bed. "Hey, man. It's time to take your meds."

He was impassively staring up at the ceiling, unblinking.

"Hey, man, I just got my word of the day: vesicant. A vesicant, or 'blister agent,' is a chemical compound that fucks with your skin, eyes, and stomach. Mustard gas. So the fucking Nazis conducted experiments at concentration camps on the most effective treatment of mustard gas wounds. The Nazis deliberately exposed prisoners to mustard gas and other . . . vesicants. What dicks. The prisoners' wounds were then tested to find the most effective treatment for the mustard gas burns. Fucking Nazis. Who could be that cruel?"

Jared was silent, waiting for the perfect moment, I assumed.

"C'mon, man," I said.

I shook him, teasingly yet firmly, like a housecat requesting breakfast. "C'mon, man," I said. "Hey, man, c'mon. Time for your punch line, man."

Jerusha called from the front room. "Hey, Kenny. Take a look at this."

"Just a sec!" I called out, turning to Jared. "Hey, man."

I shook him again. No response. Again.

"Oh, shit," I whispered. "Oh, shit, no."

"Kenny," Jerusha called. "Check this out."

I shook him harder.

I laid my head on his chest. No movement. No beat of life. Just meat, various gasses and pooled fluids.

"Come here, guys!" I cried out. "Quick! Jared won't wake up!"

Instantaneously, it seemed, Jerusha first and then Nephi burst into the room.

"What did you say?" Jerusha cried.

"I don't feel a heartbeat!" I said, crying.

Jerusha shot to her knees, placing one hand on her brother's chest and the other on his forehead, haltingly, like an acolyte touching the flame to his first candle.

"What do you feel, Jerusha!" Nephi cried. "What is it?"

"Dad, call an ambulance!" she cried. "Call an ambulance!"

Nephi bolted from the room, calling out, "God, no!"

Jerusha pulled up Jared's shirt. "Who the fuck knows how to do CPR?"

"I know," I stammered.

"Do it!" she demanded. "Do it!"

By now I was bawling, unable to dredge my MTC CPR training from the bomb shelter of my brain. "I can't! I can't" I said.

"Goddammit, yes, you can!" Jerusha demanded. "Yes, you can!"

"No, I can't!" I cried. "I can't remember."

"Do something!" she cried. "God!"

I placed my hands over Jared's solar plexus and began to pump on his chest, clumsily. "Oh, fuck, what now?" I said to myself. I grabbed the sides of my head, clutching hair.

"Do something!" Jerusha cried.

I pinched Jared's nose with one hand and placed my mouth over his open mouth. One . . . Two . . . Three? Now . . . pump his chest. How many times?

"I can't!" I sobbed.

"Do something!" Jerusha cried. "Oh, God!"

Nephi burst into the room just then. "The paramedics are on their way!" he breathed, kneeling by the bed and placing his hand tenderly atop his son's head.

"My son!" he cried, placing his forehead on Jared's forehead as I continued pumping Jared's chest. When I moved to breath my life into Jared, I said, "Excuse me, Dad."

As I blew air into Jared's chest cavity, his body offered no resistance, thudding dully against the bedrails.

Jerusha collapsed into the corner, legs akimbo, like a doll's, and buried her face into her hands. "No!" she cried.

"You son of a bitch!" Nephi wailed. "Curse you to hell! Why didn't you kill me? I'm the one!"

The EMTs burst through the door. "Move!" one of them commanded. "Move!"

They began to minister to Jared. Finding no pulse, they placed him on the floor, ripping off his shirt and beginning CPR. Nephi and I drained from the bed. I rolled to my side. Nephi collapsed back onto his heels and fell into the nightstand, knocking the lamp to the floor. Jerusha had bolted upright and jumped to the foot where the EMTs were working on Jared. "Please save him," she pleaded, fingertips on her lips, to three of the EMTs, who were performing CPR on Jared. "Please."

The fourth EMT was asking us for any helpful medical history on Jared, anything about the events leading up to this situation. We stuttered and stammered incoherently, barely able to keep our feet beneath us in the upside down universe.

As this was going on, the paramedics burst in and set up their defibrilator unit. They started an IV, urgently pushing epinephrine, Atropine and Calcium Chloride through Jared's arteries. One of the paramedics put the defibrilator paddles to Jared's chest, crying, "Clear!" and a spasm of useless juice raged through Jared's ridiculous body. Again and again they tried. Jared shook like a compass needle seeking true north.

When I talked to the paramedics much later, they admitted that they knew Jared was long gone soon enough but they kept "trying" because we were standing there freaking out.

"Even if the person is dead and not coming back, we do whatever possible to make sure the event is as tolerable as possible for family and friends. You never want to give false hope, but they need to know there was nothing else that could have been done," one of them told me later. "At that point, we're treating the family, not the deceased. He's gone and not coming back. There's a reason that people call resurrections a miracle. They don't happen—well, maybe one in a zillion, but you know what I mean."

After about 15 minutes of laboring over Jared, the paramedics appeared to look at one another and nod all but imperceptibly. One of them stood and addressed himself to us.

"We've done everything that could be done, but . . ." he said.

At this, Jerusha wailed and collapsed to the floor. Nephi, his only son dead at his feet, instinctively did what he always did and focused on the person who could most benefit from his help and went to his knees next to his living daughter.

Jared was gone. Heavenly Father took him, I guess, or Jah.

Shit, I don't know.

CHAPTER TWENTY-FOUR

A s best as I can figure, here are the missions from God I've been on, all of them.

The first mission was my mission, my two-year Mormon mission. Make what you will of that.

The second mission and third missions were, respectively, to help Jared cope with his disease and to help the Basermans cope with Jared's death. Didn't really receive a call for either of those from God, the second and third missions. Doesn't seem like it's His job. That's on me. I just saw a need. That was the "call." They were missions to me, from God. They were both very hard, much harder than having doors slammed in my face during the first mission—if that counts for anything.

Particularly the third mission—we were devastated. I was devastated. My first friend, gone. A brother. A son. Torrents of grief. No one talked much. Someone always seemed to be crying, the white noise of the ocean. Often, a moan of agony and bafflement. Jerusha could barely stand at the funeral. She leaned into me like a drunk from Curley's. Nephi stared at the ground as the casket was lowered into the earth. He seemed to be muttering communiques to the Celestial Kingdom, SOS's, more or less. Mavis pressed her face into Bloodworth's chest and sobbed. Bloodworth held young Jared in his free arm and seemed to be unable to stop shaking his head.

I was hurting, but I tried to be there for everyone. Mainly, that meant lending a shoulder to cry on. Often, it literally meant sitting forever in uncomfortable poses while someone wetted the front of your shirt. And, what's more, usually I cried, too. What could I say? What could anyone say?

Mostly, we were miserable together, month after month. Then into a new year.

At a certain point, I realized there was only so much I could do. The grief had to run its course, whatever that was. Four stages? Five stages? It all sucked. It was going to take as long as it took. Maybe we'd never be better.

Jerusha seemed to emerge first from the gloom, haltingly, dumbfounded but alive, like a cartoon fox with a dynamite cigar. Not surprising. She was the strongest of us all, after all. She still cried often, but she could talk. Nephi followed her. He insisted that what we needed was to volunteer somewhere—a soup kitchen. "Take our minds off our troubles and let us help others," he said. Eventually, Mavis had a quiet joy all her own, even when she was sad, thanks to little Jared. Bloodworth, too.

Then it hit me, one morning in bed, epiphany-like. I turned over and wiggled Jerusha's hair on her nose until she woke up.

"Stop it, you!" she said and hit me playfully.

"Good morning, love," I said.

"Good morning, love," she said.

"I got something."

"You do?" she said, rubbing the heels of his hands into her eyes.

"Well, I've learned that God doesn't work in my life doing stuff, you know, directly. I prayed and prayed for God to give me the power to deal with Jared in love, but nothing came. It was just hard work. And helping you and your dad and everyone after Jared's death, that was just a lot of hard work, too."

She propped herself up on one elbow and look at me dubiously.

"What's your point?" she said.

"I'm still a selfish son of a bitch. I mean, Jared's sickness drove me fucking crazy. I'd rather be sitting on my ass than helping Jared —or anyone, really. Here's the thing, though," I said. "Are you listening to me?"

"Yeah, I'm listening to you," she said.

"Good. Here's what I've learned from all this shit. You ready?"

"Yes, I guess."

"You sure?" I asked.

"Sure, lay it on me."

"Okay," I said. "If God gave me the power to make the sacrifice, then it wouldn't be a sacrifice, would it?"

"What?"

"A sacrifice has to cost you something, doesn't it?" I said. "Otherwise, it's not a sacrifice, is it?

"Uh."

"You think God wants you to sacrifice for others. You've got that part right. But God can't give you the power to make the sacrifice."

"Can't? Is that the truth?"

"That's what I said."

"So what good is God then?"

"God has to be of some use to you in order to be God?" This was me—me!—talking so confidently about what God would or wouldn't do. Or couldn't. "God didn't allow Jared to get sick. It happened because He couldn't stop it from starting and He couldn't turn it around once it started."

"Do you mean He couldn't in that He chose not to?"

"I said what I said," I said. "My stepfather says that God does

what we can't do after we've given it our best shot—110 percent.
After all the shit we've gone through, seems to me he had it
backward."

"Pardon?"

"We do what God can't," I said.

"Wow," she said. "I think I see what you're getting at now. And
God can't make you sacrifice for me—any more than He can give
me the power to forgive Jo. I've got to do that myself, else it's not
forgiveness."

"Here it is," I said. "The bottom line is God can't be both all-
powerful and good. It's a classic argument. Theodicy"

"Look at you with the big words," she said with a crooked smile.

"Don't make fun," I said. "If He's all-powerful, then bad things
wouldn't happen. Jared wouldn't have gotten schizophrenia.
Should we believe in a God Who controls everything that happens
and causes a lot of terrible things to happen—or even allows them
to happen? Or should we believe in a God Who is good but isn't
powerful enough to stop the shitty things from happening? Yes,
God is powerful, but He's not all-powerful in the way we think of
all-powerfulness, mostwise."

"Mostwise?"

"I think," I said, fishing the tip of my ring finger in her belly
button, "God works in the universe like you work with me."

"Oh, yeah?" she said, closed her eyes and made exaggerated
kissing motions with her lips.

I leaned in and kissed her.

I pulled back and looked at her. "See?" I said. Her eyes were
closed.

"Mmm," she said, keeping her eyes closed and looking beatific.
"I see." She remained in that state for one, two, three seconds and
then she looked at me, reaching with her free hand down to my
gizmo and saying, "I have an idea."

"Oh!" she said in mock astonishment. "Looks like you're paying
attention."

"It's one of my gifts," I said. "It's a burden."

"Let me unburden you," she said.

So she did.

Believe me, I've had plenty of sexual encounters with Jerusha that I would classify as "transcendent." But, even then, we were slaves to the mechanics of it. That is, even in those sessions of transcendent sex, we both knew that it was only a matter of time. Jerusha, she could go on all night. But, I would eventually explode. If you rub two sticks together long enough, you'll get a spark. I think it's the Second Law of Thermodynamics or something. Likewise, if you rub two bodies together long enough, climax will occur. With this sex, though, it wasn't like I was a dam waiting to burst. We were circulating sexual energy back and forth between each other—an endless loop. We could have gone on forever. Funny thing was, we actually stopped several times and had these mind-blowing discussions. Then we'd circulate more sexual energy. Then we'd talk some more.

It was a sign from God. To the extent that He's able to give signs.

So I emerged from the session with my fourth mission.

It was all about telling Jared's story.

The point was not to worry about what I'd get out of it, the whole experience—I had to talk to everyone. Everyone. Piece by piece. I had to talk to people who knew Jared before, during and after his mission. I had to take down everything they said, every nuance.

It was a mission from God, after all.

At first, I went a bit overboard, I admit, perhaps because I began with Briskey and the characters surrounding him. The Briskey Enigma fascinated me. So energized, I went on a road trip. I took Jerusha with me because she made me a happy man. She was all for the mission—though she was coy about whether or not she thought it was really a mission from God—and she was a big help, calling BS when she saw it. And people did evade my questions.

You can imagine how cooperative the Senator was—or Cassius Parthemer, live-in landlord of the forlorn Regency Inn on the ragged flatland due south of Boise! Yes, I cornered Cassius Parthemer, every third word being fuck or a derivative thereof. Jerusha began to hint that I might be taking this whole thing too far. But I persisted. We headed down to Utah to question Prof. Bill Grout, the unfortunate kid who had had his neck wrung by the boyhood Briskey. From there, it wasn't too far, in a Cosmic sense, to drive out to Riverside, California, and see Todd Horus, one of the missionaries who had converted Bloodworth to the Restored Gospel. Then I got it into my head to backtrack to Utah and get an Official Comment from the Powers That Be in Salt Lake City.

That's when Jerusha put her foot down.

"They don't know shit," she said.

She had a point.

So back to Sedro-Woolley for the spade and pick work, bit by bit drawing out the impressions of ward members. And Dewey. And let's not forget Sunshine Toledo. How could one forget Sunshine Toledo, bane of cultists and wicked witches? Then I re-interviewed all the main players, Nephi, Jerusha, Bloodworth, Mavis. I had come up with all sorts of follow-up questions on my road trip.

Then I put it all down, let it gestate.

Then I wrote it up. And now you've read it. Mission completed.

However, I suppose I should sum up.

After Jared's death, we endeavored with real intent to put roots down in Sedro-Woolley. We gave it the old college try, but it was just too conservative for Jerusha. "Inbred," she called it. The place gave her the rickety shivers. She wanted to get as far away as possible from Sedro-Woolley and still stay in Skagit County, which she had grown to love: the green rolling mountains, nuzzling down in a blanket on a wet day, dirt-under-the-fingernails farmers waving amiably as you passed by. The ample bud. So one option was to keep going east, upriver. Problem was, it was a long time until you encountered a demographic that Jerusha could stomach. I felt the same way. You were far, far upriver before you hit the artists, the communists—in that they lived in communes, not that they were necessarily Marxists, though I'm sure there were plenty of those— and the other non-conformists. To get there, you had to travel through mile after mile of hidebound constitutionalists and relocated Tarheels. Inbred hicks. And when you finally got there, you were just too separated from civilization to suit Jerusha. I felt the same way.

So we went west, downriver. That was our only option. About twenty miles downriver was LaConner, home of counter-cultural freethinkers and fiercely independent small businesspeople. I became a cub reporter at the *Channeltown Press*, the weekly paper in LaConner.

And that suited Jerusha, until she discovered Fish Town, a scattering of abandoned gillnetters' shacks in the estuary between LaConner and the Puget Sound. No electricity. No plumbing. No zip code. No roads in or out. Jerusha loved it. So we moved there. The residents of Fish Town paid nominal rent to the owner of the land, a timber baron's heiress. Nominal was about the best she could hope for. As it was, if the Fish Town residents were late with the rent, or if they just didn't pay, it was unlikely she or one of her agents was going to make the trek out to the village. The citizens of Fish Town were notable deadbeats—they made the residents of LaConner look like upstanding citizens— and they were militantly unemployed. That is, except Jerusha and me. As I said, I had finagled a job at the *Channeltown Press* and Jerusha, she made enough to keep us in ganja by working, languidly, at a juice bar in town. LaConner was willing put up with a paper as cheeky as the *Channeltown Press*. And for its part, the paper was willing to put up with an untrained schlep like me as their editorial voice. No big risk on their part. The way they figured it, if I didn't pan out, there were ten other schleps behind me, pencil-thin poets mainly, willing to work for a handful of mixed nuts.

At his job as janitor at the crisis counseling agency in Sedro-Woolley, Nephi found himself doing his own counseling on the burned-out employees. It's a tough job to listen to people in crisis all day. Nephi would be eating his lunch in the breakroom and these employees, mainly women, would come in and commiserate with him, and he was more than willing to oblige. He's actually a pretty wise guy—insightful. Bottom line, he helped a number of women with their job fatigue. Soon enough, the women were encouraging their boss to give Nephi a try as a phone counselor. He was skeptical but he agreed. But Nephi soon became the most perceptive, empathetic counselor at the clinic. Repeat customers would call in asking for him by name. Nephi started forming a particular bond with another employee, a woman who practiced "energy healing" and who wore feathers in her hair. In particular, in her off-hours, she offered a service in which she'd minister to an unwell person by knocking on Tibetan bowls and gongs. As she was making these hypnotic noises, she would guide the person through relaxation meditation, grounding them to Earth energy and connecting them with the Highest Consciousness. That was what she said. Eventually, she and Nephi became an item, and Nephi moved into her apartment in Sedro-Woolley. The woman convinced Nephi that LaConner would be far more receptive place to market her services, and they moved. Nephi was overjoyed to be closer to Jerusha and me, though he shed quite a few tears about moving away from Bloodworth, Mavis and little Jared. I think he made his peace with God. In fact, he told me as much. God wasn't his father. His father wasn't God. Amen. Of his girlfriend's techniques, Nephi would say, "It's not for me, but if it helps other people, more power to them." By all appearances, they were a happy couple.

Likewise, Mavis and Bloodworth were the picture of wedded bliss. They both felt a void in their lives, though, from not having a home church. Having married a Latter-day Saint, Mavis was no longer welcome at her church. They shopped around and settled on the local Episcopal church, St. James. It seemed to be the best fit, as the church allowed a lot of latitude in dogma. Pretty much, parishioners could believe whatever they wanted as long as they could demonstrate some philosophical/theological lineage to Christianity. After everything, Bloodworth had pretty much come to conclusion that God didn't really care what you believed. Not really. I mean, He probably looks askance at voodoo, but past that, He's cool with it, the conclusions you reach. That said, Bloodworth felt there was something about Jesus Christ. History hinged on Christ, somehow. God was saying something with Jesus Christ. Bloodworth wasn't just exactly sure what that was. God left it up to us to decide what Jesus was all about. As usual. And, indeed, much of human history has revolved around arguments about Jesus. Really, God could have been more plain about Jesus. Just goes to show: He's—what?—reckless, I guess. So St. James suited them fine and they were warmly welcomed. Soon enough, the priest asked them if Jared had been baptized. This led to some disconnect for Mavis and Bloodworth with the church. Mavis was raised to believe that infant baptisms were a doctrinal deformity sutured onto the true faith by the Catholic Church. As a Latter-day Saint, Bloodworth was taught that the time for baptisms was age eight since children were unable to sin prior to their eighth birthday, per Mormon doctrine. (The rule was clearly inked by someone who had never known a 7-year-old.) Eventually, they decided on a baptism. We all were in attendance. Jared screamed like a strangled rabbit when the priest sprinkled the water on his forehead, which amused everyone present.

Mission President Dewey was called as Stake President to replace the late Artis Watson, moldering in the dirt as I write these words. Nothing pleased Dewey more than a chance to flex his entrepreneurial muscles, I think. President Dewey went on to oversce an unprecedented period of growth for the stake. Even the

Sedro-Woolley ward, first left reeling from the Jared fiasco, ended up growing in membership. Good for him. It never occurred to me for one short second to spill the beans on Dewey.

Shortly after Jared's death, Briskey convinced the local Seventh Day Adventist church to rent him their chapel on Sundays for his services. Attendance was robust at first. After all, Briskey had been officiating when Watson was struck dead by the power of the God, so, to many members of the Sedro-Woolley ward, it was a show worth watching. (Also, many women from the ward were attracted by the idea of receiving the power of the Melchizedek Priesthood. Who can blame them?) A fair number of other folks from the community showed up as well, perhaps lured by the flyers Briskey posted around town that promised that visitors would "experience the power of the New Testament church in the modern age!"

However, when no further miracles were forthcoming, attendance began to dwindle. All but one of the Mothers of Invention went elsewhere, probably not back to the Sedro-Woolley ward, I'm guessing. Only Sister Skeemer stayed, and she ended up tying the knot with Briskey. Jerusha and I sat in on a service incognito about a year after Jared's death. It was clear that some of Briskey's enthusiasm seemed to have waned. However, Briskey never admitted the whole thing was a scam. Nor did he just vanish into the green scenery. He just kept on keeping on, which to me is a good argument in favor of his sincerity. Jerusha doesn't buy it. She said it only proves that he had come to believe his own bullshit.

Turns out Jo and Emily put down roots in LaConner as well. A fresh start for Jo. LaConnerites didn't give a rip who she loved—just make sure you pay your tab, goddammit.

Life was good. The universe truly is random and chaotic. But, on the whole, it has more good things than bad things in it. Like my "family." All of us—Nephi, the Bishop, Mavis, little Jared, Jerusha and I—get together often, as a whole group or in subsets, out for coffee or something. We never fail to talk about those crazy months in Sedro-Woolley. We laugh and we cry. And, for all I know, somewhere far, far, far away—past the reach of reasonable hope—Jared is orbiting Kolob, probably cracking wise while Heavenly Father jams savagely, sending a shimmering chainsaw note through the universe.

Or so I'm led to believe.

ACKNOWLEDGMENTS

Mainly, I spent a lot of time alone writing this book. Constructing a novel is a lonesome, windblown affair. That said, some helpful souls came to my aid. I'll always be grateful for Chris Guthrie's expertise—and encouragement—early on. The folks in two writing groups offered me invaluable feedback: Brian Bleau, Diane Bunnell, Lynn Campbell, Shawn Inmon, Anne McIntyre, Michele Reamey, Peggy Ross. Aubin Barthold's insight was excellent. A number of people provided, well, technical expertise: Ken Clark, Lee Copeland, Holly Welker, John Williams, Daniel Shirley. My excellent proofreader was Debra Ann Galvan.

AFTERWORD

Did you like *A Danger to God Himself*? Then you'll probably like my blog by the same name. Why not subscribe? It's free! As a thank-you for subscribing, I'll send you a chapter I left out of this book. It's called "Kenny's Testimony." Learn how Kenny found—and then lost—his testimony before his mission. Click on this link (http://eepurl.com/cSuqj9) to get your extra chapter.

ABOUT THE AUTHOR

I've known I wanted to be an author since I was 9. Life got in the way, though. Specifically, I finished college, landed my first newspaper job, got married, got divorced, raised my three amazing kids with my wonderful ex. Turns out, life's a lot of work. During this entire time, I was employed as a full-time writer, strictly nonfiction —though dramatic nonfiction, I like to think. Anyway, when my kids got old enough, around my 50th birthday, I was able to devote the time necessary to write a novel. So I did. Little did I know how much time would be "necessary." Why didn't someone warn me writing a novel's so hard?

A Danger to God Himself is my first book, written almost entirely at a coffee shop in Puyallup, Washington, and a bar in Tacoma, Washington—mornings and nights, respectively.

You can email me at adangertogodhimself@gmail.com

For More Information:
johndraperauthor.com
adangertogodhimself@gmail.com

Made in the USA
Monee, IL
20 October 2022

16240286R00184